W9-DAS-999

**Applause for the K-9 Rescue series by D.D. Ayres**

"*Irresistible Force* is simply fabulous! With exhilarating action and stunning sensuality, Ayres draws you in and doesn't let go."
—Cherry Adair, *New York Times* bestselling author

"Incredible! You'll be on the edge of your seat to see if the heroine can make it out alive."
—Catherine Coulter, *New York Times* bestselling author

"Ayres brings gritty realism and sexy heat to this romantic suspense series."
—*Publishers Weekly*

"Intrigue, danger, and romance . . . if you think dogs and romantic suspense are an excellent mix, then this is the series for you!"
—*RT Book Reviews*

"Sexy, romantic, and with enough humor to keep the pages turning."
—*Cocktails and Books*

"A steamy, exciting, suspense-filled love story."
—*Clever Girls Read*

"A story about a HOT cop and his K-9 partner? I was all in! And boy, did Ayres deliver! I count this book as a DEFINITE read. Cops and canines, two things near and dear to my heart!"
—*Charlotte's Book Review*

St. Martin's Paperbacks Titles
by D.D. Ayres

*Irresistible Force*
*Force of Attraction*
*Primal Force*

# PRIMAL
# FORCE

D.D. Ayres

St. Martin's Paperbacks

**NOTE:** If you purchased this book without a cover you should be aware that this book is stolen property. It was reported as "unsold and destroyed" to the publisher, and neither the author nor the publisher has received any payment for this "stripped book."

PROM
Ayres

This is a work of fiction. All of the characters, organizations, and events portrayed in this novel are either products of the author's imagination or are used fictitiously.

PRIMAL FORCE

Copyright © 2015 by D.D. Ayres.

All rights reserved.

For information address St. Martin's Press, 175 Fifth Avenue, New York, NY 10010.

ISBN: 978-1-250-04219-4

Printed in the United States of America

St. Martin's Paperbacks edition / September 2015

St. Martin's Paperbacks are published by St. Martin's Press, 175 Fifth Avenue, New York, NY 10010.

10  9  8  7  6  5  4  3  2  1

*This book is for my readers: past, present, and future.*
*You make the effort worthwhile. Thank you.*

# ACKNOWLEDGMENTS

I took some liberties in this novel. The dog training program set in Arkansas that includes a component in a women's correctional center is fictional. My inspiration for such a program came from Patriot Paws located in Rockwall, Texas. Patriot Paws is a not-for-profit agency that trains service dogs for vets. Their mission says it all: "*. . . to train and provide service dogs of the highest quality at no cost to disabled American veterans and others with mobile disabilities and PTSD in order to help restore their physical and emotional independence.*" Patriot Paws, and many other organizations like it, are providing a vital service to our veterans.

Thank you, Patriot Paws, for allowing me to ask a hundred questions, observe classes, and meet the wonderful staff: Lori, April, Jay, and all the others. You run a first-class operation with skill, heart, and generosity.

Thanks to my K-9 law enforcement expert for the entire series, Brad Thompson. A former senior handler and instructor/trainer of the Fort Worth PD K9 Unit, he's currently assigned to the Special Investigations Unit, where he's responsible for public integrity investigations, executive and dignitary protection and surveillance, and counter-surveillance activities.

As always, my editor Rose Hilliard. She sees no obstacles, only opportunities to make it better.

And my agent Denise Marcil. You're the best!

# *PROLOGUE*

"What the hell do you mean by calling me on this line?"

"Sorry, sir. I couldn't get through on the other."

"Hang up, dammit."

"What's wrong, dear?"

Harold Tice smiled at his wife, who had rolled over in bed to look at him. "Business. Always business." He patted her thigh. "You go back to sleep. I'll take this into my study."

He checked to make certain he was on a secure line before returning the call from his desk phone. "Yeah?"

"There's been an inquiry into one of those files you asked us to keep an eye on, sir. The military file on former U.S. Army Military Police criminal investigations 31D Special Agent Lauray Battise was pulled this week."

"Who pulled it and why?"

"I didn't get that information. Would you like me to look into it?"

"Don't bother."

After he hung up, Tice remained seated, drumming his fingers on his desktop. In Arkansas, the name Tice was synonymous with wealth and influence. If there was big money to be made, Tice Industries, a trucking and transportation company, usually had a cut of it. He wasn't a sentimental man, or an idealist. He was hard-nosed and pragmatic. It was his job to keep the family company going, by whatever means necessary. Only two incidents, both occurring four years earlier, had threatened his turn at the helm. One was local, and had been resolved. The other had taken place half a world away.

Tice's fingers paused in mid-drumming. The problem of MP Battise had been the more dangerous. Yet that incident had seemingly gone away after Battise was wounded in the field in Afghanistan. Lucky coincidence?

He'd never asked for the details. Even so, he had continued to keep an eye on mistakes that carried the potential for harm, however remote. The fact that someone was looking into Battise's file could be nothing. More than likely was nothing. Better to do nothing. A man in his position couldn't afford to be too curious.

"Are you coming back to bed?"

Tice looked up to find his wife in the doorway. "Will it be worth it?"

She smiled and whipped back her robe to flash him a leggy length of bare skin.

"In that case." He stood up. "You warm up the sheets while I make one last call."

When she had gone, he picked up the phone and dialed another number.

"I hear we have a wounded vet, a former U.S. Army criminal investigator named Lauray Battise, living in my son's district. Might make for good PR. Find out where he is and what he does for a living."

Enemies kept close. A man in his position couldn't afford to be too careful, either.

# CHAPTER ONE

*He was running.*

*The best part of any day. Straight up a steep mountain incline. Knee lifts as important as footfalls. The jackhammer explosion of quads and calves propelled him off the ground and up the terrain in a zigzag pattern. One after the other, his boots hit the rocky earth, springing him forward, taking him higher.*

*His heart was pumping like a motor with a hemi attached. The sky above a pale-yellow dome of heat. The earth beneath him hard, desert dry, unforgiving.*

*It didn't matter. He was almost there. Almost at the summit. The scraping of air in and out of his lungs was the end-all, be-all of the moment.*

*Finally, there was no more ground in front of him.*

*He bent at the waist, gasping greedily for all the oxygen his lungs could wring from the thin air. His quads trembled. His calves burned. Sweat*

*evaporated right out of his pores. He'd be danger-
ously depleted soon.*

*He stood up, arms thrown wide, staring out
across the natural cauldron where the Afghani town
below lay sprawled like lumpy brown fungus. It
didn't matter. Nothing mattered. He had achieved
his goal.*

*Top of the world, Ma.*

*One second, silence in the narrow but familiar
street of an Afghan village, interrupted only by his
partner's excited bark. The next, a consuming white-
hot brilliance. Then the searing pain of a body on
fire.*

*Someone was screaming. Echoing in his head
the sounds he could no longer make. Where was his
K-9 Scud?*

*Rifle fire and then a canine yelp of pain came
from just above him. Scud! Scud was hurt! He tried
to turn his head but the effort was too great.*

*He was shaking uncontrollably. Shock was set-
ting in. He was trained to resist it. Must control that.
But . . .*

*Can't breathe. Can't—*

Lauray "Law" Battise jerked awake to the wettest kiss
of his life. There was plenty of tongue and heated breathing and—um, she might have brushed first. Her breath was
two Tic Tacs short of yummy. Well, hell. It was wartime.
He needed release, anything to block out the memories.
Resigned, he reached for his bed partner, already hoping his
nightmare hadn't preempted the possibility of a morning
hard-on.

Instead of an armful of warm naked woman, he embraced a heavy muscular body encased in curly dense fur.

"What the fuck?"

Law opened his eyes and frowned down the length of his nose at his unwelcome bed companion. Sixty-five pounds of dog the color of a rusted-out car lay stretched out on top of him, her muzzle just touching his chin.

Even through the haze of his flashback, he knew the dog was evaluating his odor, teasing apart the cocktail of chemicals called pheromones, to test whether he was still in the throes of a full-blown episode.

Calm but alert, she licked at the sweat running from his chin whiskers down onto his throat then paused to gaze at him with golden-brown eyes of concern.

He pointed at the floor. "*Heruntersteigen.*"

She merely stared at him.

"*Heruntersteig*—" Oh, right. Civilian dog. She didn't know German commands, the language of most military and civil law enforcement K-9s. This docile pooch only knew words like *fetch*, *sit*, *heel*, and *go potty*.

"Get down."

She immediately did as he asked. But moved no farther away than the side of his bed, where she stared at him with soft doggy eyes.

Law sat up and stripped a hand down his face, wiping away the sweat of anxiety. The acrid smell of rocket propellant had yet to evaporate from his imagination. He flicked on the nightstand light as his gaze tracked the small perimeter of the hotel room for intruders. The action was so ingrained in his psyche that he wasn't fully aware of it.

The room was empty. Even so, he was about to rise and double-check the door lock when the cell phone tucked under his pillow began to vibrate. He grabbed for it.

"Got yourself a dog?" His half sister Yardley's voice was unmistakable.

Law's eyes narrowed on the mix of golden retriever and poodle with a rusted-red coat, coal-black nose, floppy ears, and enormous curling tail. "What I've got here is a giant Cheez Doodle. Jesus. Who names a working dog Sa-*man*-tha!"

"Still having flashbacks?" Yardley Summers always cut to the heart of a matter.

Law didn't lie. And he never backed down. His go-to response for any question he didn't want to answer was silence.

"I'll take that as a yes. We had a deal."

"More like extortion."

He grunted at the memory of his half sister arriving without warning at his door six months earlier. He'd just failed his law enforcement physical, for the second time. His prosthetic leg was good, but not hard-charging pursuit-and-apprehension-reliable enough to put him back on patrol with the Arkansas State Police. So he'd handed in his resignation. Instead of accepting it, his trooper sergeant had put him on extended leave and called Yardley, the only kin Law listed in his personal file.

"I didn't ask for your help."

"You were in no condition. I've never seen anything more pathetic than you drunk and drowning in self-pity."

Law ground his teeth to keep silent.

After showing up on his doorstep, Yardley had cussed a blue streak as she'd bullied him into the shower then all but spoon-fed him her "special" homemade soup. She didn't mention it contained a cocktail of all the meds he had been avoiding until he was cross-eyed and sliding out of his chair.

Three days later, when she was certain he was wide-awake and could function, she'd left behind a filled-out copy of an application for Warriors Wolf Pack. Attached was a note that said: *Do this and I will do what you asked.* That was six months ago. She hadn't been in touch until now.

"You called at the ass crack of dawn for a reason, Yard?"

"I need to know that you're taking this PTSD dog idea seriously."

The hair on Law's neck rose as his fist tightened around the phone. "You found out something."

"I don't have the full intel yet. These days snail mail is safer than the Internet. By the time you've done your ten-day training, I'll have it."

"Right." Law punched the END button and lobbed his phone onto the mattress. If Yard knew him, he knew her, too. She wouldn't have called unless she already had something. He didn't need to ask how she'd gotten the information. Yardley Summers had connections that would make a CIA spook jealous.

Staring off into space, Law flexed his hands to pump off a little of his anger as a familiar resentment swelled in him. He hated asking for help. Even from Yardley. Had never in his life asked for it, or accepted it. Even now he hadn't reached out to members of his former unit because instinct or stubbornness—or paranoia—told him not to.

But his life had turned to shit after the explosion in Afghanistan four years earlier. He needed answers, about what had happened to him, and to his military police K-9 partner, Scud.

During his last tour of active military police duty he'd been paired with an Alpha-male Belgian Malinois named Scud who could control crowds, take down a sniper, and locate IEDs all in the same day.

Scud was loyal but he wasn't always friendly. Most handlers wouldn't take him on. Yet Law had seen in the tough loner a reflection of himself. They weren't buddies, yet they became a team, moving and working as one, anticipating the needs of the other in daily life-and-death situations.

Law rubbed hard at one of the scars hidden beneath the bush of beard along his left jaw. The explosion he never saw coming had strafed his body and shredded his left leg, and killed Scud outright. He knew what to counsel himself. *It wasn't my fault.* But the thing about that was, if it wasn't his fault, whose was it?

Pain squeezed Law's heart but he fought the emotion. If tortured, he would have lied about his feelings for Scud with his final breath. Never again would he allow himself to be that vulnerable.

His guilt over Scud had strengthened during the last year. Before that, he'd been too busy trying to heal and restore what was left of his mangled body. It wasn't until nine months ago, as he was trying to reclaim his life as a state trooper, that symptoms of PTSD kicked in hard, taking a turn at wrecking his psyche. Was his subconscious, finally, trying to tease out the answers to what had happened that day? Or was he now just a messed-up loser who needed a dog to keep him from freaking out in public?

"Screw it." He could handle this on his own. Alone.

He stood up. And hit the floor with a thud.

"Shit!" It had been a long time since he'd forgotten to compensate the distribution of his body weight for one leg. The delusion of having two legs must have been the leftover result of his running dream.

He swung out a hand for his prosthesis lying on a nearby chair. It was out of reach. Before he could scoot closer, Samantha moved quickly to pick up the artificial leg with her mouth. She brought it over and placed it gently in his lap without being asked.

"Good dog, Sam—dog." He felt silly calling her by that long-ass Samantha name.

Law hoisted himself back up on the mattress and reached for the pouch of doggy treats WWP had given him to reward his companion for her work. Half a service dog's daily food supply was handed out in the form of rewards. He held out a few small nuggets, which she gobbled up. He dug into the bag again, figuring he owed her.

"So here's the deal. I'm calling you Sam until I turn you back in. You good with that, Sam?"

She gazed up at him with calm adoration and tongue-lolling satisfaction.

*Crap.* Sam even had a nice smile.

Okay, so the dog was getting to him. She was more than a pampered pet. She was everything the WWP promised: attentive, smart, intuitive, and helpful. The perfect service companion . . . for someone else. He didn't deserve this dog's help or loyalty. He'd lost that right when Scud died. He couldn't be responsible for another companion's life. Ever again.

Law turned to inspect his injured limb to make certain his fall hadn't caused any damage. Some pain, more or less, was always with him. There were better things to think about. For instance, the attractive dog trainer Jori— something. He hadn't caught her full name.

His K-9 instructor side appreciated watching her technique while working with the dogs. The purely male part of him enjoyed watching the way her pants pulled tight across the very nice curves of her butt and how her tee pulled taut against the swell of her breasts as she worked. She was the kind of woman who didn't need to show skin to be sexy. It was in the way she handled herself. The subtle huskiness of her voice was sexy as hell, too. Her straightforward manner kept the other four vets smiling and at ease as she helped them understand the capabilities of their specially trained new service dogs. Except him. *Him*, she ignored.

Law smiled to himself. She must have read something predatory in his expression that first day. He couldn't argue with her judgment. Jori gave him an itch.

Maybe it was the long honey-brown braid she wore, twitching down her back as she moved. Made him want to wrap that braid around his forearm and haul her in by it. Each time she touched his hand to loosen his grip on the leash or to adjust his position with his dog, he fought the urge to reach out and touch back. And then go on touching and holding, wanting to kiss and caress her until he had persuaded her to be naked under him.

Law pushed an impatient hand through longish thick black hair. He probably shouldn't be thinking dirty thoughts about his instructor. Jori didn't look like an easy lay. He didn't have time for anything else.

He knew what women said about him: *Good in bed but impossible to love.*

True enough. He was insensitive, untrustworthy, possessed of a quick temper, and selfish. He'd enjoy the company of any willing woman. But he never let it get personal, or stand in his way. In that, he was his father's son.

"Nothing short of all fucked up," he muttered to himself.

He picked up the liner to sheathe his stump, rolled and smoothed it on, then picked up his prosthesis. Now, *this* baby was worth being excited about. This techno wonder was going to get his trooper job back. Without that concrete measure of his worth as a man, his struggle to get better was worthless.

Three months ago, he'd succeeded in getting his old prosthetic leg swapped out for one with sophisticated military-grade microprocessor-controlled devices. With gyroscopes, accelerators, hydraulics, and sensory points to turn muscle contractions into device response, the new leg gave him great stability and mobility. With it he could walk, climb stairs, even run without thinking about it— as long as he remembered to strap it on.

He stood up, this time with the expected results. As close to good-as-new as he was going to get.

If he hurried he could get in some gym time before he left for Richmond, Virginia, the nearest airport to where Yardley lived. The best cure for a PTSD episode was to push himself, hard, until his heart was pumping like a jackhammer and his muscles trembled with fatigue. Only at the peak of exhaustion did his mind sometimes shut down long enough to give him peace.

Unless . . . he could convince Jori to do the dirty with him before he left. In and out? A one-off in their lives?

He shook his head at his unruly thoughts. *Bad, Law. Phooey, Law. She's not for you.*

Samantha watched with concerned eyes as her Alpha dressed himself. She knew he was Alpha because of the tone of his voice and the strong virile scent that labeled him the dominant partner.

She smelled others things on him as well, like anger, fear, and anxiety. She didn't like those smells. They made her uncomfortable, much like the veterinarian's office. The cloying odors of injury, sickness, and fear from other animals could not be scrubbed away by antiseptics. Those smells were worse than the shots she occasionally received.

As the Alpha passed her, Samantha pushed her nose forward and sniffed his pant leg.

"Don't."

She drew back. His tone was harsh. As if she'd done something wrong. Didn't he know? She was trained to pay attention, and to find ways to make the fear and anxiety stop when those pheromones emanated from him. She had done that this morning, even if he didn't seem to understand at the time why she had woken him. That was okay. He would learn. He was her chosen Alpha.

Three days ago five men and their family members had come to WWP. Each brought a reek of smell fragments from his daily life. Some were familiar, others the unique combination of their own bodies, homes, and habits. One man was ill. Two had had coffee and cigarettes for breakfast. She even knew by their shared smells which humans belonged to the same pack.

But one man's scent was different. His odor was a cocktail of emotional markers that included anger, pain, and sadness. And more. He smelled alone. There were no other human scents on him. No animal scents, either.

Most of the people Samantha had encountered in the twenty-five months of her life carried the scents of their companions, human and/or pet. This Alpha smelled of isolation. That was not good for a pack animal.

The only time Samantha had felt this way was when, as a puppy, she'd been abandoned at a shelter. All the smells were strange. None of her litter or her mother. She was fed and watered, but otherwise left alone in a cage that prevented her from running or playing with the other dogs. Until Alpha Kelli found and brought her to WWP.

She loved being in the WWP pack. There were lots of dogs to play with, and human Alphas to love and teach and protect her. Even when she moved from Alpha to Alpha for training, she was always treated as part of the pack.

But now things were different.

She had felt the excitement in the WWP pack the day the strangers came. She sensed that things were about to change, yet again. One of the strangers would take her home.

Yet no one handed her off. They simply dropped her leash and let her roam among the strangers, sniffing out a need. Her choice. It was not hard.

The sad man needed her to be his pack. She'd picked

that up the first day. No Alpha, even the strongest, was healthy when he was without his pack.

The Alpha dropped his wallet and cursed.

Samantha hurried over and scooped it up in her mouth before he could bend down for it. He looked surprised then frowned. She felt confused by his frown. Then proud when he took the wallet from her.

He nodded at her but did not offer the affection of his hand or a treat. *"Gute Hund."*

She licked his hand to show that she didn't mind that he didn't know how to behave. He would learn.

She did not always understand his words, but she would learn.

When he sat to tie his shoe, she moved close and weighed her big head on his thigh. She watched him, her eyebrows twitching up and down as if she could signal to him that he was not alone anymore. She would help with the sadness, and calm his worries. She was now his pack.

# CHAPTER TWO

Jori Garrison wasn't having a great morning. She'd been awakened by yet another phone call from the person she'd been dodging all week. Then she'd discovered she didn't have food for Argyle. So here she was, not even showered, looking for cat food on the shelves of a nearby convenience store.

She had just located the single box when she noticed someone passing the end of the aisle. Her stomach did a jump of recognition as she came to her feet slowly, so as not to draw his attention. She needn't have bothered. He was headed straight for the back of the store with a determined stride.

Though she had had only the briefest glimpse, there was no mistaking those broad shoulders stretching the limits of his olive-drab T-shirt. Or the Native American tribal tattoo riding the heavy biceps of his left arm. *Lauray Battise.*

For three days she'd been working with him and the other four veterans who had come to receive a service dog from Warriors Wolf Pack. Despite all her efforts to dismiss her feelings, heat simmered beneath her skin whenever he was around. She literally had the hots for the man. Too bad he wasn't even remotely likable.

Jori clutched the cat food box to her chest as her gaze followed him. He might be rude and standoffish, but he certainly was nice to look at. He had been exercising, hard. Dark circles of sweat made his tee cling to his back, revealing the taut contours of muscles beneath. Everything about him radiated strength, determination, a force to be reckoned with. That solid muscular physique was a testament to months of hard unrelenting therapy.

If he'd been wearing long pants, she doubted casual observers would have known he had a disability. Instead, he wore basketball shorts that revealed the prosthesis where his left leg should be. She liked that he wasn't self-conscious about that. She, on the other hand, was uncomfortably aware of him.

As he stopped to fill a cup with hot coffee from an urn, she noticed how his dark hair stuck out from under his ball cap at weird angles. His thick black beard was in serious need of pruning, too. No need to wonder if there was a woman in his life. No one who cared for him would have let him go out looking like that. Not that his relationships with women were any of her business. Or ever would be. But she couldn't help admiring the solid definition of the man, or wondering if every part of him was as impressively large.

*That's just prison talking.*

It's what her second cell mate Ethylene would say whenever conversation at the women's correctional center rolled around to talk of men and sex. Which it had at some point each day.

After a few seconds more, she realized that he had stopped pouring and was staring off to one side. She followed his gaze to the refrigerated cases next to him. She could see his reflection clearly in the glass door. *Oh*. If she could see him that meant he could see her, too. He wasn't staring at the drinks, but at her.

The impact of his gaze hit Jori with a scorching effect. It was intimate, exhilarating, and completely male. Which was saying a lot, considering his stare was reflected by chilled glass.

Embarrassed to be caught eyeing him, she hitched up a hand in greeting.

He didn't respond but, after another second, opened the door and reached for a bottle of water.

She turned away, uncertain about what had just happened. Maybe he hadn't been staring at her, after all. Yet the hot knot of sexual awareness balled in her stomach told her he'd seen her, all right. And dismissed her.

She grabbed a bag of chips at random from a rack as she hurried away.

Okay, so they hadn't exactly gotten along the past three days. The intensity of the way he watched her work with the dogs and other vets unnerved her. Though she'd been working with WWP for six months, this was her first experience working directly with the vets. Maybe it showed. Unless he had figured out what she thought she'd been successful at hiding.

"You'll fall a little in love with all of them." Kelli Miller, the owner of Warriors Wolf Pack, had warned her when she began working full-time at the WWP main office near Conway. At the time, she thought Kelli was talking about the service dogs they lived with and trained every day. Now she suspected Kelli had meant something else.

Most veterans brought along family members or a friend when they first visited Warriors Wolf Pack. Many were young men and women in their prime when war brutally ripped from them vital parts of their physical functioning. Years of military training and strong families had helped them work through a defined set of objectives and treatment to get to the point where they could manage a service dog. Once a trained animal was added into the mix, their efforts at self-reliance became downright jaw-dropping.

But there were others, loners by circumstance or choice. They had no support system. Battise had come alone.

Jori resisted the impulse to glance back over her shoulder. Not that Battise looked like a stray. He seemed more like a lone wolf. The kind that wouldn't run long with any pack. Instead, he prowled around the edges, watchful and alert. The missing leg seemed to be a mark of his courage, as if he were a wild animal willing to gnaw off his limb to retain his freedom.

Jori shook her head to dispel her fanciful notions. Battise was at WWP for a PTSD dog. That meant he was plagued by demons he alone understood. She knew about personal demons.

"Don't." She said the word under her breath as she hurried toward the cash register. She didn't need to cloud her judgment with too much compassion.

"Hello, Miss Jori." The clerk smiled a toothy smile as she stepped up. "Looking good today."

"Thanks, Sanjay." Sanjay was so polite, he'd say that if she came in wearing a paper bag. "How's Mena?"

"Not so good. The tooth pains her." He tapped his upper jaw. "I tell her, go to the dentist. But she says no. She's using ground cloves for the pain."

"If the pain continues, she'll need to see a dentist."

"I try to tell her. Lottery ticket today?"

"Only if you can guarantee it's the winner."

Sizzling sounds coupled with the mouthwatering smells made her glance sideways at the pigs-in-a-blanket in the warming case next to the cash register. Her stomach gurgled. "Are those fresh?"

"Made this morning." Sensing a sale, Sanjay reached for his tongs and waxed paper bag. "With or without cheese?"

"I shouldn't." Jori sighed and set aside her chips. "Well, maybe this one time."

"You going to buy something today?"

Jori looked around at the sound of that terse voice coming from behind her.

The shallow span of Battise's face visible between his cap brim and bush of beard contained black-lashed eyes the sludge-gold color of high-quality crude oil. He held a coffee cup in one hand and a water bottle in the other. Tucked in his right fist was a cellophane bag through which she could see an apple cruller. She wondered fleetingly what it would feel like to be that cruller.

She inhaled and went light-headed at the smell of clean salty sweat wafting faintly off him. *Oh God.* She was about to embarrass herself by drooling.

Mustering her most professional voice, she shifted her gaze to his face. "Hello, Mr. Battise."

"Law will do." His dark-amber gaze dipped and hovered at her mid-chest long enough for her to remember she wasn't wearing a bra. She'd ducked out for cat food wearing her sleep tee tucked into a pair of cutoffs. To judge by his fractional squint, her body must be reacting to his bold gaze. Yep, her nipples definitely tingled. Damn. Her hormones were in overload.

When that black-gold gaze returned to her face, Jori felt both the attraction and the repulsion of a force mightier than her own. "I'll ask again. Are you planning to buy something today?"

"Yes, of course." Jori dumped her things on the counter. What a grouch.

When she had paid, she turned back to him, determined to show him the kind of manners he didn't seem to possess. "See you shortly." No need to prolong the moment. Not when her senses were outmaneuvering her brain.

"Wait a second." He pulled a twenty from his pocket and handed it over to the cashier before continuing. "Might as well tell you, I'm turning the dog back in today."

Surprise darted through her. "Samantha? Why?"

He gathered up his items and change before turning fully toward her. "Let's just say I'm not a doodle kind of guy."

It didn't take effort to process that bit of macho attitude. No doubt a poodle mix was too cuddly for his image.

She offered him a sly look. "Too much dog for you?"

He slanted a stare-down at her that made her vividly aware of the six-inch difference in their heights. Did he have to make everything a contest? Yes. Probably. Because he could so easily win. Walking intimidation.

She held on to her smile. "Come on, Mr. Battise. Sam's so well trained, a two-year-old could handle her."

"Do I look like a toddler to you?"

What he looked like was a man-sized helping of trouble for a woman with too much imagination, and too little opportunity to exercise it. But he wasn't offering her a chance to dance. The *back off* sign was bright in his gaze.

He slid on his shades, finishing the impression that he was barricaded behind his cap and beard. "Give the dog to someone who needs her."

Jori quickly recalibrated. Kelli wouldn't be happy if she didn't at least try to dissuade him from that action.

As he moved toward the exit, she fell into step beside him. "If Samantha's not behaving, I can sort her out for you. You wouldn't be the first client who hasn't had a dog before. You'll get the hang of it."

Instead of stepping through as the automatic doors whooshed open, he paused and looked down, his stare zeroing in on her ninety-nine-cent flip-flops. One was neon green, the other bubble-gum pink. Each sported colorful plastic flowers over the big toe.

Some emotion rounded his cheeks above his tangle of beard as his gaze rose quickly up her bare legs and torso to her face. "What do you get out of bossing grown men around?"

The question was meant to back her off but Jori absorbed it with a blink. "What I get is results, Mr. Battise. See you later."

She moved first through the exit.

"Nice butt."

He said the words so softly she wondered if he meant her to hear him. She turned around, eyes narrowed. "In your dreams, Mr. Battise."

"All the time." He smiled then, the first time she'd seen anything like humor in his expression.

She turned and put one flip-flop in front of the other, ignoring the slapping sounds they made as she moved out across the parking lot. But she was smiling.

Yep. He held in check more force of personality than most men possessed. The reason she was sweating was entirely her own fault. Battise was hot. All he had to do was appear and she was all sweaty slut in heat. At least she had good taste. Battise was prime slut muffin material.

But not a nice man. He was rude, and curt, and condescending. And he was probably troll-ugly beneath that beard. Yeah, gorgeous body but a weak chin, buck teeth, and pizza-textured skin from years of bad acne, or steroid abuse, or both. He probably lived in a room that smelled of stinky socks and sweaty balls. That's why he was so rude. He knew women were turned off by his—

"Oh hell!" Jori laughed out loud. He'd be gorgeous without a head. And he didn't smell. Well, only of fresh sweat. She was just annoyed that he didn't seem to find her, despite his comment, attractive. His pupils never dilated when he looked at her.

Jori caught her reflection in a passing car window and gulped. With her non-matching flip-flops, bed-head braid, and homemade cutoffs, what was there not to like?

The November breeze made gooseflesh of her thighs as she hurried across the parking lot. Yet the sun rising clear and bright through the remaining autumn leaves promised a true warm Indian summer day.

Once behind the wheel of her vehicle, two thoughts struck Jori. One, she couldn't really afford the pig-in-a-blanket she was about to devour. And two, Samantha hadn't been with Battise. Service dogs were supposed to go everywhere with their owners.

She looked up and saw Battise standing next to a truck several yards away. It was an F-150 Super Cab with a narrow second row of seats. Painted a no-nonsense gunmetal without trim work or even a bumper sticker, it reminded her of its owner: big, practical, yet impressive. Samantha had poked her muzzle through the open space in the passenger window and was watching him eat his cruller. As she watched, he offered the dog a bite. Samantha wolfed down the entire remains of the fried dough in a single gulp.

"Huh." Jori sat back and unwrapped her own meal. Not good canine nutrition but at least Battise was interacting with his dog.

Just as she took a bite, she saw him reach for the back of his T-shirt and pull. The deep valley of his spine came into view like a canyon. The edge of his shirt slid higher, revealing skin the color of copper pulled tight over dense muscles that rippled and bunched as he moved. The broad mesas of his shoulder blades appeared as he pulled the tee over his head.

The glorious male striptease was not all that had her paused in mid-bite. There was a series of long scars running like silver through the bronze contours of his lower back and around his left side before disappearing into the waistband of his shorts. Suddenly the violence that had taken his leg was all too real for her.

He tossed the damp shirt in the back of the truck then moved around to the driver's side, revealing a slight limp he could no longer hide. Jori followed him with her eyes. The keep-out intimidation of his attitude suddenly had another interpretation. Pain. The emotion in his gaze, so sharp, so familiar—was it an echo of his lingering pain?

She'd read a lot about the needs of disabled veterans in preparation for the week. Pain both real and what was called phantom, because it came from limbs no longer there, was often a constant companion for amputees.

Jori let her breath out slowly. She hadn't needed a whopping helping of sexual magnetism to start her day. Especially when there was nothing she planned to do about it. But the scars made Battise all too real.

She felt a twinge of shame. She'd been ogling him as if he were some book cover model showing off his perfect body for her enjoyment. But he was all too human. His arrogance was more likely the shield of a proud man who had lost, and suffered, and survived.

Jori set her breakfast aside uneaten. Suddenly all she wanted to do was make his life better. If he'd let her.

Jori put her SUV in gear, wincing as the gears of the 150,000-plus-mile vehicle clunked before meshing. Trust her to fall for the moody guy who wouldn't know a good time if it fell on him. Maybe if *she* fell on him . . .

*That's just prison talking, Jori.*

# CHAPTER THREE

"Maybe if we paired him with Bruno?"

"Bruno's not ready." Kelli Miller, owner of Warriors Wolf Pack, sat with her sneakers propped on the desk in her office. "Besides, the dog chooses the vet. That's our policy."

Jori nodded. Samantha had practically Velcroed herself to Battise the first day. She wouldn't leave his side even when beckoned by other vets. "But Mr. Battise said, I quote, 'I'm not a doodle kind of guy.' I don't think he even likes dogs."

"That's your impression?" Kelli's lips twitched as if she knew something Jori didn't. "Hold that thought." She rose from her chair.

Immediately the coal-black Lab mix named Troy, dozing at Kelli's feet, sat up and thrust his muzzle forward as he gazed up at her for instruction. Kelli made the sign for *stay* then went to push her office door closed before turning back to lean against it as she faced Jori.

"Veterans come to us for help. We don't need them to

be grateful, happy, or all fuzzy about what we do. Mr. Battise came for a reason. What do you know about him?"

Jori shrugged. "He suffers from PTSD." And he was hot. But she doubted Kelli wanted to hear that.

"Anything else?"

Jori shook her head. "Unlike the other veterans, he doesn't talk much." And then only in intimidating terms.

"Then I suggest you make it your business to get to know him. I'll pair you two together today for individual work. Once you know his story, I'm sure you'll be able to find a way to make Samantha work for him. That's the most important part of our job."

Jori knew this was true but wasn't at all certain about her ability to fill that need with Battise. "Shouldn't he be with someone who has more experience, like you?"

Kelli eyed her appraisingly. "You're a certified service dog trainer, Jori. You're a natural with our animals and they know it. I understand why you have trust issues. But WWP believes in you. Don't you think it's time you trusted yourself enough to do the job you're qualified for?"

"Yes, ma'am." WWP had a motto they lived by: *There's a useful place for everyone and everything.* She had more reason than most to know that it was true. Now she'd been assigned to prove it. To Battise.

However, getting close to a man who could kick-start her libido with just a glance was going to be a challenge. Getting him to talk about himself when he seemed to think "Hi" was a complete conversation was going to be even harder.

Jori reached down to scratch Troy behind the ears. "I'd better go. Class is about to start."

Jori's cell phone vibrated in her pocket as she entered the main room. She glanced at the display. Her mother. Again. Time to stop avoiding the inevitable. She took a deep breath before answering. "Hi, Mom."

"Thank goodness. I was getting worried. I'm trying to respect your boundaries, Jori. But honestly, it's not easy when you won't even return my calls."

"Sorry." Jori felt her throat tightening. "Hang on."

Jori caught the eye of Maxine, one of the volunteers covering the front desk, and made finger-walking movements before she ducked out a side door onto the parking lot. It was empty of people. She wouldn't be overheard.

"Mom, I'm really busy. We're graduating a class of veterans and their new service dogs this week."

"That's nice." While a worthy cause, her mother didn't think WWP was an appropriate full-time job for her college-educated daughter. At least she had stopped saying so each time the subject came up. "This won't take a minute. Did you receive Kieran and Kaitlyn's wedding announcement?"

"Yes." Jori searched for a more enthusiastic response to her older brother's upcoming nuptials next month. "The intertwined *K*'s are a nice touch."

"Aren't they? Your brother and his bride are working so hard to make their day special. Eureka Springs in December will be gorgeous. They decorate the town like a Victorian Christmas village. Oh, and the bridesmaids' dresses are in."

As her mother continued, Jori's mind wandered. For nearly four years, fear and worry and bewilderment had been the subtext of every conversation. So far, there was no new normal. Only awkward moments like this. Maybe if she went home for a few days after the wedding they could begin to reconnect. Maybe at Christmas—

"Wait, Mom." A name in her mother's ramble jerked her thoughts back to the present. "Did you say Erin Foster is a member of the wedding party? When did that happen?"

"Last week. After Kaitlyn's sister was told she can't travel due to complications involving her pregnancy, so

Erin offered to step in as maid of honor. They are sorority sisters, after all. By the way, Erin's a Tice now, remember? She married Luke Tice right after . . . the unpleasantness. I sent you pictures of the wedding from *Soiree Magazine*. Remember?"

"Uh-huh." Jori hadn't read any of the social news her mother had bombarded her with for the past four years, all about the wonderful lives being lived by her former friends. But that wasn't the reason this news surprised her. "I can't believe Erin would agree to be involved in anything to do with the Garrisons."

"I don't know why you'd say that."

Exasperation colored Jori's tone. "Maybe because she's married to one of the attorneys in the D.A.'s office that prosecuted my case?"

"Now, Jori, Luke isn't in the D.A.'s office anymore. He's in private practice, and running for state senator. So, see, it's all working out nicely. The wedding will give you a chance to reconnect."

Jori rubbed at the knot of tension that had drawn her eyebrows together. Her mother was a relentlessly upbeat person who never admitted to a problem until it slapped her in the face. She just hated to be the one to deliver the blow.

"Kieran and I talked about this, Mom. He understands why I won't be at his wedding."

"Well, I don't. No one would dare spoil a wedding day with old gossip."

Gripping the phone tight, Jori dropped her voice into a desperate whisper. "Get real, Mom. *Everyone* will gossip about me if I'm there. Your daughter's an ex-con."

The stunned silence on the other end sent shame arrowing through Jori's middle. Why had she answered the phone? "We'll talk later. Got to go. Love you."

Jori held her eyes wide to prevent tears from forming.

She'd learned the first week of incarceration that showing vulnerability of any kind identified an inmate as weak, and therefore a potential victim. Too bad she hadn't learned that lesson before Brody Rogers entered her life.

In her darkest moments she had wondered if her fate would have been any worse if she'd shot her fiancé. Everyone seemed to understand crimes of passion. But when she was arrested after Brody's accidental death in a car wreck, their friends had scattered like roaches before Raid. Controlled substances were found in Brody's body and more in his car, along with lots of cash. A warrant had been issued that night allowing police to search his apartment in Fort Smith—and her apartment in Fayetteville, because the lease was in Brody's name. Drugs were found in both places, enough to get her arrested and charged with drug possession with the intent to distribute.

The statewide news media had had a field day with the scandal of two prominent families caught up in a sordid drug story. Few besides her family believed her when she said that Brody had hidden cocaine packets in her closet without her knowledge. In fact, she didn't know anything about his dealing. The judge certainly hadn't believed her. She'd been sentenced to ten years. Eligible for patrol after three and a half. That was six months ago.

Jori sighed as she pushed through the door into the building. She was learning to live with the stigma of being a felon. That didn't mean she would inflict it on her family.

When she reached the training room and saw that Battise and Samantha weren't with the other vets, she backtracked to the main room to ask for his phone number so she could remind him he was late.

"Let me make that call." Maxine grinned and pushed a handful of dreads off her shoulder. "Any excuse to talk to that man will do me fine."

"Okay. Just don't expect a friendly response."

Maxine nodded. "I know. He rubs you the wrong way. Personally, I wouldn't mind which way he rubbed me. But I'm not the one he's been sniffing around."

Jori rolled her eyes. Corny canine references between staff members were a daily event. "He's not dogging me."

"No, he's been stalking you with his eyes." Barbara, another volunteer, looked up from feeding the guinea pigs they kept in cages in the main lobby. All sorts of household pets were kept at the facility as part of the training of their service dogs. "And you've been watching him like he was going to suddenly morph into Wolverine."

Too true. But Jori wasn't about to own it. "Whatever. Let me know if he's not coming, Maxine."

Class was well under way when the door to the practice room opened and Battise entered with Samantha.

Jori frowned when she saw that the service dog wore a traditional collar that hadn't come from WWP. Her gaze followed up the leash to the bronze hand holding it and finally up to Battise's face. There was little to read there, aside from the light of challenge in his sludge-gold eyes. He was probably waiting for her to say something about his being late. But Kelli had given her a mission. Make nice and get to know him.

"Good morning." She smiled brightly as she left the ring of trainers, vets, and dogs to engage him. "Kelli's just reviewing how to use the gentle lead."

His heavy shoulders jerked up and down beneath a clean navy-blue tee, drawing her eye to the inked feather visible below the hem of his left sleeve. "Didn't bring it."

Jori held on to her smile. "Not a problem."

She bent down. "Hello, Samantha." She gave the dog a treat from the pouch at her waist and cooed affectionately as she detached the leather collar. "Such a good girl. Did you have a good night with your new handler?"

Samantha looked back at Battise, as if she understood Jori's question. He didn't meet her eye.

Jori produced a gentle lead from a pocket of her cargo pants. It was made of a flexible loop worn around the top of a dog's muzzle and a second strap that went under the chin and clipped behind the dog's head. A dog could bark, eat, and even pick up an object in its jaws while wearing it.

When she had given Samantha another treat, she looked up at Battise and held out her hand for the leash. "May I?"

He handed it over without hesitation. The jolt of surprise she felt as their hands touched was a purely involuntary response to a passion, she told herself, she had no use for.

"Heel, Samantha." She tugged the leash lightly and pressed the clicker used to train dogs when they had to respond to more than one handler in the environment.

To her amazement Samantha didn't budge. The canine continued looking up at Battise. "Give her permission to leave your side."

Law frowned at the dog. "*Geh*—uh, go on, Sam. Go with Jori."

Samantha licked the hand he had used to emphasize his point before turning away obediently.

Law watched the pair walk away in misgiving. He should have left the dog at the reception desk, as he'd planned. Regardless of Yard's advice, he was leaving without a dog. So what was he doing standing here, when he needed to be headed to the airport to catch his booked flight to Richmond, Virginia?

He knew the answer. He was behaving like a POG, lusting after something he couldn't have.

When he'd noticed Jori at the convenience store this morning, something about her posture had caught his attention. It was so unlike the friendly young woman he'd seen at WWP the past three days. With shoulders hunched and a thumbnail hooked into her teeth, she'd looked as if her day hadn't begun well and wasn't going to get any better. That shouldn't have bothered him, but it did.

He'd nearly stopped to speak to her. But then she'd bent to pull something off a lower shelf. Better to keep moving, he'd told himself. Her problems. No need to make them his.

Then he'd caught her reflection in the glass doors of the refrigerated cases. The intensity of her gaze had grabbed him by the short hairs. He'd frozen, not certain how he should react to that frankly lustful gaze aimed his way. His body didn't hesitate. His dick had gone hard as a lead pipe.

Something like humor tugged at Law's mouth. Even after her friendly wave he couldn't think of a goddamn way to respond that wouldn't end up involving the clerk calling the police about two customers engaged in a lewd display of public affection.

At the checkout line, he'd behaved like an asshole. All to cover up his real feelings. He wanted her. Bad.

That's why he was here now, staring at her ass while barely registering the presence of the other vets, dogs, and trainers. He checked his phone. Three hours until his flight. It was an hour's drive to Little Rock's airport. He should leave now.

To his surprise, his stride carried him toward, not away from the class.

Across the room Kelli welcomed Jori back into the semicircle of people. "Why don't you give us a quick refresher on the gentle lead, Jori."

Jori ignored Battise as he took up a position a little apart from the rest, his back to the wall. "We use gentle leads because even the tiniest tug on a leash will turn your dog's head in your direction for commands. This type of leash is a bonus for someone in a wheelchair, or an amputee using one or more prosthetic devices. You won't get jerked off your feet, or out of a chair by a stubborn animal. Not that we have those here."

To demonstrate, she took a few steps then made a sudden right turn, surprising Samantha. After the slightest tug on her leash, Samantha instantly changed directions.

"Very good." Kelli waved her back into the group. "Right now one of our puppy raiser families is training a hundred-and-five-pound black Lab named Bronco. Their seven-year-old daughter Harley can completely control him on a gentle lead."

"And a little child shall lead them." Abe, a Vietnam vet in from Michigan and the eldest of their clients in this graduating class, was missing his right leg above the knee. He wore a T-shirt that read: *THIS SHIRT COST ME AN ARM AND A LEG. I GOT IT ON DISCOUNT.* His new dog was Ginger, a big blond shelter dog who was part Lab and parts unknown.

When each veteran had been allowed to test his skill with the gentle lead, Kelli stepped in again. "Before we break up into individual sessions, do any of you have problems or successes from last night that you want to share?"

Seth, a fresh-faced twenty-eight-year-old from Vermont in a wheelchair, raised a hand. "Does falling out of bed at three a.m. constitute a problem?"

"Depends on what you did while you were down there," Abe answered. "I've been known to locate quarters and missing socks while lying there waiting for help. Even found a busted TV remote under my sofa one time."

That drew a round of friendly laughter from all five vets.

Seth reached out to pat the big chocolate Lab sitting by

his chair. "Johnny, here, is stronger than he looks. Between us we had me back in bed in no time. Then he climbed in beside me and laid on the outside. Guess he didn't want to be awakened by me falling out a second time."

Kelli grinned and patted Seth's shoulder. "So you're happy with Johnny?"

"Beats all the hell out of spending the night on the floor, or calling my parents for help."

"Or using them toddler bed rails," the man beside him contributed.

After each of the other vets had related a story about his first night with his dog, Jori glanced at Battise. At least he was still here.

She approached and offered him Sam's leash, which he took, if reluctantly. "Is there anything you'd like to share, Mr. Battise?"

"Share with you? Sure, sweetheart." A toothy grin appeared in his beard. "But right here, in front of God and everybody?"

The other men smirked or tried to hide their smiles. Right. She'd handed him a big slow-pitch softball of a line that didn't mean anything. She just shook her head and moved away.

"All right," Kelli said briskly. "We'll take a break to allow our dogs to be walked and watered. Then we'll begin our day's one-on-one training. Mr. Battise, you'll be with Jori. Abe, your trainer will be Will."

As Kelli paired up the remaining vets and trainers, Jori's heart began to pound in slow heavy strokes. Battise was looking at her with the light of battle bright in his gaze. She smiled but made the gesture for drinking. She needed a moment to collect herself if she was going to go one-on-one with him all afternoon. At least he hadn't left.

The drink machine was located in the hallway. Abe and Ginger had beaten her there.

Abe rolled his chair back out of her way while Jori dug in her pocket for change. "That was a nice bit earlier about the soft leads." He cupped Ginger under the chin, stroking her with the familiarity that one would expect from a longer association. "Did you two put that together to make the rest of us feel better?"

"What are you talking about?" Jori fed the machine her change.

"That business of Sergeant Battise pretending like he doesn't know how to handle dogs. Since the others bought it I guess I'm the only one who recognized him."

She collected her bottle. "What do you mean?"

"He was all over the news about three years ago. Military K-9 police. CID. Special agent. Wounded in Afghanistan. Got a medal and everything."

"Oh." Jori twisted open her water bottle and took a long swallow. The cold hit her stomach like icicles. *Battise was military K-9 police!* Compared with his experience with dogs, she was a rank amateur. That certainly explained his attitude toward her. Even worse, he'd let her make a complete fool of herself, thinking he didn't know or like dogs.

Jori could feel her pulse begin to beat in her temples. Privacy was a top priority at WWP. But Kelli, who personally conducted all intake interviews, would know Battise's history. She could have told her a little about Battise this morning. Instead, she had told Jori to get to know him. As if she'd had the time before and deliberately neglected to. Or had she?

Jori glanced at Abe. She knew the names of his grown children and that he had six grandkids. She knew Seth had gone to college on a baseball scholarship. She also knew that James had fathered two children since losing both legs. And that Joshua was about to get married. But Battise had made her too uncomfortable to make small talk with.

Or maybe she'd avoided getting to know him because she couldn't keep her own emotions under control when he was around.

Furious with herself for letting her issues get in the way of doing her job, Jori turned to find that Battise and Sam had followed her into the hallway.

She gulped, feeling guilty for no good reason. Nothing in his attitude said he had overheard her conversation with Abe. That didn't mean he looked happy to see her.

"You done with your break yet?"

His tone went straight through her, sparking anger she didn't pause to identify. "No, we get two whole minutes per break, Mr. Battise. We're civilians." She took another long sip from her bottle to cool her annoyance.

Abe grinned, looking from one to the other. "If you lovebirds will excuse me." He rolled on down the hallway, chuckling.

Jori waited until Abe was out of hearing before she leaned in toward Battise. "You're rude."

"I know." He reached out and took her hand, placed Sam's leash in it, then folded her fingers closed with his other and squeezed. Strong even teeth appeared in the middle of his beard. "But you're curious."

He bent down and grabbed Samantha under the chin and scratched her behind the ears. "You take care of yourself, Sam. I'm sure a nice new owner will be along any day." He leaned in to kiss her between the eyes and stood. "Give Kelli my thanks but tell her I have somewhere to be."

"You can't just walk out." Jori took a step after him. He didn't pause, sliding on his shades as he strolled toward the exit door.

"Mr. Battise."

He didn't even look back.

Jori stopped herself from following him, aware that

nothing she could say now was likely to turn him around. But watching him push through the glass doors was an exercise in frustration. Back erect, shoulders squared. The slight limp was subdued once more by sheer willpower. Even from behind he looked good enough to lick.

Jori looked down at Samantha, who was staring after him and whimpering as she strained on the leash. "You, too? We must be out of our minds. Out of our minds."

She fed Samantha a couple of treats to distract her from the stress of losing her handler, then marched them both straight into Kelli's office.

"Mr. Battise just walked out."

Kelli cocked her head to one side. "Where did he go?"

"He didn't say. Just to tell you he had somewhere else to be." She stopped short of voicing her opinion that he wouldn't be back. What little she knew about him made him unpredictable.

To her surprise Kelli just smiled. "Have Maxine put in a request to one of our puppy raisers to take Samantha until he returns." WWP seldom left their dogs in kennels on the property overnight. Service dogs needed the constant reinforcement of home and family life.

"I could take her for tonight." Jori wasn't sure why she offered but there it was.

"Suit yourself."

"One other thing. I'd like permission to read Mr. Battise's file."

"It's in there." Kelli pointed to the row of tall file cabinets then reached for her purse. "I have a meeting in Little Rock this afternoon so I'll be out the rest of the day. See you in the morning."

When her boss was gone Jori shut the office door, not wanting to be disturbed. She searched until she found the folder she wanted from the wall of files. Propping a shoulder against one of the metal cabinets, she began to read.

She skipped the personal information, flipping the sheets until she came to Battise's injury assessment. It was more thorough than she expected.

Amputee, above the left knee. Battise, like many soldiers wounded by a blast that had a thermal element, had spent seventeen months in and out of hospitals, while surgeons dealt with additional injuries, did skin grafts, and reduced heavy scar tissue, all while initially attempting to salvage his leg. Just reading about it made her ache in sympathy for him. He had suffered so much.

In notes added in the margin she read how he had fought the doctors, wanting to maintain all of his ruined leg if he could. Only after he gave in to the need for amputation did his pain become manageable.

Jori paused to catch her breath. Managed pain. That meant there was still pain. All the time. That could erode a man's attitude. She hadn't made room for that possibility in her assessment of him. Maybe because he wanted it that way. Better to be thought an asshole than needy? Sounded like Battise. She glanced back down.

Instead of checking individual boxes, he'd made one big checkmark on top of the list of PTSD symptoms. In the area where he was asked to describe his symptoms, he'd written *HELL*. That covered a lot of ground.

She flipped to his work record. Right after college Battise entered the police academy and was then hired as a K-9 officer with the Arkansas State Police, Troop L, handling drug interdiction. Jori frowned. K-9 officer slots were at a premium in nearly every law enforcement department in the country. Even with the bushy beard, Battise didn't seem much older than thirty. She flipped back a few sheets. Born in Polk County, Texas, 1984. Yep. Thirty-one next month. How had he gotten into a K-9 unit position right out of the academy?

She flipped the pages back to his personal information. Name: *Lauray Bronson Battise*.

"Oh crap." Why hadn't the name clicked in her head before? He was the son of Bronson Battise, one of the most famous trainers of military and police K-9s in the United States.

She had read everything she could find online about professionally trained K-9s once she was accepted in the WWP service dog program at the correctional center. Bronson Battise's name came up often. As the founder and original owner of Harmonie Kennels, he had developed methods now used by other facilities to train specialty dogs for law enforcement, government agencies, and the military.

Jori blew out her breath and reached for her water bottle. A dozen questions chased around in her thoughts. For instance, why had he come here for a service dog when he could have trained any animal he wanted from the famous Harmonie Kennels?

"Find anything interesting in there?"

Jori hadn't heard a sound but looked up and right into the black-gold glower of Lauray Battise, aimed at her from the open doorway.

# CHAPTER FOUR

Samantha sprang to her feet and woofed happily, her long Cheez Doodle tail swishing back and forth as she padded over to greet him. Battise bent and scrubbed under her chin with both hands, murmuring words only they understood.

Jori's reaction to his arrival wasn't nearly so welcoming. When he straightened and looked at her, her voice was cool as ice. "Why are you back?"

Law wasn't about to tell her about his sister's text. She had sent him three words as he was climbing into his truck: *Bring the dog.* Yardley was spooky.

Instead, he looked down at Sam, who was leaning against his pant leg. "Sam. Down. Stay."

Samantha plopped down on her belly but continued to look up at him with adoring eyes.

Law glanced again at Jori and pushed the door shut behind him.

When he closed the gap between them he could see his name typed on the tab of the folder she held. She was checking up on him. He couldn't decide whether that was a good or a bad thing. He poked the file. "Know enough now?"

Jori shook her head. "Why didn't you tell me you're Bronson Battise's son? Your family's famous!"

His eyes narrowed. "Is that important to you?"

"It's important that you're a professional dog handler." She smacked the folder against his chest. "You let me spend three days instructing you as if you've never owned a dog. I want to know why."

"Maybe I was curious about your technique."

"But other people knew. I must look like a fool to them."

"You've nothing to be ashamed of." Those dark eyes of his were shifting over her again, as if he thought he had missed something the first two times he'd stared at her today. This time his gaze dropped all the way to her feet, where it stayed for a few seconds. "Well, maybe there's something. Your shoes don't match."

"So what?" She deliberately wore one red sneaker and one yellow one.

"You wear mismatched shoes or socks every day." His accessing gaze came back to her face. "That must mean something."

"Only to me."

"As long as you aren't ashamed of it."

His expression softened a bit. With humor? It was the closest thing to a real conversation they'd ever had.

He took the file from her hand and closed it. "Anything else you want to know about me? Ask."

"Okay." There were things. Lots. She just couldn't think of any of them with him standing so close.

She backed up a step, trying to be casual as she draped her elbow on top of the file cabinet. She gained only six inches. "With your background, you could have gotten a service dog from any breeder in the country. You came here. Why?"

His lids lowered to half-mast over the dark-gold brilliance of his eyes. "I was blackmailed."

Jori couldn't imagine anyone who could force this man to do something he didn't want to do. There had to be another reason. "Is it because we specialize in PTSD dogs?" She glanced at the file he held. "The extent of your injuries indica—"

"—I got blown up. That's not exactly news to me."

He dropped the folder on top of the file behind her and braced his hand beside her arm on the file cabinet, effectively enclosing her between his body and the cabinet. "Next question."

Jori tried to ignore his attempt to dominate her space. "Samantha's specially trained to help with PTSD episodes. I've been working with her for four months so I know she's good at her job."

"That's not a question."

"Do you think she's well trained?"

"Very."

Jori thought about that one-word answer for a second. The only way he would know that was if he had seen her in action, too. "Did you experience an episode last night?"

He stared at her, every muscle in his face gone Mount Rushmore hard. Then he jerked his head to the left, as alert as if Kelli's desk had reared up on hind legs and snarled at him.

For a split second Jori didn't understand his reaction. Then she realized she'd heard the sound, too. A pile of papers on the desktop had shifted. Nothing to alarm even Samantha. But Battise was blinking as his head swiveled slowly right and left to scan the corners of the ten-by-twelve-foot office space. Though he wasn't touching her, she could feel the tension making his body rigid.

She'd read about and watched other trainers working

with service dogs simulate it. But she'd never seen a real exaggerated startle response in anyone.

Samantha, ahead of Jori in processing what was going on, had risen and come over to Battise. Immediately she pushed in close to him, wedging her heavy body behind him at knee level. Battise didn't seem to notice.

Wanting to help, too, Jori reached out and touched him just above the elbow. His biceps was more than warm. It was almost scalding.

"It's okay, Mr. Battise."

She watched his whole presence change in the wake of her words. His attention snapped back to her. He looked first at her fingers curled lightly on his biceps and then up at her face. His blinking slowed.

"I don't need your help." His voice was as hard as the muscles under her touch. His gaze seemed to repel her by force of will.

Determined not to lose him, she clamped her fingers tight on his arm. "I can see that you're very capable in many ways, Mr. Battise. But this isn't war. You don't have to gut it out alone."

He didn't answer but he didn't pull away from her touch.

Maybe she just needed to change the subject. "Look, if you don't like Sam—"

"I never said I didn't like Sam." He didn't move yet he suddenly seemed closer. "I said I don't want her." The words came out as if each one were a whole sentence.

"Okay. Tell me what you do want."

"What I want?" When his rough and ready gaze rose to tangle with hers, a surge of pure lust burst through Jori. Sexual heat radiated off him like waves from glowing coals. And his eyes. Direct, penetrating. Pure Alpha in search of every advantage against a perceived opponent. At the moment it was all aimed at her.

Self-protection was telling her to run like a scared little

rabbit. Not that there was anywhere to go. She was cornered between the file cabinet and his rather impressive body. Another part of her wanted to lean in to him, to touch and taste that heat. Yet the biggest part was urging her to bark back at the Alpha invading her space.

She slapped a palm flat on his chest. "Back off, Mr. Battise. I'm not your enemy."

Something glinted in his gaze. "Then why do I feel in jeopardy whenever you're around?"

As if. There was too much male presence in his stance to make her feel safe enough to enjoy his brand of humor. But that didn't mean she wasn't thinking, fast, about her next move.

She removed her hand. Her palm went cold from the loss of contact.

"Know what I think, Mr. Battise? You wouldn't recognize what you needed if it was standing in front of you."

"You want to know what *I* think?" He lifted a finger and touched her two inches below the hollow of her throat where the skin was exposed above the vee of her T-shirt. "I think you're curious as hell about what we'd be like together."

Jori couldn't lie. The raw heat surging through her was his doing. She was playing with fire. But, she reminded herself, there was only so much he would dare in a public place with a dozen people within the sound of her voice.

She straightened up, suddenly aware that a file cabinet handle had been poking hard into her back. "No thanks. I'm busy."

"Boyfriend?" He said the word all snarky and dismissive of the imagined man.

She shrugged, trying to see past his shoulder. "I'm just not interested."

"Liar."

He leaned in until his beard tickled her left cheek and

his voice was a deep dry gush of male temptation in her ear. "Let's get the hell out of here and go somewhere we can satisfy our . . . curiosity."

"Not going to happen." She again put up a hand to push him away. Yet when she encountered the contours of hard warm muscle beneath his shirt, instead of shoving him away, her fingers curled reflexively into the fabric.

One side of his beard hitched up in what could only be a smile. He leaned toward her, applying the pressure of his chest until her hand retreated and there was no space left between their bodies. His chest crushed her breasts.

He was watching her, no doubt trying to determine just how far he could go before she screamed. "Don't worry. I just want a taste of what I can't have. Call it a consolation prize."

For about a tenth of a second Jori thought, *What if someone sees us?* Then she stopped thinking of anything else but the man locking lips with hers.

Law just meant to touch his lips to hers, to brand her with a taste of what she'd be missing if she didn't take him up on his offer. But then she surged in against him, her fingers grabbing fistfuls of the front of his tee as she opened her mouth under his.

It was like waving a red flag at one very touchy bull.

He had long ago outgrown having a teenage omni-directional dick that any passing pretty girl could make painfully hard. Yet all it took was Jori's lips parting and her tongue sliding out over his lips to stretch his cock full-length. She wasn't supposed to kiss like this. Like she knew what he wanted, and how he wanted it, and was ready to provide it as long as he needed it.

Even so, he knew what she was doing. Teasing herself, and him, with possibilities she had no intention of making good on. That was her mistake. Because right now he wanted her. *Bad.* And he wasn't going to let her off easy.

He hadn't forgotten about the fact that anyone could walk in on them at any time. This was just his one and only chance to scratch, if only a bit, his itch for her. He was going for it for as long as the opportunity lasted.

A low male sound came from somewhere deep in his chest as he gathered her in his arms and slanted his mouth, hard, against hers.

One of his hands gripped her braid near her nape and pulled until her head was tilted back under the power of his kiss. His other hand hauled her in by the waist; then his fingers dived down the back of her pants, under the waistband of her panties, to grasp one full mound of womanly ass.

Under the assault of his mouth Jori felt every cell in her body react. Her nipples tightened. Her sex clenched, hard, seeking satisfaction that required the participation of a male body. In no time he had taken apart every scintilla of resistance, with only a kiss, and she was sagging in surrender.

Jori held on, fingers flexed on his chest like a climber trying to find a hold on the face of a sheer rock cliff. He kissed like he was on fire, all desperate need laced with the absolute control of a man who knew what he wanted and exactly how to get it.

Law felt her surrender. Her body went soft in his arms. His hands slid lower, one to embrace her shoulders while the other curved down deeper under her butt to lift and mold her body to fit his. She helped, rising up on tiptoe. He was home free.

The sudden burst of laughter from the main room was as startling as a gunshot.

Law jerked his mouth from hers and twisted his head back to check the doorway. No one stood there. But it was only a matter of time before someone noticed their absence and came looking for them. Not that he really gave a damn.

He was hard enough to pound steel. Was ready to take her on the desk right in front of every bug-eyed veteran, volunteer, and dog in the place. But she wouldn't like that.

Law released her. Well, he tried. His hands weren't listening to his head. His fingers made it all the way out of her panties, only to grip her upper arms as if they knew that releasing her was the very last thing he wanted to do. If he couldn't let go of her, he needed to think of something else.

"Are you finished?"

Jori was staring at him with pupils so wide he could drown in them. Her mouth was wet. Finished? He hadn't even gotten started.

When she licked her upper lip his whole body jerked as if she had just slid that hot pink tongue up the underside of his cock. He glanced around, looking for a suitable surface. Desk. Floor. He wanted her now.

His gaze came back to her and his belly clenched. "You asked me what I want. What I want is you."

The bluntness of his words left her blinking. Jori strained to think with her heart pumping double-time. "This is nuts. I don't know you."

"Wrong answer." His fingers opened free like bolts blown by explosive charges. He took a step back, but it was only enough to leave breathing room. "You want me. I want you. We know enough."

She gave her head a tight shake as her gaze slid from his.

He glanced at the clock. There'd be other planes. There wouldn't be another time for this. He focused on the woman who had put a heartbeat in his dick. "Tell me three things."

She gaped at him, caught between amusement and shock. "This is crazy."

He leaned forward and covered her mouth again with

his. When he broke contact, he was the one who sighed. "Three things."

"I like being outside better than inside."

"One."

"I like to dance."

He nodded. "Faster."

Jori swallowed the hollowed-out feeling expanding in her chest as if she had stepped off a cliff into thin air. "I'm absolutely the last woman you should be with."

His eyes widened. "Why?"

"Because you're—were a cop." Jori was too surprised by the words that had come from her mouth to notice his reaction.

Law went very still. The itch that had been driving him crazy remained, but with a very different vibe. Why should she care that he'd been a cop? No. She'd said *because* he was a cop. Cause and effect. Who didn't like cops? People who'd been on the wrong side in an encounter with one.

Something clicked in his head. Something that had been staring him in the face all week yet hadn't registered. He turned and walked out of the office. Samantha, ever on the job, trailed after him dragging her leash.

Jori let him go. She'd seen the light go on behind his eyes and suspected where he was going, and why. She had hoped he already knew. That maybe someone had told him.

As her breathing slowed she realized her clothes were a mess. When had he pulled up her tee and freed a breast from her bra? And how had her panties become wadded in her crotch? He hadn't opened a snap or lowered a zipper but she was half undressed inside her clothes.

After a quick rearrangement, she followed him reluctantly into the main room.

She saw he had stopped before the Warriors Wolf Pack's

Wall of Heroes, scanning the faces of the vets who had become WWP family. He moved quickly past them. Farther along there were framed pictures of staff and volunteers. She knew the second he found what he was looking for in the final set of photos. All the air seemed to leave her lungs.

He leaned in, his finger touching the glass of the picture as if he needed to verify with a touch what his eyes were showing him.

Jori knew the photo all too well. It was taken at the women's correctional center. The inmates, all in matching white jumpsuits, were part of the Warriors Wolf Pack rehabilitation program while serving their sentences. She was the third woman from the right, holding up her certificate as proof she had fulfilled the requirements to be a service dog trainer . . . once released.

She was an ex-con. Law hadn't known about that until this second.

Jori sucked in a breath, trying to steady her pride and absorb the hurt coming at her like a major-league fastball. No way to dodge it.

When he levered away from the framed portraits he didn't even glance her way. He walked straight across the room and out the main doors. Samantha hurried but the closing door halted her on the inside. Unhappy, she pawed the door and whimpered.

Jori glanced over at Maxine, who was gaping at her from behind the reception desk like a fish jerked out of water. She came rushing over. "What was that about?"

Jori thrust out her chin. "Nothing important."

As she turned away the main doors flew open again, shoved by a powerful arm. Battise stood in the breach. He looked seriously pissed.

"I don't give fuck about your past. Are you coming or not?"

Jori folded her arms, staring daggers at him. "What about Samantha?"

His gaze flicked to Sam, who still stood by the door. "Bring the damn doodle with you."

She turned to Maxine. "I'll be back. Lunch break."

"Oh, somebody's hungry all right," she heard Maxine say as she picked up Samantha's leash. "I just doubt curly fries are involved."

# CHAPTER FIVE

Law sat in his truck before Jori's apartment, thinking. He'd just learned that the woman he was about to screw was a convicted felon. He didn't know what she'd done, or why. And guess what? He didn't give a damn.

His interest in her had nothing to do with who she was, or what she'd done, or even whether or not she might be good in the sack, though preliminaries said she'd be great. He could have had sex every day of the week but had lost interest in recent months. Yet something about Jori brought every hair on his body to attention. He wanted her so bad his zipper had been making teeth marks in his rigid dick for three days straight. Jerking off in the shower didn't begin to satisfy his itch.

And here she was, sitting and waiting for him to make the first move.

So why had his conscience suddenly jumped up to bite him in the ass? Because every thought in his head so far was about himself. Jori was the goal, the objective, nothing more. And unaccountably, he felt bad about that.

He glanced over at her. She sat staring out the windshield, chewing a corner of her lower lip as she fiddled with the end of her braid. He could tell she was having a conversation in her head, too. And it probably wasn't as lust-driven as his was.

"This doesn't work if you think about it."

Jori nodded, not looking at the man whose bones she wanted to jump right here in his truck. But if she kept thinking, she might just talk herself out of satisfying the hunger for him simmering beneath her full-body flush.

"Look at me." He waited until her gaze shifted to him. "I don't do relationships."

Jori watched him, drinking in the implication of his words. *Hard to handle. Impossible to hold on to.* That might just be the good news. She could barely keep up with herself. She didn't need strings or commitment, or even checking up on.

Sex, then gone. That she could handle.

She gave a little nod.

A smile jerked one corner of his mouth as he reached past Sam to wrap a fist around the thick shiny braid flipped across her shoulder. "Let me put this another way. I don't want a girlfriend. But I do, very badly, want to fuck you."

Law watched her complexion catch fire, but she didn't look away. When his gaze lowered to her breasts, her nipples pebbled as if he had actually touched them. He suspected if he reached into her pants he'd find her wet and warm with anticipation. But lust wasn't the same thing as accepting what he had said.

"Tell me this is what you want."

Jori frowned at him. Why was he giving her warnings? Couldn't he tell she was so ready for him she was about to burst into flames? Maybe not.

She reached across the space between them, tangled her

fingers in his beard, and tugged. "You promised me sex. So shut up and put out."

His laughter startled her. At most she would have expected something dry and mirthless from him, as if dust had collected on his humor. But this was a belly laugh, full and rich, and sexy as hell.

Law reached for her hand to guide it down to a hands-on demonstration of his interest. But Sam suddenly sat up and shoved her curly head into his face, blocking the move.

Pushing the pooch's head aside, he gave Jori a glance that made her thighs clench together. "Let's do this."

Once inside her door, he didn't give her a chance to even turn on a light. He took her by the shoulders, spun her around so she faced him, then back-walked her up against the nearest wall and kissed her.

Law had never been much for kissing. It was just the opening move for sex. But kissing Jori was different. Like potato chips, one of her kisses was not enough.

Heat slid through Jori as his hand slid up and grasped the braid at her nape to hold her still under the assault of his mouth. He kissed the way he did everything else, full-on, hard-charging. With no possibility of retreat. More than that, he kissed like a man with a hunger he couldn't quite control. A little rough and eager.

That was okay. She had an appetite of her own to satisfy. She reached up and fisted the thick hair at the back of his head with both hands to pull him closer.

She'd never kissed a man with a beard. It was a warm soft surprise that contradicted his hard-ass outside. He tasted clean and sexy and male.

She wanted to kiss him until she was saturated with his taste and smell and feel. Yet the world was spinning too fast for her to stay balanced. Her knees began to shake, her thighs loosening with anticipation.

Law was not about to move even an inch away. He wanted her to be much *much* closer. He moved a hand from her waist down her back. His hand traveled over the fabric that covered her hips until he cupped it under her butt. Then he pressed her hard against his throbbing groin, dry-humping her like a teenager for the sheer pleasure of it.

Jori's hands moved to his shoulders and gripped hard. He had worked her shirt up so that she felt cool air against her bare midriff. Then he grasped her with both hands just above her waist. His thumbs massaged her ribs just below the cups of her bra, then slipped up into the spaces left as she gasped in response to his touch. Once inside, his thumbs skimmed the soft undercurves of her breasts.

His kisses went roaming, leaving her mouth to trail across her cheek, whiskers tickling her, until he reached her ear. He sighed into it and then licked the center.

Jori jumped in shock at the touch of that warm wet tongue. But his hands were moving again, skimming her shirt up and over her head.

Law stepped back a little to better see what he had revealed. One of his slightly abrasive fingers skimmed along the top of her bra from side to side, then hooked into the low point. Grinning, he drew her in by it and kissed her, hard and quick before releasing her.

"Turn around."

When she had, bracing her hands against the wall, Jori felt him move in behind her until the proof of his interest in the main event was pressing into her backside. His hands slid up her back until they could work the hooks of her bra.

It surprised her that he didn't just jerk them open in his eagerness to see what lay beneath. Instead, he took his time, releasing each hook separately, as if each were a little present not to be missed. It was an excruciating tease as he paused after the second hook to run a finger under one strap and then the other, lifting them up and sliding each off the curve of her shoulders to hang loose along her arms. It was a delicate act for so powerful a man and it made her aware that he was enjoying this as much as she was. Finally, he unhooked the last catch.

She caught the bra against herself. His hands went about her waist once more but he didn't turn her around. The shock of his tongue, warm and sinuous between her shoulder blades, made her gasp. Her nipples beaded up behind her hands as he slowly traced her spine with his tongue. No man had ever done anything quite like that, so simple yet so intimate, as if he was enjoying her whole body. Not just eager for the main attraction.

The shocking heat of her own arousal melted her knees. In another second she'd be sliding toward the floor. But he seemed to sense that weakness and quickly spun her around. When she faced him, she dropped her hands, watching his face as the bra straps sailed down her arms and off her fingertips.

He stilled, the features of his face rigid as he looked his fill.

When his eyes came back to hers, Jori held his simmering stare. The intensity of that serious golden gaze weighed like sunshine on her face. In response, a bead of sweat worked its way down between her breasts, trembling with each breath she took. She closed her eyes, the better to pretend that it was Battise's tongue tracing that damp trail down her torso. The thought made her arch her back and take a deep breath, which thrust her breasts forward. Slowly, she let it out between parted lips.

Watching that slick of sweat surf her cleavage, Law's mouth went dry and then flooded back, so that he had to swallow before he could breathe. Unable to resist, he leaned forward to catch the salty drop on his tongue just before it reached her belly button. The knot in his cock doubled down.

With a rough groan of intent, he stripped off his shirt, tossed it aside, and reached for her with both hands.

But Jori moved to hold him away with a palm flat against his sternum. It was her turn to look. He went still as stone, his expression again as guarded as it had been every other time they'd gazed at each other. She held that daunting expression a beat and then lowered her gaze.

He was beautifully made. Powerful shoulders flowed into smoothly sculptured pecs beneath a trace of dark hair. The ripples of his abs were like the pattern water made on a beach as the tide ebbed. Besides the unusual tattoo circling his left biceps—something she wanted to ask about but didn't dare—there were other markings. Things that made her breath hiss inward between parted lips.

A scattering of scars, some smooth and others puckered, marred the perfection of his lower torso. The scar she'd seen from the back that morning in the parking lot now revealed itself as wrapping forward over his left hip before disappearing into the pants riding low on his hips. There was a patch of skin grafting the size of her palm to the left of his belly button. Heavier scars disappeared into the waistband.

She blinked twice before lifting a misty troubled gaze to his. The *keep out* sign was back in his eyes.

"The scars bother you?"

"Of course." Jori wanted to touch but his expression revoked her permission. "You've suffered so much."

"That was long ago." He said the words carefully, but the rough edge of those last words told her that *long ago* still occasionally roared back with disturbing clarity. Samantha was proof of that.

He back-stepped, palms going up in surrender. "If you find me ugly—"

"No!" She took a step toward him, but he backed up again.

His lids shuddered down. "My equipment's all original and in working order. If that's what's worrying you."

"It's not that, either." Gazing at his torso, the push of tenderness, sorrow, and desire to make it better welled up in her.

She approached again. This time, he didn't retreat as she reached out and ran a finger lightly over one of the scars. She felt a heavy tremor roll through him and knew it was costing him a lot to be inspected this way. That wariness was too much for her to respond to with mere words. Easier to just lean in and press her mouth to the scar at the top of his rib cage. His skin was warm, no, hot to the touch beneath her lips.

He took her by the shoulders, lifting her away from his body. Then a hand came up, forcing her chin to rise so that he could look her full in the face. "I don't need pity."

"You don't have it."

"Are you sure?"

Jori smiled and reached for his belt with both hands. "Aren't you?"

Something like humor flickered in his sludge-gold gaze. "All right then."

When she surged in against him, all heat and womanly curves and hunger, and eager moving hands, Law gave up any scruples about what they were doing.

She unbuckled him and then slid down his zipper. That little zipping sound was the most erotic thing he'd heard in months. No, it was the yummy sound she expelled into his open mouth when she reached in and released his cock.

*Well, hell.* He wasn't going to be able to be gentlemanly about their first time after all.

He grabbed her arms, lifting them back against the wall and pushing her body flat with the power of his. "I'd love to do you right here but it's not practical for me."

She smiled at him, laying her arms about his neck. "I do have a bed."

He grinned.

They entered the bedroom to be greeted by a hissing and spitting ball of black, white, and orange fur dancing sideways across the middle of the bed.

Until that moment, Jori had completely forgotten about the fact that Samantha was with them. And that her kitten, Argyle, wouldn't necessarily be happy about that fact.

Argyle's tail stood straight up and bristling, her kitten body like a McDonald's arch, every whisker stiff with rage at the intruder who came and rested her doggy head on the coverlet.

Law looked back at Jori. "Friend of yours?"

"Yes." Jori scooped Argyle off the bed. She cuddled the kitten in the curve of her arm as she stroked her. "Now, Argyle, you've seen a dog before." She walked slowly over to Sam and bent down. "Sam, this is Argyle. Argyle, this is Samantha."

The kitten shrank in her arms for a second then poked her head out and batted at the dog's nose with a paw. Jori noticed she hadn't used her claws.

Samantha calmly accepted the feline inspection. Just added a whiff of kitten to her collection of identification smells of things in the world.

"That's right. Sam is a friend." Jori patted Samantha. "You two play nice."

"Somewhere else." Jori looked up to see Law pointing toward the doorway. "All nonessential personnel out. Now."

Offended, Argyle let out a loud *mee*-now a whole octave higher than usual before leaping from Jori's arms and disappearing through the doorway.

Sam glanced at Law, who gave her the *go out* sign. With what Jori would swear was a doggy sigh of exasperation, the goldendoodle exited the bedroom at a more cautious pace.

Law quickly closed the door behind the pair. "Now, where were we?"

Jori pointed to the bed. "Almost there." Her voice sounded calm but she was looking at his erection with eyes wide. His pants were splayed open, and his thick rigid cock was arching out of the opening. And she had very hungry eyes. Maybe they were a little too bright?

"How long has it been for you?"

Embarrassed, she glanced up at the water spot on the ceiling of her cheap apartment. "Four years."

"Four—?" She was practically a virgin again after all this time.

Unless she'd gotten freaky inside.

"You still prefer dick to pussy?"

Shocked by his crudeness, Jori jerked her gaze back to him. Right, why should he be any different? All ex-cons must be lesbians. It was one of the clichés everyone wanted to believe about incarcerated women. Her armor of emotional distance clanked into place. "What's the matter? Worried I might disappoint you?"

"Just the opposite."

Jori studied his expression to see if he was baiting her. He looked completely serious. And a little uncomfortable. "If you've changed your—"

He was on her in a flash, a wall of warm smooth skin covering muscle and bad intentions. "I don't give a rat's ass about anything before now. I want to fuck you, bad. Do you still want to fuck me?"

A flush warmed her neck at his language. Like him, it was direct and to the point. No flowers. No easing into the moment. Just the bald honesty of his erection pressing into her belly.

"Say something, Jori." The demand, whispered into her

ear, made her belly quiver and her sex tighten in delicious anticipation.

She smiled. Battise was asking permission, even if it sounded like a command. So his style. She could be as direct.

In answer she reached down between them and fisted him. He was hot and hard and trembling with the need for action. As he groaned in pleasure she took advantage, pumping him a little just to make certain he knew he wasn't the only one with control. "No more talk."

Within moments they were entangled on the bed. Law had a new directive in his head: *Do this right. For her.*

He took advantage of her prone position to trail his fingers down her arms and cover her breasts. Lifting them to his lips, he took a nipple between his teeth, tugging and licking first one and then the other. He loved the way she squirmed under him. No doubt his whiskers tickled her as he whisked his beard lightly back and forth over her tender nipples. She was moaning low. Maybe he was hurting her. But she grabbed handfuls of his hair to hold him in place when he lifted his head to check. Her eyes were tightly shut, her mouth slightly open. The sight was even more erotic than the sound of his zipper being lowered by her. His cock was weeping with need, and they hadn't even gotten past second base. But that was about to change.

He shucked her pants and panties down her hips and slid a hand under her butt. He pulled her in tight. That action spread her thighs an inch. Enough for his fingers to slide under and then up. She was wet, so ready for him.

Jori sighed in surrender to the sensations swirling through her. His stroking was gentle at first, working her tender folds until her body lubed the passage of those thick, clever fingers. Heat pooled in her pelvis and spilled from her body onto his hand from the friction created by his fingers.

Jori lifted her hands away from the hard expanse of his shoulders and placed them back against the bedding, a moment of complete surrender.

"Oh yeah. I want you all wet and coming in my hand." He smiled at her an instant before covering her mouth with his.

He slipped his other hand up between her soft thighs to tease the feminine nub at the top of her sex. Her shuddery moan made him smile in response. She was juicy and warm, and ready for him. She whimpered as he parted the wet silk of her lips. The jackhammer need pushing him almost made him forget.

He rolled off her suddenly and sat up.

Gasping at his sudden withdrawal, Jori sat up. "What? What's wrong?"

The annoyed look on her face made Law smile. Oh, she was into him.

"My leg." He pointed to his prosthesis. "I need to take this off. Okay?"

Jori batted the sweat out of her eyes, only now aware that he was completely naked. She must have made a sound as he removed the prosthesis because he looked back over his shoulder at her.

"Am I freaking you out?"

She shook her head tightly. What was freaking her out was that he had stopped making love to her when she was on the verge of her first male-induced orgasm in nearly four years. "Just hurry."

Nodding, he rolled the sheath down and carefully lay it to one side and then did the same with the protective sock. Finally he turned back to her. "Good to go."

His rough beard scraped lightly down her belly until it lost its effectiveness in her own curls. And then his tongue slipped out and began to explore her wet folds.

"Oh . . . geez!"

Law couldn't agree more. But at the moment he was too busy using his tongue to speak. He spread her thighs a little more to get to the core of her and then proceeded to offer her his own special brand of tongue-loving.

She came suddenly and hard against his mouth. He held her in place with firm hands on her hips while he gently nibbled her until she stopped erupting in little rhythmic cries of pleasure. Even as she tried to come down the flicks of his tongue were urging her toward another peak that rose so steeply, it bordered on pain.

"Too much!" She pushed against him, bracing her hands on his sweaty shoulders. "Oh, what are you doing to me?"

"Easy, easy. We're just getting started." He slid up her body and pressed his rock-hard cock against her so that she understood how ready he was.

When she could catch her breath, Jori looked up to find him hovering above her, balancing his weight on his hands. "Please tell me you have a condom."

He smiled and produced a packet. "I was born prepared."

That wasn't as reassuring as she knew he meant it to sound. No, screw that! She felt wonderful and wanted more. Wanted him.

She grabbed the packet from him.

"What are you doing?"

She tore it with her teeth. "You're moving pretty slow for a heartless fucker."

He laughed. She made him laugh. Right in the middle of the most intense moments of sex, she'd made him laugh. And it felt good. But she felt better. When she couldn't get it on him fast enough, he took matters into his own hands.

When he was done, she lifted a leg and hooked her heel behind his good knee. Law used the advantage of her parted thighs to slide two fingers deep into her sex. She lifted her hips up off the mattress and into the push–pull of his fingers. But that wasn't how he wanted to be inside her. He wanted to cram the full length of his rigidly erect cock into her. He reached between them to direct his shaft into the hot silky folds of her sex.

A faint cry escaped Jori as the head of his cock entered her and met resistance. A worrying thought struck her. It had been a long time. Did a woman's sex close back to virginal status after years of nonuse? Or was he just bigger than she had experienced? She took a couple of quick breaths, telling herself that she could take whatever he had to offer. But a little cry of distress escaped as he pushed into her.

"*Shhh!* Don't force it. It'll happen." His whisper was thick with a sex-drugged urgency yet calm, too. As if they had all the time in the world to work out a capacity problem. Only the sweat dripping off the end of his chin onto her neck betrayed how much force he was exerting not to just ram into her.

Jori gripped his biceps though her fingers didn't begin to meet around those taut muscles. Then she lifted her legs to wrap them about his waist, hoping to give him easier access. The head of his cock was positioned so naturally between her lips that when he flexed his butt muscles, he slid home easily.

"Ah yes. That's good, Jori. Now hold on tight." One hand braced against the bedding, his other tightly clamped under her butt, Law began to move her body in a slow, circular in-and-out grind, his whole body flexing when he ended each circle with a deep thrust.

Jori expelled a soft cry of pleasure each time he thrust, letting his rhythm carry her along until the friction became too much.

When she came Law didn't alter his rhythm. He just kept up that slow, mesmerizing grind. Every instinct urged him to move quicker, harder, pound home. But with a kind of perverse pleasure, he held off. Control, in everything. He could do this. Prolong the pleasure. Fresh sweat popped out on his forehead. His face was tight with concentration. The sensation of holding back a dam about to burst, building and building in his groin.

Finally he felt it, the sudden tension in his shoulders and back, and the extra swelling of his cock inside her. He came in a long hard rush of liquid release that paralyzed him for a second. And then he was riding it out, in long hard strokes that prolonged the sensation of free-fall satisfaction.

He heard her gasp out his name. Nothing faked about her stuttering breathless response to her third orgasm. Smiling grimly, he clutched her tighter, hips still moving to wring out every ounce of pleasure to be had from her body.

# CHAPTER SIX

Law lay on his back, counting the seconds before he got up.

Jori hadn't moved a muscle since he'd rolled away from her. Was she okay? Most women let him know, sometimes in very explicit terms, that he'd satisfied them. Jori had just hugged him once, tightly, and then let him go. It had taken him a few seconds to realize that he was the one still holding on to her for dear life.

It had been awfully hard to pull away from her soft warmth, harder than he'd thought it would be. But he'd done it. Because to do anything else would mean that he wasn't ready to leave. And yet, he was still here.

Worried, he glanced over at her. Her eyes were closed but she was smiling. That smile made him feel proud, as if he'd done something wonderful. Damn! No strings had just sprouted a few tendrils.

He felt her roll toward him and then her warm little fingers were moving across his thigh toward his groin. If she touched him again, he wouldn't get out of this bed for a long *long* time. He grabbed her hand before it found its goal and moved it away.

She looked puzzled. "What's wrong?"

He didn't know. Well, maybe he did. But it didn't matter. It couldn't matter.

He shrugged. "Nothing. I'm just, you know, satisfied for now."

He saw the light dim in her eyes and could have kicked his sorry ass to Memphis and back. He didn't have to hurt her. Or lie. He was more than half hard again. But he couldn't do this again, not with her. It was there in her expression. She was beginning to like him. And that made his stomach feel funny.

He wasn't a good guy. He'd warned her. Some men knew how to handle women with charming words and easy smiles. He'd never had what people called finesse. He only knew how to be a bastard.

*Leave 'em quick and leave 'em mad, son. That way they won't be eager to come back for more.* Did all fathers give their sons such advice?

He felt her move away and flop back on the mattress beside him. After a moment she spoke, her voice now devoid of emotion. "Thanks."

"For what?"

"For making me feel normal again. I'm trying to get my life back." He heard her swallow some emotion before continuing. "That helped."

Her confession hit him smack in the chest. He knew all about wanting one's life back and fearing it would never happen. He should be thanking her, too. Being with her made *him* feel normal. His stump didn't ache, not even a twinge.

The absence of all pain was so rare he nearly checked to be sure it was still there. Instead, he felt the need for her tightening in his groin. She had brought him roaring back to life. Made him feel lighter. Loosening, if only for these moments, the fist of anger and ache in his belly that had been part of him since he'd woken in the field hospital in unspeakable agony.

He felt the room shimmer, as if possessed of a second reality. The sensation, while familiar, clenched his gut. No. He wasn't about to go there. Dear God. Not now. Not in front of her.

He heard Sam whimper softly on the other side of the closed bedroom door.

"Should I let her in?"

Jori half rolled toward the edge of the bed but Law stopped her with a hand on her shoulder. "No."

There were some things he couldn't hide from a trained canine. But he was a master at deflecting his real emotions from the prying eyes of people. He only needed to distract her, and himself.

He pressed her gently back onto the bed. "I changed my mind. You don't get rid of me that easy. In fact, I'm about to close the deal a second time. You good with that?"

She smiled despite her annoyance with his attitude, because he had begun rubbing a thumb around one of her nipples. That hand moved lower, then lower still.

She smiled and closed her eyes.

An hour later, as Jori was getting dressed, the sound of a cell phone playing "Bad to the Bone" drew her attention to Law's pants. They were still in a pile on the floor where he'd stepped out of them.

She could hear him in the shower. It was probably best to let it ring and tell him when he came out. It rang several more times before rolling over to his mailbox.

Just as she relaxed and went back to zipping up her jeans, the musical ringtone began again. This time she ignored it. But when it began to ring a third time, she couldn't. Maybe it was something serious, an emergency.

Jori snagged his pants from the floor and found his phone. "Hello."

"Well, hi there." The woman's voice was as sultry as a southern summer night. "I'm looking for Law."

"If you mean Mister Battise, he's unavailable."

"I'll bet he is." The woman's chuckle made Jori blush despite the fact that the stranger on the other end didn't know a thing about her, or what she had been doing. Unfortunately, that chuckle said she knew Law all too well, and could guess what they'd been up to.

"Can I take a message?"

"Just tell Law I've got what he wants."

Jori stared at the phone for a second after the woman clicked off. *I've got what he wants.* Was that a real message, or a dig at the strange woman who had possession of Law's cell phone?

"Why did you answer my phone?"

Jori looked up to see Battise standing in the bathroom doorway, gloriously naked and shameless about that fact. Her gaze went briefly to his stump as he balanced quite easily on one foot while drying it. Then she couldn't help but notice that he was already semi-hard. Was that a permanent condition with him? Her gaze slid away but not soon enough to keep her body from reacting to his impressive provocation.

"The caller kept ringing back. I thought it might be important."

She held out his phone but he ignored the gesture, moving on to towel dry his hair. "Was it important?"

"I don't know. The caller said to tell you she has what you want."

She noticed that his expression never shifted from detached interest as he held out a hand for the phone. When he had checked the call number he tossed it on top of his jeans on the floor.

Jori knew she had no right to be curious, let alone ask any questions about the woman who'd sounded so smugly confident when confronted with another woman. No, she wouldn't ask about her.

He hopped over to the bed and sat before beginning the ritual of putting on his artificial leg. She had laid the sock and sleeve and leg out on the mattress for easier access but he didn't say a word of thanks. Not that she'd expected any. Not really.

*Now is really not the time to find excuses to have hurt feelings, Jori.*

She frowned as she dragged a comb through her damp hair. He'd given her what they'd agreed to. He'd told her not to expect anything else. It was stupid for her to be standing here like a sulky teenager unable to hold a civil conversation. "The caller called you Law. Is Law a nickname?"

Law smiled to himself, guessing the question she wasn't asking. He could put her mind at rest by saying the woman who called was his sister. But he resisted. No need to change now and confuse everything.

"Law is my first name. Well, my nickname. It's actually Lauray." He pronounced it *Law*-ray. "It's Cajun. The Battise part is Alabama-Coushatta."

"Coushatta? What's that?"

"A Native American tribe." He slanted a knowing glance her way as he slid on his artificial leg. "You've never heard of us?"

"No. Everyone I ever met who claimed to be part Native American said they were Cherokee."

His lips twitched, a quick uptick of amusement. He was tempted to tell her more. But that would just be pretending they were now going to get to know each other. He needed to get the hell out. And he knew, too easily, how to shut her down.

"How long were you inside?"

Jori flinched. Of course. He was curious about that.

She folded her arms across her chest and jutted out a

hip. She had her own way of erecting walls. "Three years, six months, three days, nine hours, and fifteen minutes. More or less."

Law frowned as she gave him the math. She couldn't be more than twenty-five or -six? That meant she'd spent the first years of her adulthood behind bars. He hurt for her just thinking about it. But he didn't want her pain.

He'd seen her in action with the other vets and the service dogs. She had a natural kindness and sympathy for living things. No doubt some bastard had taken advantage of her generous nature and it had gotten her into a world of trouble.

In his experience in law enforcement, misguided loyalty to a douchebag boyfriend accounted for why most women ended up in jail. Didn't matter if the women were soldiers or civilians. None of his business, of course. The fact that he'd like to pummel the hypothetical bastard who'd ruined Jori's life made no difference.

Jori finished braiding her hair before she said, "You haven't asked why."

He stood and zipped his pants. She sounded defensive, like his opinion mattered.

"A sentence that allowed you out in three and a half years means you probably didn't kill anyone. Did you try?"

"No." She sounded horrified by the idea while he'd sounded matter-of-fact.

"Then I don't need to know." *Don't want to know.*

Law bent to lace up his boot. They'd already said too much. Shared too much. She was in search of bonds, promises, and a future. But he didn't have any of those things to offer. He should have left her the hell alone.

He glanced in her direction but his gaze snagged on her feet. She wore socks, one blue and one orange. He felt his gut twist. Those damn socks! He'd noticed them when she wrapped her legs around his waist, the first time.

He felt even worse. He should have left it to some

upright Dudley-Do-Right type to bring back her sexual nature. Someone with more to offer than *Slam, bam, thank you, ma'am.* Someone who might want to make those plans she needed.

He looked up, hoping like hell she wouldn't see in his expression all that was roiling inside him. "Look, I'm not sure—"

A scratch at the door interrupted.

Looking like she needed an escape, Jori hurried to open it.

Sam walked in, her head moving slowly from one to the other, studying the emotional climate of the humans in the room. First, she moved toward Jori and rubbed her curly head against her thigh. Jori reached out to pet her but, after only a few strokes, Sam hurried over and lightly pawed Law's good foot, a sign she needed to go out.

A moment later, Argyle appeared. Moving like a furry dart, the kitten skipped across the room, bounded up on the bed and onto Law's chest. Claws out, she raked at his face with both paws several times before leaping off and zigzagged her way back out the door.

Horrified by her pet's actions, Jori rushed over to Law. "Oh no. Are you hurt?"

Law felt his face. "No. Lucky my beard's so long and thick."

"I can't think why she'd act like that. She's usually . . ." Jori's voice trailed away as she went in search of her cat.

Law knew the answer as he felt his stinging nose. He didn't need a pocket-sized ninja kitty with an overly developed protective instinct to let him know he was a good-for-nothing rat bastard. The damning evidence was there in Jori's sexual glow.

He walked into the living area where Jori was petting Argyle. "I'm heading out. You want me to drop you back at work first?"

Jori glanced at her kitchen clock. How was she going to explain a three-and-a-half-hour lunch?

She shook her head. "No, I'm good. It's only a three-mile walk. I need the exercise."

Law watched her a moment longer, liking her display of independence, even if it was pitifully obvious she was doing it because she was trying to take him on his own terms.

She followed him to the door, Sam trailing Law.

At the door, Law turned back. His shoulders were hunched as if in anticipation of a blow. How many women had he run out on? No, better not think about that now.

Jori had folded her arms before her chest, her green eyes looking a bit large for her face. A half smile jerked her lips to one side. "It's okay."

He only meant to say good-bye but he found himself moving back toward her and reaching for her.

He felt her stiffen slightly as his hands settled possessively on her waist. How was it that he wanted to both reassure her that she was safe from him, and yet tell her to run like hell.

"I made a mistake with you."

God, the stricken look on her face cut deep. He never apologized. But he couldn't stop himself. "You're worth more than a good time, Jori. You deserve someone who can give everything you need to make you smile all the time. I'm just not that guy."

He astonished himself by kissing her forehead quickly before releasing her. "I hope you find what you need real soon."

Jori waited until the door closed behind him and Sam before she said softly, "You, too, Law."

# CHAPTER SEVEN

"I don't give a good goddamn about excuses. Next time you screw up I'm going to come down there and give you a proctology exam with my right foot. You're a lily-livered, sorry excuse for a whore. But you're my whore, bought and paid for with my money. You got that? That's what I thought. Now take care of it." Harold Tice stabbed the OFF button on his phone.

"Easy, Dad. You're going to bust a gut over nothing."

Luke Tice had been listening to his father's end of the phone conversation with a divided mind. His father certainly knew how to light a fire under a body. And how to get his way. But now that Luke was running for office, he needed his dad to pull in his horns a bit. "You want me to follow up on that for you?"

"No." Tice swung his desk chair toward his son. "I don't want you bothering with business, son. You've got other fields to plow. How's the campaign coming along?"

"Well enough. We've got a fund-raiser over in Benton-ville this weekend."

His father nodded in approval. "Anything you need, you

tell me. I got ways of funding the campaign that won't show up as Tice money on your books."

"While I appreciate the offer, Dad, what I need right now is for grassroots people to buy into my campaign. In a special election like this, small donors count more with public perception."

"Public perception. Exactly. Which reminds me. You need to pull Erin out of Kaitlyn Ferguson's wedding. You can't afford the association."

Luke smiled and rubbed his chin. "I couldn't if I wanted to. Erin's got her heart set on making her former sorority sister's wedding the northwest Arkansas social event of the year."

"That's exactly what you can't afford. Everybody remembers that your office prosecuted the groom's sister. One thing if they had gotten married before the sister was released. But now, how's it going to look, you sitting up in the wedding next to a felon you helped convict?"

"It's going to look like I'm a big-tent politician. Jordan Garrison served her time for her crimes. She got a new start. Working with that canine service organization, Warriors Wolf Pack, that trains dogs for wounded vets. I'm big enough to wish her well for accepting responsibility and trying to steer a new path. This is a win–win. I'm courting votes from veterans, their families and friends, and dog lovers."

His father gave him a sour look. "What I'm seeing is pictures of you and your wife smiling and drinking above a headline that reads: SENATE HOPEFUL HOBNOBS WITH FELON HE PUT BEHIND BARS."

Luke laughed and shook his head. "That's not going to happen. I've already prepared a statement for the press the day of the event. Get my message out there on my terms."

"You're thinking like a schoolboy. Have you forgotten

that the young Garrison woman was nearly married to your cousin Brody? You don't need to do anything that will remind voters of that association."

"No." Luke grew serious for a moment. Harold knew his son was thinking about his cousin Brody. They'd once been very close. He'd want to mend fences with Brody's intended. His next words confirmed it.

"Backing out now would have the same effect since Erin's volunteered to step in at the last minute with the wedding preparations. She's hosting a bridal shower. Besides, it might not even be an issue."

"Why's that?"

"Erin heard from Kaitlyn that Kieran's sister won't be attending the wedding."

Harold's ears pricked up. "Why would she do that?"

"Doesn't want to embarrass the family, I suppose. Erin says Jori hasn't been in contact with any of her former friends since she was released. So if you want to do good for me, Dad, then think about tossing the Warriors Wolf Pack a few dollars."

"How few?"

Luke smiled. He could always count on his dad. "I did a little research. It costs them twenty-five to thirty thousand to train a dog."

"You don't say? And they use female inmates to train them? I have to wonder about our correctional institutions' intentions when they reward dope peddlers with participation in such a program."

"Oh no. Dad, don't even think about it."

"You don't know what I'm thinking."

"I know you. You're thinking about how to leverage a donation to make trouble for Jori Garrison."

Luke stood up, a frown on his handsome face. "I'm not asking, I'm telling you. Leave her out of any plans you have to help me. I've got this covered." He looked at his watch. "I got to go. Erin's meeting me for lunch at Bordino's over in Fayetteville."

"You should take her by a jewelry shop afterward, offer her the bauble of her choice if she'll come down with the flu just before the wedding. Always soothed troubled waters with your mother."

"Subject closed, Dad. You'll see. It'll be a goodwill opportunity."

Harold stood by the window of his office after his son had gone. Even the hand-tailoring of his suits couldn't completely disguise the silhouette of the raw-boned Arkie fieldworker he'd begun his working life as.

The Tices had what Arkansans referred to as "plenty of money." But Grandpa Tice, the founder of Tice Industries, believed that money, while a good thing to accumulate in a bank, was the root of all evil if a man didn't earn it himself. So, like his father and grandfather before him, Harold had begun his working life as a wildcatter in the oil fields of west Texas and Oklahoma before coming to work for the family business.

And in the process, Harold had begun his side business by delivering nickel and dime bags of pleasure to rigs and oil platforms. It wasn't legal but, hell, every man worth his salt got his hands dirty while making a fortune, be it digging for gold, diamonds, or crude, or mining men's darkest impulses.

Once in charge of Tice Industries, he'd kept that secret side of the business going by using Tice Trucking Company to act as deliverymen. He didn't buy or sell, he delivered drugs from point A to point B, for cash. No questions asked. Business had never been better.

Harold reached for his e-cigar, a recent gift from his wife. The weight, balance, and paper gave it the feel of reality. It even tasted, after a few puffs, like a real cigar. But it didn't have the tactile smoky appeal of a real Cohiba.

He took a puff, exhaling a long but not-quite-satisfied breath. Some things changed. But not all for the good.

He hadn't insisted that Luke work in the backbreaking industry that had forged his ancestors. Instead, he had sent him directly to college and then law school. Most times that seemed like a good decision. But today, when his son admitted he couldn't completely control his wife, he was having second thoughts. A man who hadn't dealt with the hard realities of life was more likely to make careless mistakes.

Harold pulled at his top lip with his fingers. He'd made a few errors of judgment in his life. Point of fact, Brody Rogers.

He'd been grooming his wife's sister's son to take part in the family business, freeing Luke to concentrate on building his way into political office. But the damn fool Brody started enjoying his insider position too much. Thought he didn't have to answer to anyone. Got reckless. Selling drugs to college frat boys!

If Brody hadn't died in the auto accident that brought that fact to life, he might have throttled his nephew himself.

Harold squashed a twinge of conscience over Brody. His sister-in-law still couldn't mention her son without crying. Luke and Brody had once been as close as brothers, until the natural rivalry that often develops between male relatives came between them. Still, he could feel his blood pressure rise each time Brody's name was mentioned. The damn fool had exposed them to some very unwelcome scrutiny.

Now the ghost of Brody was rearing its head in the form of Jori Garrison.

Harold dropped his e-cigar back in its useless silver ashtray. A man couldn't cover every eventuality, but he could move like lightning once a possibility presented itself.

This wedding was a media disaster in the making. His top priority was putting his son in a state senator's seat. That meant he'd have to pave the way. And paving couldn't be done without removing obstacles in the path. If Luke couldn't see that, then he had no alternative but to act for him.

Smiling, Harold reached for his phone. Jori Garrison was thinking about not attending the wedding. A possibility had presented itself.

The secret to successful manipulation was to nudge along events that might have taken place naturally. That way the pawn would swear, if asked, that it was her idea.

"Erin. It's your favorite father-in-law. How's your husband's campaign coming along?"

# CHAPTER EIGHT

Yardley waited at passenger pickup in the Richmond International Airport for a brother she'd seen rarely in their adult lives. Until six months ago, it had been five years since they were last together. But there was no mistaking Lauray as he came through the exit doors.

She had to stifle a laugh. He held the leash of a dog that was exactly what he'd described, a cutesy rust-red mash-up of golden retriever and poodle with an enormous curling tail that, sure enough, reminded her of a Cheez Doodle. The contrast between man and dog couldn't have been more startling. Wearing tan cargo pants and a dark-green tee that revealed the definition of a man in his prime, Lauray looked hard. Despite the beard and untamed black hair, he looked like a man in charge. Even with a froufrou dog on a leash.

As proof, a female flight attendant was hurrying along beside him to keep pace with his stride.

Yardley fell in behind them as they neared the baggage carousel in time to hear the flight attendant say, "So I'll see you, later?"

Law wasn't looking at his companion but slowly scanning the congested area full of impatient travelers. "I have your digits."

The young woman's wide smile faltered at the noncommittal answer. "Okay then." She bent to pat the head of the dog he had on a leash. "Such a sweet dog. I hope you can find a good home for him." She glanced up at Law, looking like she'd rather be petting him. "Bye."

Yardley shook her head as the flight attendant walked away. Despite the threat to the female population, she was pleased to see the old Law back in business.

More curious about Law's other companion, she turned her attention to his dog. Unlike many American canine breeders who focused as much on appearance as ability, Yardley took the European approach: Dogs were chosen for training based solely on their ability to perform a desired task.

The goldendoodle moved slowly but deliberately behind Law as he stood in the open waiting for his gear. It was the only clue that the shifting crowd of people in the congested area was agitating her master.

Yardley shifted her gaze to her brother's profile. His neutral expression gave away nothing, as she expected from a trained law officer. She glanced back at the canine. Perceptive dog.

Sliding into his line of sight, she offered Law a sisterly assessment. "You look like hell. What's with the survivalist beard?"

Law gave his sibling a quick once-over. "Nice to see you, too."

Law knew he looked rough around the edges but he certainly couldn't return the insult. His half sister had always been a stunner. Even dressed in jeans, a tailored shirt, and military boots, she still managed to look feminine. Her wide mouth and elegant cheekbones were striking, especially when paired with her no-nonsense gaze. Eyes, blacker than his, revealed their shared Native American genes through their respective mothers. Her long dark-red hair, today pulled into a ponytail, flagged the Cajun ancestry of their father.

Yardley bent down to dog level and spoke to Samantha. "Hi there, girl. My name's Yardley."

Samantha wagged her tail but looked back at Law for instruction. When he gave the signal, she stepped forward to be petted.

Yardley pulled a treat out of her pocket.

Samantha sniffed in the direction of Yardley's palm but then backed up and sat down, leaning slightly against Law's leg as she returned her attention to him.

Yardley stood and pocketed the treat, nodding in approval. "She's been proofed. That's unusual for a dog so young."

"Checking my ability to judge the thoroughness of a canine's instruction?"

"Maybe. Last time I saw you, you'd lost discipline and were getting fat."

Law frowned down at her, thanks to the three-inch difference in their heights. "I was never fat."

"Waddling, goosey-goose fat. *Quack, quack, quack.*" She imitated a goose walk, drawing laughter from a nearby child.

Law shook his head and lifted his gear off the carousel. "Let's get out of here before you embarrass yourself even more."

Yardley fell into step beside her brother. As they reached the exit doors they each reached for mirrored shades and donned them with movements that looked choreographed.

"What was that about you looking for a home for your dog?"

"Conversation." Law sighed. Obviously she'd overheard his exchange with the flight attendant. Nothing got past Yard. He'd have to remember that.

Once in her jeep, Yardley turned to him. "Food?"

He nodded.

They ended up in a burger joint northwest of Richmond's city limits. Once he found a table at the rear where he could position himself with his back to a wall, she ordered a burger without bread, and a salad. He ordered the half-pound bacon blue cheeseburger with a side of onion rings.

"Nice to see that you're keeping your body clean."

Law grinned wide as he lifted the massive burger to his mouth. "I'm on furlough. What about you? You heard from *him* lately?"

Yardley's face went blank as she reached for her fork.

Law watched her while he chewed. They didn't need familiarity to sense trouble in each other. "Has it been more than a month?"

"Almost two." She was still staring straight ahead.

"He works for Doctors Without Borders, right? Why aren't his people talking to you?"

"I don't have to right to ask them anything about him."

Law knew what that meant. Yardley wasn't listed on the guy's who-to-call-if list.

"What about your spook grapevine?"

She shook her head. "The usual channels aren't open to me."

Law almost asked why before his own covert experience kicked in. She couldn't ask because most likely he wasn't listed "on paper" as being wherever the hell he was.

Yardley had mentioned she was seeing a guy when she'd visited him months ago. Which had shocked him. Like him, she kept her personal life personal. Her private life was downright classified. Even now, he knew nothing about the guy beyond the fact that he worked for Doctors Without Borders. Yardley wouldn't say what he did, or even his name. But the fact that this mystery man owned Yardley's heart told Law all he needed to know about the guy. He had to be a stand-up, dedicated prince of badassery.

Yardley wasn't likely to fall for a doctor. Law suspected the man worked security, off the record, for the organization that by its very nature struggled to remain independent and neutral, not part of any government or international system. They didn't work first-world places. More like third, fourth, and falling-off-the-map places.

Now he was missing in some godforsaken shithole in the remotest part of one of the most dangerous places in the world. Two months was a long time to be out in the cold. Yard was worried. Now he was, too.

Law looked down at his empty plate feeling bad for having brought the subject up. Yard was hurting and he had nothing to offer her private pain but respect.

He didn't bother with the usual *He'll turn up* or *He's going to be fine*. Those words would be wishful thinking at best. There was nothing he could do to help. He wasn't even certain he could save himself, at the moment.

His mind slid into his own misery. He'd walked out on Jori. And that, he was discovering, was going to bother him worse than the itch he'd gotten to scratch.

"You seeing anyone?" Yardley was studying him now with the interest of a K-9 on the scent.

Why had he mentioned relationships? He never talked about his. Then he remembered Yardley had talked with Jori when she answered his phone. Time to cover up.

"Usual story. She kicked me out."

"Hard to believe."

"You helped. Thanks for being all mysterious on the phone with her."

Yardley chewed a forkful of salad to give herself time

to think. She'd spent her professional life working with highly disciplined, highly motivated professionals, mostly men, in law enforcement and the military. Sometimes those who partnered with her highly intelligent, highly motivated animals were more in need of TLC than their canines. Dogs were better at getting what they needed than many of their human counterparts. First-responder handlers, always the ones turned to in a crisis, learned to tuck their emotions away while they coped with the needs of others. Those without strong family ties sometimes lost the ability to relate to their own needs.

Her brother wasn't even on the map about his own feelings. Once he'd thought he was invincible. Now that life had shown him otherwise, he was hurting in a way that might just destroy him.

Of course, she couldn't very well point that out. He wouldn't thank her for it. He might even walk out. He'd done so before, most memorably at the reading of their father's will eight years ago. His final words had stayed with her, along with a certain amount of guilt.

*He didn't give a shit for me when I was alive. I don't need shit-all from him now.*

Law had refused the inheritance of Harmonie Kennels and never looked back. Her good fortune, but her brother's loss. No one, especially Law, needed to be alone forever.

She'd seen that micro expression of hurt when she'd mentioned the woman. Maybe she threw him out, or maybe he ran. Either way, he wasn't happy about it. And that might just be the best news of all.

If Law was emotionally involved, even if he saw it as a negative, that was more than enough to work with for a smart woman willing to do the mining of the heart of a difficult man. A woman who trained dogs would know how to work with Law's nonverbal way of dealing with his emotions.

Yardley reached over and snagged one of his onion rings. "What was wrong with her?" Law looked confused by the question, but she knew it was a dodge. "The woman who threw you out."

It took Law a split second to choose the most offputting fact about Jori. "She's an ex-con."

Yardley broke into laughter. "Oh my God. You've turned into a prude. I remember a time during your teens when Dad bailed you out regularly."

Law sent her a hooded look. "I liked you better as a distant relation. Far distant."

Yardley shrugged. "I'll remember *that* the next time you ask for a favor."

Law's interest quickened. "So where's the file?"

"At home. And we're going to finish this meal before we go there. So, dig in."

Law stuffed his mouth with his burger as his thoughts wandered to Jori.

She'd told him she'd be fine. But he couldn't forget the image of her tangled in the sheets, wearing two different-colored socks and nothing else. The image burned through him like molten glass. Thinking of her equaled a hard-on. Nothing had changed because he now knew how it felt when she came with him buried to the balls inside her. No, wait, it had.

He closed his eyes briefly. It had felt so damn good he wanted to cry.

"She's too nice for me."

Law glanced up, expecting laughter from Yardley, but she was just staring at him with a thoughtful expression. "She's a sweet girl who caught a bad break."

He was pretty sure of that even though he'd stopped short of reading the newspaper about her trial that he called up on his notebook while waiting for his flight. What was he going to do with anything he learned about her? He didn't plan to see her again. He'd deleted the article unread. But Yardley was looking at him as if she knew he'd been tempted. "What?"

"You think she wasn't guilty."

"It doesn't matter, either way." That much was true.

Yardley waited for him to continue. Instead, Law pulled an onion ring from his pile and offered it to Sam. The dog scarfed it down without chewing then sat up and nosed his thigh, hopeful of another bite.

Law broke off a portion of his burger patty and placed it on a napkin before putting it on the floor for Sam. One thing he'd discovered about his new companion, Sam liked to eat.

"Are you going to tell me about her?"

Law hunched a shoulder. "I got this damn doodle because of her. Sam's a lot like her trainer."

"You mean she's friendly, cute, down-to-earth, good-natured, patient, and constantly evaluating and adjusting to your moods? I can see why you wouldn't want to be around her. Sounds like a horror of a woman."

Law frowned at his plate. "I don't like *me* around her."

"And that means?"

"I was . . . not kind."

"Oh." Yardley swallowed her smile. Being rude had never been a problem for her brother before. "The way you left it between you, do you think she'll call if she decides she wants to see you again?"

He sent her a hard look. "I didn't give her my number."

Yardley sat back, watching him eat but saying nothing more. She didn't know her half brother very well. Growing up, they'd only had contact for a few weeks a year. Their father purposely didn't want his children to be too close.

It had nothing to do with their different mothers. Bronson Battise's philosophy was that if a man couldn't stand alone, he wasn't a man. Women were something to protect and enjoy as long as a man was interested, but no more important than that. And just as easily discarded.

Yardley had suffered through that philosophy, becoming as much like a son as Bronson Battise would allow. It had never really occurred to her until now that Law had suffered, too.

She'd always thought her brother was a carbon copy of their father. A man's man whom no woman would ever tie down for long. But maybe, beneath that Battise exterior, beat a different kind of heart. Perhaps Law was like her. He had learned to cover up his softer self the way she had, for protection.

She leaned forward, elbows on the table, and propped her chin on her fists. "It's okay to need someone in your life, Law. It's better than okay. I'm beginning to believe I deserve someone, too."

Law regarded her with a wary gaze. "You ever wonder if there are more of us Battises out there?"

"You mean beside the two of us Dad acknowledged? Yeah. I'm sure of it."

Law nodded. "When I was about twelve a woman and her daughter came to the reservation to visit. My mother wasn't very kind to the mother. The girl, nine years old if I remember right, liked to hang around me. Something about her seemed so familiar. The vibe coming off her said kin."

Yardley nodded. "I loved Dad but he was a bastard. We aren't him."

Law slid her a hard glance from beneath his brows. "I met a woman I wanted. I scratched my itch and left. Don't read anything more into that."

"If that's all you think it was, you wouldn't have mentioned her to me."

Law couldn't argue with most of that. But he wasn't

about to own it. He scratched his chin whiskers. "Think I'll shave."

Yardley grinned. He was changing the subject. That meant she'd gotten through to him. "Good beginning. If you're done, let's go home."

# CHAPTER NINE

Law hesitated. The manila envelope of paperwork Yardley had received was lying on the kitchen table of her cabin in front of him. Did he have the guts for the truth? Screw that! Scud was dead. He was a cripple. Nothing on paper could hurt more than those two realities. He tore open the envelope.

He devoured the pages with an intensity that didn't allow for blinking. Every word seared his retinas, but he couldn't stop or think or do anything except get to the end. When he did, his jaw was clenched so tightly his back teeth ached.

Suddenly he shot to his feet, flinging the paperwork across the table.

"The cowardly bastards!"

"I told you, you wouldn't like it."

Law looked over at Yardley. "My own unit shot my dog." His voice was harsh, as if a hot wind had blown over his vocal cords, leaving them husk-dry. "The bastards killed Scud."

Yardley watched him closely. "I was told Scud was shot because he wouldn't let them near you. The men were worried that you'd bleed out before another handler could be summoned to help."

"That can't be right. Scud knew every man in my unit."

"He was wounded, Law. You read the report. He might have been too traumatized to recognize them. His Alpha was down. He was scared and in protection mode." She shifted uncomfortably. "Law, you need to let this go. It's over."

Law tried on her suggestion. Nothing he had read changed what he already knew. Only one new thing did register. Scud had died trying to protect him.

Sensing the heightened emotional outpouring from her handler, Sam came over and pushed her head in under his arm.

Law looked down, eyes narrowed. "Back off. Now."

Sam's gaze rose to his face. After a brief stare-off in which her brows twitched constantly she lay down on his feet, no longer attempting to comfort him but refusing to back off.

Yardley, too, took a cautious approach. "You've got that half-crazy-Cajun, half-inscrutable-Injun thing going on. You're even scaring the dog."

Law glared at her. She held up both hands. "I'm just saying."

"I got nothing." He waved at the paperwork for emphasis.

"Maybe that's all there is. Some things don't have an upside. We both know that."

"There's nothing else? What about the details of my wounding? There's nothing here about that. I've always assumed we stepped on an IED. But it doesn't say that here."

Yardley didn't quite meet his gaze. "I was told some papers went missing from the field report."

Law knew that was code for cover-up. "So what? Was I hit by friendly fire?"

She shrugged. "Afghanistan was chaotic in those days. The surge was under way. Troops moving quickly from area to area. Shortly after your incident, your unit left the area. A paper trail didn't seem as important as tracking the enemy."

A muscle ticced in Law's jaw. Yardley was trying to handle him. Soothe his irritation. Offer excuses. Which meant, she knew that whatever had really happened to him over there had been deliberately covered up. Nothing he could do now would change that. Except that Yardley was holding back. He could see it in the way she was sitting there a little too casual for the occasion.

He straightened up and lasered his focus on her. "Tell me."

She hesitated, bringing her considerable determination to the sibling contest of wills. "Okay. I asked a few more questions. No one will officially verify anything I tell you. But there were originally eyewitness accounts. A couple of civvies found you first. American contractors."

She pulled a sheet of paper from beneath a book on the table and unfolded it. "I couldn't get verification on the particulars, but through another connection I got the names of the contractors working the area where you were wounded." She ran through the list.

Law leaned forward to read over her shoulder. One name jumped out at him. "Tice Industries was in the neighborhood?"

"You know the name?"

Instead of answering, Law picked up and glanced again through the redacted paperwork he had scattered. There was nothing there about Tice Industries. Or why he was in that village on that particular day. But he had other, older memories to help him fill in some blanks.

Frowning, he looked up. "Tice is an Arkansas company. There's a history. Been on law enforcement's radar since before my time with the state police. But they have money and connections in all the right places. Nothing ever stuck."

"What kind of nothing?"

"Why do you ask?"

Yardley shook her head.

Law was instantly alert. "What?"

This time she just stared at the carpet.

Law leaned toward her. "This paperwork doesn't say why I was at that location. Command sent me and Scud out alone for a reason. I have to know what you know."

She nodded tightly. "I made another call, to a reporter who was in Afghanistan at the same time you were. I asked about civilian crime there. He sent me a link to a copy of an old *USA Today* report with a few lines highlighted." She pulled it up on her tablet computer and pointed.

*The U.S. Army has investigated 56 soldiers in Afghanistan on suspicion of using or distributing heroin, morphine or other opiates during 2010 and 2011 . . . Eight soldiers died of drug overdoses during that time.*

"There are more stories on the Internet. Around the time of your wounding, a soldier in the Kentucky Guard died after using heroin allegedly bought from a civilian contractor. Ring any bells?"

Law monitored his thoughts as he ticked off the points in his mind. Even in a theater of war, criminal investigations were done by Army Criminal Investigation Command. CID. Him. *A drug investigation. Soldiers dying of drug overdoses. Civilian contractors involved in drug distribution.* The words should have triggered more than a hunch. Tumblers should have fallen into place and unlocked his memory.

Nothing.

Law scraped a hand through his hair. "You done good, Yard. I appreciate it."

"What are you planning to do about this?"

Ignoring her question, he pointed to the file. "This must have cost you."

"Let's just say no one in Washington will be accepting my calls for a long while."

The mention of her secret sources reminded him that she'd possibly made herself vulnerable by helping him.

"Do you trust those you've had contact with? This can't blow back on you?"

"I already thought of that, little brother. But what happened in Afghanistan is history. You'll never pick up that trail."

"I don't need to." Tice was still in business in his back-yard. If they were dirty before, they were dirtier now. "I just need to connect these new dots to the old, and wait."

"I don't like that idea. You're not the vigilante type. It's not your problem."

"I am—was a cop. It's my problem."

Law felt energized for the first time in four years. Something was now ahead of him, instead of it all behind him. He was a law enforcement officer, first, last, always.

He stood up. "Guess I'll need that desk jockey job at state police headquarters, after all."

Yardley picked up the pages and shoved them back in the envelope. "You said yourself Tice Industries is inter-twined with political and law enforcement allies. You won't know who to trust. You've been out of the loop too long."

Law didn't answer. He knew one thing. He had to get Yardley off the case. For her own good.

"Go back to your life, Yard. I got it from here."

"I did what you asked in the hope that answers would give you peace of mind. You sound more like I've given you fuel for a vendetta."

Law stared off in the middle distance. "Not your problem."

She stood up and put a hand on his arm. "About Scud. I'm sorry."

Law nodded once. He wouldn't talk about that. Not even with Yard. "Anyone I can pay to drive me back to the airport tonight?"

"You won't get a flight to anywhere this time of night."

He stared at nothing a bit longer. "See you in the morning then."

He looked down at Sam, who had risen from her place to heel at his side without being asked. "Keep the doodle here for the night. Sam, *bleib*—ah, stay!"

He picked up his gear and walked out the door without looking back.

Yardley watched him head down her steps and then across the empty yard toward the bunkhouse where guests at Harmonie Kennels stayed. His limp was more pronounced than when she'd picked him up in Richmond. The revelations in the folder weighed upon him though he would never admit it.

She folded her arms tightly under her bosom. She knew it would have been useless to ask him again to stay with her at the main house their father had built. He'd said earlier that he preferred the empty guest quarters. The family intimacy that had once discomforted both of them was now one-sided. She would have welcomed his presence in the house.

She felt a bone-deep ache watching her brother's retreating back. She was worried about him. He had suffered so much, alone. She would have been there, if he'd allowed it. Yet someone else had had to call her when it seemed like Law was about to do something irrevocable. He really needed to learn how to ask for help. At the moment he was determined to turn his back on the woman who had gotten to him in a way that scared him. She'd love to meet this mystery woman who had disturbed her brother's spirit. She could easily call Warriors Wolf Pack and ask who had trained Samantha. But her instincts kept her from doing that. Warriors were meant to hunt. Law was on the scent, whether he knew it or not. He would not accept what came easily to him.

She didn't have much connection with her own part-Choctaw heritage. But Law had been reared on the reservation. Tribal life ran in his veins. A disturbed spirit needed to be made whole and joined to the world. Peace came from acceptance and love.

Yardley sighed and closed the door against the chill. Some men were more afraid of gentleness than hardship. It was her fate to love three of them. The first was Bronson Battise.

Their father had laid a heavy burden on his children, telling them to trust and rely on no one, not even him. All they had was themselves. To need another person was to be weak. It explained why for most of her life she, and she suspected Law, had had an easier time dealing with emotions when animals were involved rather than humans.

The second man was Law, whom she knew more by that indefinable bond of blood than actual connection. Something deep and long-standing was troubling Law. It wasn't just his wounding at war. She was certain he didn't have a clue what it was. She'd felt the same unnamed emptiness most of her life. Finally, a few months ago, she had found the answer. It had been as simple as dropping her guard.

She'd fallen in love.

Yardley turned away from her door after Law entered

the bunkhouse, rubbing her hands up and down her arms. The chill she felt had nothing to do with the temperature.

The third man she loved was missing. In his world, there were no strings to pull or favors to call in. That scared her spitless.

She looked down at the sound of whimpering. Sam stood still staring out the window toward the bunkhouse.

"I know. He's a hardheaded cuss. Serves us right for caring about him. I hope that woman he mentioned has the wisdom to see through his bunker mentality."

She pulled a treat from her pocket. "Come, Sam. You can sleep with me."

Sam waited until the house was quiet. There were dog doors in both front and back in the woman's house. She went out the one closest to the bunkhouse where she knew her Alpha was. It was a dark moonless night but she let her nose direct her. Alpha's footprints were so vivid in her nostrils, they practically glowed under the inspection of her nose. All the other smells of the night, and there were thousands, faded in comparison.

She found the doggy door into the bunkhouse with ease, slipping easily through portals sized for Belgian Malinois and German shepherds, whose scents drenched every inch of the area. She glanced nervously about, unaccustomed to so many strong Alpha scents in one place. Finally, convinced that no animal lay behind those scents, she moved on through the dark, following the wisp of familiar pheromones.

She found her Alpha in a small room in the back. He was slung across a narrow mattress, fully clothed. She climbed up carefully and then snuggled in slowly against him, so as not to awaken him. Only then did she sniff him, taking careful notice of his unique blend of smells and physical signs. Heart calm. Breathing easy. He was asleep. A quiet sleep where no ugliness penetrated. It was the first time since she'd chosen him that she felt he was at ease.

She sighed, leaned her weight against his back, and dozed, relieved of duty for the moment.

# CHAPTER TEN

"Everything seems to be in order. Your work record is clean. Your bills are paid. Anything else you want to tell me?" Case Howard, Jori's parole officer, regarded her with a benign gaze across two Grand Slam plates at Denny's. His was empty, hers barely touched.

"No. Work's going fine. Argyle's fine. Everything's fine."

Case's dark eyes narrowed. "You got someone in your life yet?"

"No."

"Your eyes say you're not being honest."

Jori swallowed carefully. This man was all that stood between her and a bad report to the parole board. "I saw a guy. A couple of weeks back."

"What happened?"

Heat and desire nudged her as memories of Battise took hold. Useless to try to push the memories away. She just hoped Case couldn't see her reaction to the memories in her expression. "We didn't stick."

Case rubbed his shaved head, glistening like a shelled

pecan under the lights. "You need to go slow. Don't get caught up in a relationship you aren't ready for."

"That's not going to be a problem. Like I said. We didn't stick."

"No other casual screwing around?" He asked the question softly, but the former college linebacker backed it up with a shrewd look she didn't want to underestimate.

Jori held his gaze. "No. Just the one time."

He nodded and seemed to relax. "Wish all my clients were as easy as you."

Jori didn't know whether to be pleased or appalled. "Can I go now? I'm going to be late for work."

Case leaned back in his chair, which squeaked in protest of the shifting of 302 pounds. "You've got to learn to relax, Garrison. I'm on your side."

"It's the questions. They're embarrassing."

"Uh-huh. There's a purpose to them. I'm not just some freak getting off on your private exploits. You're doing good." He shrugged. "Go on. I got the check."

Jori stood up.

"One thing. You still not going to your brother's wedding?"

The question caught her like a kick to the chest. "No. I've told them."

Case held her in his blank stare. "You can't hide forever. You have to face them eventually. After that, we'll really know how you're doing. I'll be in touch."

Jori didn't breathe deep until she was back behind the wheel of her SUV. She started the ignition and sped away from Denny's as if a horde of zombies were on her tail.

She hated these random check-ins with Case, even if he was a hundred times better than the stories about parole officers she'd heard from the other women in prison. Case was a decent man. But answering questions about everything from how much she weighed to the results of her mandatory pee test left her feeling invaded and way off balance.

Maybe even that would have been okay, if he hadn't brought up Battise.

It wasn't as if Battise was the first guy she'd made it with. But it felt like that, now that he had been gone long enough for her to fully appreciate the *nevermore* part of their hookup.

When the flush of their encounter had worn off, she'd been left a little edgier and a lot hungrier than before. Like one lick of an ice cream cone, one day of sex with Battise wasn't nearly enough.

Jori licked her lips, tingling with the remembered pleasure of his hot mouth. Never made it with a bearded guy before. She'd been left with beard burns on her cheeks and breasts and inner thighs for days after. Not that she was complaining.

She'd been pathetically eager, and he'd made the most of it, finding and exploring every moist quivering inch of her until she was limp from multiple orgasms and he was limp with spent pleasure. She'd probably have been better off not knowing what it was like to lie under him as he slid hot and thick and urgently into her.

Maybe she should have tied him to her bed while she had the chance.

Jori smiled. At least she could still make jokes about it.

Her cell phone rang.

Jori glanced at the unfamiliar number. Usually she didn't try to answer while she was driving. No one had her number but her family, her patrol officer, and WWP.

Maybe it was Battise!

Or not.

Curiosity won out.

"Hello. Is this Jori Garrison?"

The hair on Jori's nape stiffened. "Who is this?"

"It's Erin Foster. I'm Mrs. Luke Tice now, if you hadn't heard."

Jori could feel a coldness spreading outward from her chest. This day just kept getting better. "What do you want, Erin?"

"I know it's a surprise, hearing from me after all this time. But I'm calling about Kieran and Kaitlyn's wedding. You've heard that I'm Kaitlyn's maid of honor?"

Jori searched for an appropriately neutral reply. "So?"

"This is so awkward." Erin sounded sincerely uncomfortable. "I need a favor from you. As a sorority sister and a friend."

Jori rubbed at the knot of tension that drew her eyebrows together. *Frenemies* would once have best described her relationship with Erin Foster. "We aren't friends, Erin. I haven't heard from you since the day Brody died."

"Yes. That's what makes this awkward. As the maid of honor, I have certain duties to perform. One of them is throwing a bridal shower for Kaitlyn. Which I am, this coming Sunday. So, well, your mother asked if I would personally invite you. Although she did say you don't have plans to attend the wedding itself." She paused for confirmation, but Jori wasn't about to give her anything until she knew the real reason for this call.

"Okay, you've invited me."

There was a short pause. "That's not the favor. I need you to decline."

Jori closed her eyes for a second, safe at a stoplight. "I don't understand."

"I'm sure you've heard that Luke is running for state senator. He's leading in the polls, of course. You must know that means we can't afford any missteps right through here. The media is so unforgiving."

Jori pressed very carefully on the gas pedal as the light

went green. "Having an ex-con showing up at your doorstep for a social occasion would complicate your life."

"I wouldn't put it like that, but yes."

A grim smile spread across Jori's face. "You could just resign as Kaitlyn's maid of honor."

"Now, how would that look? Backing out on my little sorority sister's wedding after I offered to save the event at the last minute? No, I always carry out my obligations. Even if it costs me personally. But it's not just me this time. There's Luke."

"Forget it, Erin. I'm still not attending any events connected to my brother's wedding."

"Oh." The relief in Erin's voice was palpable. "So then, could you tell your mother that I did call to invite you and that you turned me down?"

"As opposed to me telling her you don't want me there?"

"I think I have the right to decide who I want in my home." Erin seemed to catch herself on that harsh tone of voice. When she continued it was all southern charm. "Your mother's a lovely woman who's been through a lot. She'd be devastated if your presence was to take the focus from the couple on their special day. That's why I thought you might be willing to help me spare her feelings with a small white lie."

"Good-bye, Erin."

Jori lobbed her phone across the seat. It took a lot of nerve, even for someone like Erin, to call to uninvite her to her brother's wedding. As if she wanted to be anywhere near Erin and Luke, with the history they shared.

It just pissed her off to think that Erin thought she had the right to dictate Jori's behavior because . . . because.

She didn't realize tears were slipping down her face until one dripped off her chin onto her chest. She swiped her chin with the back of her hand. This wasn't the first time she'd wished she never heard of Erin Foster, Brody

Rogers, or Luke Tice. And she'd already come to the conclusion on her own that her presence at her brother's wedding would be disruptive.

But damn! She didn't want to be told what to do. By anyone. Ever again.

# CHAPTER ELEVEN

"What you got there, Trooper? Some kid lose their pet?"

Law looked up from his desktop at State Troop L headquarters in Springdale, Arkansas. Another trooper stood over him, a smirk on his broad face. Law had noted the man's arrival but hoped to avoid him.

He swiveled his chair toward the man. "Trooper Pecker. What can I do for you?"

Trooper Ron Becker grimaced at the misuse of his name, something he'd endured since elementary school. "Looks like they put you on poodle patrol, Battise." He pointed at Sam. "You paint her toenails pink all by your lonesome?"

Law rocked back in his chair, his expression neutral. Since returning to work as a state trooper two weeks earlier, he'd heard just about every possible joke about his service dog's girlie looks.

He gave Becker the quick once-over. Fifteen years older than Law, Becker had a broad face with features bunched together in the middle, making him look permanently constipated. He had been on the job out of Troop L's

Springdale office when Law joined the force. Three years later, when Law joined the State Police Criminal Control Unit as a K-9 handler, they'd quickly discovered they didn't like each other. Becker was a bully who didn't believe in breaking a sweat over anything less than the hot pursuit of a suspect.

"You still assigned to the Little Rock office, Becker?"

"Yeah." Becker lifted his Smokey Bear trooper hat from his head, revealing closely shaved blond hair with a bright pink scalp shining through. "Got a call about a suspected meth cooker we've been tracking for a month. He got himself arrested at a cousin's place over by Bob Kidd Lake. Came to transport him back to Little Rock."

"Running errands? Thought a transfer to main head-quarters would have upped your profile. Governor's motor-cade, at least."

Becker sneered, his gaze narrowing in calculation. "Must be kinda hard for you, coming home from the war a hero and all. Criminal patrol trooper reduced to doing criminal background checks for potential cashiers at Walmart. They ever let you out from behind that desk to do something exciting like noise checks or alarm installations?"

Law didn't bother to answer. Becker wasn't the first to bust his balls over his desk assignment. It just dug a little deeper coming from The Pecker.

Becker glanced again at Sam, dozing in the alcove beneath Law's desk. "What the hell kind of dog *is* that?"

"A doodle. She's on the job."

"You're shitting me? I mean, honest to God, the least they could do is give you a decent dog. Looks like that one couldn't protect you from a rash."

Law reached for his wallet and pulled out a twenty. He called Sam to his side and tucked the money in a pocket of Sam's service dog vest, wrapped saddle-like around her middle. He looked up at Becker. "You can have that twenty if you can get it from Sam."

"You're joking, right?"

Law shrugged. "You asked what she does. Let's find out."

Becker hitched up his pants and snorted. "You know I work a bit with dogs?" He gave Sam a bright smile, his voice rising and excited, the way K-9 officers speak to their canines. "How you doing there, girlie? Here, sweetheart. Show Papa what you got there in your fancy little vest pocket."

He reached toward the vest but Sam blocked him with her big head. When he shortened his reach, as if to pet her, Sam again blocked him with another sharp jerk of her head.

Becker spied three doggy treats lined up on Law's desk and grabbed a couple. "Come on now, you little bitch. Come get a treat from your new buddy." He opened his palm flat, revealing the nuggets.

Sam's gaze went from Becker to Law. Law made a slight negative move with his head.

With her head turned away, Becker made a grab for the vest. Sam quickly back-stepped, dropped her head, and growled low in her throat. The sound that emerged was deeper and more menacing than expected from so harmless-looking a dog.

"Whoa." Becker back-stepped, both hands raised in defense.

"Got to admire your K-9 technique, Pecker."

This drew chuckles from the other office personnel who'd come over to watch.

Becker cursed then seemed to realize that playing along with the joke on him was the best way to go. He tossed the nuggets at Sam. "I guess she's good for something."

Sam sat by Law's chair, ignoring the treats at her feet,

content to accept her Alpha's stroking as praise for a job well done. Her tongue lolled from the side of her mouth in a doggy grin, but her gaze remained focused on Becker. She didn't like him, or his smell. He didn't like her Alpha. She would remember that.

Becker's gaze dropped to Law's pant legs. "I heard you lost a leg. You get a lot of pity sex with that thing?"

Law grinned. "Women don't complain about what's missing once I drop my drawers. Want a demonstration?"

Becker's gaze shifted again to Sam, evidently noting for the first time that her vest said SERVICE, not POLICE K-9. "You really need a damn dog to get around?"

It occurred to Law that within five minutes Becker had questioned his access to the state police database, his mobility, and his dog's purpose. This was an interrogation.

"See you around." Law swiveled his chair back into position.

Becker stood shifting his weight from foot to foot as if his boots were a size too small. "You plan on riding a desk into retirement?"

Law looked up, his expression impenetrable. "You got a better suggestion?"

"Could be." Again, that probing look. Definitely fishing. "There're sweet positions for a former law enforcement officer who'd rather make money than arrests."

Law let himself show the barest hint of interest. "What would my sweet position look like?"

Becker grinned, no doubt thinking he'd sensed a nibble on his bait. "You tell me."

Law reared back in his chair. "She'd be a double-jointed bareback rider with a pathetic need to please."

Becker guffawed. "You get tired of this? You give me a call."

Law continued to stare at the doorway after Becker left. This wasn't a random visit. He'd bet his ass on that. But what, exactly, had Becker really wanted? Unless someone had noticed what he'd been up to.

Law glanced casually around the room. No one was watching him. That didn't mean that no one was paying attention to his actions on the job.

On the face of it, his first week back here had been boring as hell. His captain was shocked when he'd volunteered to run background checks, because that was the issue over which Law had handed in his resignation. But doing those checks gave him access to what he wanted, NCIC and Accurint, crime information databases. He'd been careful to sign in to them only when information about a potential employee legitimately steered him there. Once in he'd been covertly checking the data banks, looking for any drug-related information during the past four years that involved Tice Industries.

There had been several Tice truckers arrested for drug transport while he was serving in Afghanistan. A few in Arkansas, plus one in Tennessee and one in Oklahoma. But they were independent contractors with Tice Industries, and went to jail without incriminating Tice.

What he was doing was risky. Law enforcement officers couldn't just go on a fishing expedition through databases. They needed a warrant or probable cause. After a week of nothing he was about to throttle back for a few days, before someone noticed his intense searches. Then yesterday he'd come upon the file of Brody Rogers.

Rogers, a Tice corporate manager *and* related to the Tices by marriage, had been killed four years ago when his car missed a curve on a mountain road in the Ozarks north of Fayetteville. Dealer-sized amounts of coke, prescription drugs, and thirty thousand dollars in cash were found in his car.

For about three seconds Law hadn't been able to believe his luck. It was his first solid connection to Tice, but it came with a corker of a twist. Brody Rogers's fiancée and alleged accomplice was Jori Garrison.

"Going to lunch?"

Law's head jerked up out of his thoughts to find a fellow trooper standing before his desk. "Hey, Franklin. No thanks. I've got something going on."

The trooper nodded and moved on.

With his senses on high alert, Law reached into his pocket and pulled out the flash drive he carried everywhere. It contained only one file, labeled socks. He didn't need to read it again. He'd already memorized everything he could find about Jori Garrison, her arrest, and her subsequent trial. The newspaper accounts provided him with a good outline of events. Then he'd read and reread court documents, public record, three times. Each time he came to the same conclusion. She was probably innocent. The evidence against Jori was all circumstantial. But it was enough to convict her, without Brody Rogers there to testify on her behalf.

He exhaled in disgust. She should have been smarter than to hook up with a dirtbag like Brody. How could she have allowed herself to be conned by him?

Brody Rogers wasn't some random guy, his conscience reminded him. Jori had been engaged to him. Conclusion: She must have been in love.

That thought, as irrelevant as it was to his life, pissed him off.

What was it she'd seen in him? Money? Prestige? Those things weren't important to the woman he'd met three weeks ago. Or maybe Law was just seeing what he wanted to see.

But he was a cop, first, last, and always. He couldn't afford to let his personal feelings cloud his judgment just because he wanted something to be true. He had years of experience watching and interrogating criminals of every kind. Drug dealers came in all ages and sexes, and from all ethnic and economic backgrounds. No shock that Rogers was a dealer. But Jori lacked a selfish calculating personality. Her emotions were always on her face, probably to her disadvantage. Still, she might know things that would be useful to his investigation of Tice Industries.

That was the reason, he told himself, that he'd called Warriors Wolf Pack this morning to book his week of home supervision with a trainer. He needed time with Jori to learn what she knew. It had nothing to do with the itch he'd scratched. No, that was a lie. It did have to do with sex, and everything else about her. He couldn't *not* think of her.

Images of Jori still crept up on him in quiet moments. Surprisingly, the sweet moments outnumbered the nasty-girl ones. Jori taking Sam through her paces. Her slight frown as she concentrated on helping a vet understand a command. The way she fiddled with the end of her braid when she was nervous. Or the way she would sigh, so deeply, when she thought no one was watching. She was lonely, haunted, and unsure of her future. All those things had hooked into his psyche because he shared the feelings. But unlike her, he was fine with being adrift.

Other images, of her naked and sprawled on her bed, well, those just made him horny. And guilty. He'd never thought of himself as a user. But his last glimpse of her, resolute, shoulders squared against his departure, haunted him.

"Hell." Law expelled the word softly. He needed to get laid again.

When he found time. When he made time. When he had cleared his conscience about Jori.

Meanwhile, he had a job to do and Jori had become part of it. So he'd stuff every damn feeling and impulse away and work the case.

Law mentally checked his objectives. Get Jori to talk about what had happened to her. Get her to tell him everything she could about Rogers: his habits, his friends, his lifestyle. Then let her go back home. Conscience clear.

This time he mentally bodychecked his conscience's attempt to sidetrack him. Yeah, he'd been a real jerk. Maybe Jori attracted the type. She'd certainly gotten his attention. But no, that wasn't fair. He couldn't fault her for being attracted enough to take a chance with him. She'd accepted the ground rules and had played by them. The only cheat in the relationship was him. He had wanted to stay, could have stayed for days, weeks, and so he'd run.

But now he was pursuing an investigation and, as always, would go wherever that took him.

Except that, underneath all his real and important objectives, he simply wanted to see Jori again. And now he had the perfect excuse.

Law ran a palm down his pant leg to wipe away the sweat. He couldn't believe how nervous that thought made him. Not the deep-down gut quiver he got before going on duty with Scud. This was more an out-of-my-depth sensation. He had the feeling he was going to have to protect her from himself.

Because if she gave him an inch, he was going to take the whole nine yards.

"This little gadget teaches your dog how to think and solve problems."

Jori loaded a nugget of dog food in each of the slots at the back of the puzzle then held it up for the class of trainers to see.

"Every door opens by a different method. This one has a button. This one has a lever. Another slides." Jori demonstrated each as she went along.

"Our dogs must be able to help a veteran who can't

reach to flip a switch or slide a bolt, or press a panic button if down or incapacitated. Some puzzles open easily for a quick reward. Others require repeated effort. This way your dog learns that there is a reward for persistence. By figuring out how things work, the dog gains the confidence to try new things, become self-motivated and diligent."

One of the student-trainers, Amy, held up her hand. "I don't know what *dill*-gent means."

"It means hardworking. And careful." Kelli, who had been observing from a distance, stepped closer to the line of women and dogs.

"Cassandra wasn't diligent yesterday." Amy turned to the woman next to her. "I had to clean Shiloh's teeth for you."

"That's on account I got sent to the nurse." Cassandra cupped her lower belly with a hand. "I had the cramps something awful."

Amy smirked. "You ate two ice cream bars last night. That's what that was."

The other women laughed. There were no drink machines or candy or snack machines permitted at the women's correctional center. The occasional ice cream was the sole food reward for good behavior.

"Okay. Let's see what your dogs can do. Leanne, you and Bitsy go first."

Jori placed the puzzle on the concrete floor then stepped back and folded her arms. Though she was supposed to be concentrating on the dog working the puzzles, her gaze kept straying to the line of women in white baggy jumpsuits waiting their turn to show what their service dogs could do. The sight was painfully familiar. Once she'd been one of them. Eager to please in a uniform that was nearly impossible to keep clean when one lived in a building with eleven other women and twelve dogs.

Occasionally the gaze of one of the women darted

toward her. Those looks made her palms sweat. They were sizing her up, yet treating her with a distance made up of much more than the six months since her release. She was no longer one of them. She'd made it to the outside.

The sudden sense that she didn't belong anywhere— never far from her thoughts—settled like an invisible blanket over her.

Though the training of inmates went on weekly, this was her first time back at the correctional center. The thought of reentering the prison had had her lying wide-eyed awake all night, feeling many things and wondering how she'd react. Yet all she had felt upon entering the facility near Newport, Arkansas, was the certainty that she was here as an instructor. That, and the relief in knowing that when the doors closed this afternoon, she would be on the outside.

That knowledge made her feel both giddy and guilty.

Jori shushed her thoughts. Today wasn't about her. It was about offering a future to these inmates, the dogs they trained, and ultimately the veterans the dogs were destined to aid. Her petty where-do-I-belong troubles were nothing compared with that.

For the next two hours, Jori and the other instructors from Warriors Wolf Pack worked with the canine teams, evaluating the responses of the dogs and student-trainers.

The sounds of the plastic clickers used to attract the young dog's attention to his or her trainer made it seem as if a dozen giant crickets had invaded the large space. The inmates trained young dogs, beginning at eight weeks, for eight to ten hours a day, in the basics.

The dormitory-style building within the prison grounds was erected to exclusively house those female inmates working with Warriors Wolf Pack. Metal beds were placed in two rows with a metal kennel for a dog beside each bed.

They trained and slept apart from the general population, though they did share meals and work details when not training their assigned dog. It wasn't fancy. There was no air-conditioning. Heating was used only when the temperature dropped to near freezing, as it had this early-December morning.

Jori was actually enjoying herself when the lunchtime buzzer sounded, followed by the arrival of several female corrections officers. One whom Jori recognized as Mrs. Mitchell made hard eye contact. The hair on Jori's arms lifted. Mrs. Mitchell had been a hard-ass about rules, and a bit of a Bible-thumper. Even as she told herself the woman no longer had any control over her in any way, Jori couldn't stop four years of institutionalized fear from flooding her.

Heart thumping like a jackhammer, she turned to her trainee. "Make certain Happy is checking in with you each time she completes a task, Cora."

Cora nodded but didn't make eye contact. Her chin wobbled and her shoulders rounded in self-protection. "They're coming for Happy at the end of the week."

Jori knew immediately what the problem was. Happy was Cora's first dog. After four months the puppies left here to continue their socialization with puppy raiser families. "You'll see her again."

"I know. Only she won't be mine when she comes back."

That was true. Happy would be assigned a different inmate trainer when she returned. Part of WWP's purpose was to teach inmates to serve others and stop the selfish behaviors that had landed many of them here. Still, loneliness was the Black Plague of incarceration.

"You should be proud that Happy's learned enough to move forward. You've made a difference. It's not about us. It's about the people we serve." Jori scotched the impulse to pat Cora's shoulder. She was a trainee, not a friend. "Let's get some lunch."

Minutes later, Kelli waved Jori over to her table. "I held a seat for you."

"Thanks." Jori plunked her lunch tray down and sat.

"Mr. Battise just called the office to schedule his three-week check." Kelli waggled her brows at Jori. "He asked for you."

"You got a man?" One of the inmates who shared their table was staring eagerly at Jori.

"No." She didn't have a man. She'd had sex with Lauray Battise. Hot, sweaty, delicious sex that gave her a rush every time she thought about it. But Battise was gone. Not one word in three weeks. Three weeks! And now he thought he could pick up the phone and summon her?

No one at Warriors Wolf Pack had said a thing about them going off together. Not even when she came back alone. They had speculated like mad, though. She could see it in their sideways glances. But she wasn't the kind of person who shared intimate details, the emphasis on *intimate*.

Heat and desire licked through Jori as she stared at her plate. Useless to try to push the memories away. She'd tried often enough. Now that he had been gone long enough for her to fully appreciate the *nevermore* part of their hookup, it was all she could think about when she wasn't working.

Sex with Battise had made her wonder if she'd ever really had sex before. Oh, she'd rolled around with a few guys before Brody, hooked up body parts and thought, *Yeah, this is nice.* But getting it on with Battise had been— well. The earth moved.

Her thighs tightened involuntarily with an urge she had no way to satisfy at the moment. Oh no. She wasn't going to let Battise ruin her day.

She tucked into her beans and rice, and choked. The

food tasted of prison life. And just now, she couldn't swallow that.

"You need to get you some Beano." Jori looked over at the same inmate who was still watching her. "Them beans can bind up a body somethin' awful."

# CHAPTER TWELVE

In the time it took to walk to her SUV with the last of her supplies, Jori started having second thoughts about agreeing to spend a week with Battise. She was just asking for heartache.

Or maybe a helluva week of mind-blowing sex.

A smile tugged her mouth as she climbed behind the wheel, but she resisted. As difficult as Battise could be at times, she hadn't regretted for even a second what had happened between them. She just needed to dial back her expectations before she saw him again.

Yeah. Like that was going to happen. Just remembering watching him towel off after a shower, all damp and squeaky-clean naked, made her mind sweat and her body tense.

A horn sounding sharply from behind her vehicle startled Jori. She'd been so busy thinking about sex she'd put her SUV in gear and begun backing up without really looking behind her. A big brown delivery van was now taking up her full-review mirror.

Jori hopped out. "Sorry. Didn't see you."

"No harm." The woman driver looked at her invoice. "Are you Jori Garrison?" Jori nodded. "This is for you." The woman handed over a huge box. "And I need you to sign here, please. Thanks. Have a good one," the driver tossed back over her shoulder as she hurried away.

Jori did not need confirmation of the return address to realize who the box was from. But there it was anyway, written in her mother's cheerful print. Nor did she need to open it to find out what was inside. Dresses for her to choose from for the reception and wedding coming up in a few days. Her mother had sent a text message telling her to expect them.

Annoyed that her mother hadn't taken no for an answer, Jori stalked back to her SUV, jerked open a back door, and tossed the box on the seat.

"Doesn't anyone listen to me?" She slammed the door so hard the SUV rocked.

*Mee-ow*ing in concern, Argyle poked her head up through the top of the cat carrier sitting on the floor of the passenger side to check out the source of that frustrated voice.

Jori slid behind the wheel. "Not now, Argyle." She pushed her kitten gently back inside and checked the lock. Then she started the ignition, threw the SUV into gear, and took off as if she could outdistance her problems by driving like a bat out of hell.

"No. No. No. Not here."

Jori thumped her palm repeatedly against the steering wheel. Her vehicle had just sputtered, choked, and then rolled to a halt on the half shoulder of a two-lane blacktop in the Boston Mountains of northwest Arkansas.

She twisted the key in the ignition. The dashboard lit up and then her gaze shifted to the gas gauge. It was mostly broken. It had two settings: half full and desert-dry empty.

At the moment the little red needle lay flat on its back like a victim of a heatstroke, despite the December chill in the air.

"Crap in a can!"

She reached into the glove compartment for the notepad on which she kept her record of fill-ups. The numbers didn't lie. She was out of gas.

Jori shook her head in self-disgust. How could she have forgotten to buy gas? Of course. She'd been too busy trying to outrun her anger over her mother's package to think about filling up.

Not knowing exactly where she was, she pulled out her cell phone to look at her GPS. She had one signal bar that kept winking out. That meant she probably couldn't make a call, either. Not that she had anyone to call. Roadside service wasn't in her budget. Calling Battise would be too embarrassing. She was supposed to be coming to help him. It wouldn't be very professional to begin the other way around.

Muttering, she tucked the phone back into her pocket and got out of her SUV. She was in the hollow of hills surrounded by autumn-striped trees that marched off in all directions. The strip of blacktop, she knew from the printed directions Kelli had given her to Battise's home, was named High Sky Inn Road. That should have been a warning to stop for gas. The more colorful the name, the more likely the road would be narrow, winding, and a long way from anywhere.

The sky was a high, clear Ozark Mountain blue, but the radio had earlier been filled with predictions of a potentially dangerous cold front headed toward the area over the weekend. The chill in the air was quickly draining the car heat from her body despite her puffy vest.

She plunged her hands into her vest pockets as she stared in first one direction and then the other down the empty road. Though she could see a long way, there wasn't a single house in view. No traffic, either. When had she last passed a service station? Three, five miles ago? She guessed she'd find out because walking for help seemed to be the only option. She checked her SUV, leaving a window cracked for air for Argyle, and headed off.

She'd walked no more than a dozen yards when she heard a vehicle in the distance coming from the other direction.

The state trooper car pulling up before her SUV seemed a mixed blessing. The last thing she wanted to do was deal with law enforcement. But she did need help.

The man who unfolded from behind the wheel was tall and broad, all crisp uniform, mirrored shades, and trooper hat set at an angle of intimidation.

Jori felt a nudge of unease as she walked back to where he was parked a short distance away. He had paused by his front fender to speak into the radio on his shoulder. As he stood there, she tried to penetrate the impersonal mask formed by the broad brim and opaque shades. *Clean rigid jawline, pronounced cheekbones, and a generous pair of lips.* Nice-looking man, er, officer. It didn't stop the jelly feeling in her stomach as she paused within a few yards of him.

"You got a problem?"

His voice, pitched low and penetrating, sent a shiver of alarm up her spine. Badge intimidation? Definitely. Yet he sounded familiar. She was just thinking of Battise. That's what it was! She supposed all overbearing Alpha males sounded the same when in I'm-in-charge mode.

"You need help?" Obviously he thought she hadn't heard him.

She swallowed her unease. She was being ridiculous. "I'm out of gas." Her tone sounded more defensive than she meant it to be. But she was embarrassed by the stupidity of her mistake.

"You call roadside service?"

"Can't afford it. I was about to walk back to town." She glanced over her shoulder. "Wherever that is."

"You're about to lose a passenger." A long blunt-tipped finger pointed past her at her driver's window.

She turned just in time to catch the kitten wriggling through the two-inch breathing space. She hugged the fuzzy animal to her chest. "You're a menace."

"Argyle, right?"

Her head snapped around. The officer watched her with the slightest trace of amusement tugging up one corner of his mouth.

"Still don't recognize me? Maybe if I shucked my pants."

Her gaze dropped to his legs. The wind was whipping at his pant legs. The left one was suspiciously loose. "Battise?"

"Officer of the Law, to you." He pulled off his glasses. That high-grade-crude gaze was unmistakable. But the face was that of a stranger.

A stranger she'd done the dirty with.

Oh no, not a good time to think of that. Not when he was looking at her like, like he was the big bad wolf.

Law watched her trying to absorb his new look. The uniform, the shorter hair, and the lack of a beard. It had taken him a couple of days to stop doing double takes in shop windows after he'd shaved. Yet the look was a reversion to his old self. She was recalculating her opinion of him based on what, for her, was a completely new persona. He didn't like the way it was adding up in her eyes. Her gaze was guarded, and this time Argyle was fiddling with the end of the braid slung forward over her shoulder.

He frowned. "You're staring."

"I didn't expect to see you like this."

He rested his hands on either side of his belt, elbows flared. "You mean on the road?"

"No." She waved at his patrol car. "The whole law enforcement thing."

"What bothers you most? The uniform? Or that I'm wearing it?"

It wasn't even close. It was the man himself. She'd wondered what his bushy beard disguised. Now she knew. The man was flat-out gorgeous in a totally rugged male way. She let out a slow breath of admiration, a purely feminine response. Not good. She needed her body to stop reacting to him.

She tucked Argyle into her vest, needing an excuse to stop staring. "You got your job back. Congratulations."

"The chance to pass the physical is next week. After that, I'm back with full duties." He slanted a speculative gaze down at her. "You could ask me for help."

Jori noted the glint in his eye. He was enjoying this.

She folded her arms across her chest. "I didn't think law enforcement officers ran errands for civilians."

"How about asking a favor from a friend?" It was a flip reply, and she wanted to answer it in kind. But friendship was one thing she'd never considered with this man.

"We're friends?"

"Unless you got a better name for it." He was looking at her with an expression that said he was considering a few other possibilities. All of them sexual. This was the Battise she remembered.

The heat rising up her neck and behind her ears betrayed her vulnerability to his potency. Discretion was called for. "Yeah, let's go with that. Friends."

"I live just up the road." He jerked his thumb back over his shoulder. "I keep a full gas can in my garage. Come on."

Jori followed with reluctant steps to his patrol car. By then her goose bumps had goose bumps of anxiety.

"Where should I sit?"

Law frowned at her over the hood until reason dawned. She thought he was about to put her in back. She'd probably been in the back of enough squad cars to last her two lifetimes. "Sam's in the back and she's very territorial about her space. It's either the trunk or the front seat with me."

Jori smiled. He'd actually made a joke though nothing changed in his face. "I'll take my chances in front."

He grinned at her. The experience was revelatory. Without a beard to cover it, his smile was shark-bright and just as dangerous. It hit her like a shot of tequila. Maybe the trunk was the safer choice.

She slid into the small passenger side crowded by his computer and other equipment and was immediately accosted from the rear by a wet tongue. "Samantha!"

Sam had watched her Alpha leave their vehicle with careful eyes. Usually there was no uptick in his pheromones as they rode together. But something had kicked Alpha's output into high gear. He was shedding emotions. Not anger or fear but excitement of some kind.

Sam was on alert because he hadn't let her out to accompany him. Alpha had yet to learn that was her job to be with him, always. But then she spied the WWP trainer through the front windshield and her worry faded.

Her Alpha was happy to see the Alpha female. Happy was a good place.

Sam was happy, too. The Alpha female always brought treats and toys. Sam's whole body wagged with anticipation.

And then Sam saw it. The cat.

Sam's happy dance wiggled down to a squirm. No happy dance for the high-anxiety feline whose claws were sharper than the veterinarian's needle. Too bad the Alpha female brought it. Cat was definitely *not* pack.

Still, Sam greeted the Alpha woman with a sloppy lick. She would not lick cat.

Cat hissed when she spied dog.

"No, not nice." Jori tucked Argyle deeper into her vest. "Play nice."

Argyle just *grrrr-oowl*ed low in a strangled cat way that was part snarl, part yowl.

They hadn't traveled more than two miles when Law turned off High Sky Inn Road onto an even narrower unpaved lane that didn't have enough room for a center stripe. The patrol car was no sleek machine but a big powerful vehicle that took the sudden rises and sharp turns of the hill country with the souped-up aggression of an armored tank crossing enemy territory.

"You good?" Law glanced at her with an edgy grin after a particularly sudden swoop in the road left Jori gasping from a sense of free fall.

"Good." She gave him a thumbs-up but shut her eyes, feeling that just maybe what she couldn't see wouldn't hurt her. He must know what he was doing.

They came to a sudden stop after the final fifty feet of unpaved road that sent gravel spraying from beneath the tires. Jori opened her eyes.

She hadn't given much thought to where Battise might live. Standard apartment in town, whatever that might look like. Or a trailer, maybe. She hadn't expected that he would live off-road, up a secluded gravel track in the woods. She was looking at an A-frame log cabin perched on a bluff. It was small but neat, with a porch running the width of the front and wrapping around the side toward the rear. A cord of wood cut for the fireplace lay stacked just nearby.

Law turned to her. "You can come in or wait here while I get the gas."

The words were neutral, but the invitation in his eyes was intimate and a dare.

"I'll wait."

Sam jumped out of the back of the car when Law opened the door and fell into step with him as he climbed the few steps, leading the way. When they reached the porch, Sam suddenly moved in front, barring Law from opening the door.

Law frowned. "What's up, Sam?"

Sam looked up at Alpha and then back at the door. As she did so, he moved to go past her. Sam stood her ground, lowered her head, and braced her front legs. Alpha should not pass.

Instantly alert, Law reached with his left hand to release the safety holding his gun in his holster.

"Is something wrong?"

Law looked back. Jori had exited the car and stood a few yards away.

"Get back in the car. Now."

He didn't bother to see if his order was obeyed. With his right hand, he unlocked and pushed open the front door.

"Sam. Search."

# CHAPTER THIRTEEN

Sam moved reluctantly through the door. She wanted to stay beside her Alpha and protect him. Yet this was part of their routine. She did a perimeter search each time they entered this place. However, this time was different. Something had changed. She smelled it. Perhaps he did, too.

She paused, the fur on her back twitching with tension as she lifted her nose and then lowered her head. Something faint. Very *very* faint. But real.

She moved around the room beginning on the right as she went from point to point, window to window, sniffing, studying just as she had practiced for months at Warriors Wolf Pack. All the smells here were ones she'd come to know during the past three weeks. The odors of varnish and aging wood. Fainter still were the aromas of months of cooking, the oil her Alpha used to clean his weapons, the sweet tang of soap, sharp notes of cleanser, old sneakers, ashes, and a thousand other now familiar smells of her new home. She even knew there was a very stale potato chip under the sofa where she couldn't reach it. She'd tried often enough.

Once every few feet, she stopped and sniffed the air, looking for a trace of that *other*. She licked her nose several times, an instinctive action that would improve her ability to capture scent particles. Finally, she caught it. The scent that had made her pause at the entry. She had smelled it only once before, a few days ago.

She did a quick look back at Alpha. He remained in the doorway. Usually, he walked close behind her when she did the search, holding her leash. But this time he had released her. Even from a distance she could smell the rise of pheromones sliding off him. He must smell it, too. The ugly scent. Anxiety rippled over her back in response.

"Sam. Search." Alpha's voice was high and urgent this time.

Shivering in anticipation, she turned back to the scent stream in the air, swinging her head from side to side until she had pinpointed the source. It came from the plank-board kitchen table at the far end of the room.

She hurried over and sniffed. Yes. This was it. She hoovered the chair seat and then the laptop lying closed on the surface. The smell of the man from the Alpha's office filled her scent glands. A harder shiver rocked through her. Alpha did not like him. She did not like him, either. He had tried to take something from her.

She sniffed again at the laptop and then sat, looking back over her shoulder at Alpha. He would know what to do.

Law was watching Sam but he was seeing Scud. His thousand-yard stare was extending over miles and ocean and sand, and backward in time.

> *The smell of gunfire pricked in his nostrils. The room was flickering, brightening to reveal desert terrain.*

*As usual, Scud was itching to go ahead on Law's order at the first sign of trouble. He barked an order to keep his partner under control. Scud was a stubborn son of a bitch. Just like him. He wanted this takedown so bad he could taste it. But today was a reconnaissance operation. No advance warning to troops.*

*Law's heart jackhammered in anticipation. World's fucking greatest K-9 team! Fearless. Ferocious. Born fighters.*

*But there was danger here. No names. No faces. And no backup. CID didn't trust even other soldiers on a mission like this.*

*They would need to ratchet it down. Keep things quiet until everything was in place.*

"Battise?"

Jori's voice sent Law's head swiveling toward her. She hadn't moved from the spot he'd last seen her.

"Are you okay?" Her expression was neutral but her eyes were a little too wide. She back-stepped when he turned his stone-cold warrior expression on her.

Law watched her with hard eyes, riding the adrenaline surge of his breath moving in and out as reality settled back in around him. Not desert. Mountain. Home. But the danger was real. Sam was real. Sam had alerted to the presense of another, something she'd never done before during their daily perimeter checks.

"Don't move again until I tell you to. Got that?" The words were said quietly but with such force he felt them in his chest.

He waited until she nodded. Her eyes were too wide and her mouth was slack. Not a good way to start their time together. But he had a job to do. He turned and walked inside.

The main room consisted of a living area with a sofa, TV, and fireplace. His eyes moved systematically left to right as he did a perimeter check of the room. His left hand remained on the handle of his weapon. Above was a loft open to the floor below. Law wasted no time searching there. His focus went to Sam, who still sat beside the table. She wasn't agitated or looking around in expectation of spying an invader, as even a family pet would do if it suspected a stranger was nearby. Sam's action was clear. The intruder had had one destination. Law went to the table.

The only thing there was his laptop. Beyond the dining area, sliding doors led onto a back deck. Could someone have gotten in that way? He checked. A cutoff broom handle lay in the door's track to prevent it from opening even if unlocked.

Satisfied that the intruder was gone, Law walked back toward the front door. As he did so, he refocused his attention on Jori. He'd left her standing alone without explanation. He needed to do something about that.

She stood on the gravel drive where he'd left her. He took a careful breath, taking in the details of her for the first time. She wore a blue turtleneck sweater, puffy vest, leggings, and knee-high boots. The briefest sketch of a smile widened his mouth. The boots matched! Then he saw her face. It was pale and pinched. She was afraid. Of him? It hit him like a punch in the gut.

He stepped onto the porch. "Someone's been here."

"Okay." She didn't move, but he saw her gaze shift and fasten on his left hand.

He looked down at the Sig Sauer in his hand. When had he pulled his weapon? It was an automatic response to a perceived threat. He holstered it and set the safety. He needed to distract her, fast, before she ran screaming for her life.

"You can come inside." He made an elaborate gesture

of welcome with his hand. "I won't bite. At least not without an invitation."

Jori found she couldn't return his smile. It didn't reach his eyes. The shaggy wounded veteran who had come to Warriors Wolf Pack three weeks earlier had been a very bitter, angry man. Now something had shifted that anger into purpose. She could hear it in his voice. See it in the gleam in his eyes. She wasn't at all certain of its origin. Did it have anything to do with his suspected intruder? Or had he slipped into a place where he made up his own reality? And how was she supposed to handle that? Nothing about that was in the doggy training handbook.

Once inside she looked around, trying to sound casual. "Did you find any signs of forced entry?"

He shrugged and wiped at the sweat at the back of his neck from the adrenaline rush of moments before. "I don't always lock my door. I've nothing here I care about."

She would have cared if she'd lost the laptop she spied on the table. But that didn't seem a tactful thing to point out just now. "Could it have been kids messing around?"

Law moved to check his kitchen, even opened the refrigerator. "Not kids. They would've eaten something. Drunk my beer. Trashed the place looking for money and weapons. Meth heads would have taken the computer to fence. This person wanted something specific. He didn't mean to leave a trail."

"Oh." He still thought there was an intruder.

His jaw began to work. "Go ahead. Say it."

Jori took a deep breath. He wasn't going to like her thoughts. She could see it in his expression. But she had seen him moments before. On his face had been the look of a man a million miles away from their reality. Caution told her to take an indirect route.

"Someone would have to be pretty stupid to break into

a law enforcement officer's home." She pointed to his holstered gun.

He grunted as if she had made a joke. "Are you afraid of me now?"

"No." And she meant it. *Afraid for you.* But she couldn't say that. He wouldn't thank her for her concern. Not her place to be afraid for him. Her job here was as a trainer. So she'd use that.

"If you'd stayed for the full ten days of training, you'd know we teach our dogs to do perimeter searches."

"But you don't expect them to ever find anything." His expression said he knew exactly what she was implying. "The perimeter search training is just a placebo to reassure us paranoid head cases that the Bogeyman isn't real."

His sarcastic tone rubbed her the wrong way. "Our dogs provide a reality check. Don't underestimate the value of knowing, despite what your senses are telling you, that your dog says there's nothing to worry about."

"But your service dog did just alert."

Law walked over to the table and held his hand a scant inch above the closed laptop.

"What are you doing?"

"I turned my computer off this morning. It's warm. Someone turned it on recently."

Jori folded her arms. "Or maybe you left it plugged in and the heat is from the battery charging."

"Do you see a cord?"

Jori didn't. "Why would someone want access to your computer?"

"Good question."

"So, Sam really did alert on an intruder?"

Instead of answering, he reached into a pocket and produced a few treats. Obviously he wasn't going to share his thoughts with her. "Sam. *Heir. Gute Hund.*"

Jori noticed he'd reverted to German, law professional K-9 command mode.

Sam didn't seem to mind. She came forward and got her petting and kibble treats for a job well done from her Alpha.

"Has she learned much German?"

Law frowned. "There's an ongoing debate about how much language a dog really understands. A few words, certainly. It's more the tone of voice." He petted Sam absently, as if something else was on his mind. "She did all right. For a doodle."

*For a doodle.* The phrase bothered Jori. It was obvious that Sam was totally devoted to Battise. But Battise had yet to return that full-hearted affection.

She bent and let Argyle, squirming like a dervish, down onto the wood floor.

Argyle *meow*ed as if someone had stepped on her tail, became an arched ball of fur that skipped sideways, and then shot across the floor and down an unseen hallway.

Sam, spying the cat, followed their uninvited guest at a cautious stalking pace.

Jori sighed. It seemed as if every other living thing in the room was operating off some high-frequency intensity she couldn't hear.

"You want a beer?"

"No thanks." Jori supposed this was his way of saying the emergency status was over. "I need to get back on the road. I didn't leave a deposit with the motel in Springdale. I just planned to stop by to let you know I had arrived."

"You could have just called."

Jori held his gaze. *So could you.*

And there it was, the reason they were dancing around each other.

Not wanting to sound like a woman left behind, she concentrated on the reason she was being paid to be here.

"Do you have those moments often, where you need Sam to reset reality for you?"

He blinked twice, as if calibrating his thoughts. But if she hoped he was going to answer the question, she was disappointed. "Why did you agree to come, Jori?"

Another, more dangerous question. But if he could ignore questions he didn't want to answer, she could, too.

She looked around. "Nice place."

"I rent." The *keep out* sign went up in his gaze. "It provides the privacy I like."

She rounded on him. "I wasn't hinting that I wanted to stay with you."

"Too bad. You would make a nice change from having Sam in my bed." He hadn't moved an inch closer but she suddenly felt crowded as he watched her with his lids at half-mast.

He seemed so calm, so in control. The challenge in his expression said it didn't matter if she jumped him or walked away. He had six other things on his mind and none of them, or all, might be about her. He wasn't giving away clues. His cool made Jori want to wipe that smug look off his gorgeous face and replace it with a lustful grin from lips swollen and damp from her kisses.

He set his Smokey Bear hat on the table then reached to unhook his rig and lay the twenty-plus pounds of his utility belt on the table beside it. "I'm going to make this easy for both of us."

When he looked up she didn't have to wonder what *this* was. It was there. Direct. Hot and volatile as his sludge-gold gaze. Absolute lust.

He stopped just inches away and leaned in to bring his lips on a level with her own. "We already know how good it can be between us. That makes it simple. We either act on it. Or we don't."

He reached up and took the tab of the zipper on her vest

and began dragging it slowly down. "What about it. Want to get naked?"

Jori held still. She knew he was trying to steer her away from her assessment of his earlier actions as symptoms of PTSD. The problem was, it was a damn effective tactic. The carnal hunger that she'd been ignoring for three weeks was out of its box and stomping around her bloodstream in military boots.

He kissed her, expelling his warm breath into her mouth.

Law's arms wrapped around her, drawing her up against his muscular length, crushing her to him as he took control of her, and of the hunger scorching through him. He palmed her butt, lifting her to grind his instant erection on her. Then he lowered his head and kissed her again.

That's all it took. All her good intentions went down the drain with the touch of his lips. Jori wrapped her arms about his neck to pull him closer.

Part of Law was more than satisfied by her response. The other part warned him just how far over the line he was headed. He'd only meant to distract her. Expected her to back off. But he couldn't hang in there when she kissed him like this. His head was in his pants and his dick was doing all the thinking. The urge to push into her and screw them both blind had him trembling.

What had he been thinking? He could no more control the heat between them than he could fly to Mars.

Feeling pretty damn desperate, and a split second from taking the decision out of her hands, he pulled back from the primal blaze that was Jori Garrison.

One second, Jori had half climbed his body. The next, she was dropped back on her heels to steady herself as best she could on legs made liquid by his embrace.

Winded and a little stunned, she grabbed his arm to keep from dissolving in a puddle at his feet. When she looked up at him, eyes dark with desire, he was sorry he'd touched her. "Why did you do that?"

"Just curious. You still want me." He grinned. "Bad."

Hard to look at the astonished hurt on her face. Harder still to resist the temptation of her mouth blurred and swelling from his kiss. No surprise when the hurt in her gaze flickered into outrage. He was just pathetically grateful. Without it, they would both have been lost.

"Don't flatter yourself. So, I'm horny. You're horny. Big fat deal. You need my expertise with Samantha more than you need in my panties. Keep it tucked in your pants for the other women in your life. I'll handle my end."

She was doing great. Letting them both off the hook with that jolt of common sense. It was working right up to the moment he got sucker-punched by something as harmless as her lower lip trembling.

He looked away, his gaze going everywhere, like that of a man overboard searching for a life preserver in a stormy sea. And there it was. His laptop.

"I have business I need to take care of before we continue . . ." His eyes tracked back to her. ". . . with training. Make yourself comfortable."

He saw her split-second hesitation before she answered. "Right."

Goddammit! She didn't play fair.

The urge to reach out and soothe, even to apologize, was so strong he felt the pain of restraining himself. His fists clenched and his chest ached. He'd never felt regret whether he was taking or rejecting a woman. And never, even when he knew he was wrong, had he considered apologizing. What the hell was going on?

Jori didn't notice his dilemma. She had turned away, staring blindly for a second. Bastard! She knew better. He'd warned her. Worse, she couldn't believe she'd practically begged him to continue.

She sucked in a breath and almost choked on it. "I need some air."

She pushed back through the front door and moved quickly across the porch and around the side of the house toward the back, anywhere to get away from him so she could breathe.

She inhaled early-December air, the chill a welcome relief from the sexual heat of moments before. It took a few seconds for her vision to clear. But gradually the view won her attention.

The vista was impressive. The land behind the cabin dropped away steeply from an outcropping of shale on which it was built. Below, a thickly wooded valley rippled down and out before climbing the next ridge. Most of the trees had lost their leaves but in the deep underbrush there were still deep veins of green that winter had yet to reap. Higher up, where the foliage had been pruned away by a series of frosty evenings, a throng of trees thrust bare limbs through the slanted sunlight.

If a car hadn't passed by under her gaze, she would never have noticed the road that snaked through the ridge across the valley. With her vision adjusted, she soon spotted her SUV, too. Had Battise been watching for her, seen her become stranded on the road, and come to her rescue? Why wouldn't he just say that?

She groaned and bent to lay her head on her arms, folded on the railing. What sort of man treated even kindness as a covert operation?

*You don't know him, Jori. You better not try.*

Good advice. If only she'd take it.

"I didn't find anything. But that doesn't matter now. I've got something better."

Becker grinned to himself as he sat behind the wheel of his truck in a sharp curve of High Sky Inn Road. Dressed in scent-blocker camo pants, a bubble vest, and cap, he looked like any other Arkie who might have pulled off to enjoy the view, or take a leak. The Steiner binoculars resting on his thigh hinted at the real reason for his stop at this particular spot.

He'd gotten lucky. Now, whether it was good luck or bad would depend on if and how he could capitalize on his new information.

"Battise has a guest. Called the license plate in. You're not going to believe this. It belongs to Jori Garrison."

He listened carefully to the response, straining to detect the degree of concern in the voice on the other end rather than in the actual words.

"Hell, yeah, I'm sure. Looking at the woman standing on his deck as we speak."

A slight rise in pitch from the voice on the other end. He smiled. That's what he was listening for.

"How the fuck should I know? My three days off are up. I'm headed back to Little Rock. We have an agreement. Nothing's changed."

# CHAPTER FOURTEEN

Law looked over at Jori. "Coffee?"

"Yes."

"How about a little breakfast, too?"

Out of the corner of his eye he saw her shake her head. "Are you sure? It's going to be a long boring morning before lunch."

"No."

He glanced again at her. She was staring straight ahead out the front window of his patrol car at the streets of Springdale clogged with the morning commute. No expression. No apparent interest in him.

The only thing possibly more hostile toward him was that cat crammed in the travel crate on his backseat. Even Sam, who usually took up the entire backseat, was giving the feline a wide berth. Argyle had already demonstrated her reach through the bars with a paw full of needlelike claws.

Jori said she couldn't leave Argyle in the motel room all day. So there was an aluminum pan and a sack of kitty litter in his vehicle. Perfect.

The day was overcast, threatening rain. Sunrise had yet to have much of an impact on the darkness, making everyone feel like their day had begun much too early. But it was a sunny spring day outside compared with the atmosphere inside his cruiser. Iceberg in his passenger seat.

He'd picked Jori up at her motel this morning so she could watch him and Sam go through their paces on a normal workday. He'd cleared it with his captain by getting permission for her to do a ride-along. Of course, it was mostly going to be a sit-and-watch-him-at-his-desk-in-the-office-along. He'd said he was working with a wounded warrior program to ensure that their service dogs could function even in a high-energy environment like a state police station. He'd omitted the PTSD issue. As far as he was concerned, Sam had already proven an ideal station dog, quiet, attentive, but never drawing attention to herself. If only her trainer were as easygoing.

*Heat of the moment.* That's what she'd said to him after he'd finished checking his computer the day before and found her on his back deck. She hadn't even allowed him to begin some version of maybe-I-made-an-error-in-judgment, just-short-of-an-apology speech.

She'd lifted a hand to silence him, her right eyebrow arching slightly. "Forget it. It happened. It won't happen again. Heat of the moment."

And that was that. After he gassed up her SUV, she'd driven away without even a backward glance.

Law cursed under his breath as the eighteen-wheeler, three cars in front of him, began rolling forward at a pace a chicken could outrun. At the rate he was creeping along they'd miss the light, again. This wasn't L.A., Houston, or Manhattan, but the Fayetteville-Springdale half-hour version of rush hour was just as slow, boring, and frustrating.

When he'd called Jori's motel at six a.m., he half

expected to hear she'd never checked in. But she answered, sounding wide awake.

So he manned up, told her he was going to the gym for an hour and then he'd be by to pick her up to do her first day of shadowing them.

All she'd said was, "Fine." One lousy syllable.

Since then, she hadn't spoken a word he hadn't had to pry out of her.

Law ground his teeth as the light in front of him turned red for the second time without him getting through the intersection. "Forget this."

He turned on his blue lights, pumped his horn a few times, and gave his siren several short blasts.

He watched as the middle-aged man in the Toyota in front of him glanced in his rearview mirror, jerked in surprise, and then glanced nervously right and left, looking for a way to get out of the state police cruiser's way. It took a few seconds for other drivers to make their way. But little by little Law was able to nudge his cruiser to the head of the line.

As the cross traffic slowed, he swung over in the left-turn lane, blasted his siren, and then when traffic halted for him shot through the intersection.

"Was all that really necessary?"

Jori's dry tone hitched up his grin as he swung a glance her way. "Hell, yeah."

She just shook her head but he would swear she was pinching off a smile. Okay then. She was angry. He was angry. But she might thaw. She needed something hot— don't go there. She needed coffee.

He swung into a convenience store parking lot.

"You're not planning on buying coffee here?" She sounded as indignant as if he'd scooped up a cup of mud and offered it to her. It wasn't the thanks he was hoping for.

"You want the real law enforcement experience, you're

getting it." He pulled into a space before the store's bank of picture windows decked out with a few strings of twinkling multicolored Christmas lights. "How do you take it?"

"I'll get it." She pushed her door open and was out before he could move.

Sam nudged her head through the back window to watch her exit.

Law reached up to cup a friendly hand under her chin. "That didn't go the way I planned. Women. I swear the sex is alien."

But he smiled as he watched her walk toward the store. She was mad as hell at him. She had every right. But that didn't stop him from looking, or appreciating, or wanting.

Her khaki cargo pants fit tight across her gorgeous ass. That flare emphasized her narrow waist. The way her braid bounced down her back had him hard within seconds. All those things—and more, the woman herself—would be sitting inches away from him for the rest of his shift. Untouchable.

He sighed. It was going to be a long day.

Rodeo-ing his way through traffic lights wasn't like him. Letting off steam and showing off in public wasn't his way. But something about Jori had him flexing his fingers on the steering wheel, edgy and needing to work off his frustration. Maybe he'd hit the gym again at lunch hour.

He reached over to check his computer when he realized Jori hadn't moved very much since she'd entered the store. She was stock-still, staring in the direction of the checkout counter.

At that moment she turned her head back toward him. Her eyes were wide with alarm.

Something cold slid down Law's spine. Time slowed as he tracked back along her gaze, taking in every detail of the scene all at once.

A man stood at the counter. Short. Slim. In a gray hoodie.

He could have been paying for a Slurpee except that his right hand was moving about wildly while his left was stuffed in his hoodie pocket. Was he hiding a gun, a knife? The cashier was busy at the register, stuffing what appeared to be money in a plastic bag. Several customers stood well back instead of forming a line.

Jori was between Hoodie and the door.

Law reached for his radio and called it in, identifying himself. Robbery in progress, giving the location and asking for backup. All before his brain caught up with the automatic response of years of training. "Potential hostage situation."

Law sat two more seconds running scenarios in his head, seeking every tactical advantage. If he found himself in a standoff, or a hostage situation, he would have failed.

One. Too late to back up out of Hoodie's line of sight. If he hadn't already noticed the cruiser, he might notice if it moved.

Two. Look for signs of an accomplice in the parking lot. His head swiveled left and right, clocking the perimeter in degrees. No accomplice apparent in parking lot. No unattended vehicle with engine running. Maybe Hoodie was on foot.

Three. Better if he could wait for him to come out, away from those trapped inside, thinking he was getting away with the heist.

Only six, maybe seven seconds had passed since he'd seen that look on Jori's face.

Law reached to open his door handle and forced her image away. He had a job to do. She wasn't the only one in jeopardy.

Several young Hispanic men in roadworkers' gear were headed for the doors. He drew his gun, held up a finger for silence, and motioned them back. He didn't have to say a word. They backpedaled double-time then scattered, seeking cover.

Law heard a shout from inside. He stepped behind the ice machine, putting something heavy between him and the exit. His nerves stretched, ears straining for but hoping not to catch the *pop pop* sounds of a weapon being discharged.

Jori was between Hoodie and the door.

Nothing.

Who robbed a convenience store at seven thirty in the morning when traffic would be at its maximum? One desperate amped-up dumbass.

Jori was cross-eyed angry when she exited Law's cruiser to buy herself coffee. He wouldn't apologize? She didn't need him to drop even a dime on her. She'd buy her own damn coffee.

That's what she couldn't get over. She'd lost a night in restless agitation over his inexplicable behavior. Then to get a call from him before dawn making some crack about how he was probably interrupting her beauty sleep. She should have told him where to go and how to get there, and then packed and driven back home.

As if getting her a cup of coffee would make up for his Neanderthal—wait, that might be disparaging Neanderthals. She'd recently read something about them being more intelligent than formerly thought.

She pulled open the door, bells jingling. The air inside rushed out to greet her like a drunken Santa, wrapping her in a too-familiar embrace and greasy peppermint breath. It took her three steps to realize that everyone else in the store was staring at her. No, not her. But staring all the same.

A creepy-crawly sensation zipped up the back of her neck into her scalp as she saw too late what was going on.

*Oh God. Oh God.* The words went into a permanent loop in her brain as she realized that a robbery was taking place.

A scraggly man in a hoodie stood at the counter talking loud and fast. His head swiveled toward her, exposing a lean face, sunken eyes, and wisps of long brown hair sprouting from the edges of the hood. He shouted something at her.

She couldn't hear him above the roaring in her ears. She could only stare dumbly back at him. His hand was in his pocket. Something bad was in his pocket.

Another of the customers motioned her back but her legs no longer worked.

Only when the man in the hood turned away to shout at the cashier to hurry could she move.

She turned her head back, telescoping her mantra into hope as she sought through the plate-glass window the gaze of Lauray Battise. He would make it okay. She knew that with absolute certainty.

Hoodie pushed through the doors, shouting over his shoulder, "No police!"

Law held his breath as Hoodie took but a few more steps, then he moved rapidly to place himself between the perp and the store door. No going back in.

"Police officer. Stop. Drop your weapon."

Hoodie stopped short, turning to look at Law. He saw the gun, going bug-eyed and slack-jawed with amazement.

Law steadied his weapon, his voice loud and sharp. "Stop. You're under arrest. On your knees."

"Fuck that!" Hoodie dropped the bag of cash and took off across the parking lot, using both weapon-free fists to pump the air as he ran.

Law was after him even before he'd completed the split-second decision: shoot or pursuit. The reasoning took a slow second.

No way to know if the pocket held a gun, knife, or nothing.

There were bystanders in the parking lot and beyond. A shot might go astray.

No K-9 to chase down Hoodie's sorry ass.

Pursuit.

Hoodie beat sneakers across the concrete, heading for the street and traffic. Law could hear sirens closing in fast as he gave chase. All he had to do was get Hoodie on the ground and hold him until the cavalry arrived.

Law increased his stride and pace. Each footfall jolted his left side, but it didn't matter. Nothing mattered but that he didn't trip, didn't fall. He was closing in on his target with each step.

"Stop. You're under arrest." The words exploded out of him.

He caught Hoodie by the back of his jacket with his gun-free hand and jerked, hard. The action sent them stumbling then sprawling onto the curb and half into the street.

He didn't think about his prosthesis as they went crashing onto the concrete. Or as Hoodie thrashed around, kicking and bucking, knocking them both repeatedly against the curb. All he felt was the shot of satisfaction that he'd outrun a sumbitch who had two good legs, and taken him down.

"You're under arrest. Hold still, dammit."

"Good takedown, Trooper Battise." The Springdale police officer, a young man fresh out of the academy grinned as he glanced back at his vehicle where Hoodie sat cuffed and sobbing like a child. "Outrun by a one-legged man. He won't live that down in lockup. Wait till my sergeant hears about this."

Law smiled and nodded, still a little winded as he sat on the curb. He needed to get up but he was pretty sure he wasn't going to like what happened when he did.

"Law."

He turned and saw Jori coming toward him. He pushed himself to his feet, wincing against his body's protest of pain. He didn't have time to register it. Jori plowed into him, her arms going around his waist to lock her body into his. He gritted his teeth as he felt a great wave tremble through her. "Thank you. Thank you."

Law met the gaze of the patrol officer over her head. The fresh-faced officer winked at him and made a jerking motion with his fist. Law frowned and put an arm protectively around her. Had he ever made light of a victim's gratitude? He hoped not. Because right now he wanted to punch his fellow officer in the face.

"Officer Todd, this is Jori Garrison. She's doing a ride-along with me as a representative of the Warriors Wolf Pack organization. We're trying out one of their dogs in a law enforcement environment. Ms. Garrison was in the store when the robbery went down."

"Oh. Nice to meet you, ma'am." The younger officer's face sobered. "Sorry about the circumstances. But since you were in the store at the time of the robbery, I'll need to get a statement from you. If you'll step this way with me."

"Sure." Jori unwrapped herself from Law's embrace, her solemn gaze probing his. "Are you okay?"

"Nothing a little soap and water won't fix. Make your statement. I'm not going anywhere."

She glanced down at his torn pant leg, revealing his prosthesis. He could see in her expression that she wanted to ask about it. But she held back. And he was grateful. "I knew you—I just knew." Her face reflected deep emotion, but she turned away before finishing her sentence.

Law watched her go, waiting until she and the officer were occupied before trying to test his weight on his artificial leg. He'd heard a crack as he hit the pavement. He only hoped he'd be able to make it to his cruiser without assistance. Some hero that would make him. On leave for medical reasons before he was officially on patrol again.

He saw an EMT coming toward him and waved her off. The ambulances had arrived with the police cars. He tasted blood in his mouth and his hip felt skinned to the bone, but he wasn't going to be carried off like a fallen warrior. He'd had enough of hospitals, ambulances, and medical attention to last him at least ten lifetimes.

He shifted his weight, rocking slowly back and forth. Something was loose in the leg but he felt like it might hold him up. However, there was a serious limp in his stride. He just needed to make it back to his vehicle before the euphoria of his takedown wore off and the pain set in.

He was standing by his cruiser when one of the officers finally told them they could leave. He'd let Sam out on a long leash to take care of her needs in a patch of grass by a streetlight. He reeled her back in now.

Sam eyed him eagerly as she came quickly back to his side, catching the backwash of excitement pheromones still rising off him. But also his pain. Alpha was hurt. She sniffed around his strange leg, the one that smelled like metal and oil and electronics, and up to where the sweat of the man himself was strong, along with faint traces of blood.

Whining softly, Sam tried to lick the wound through his trousers.

He did not return the affection. "Get off, Sam."

Law pushed her snout none-too-gently away. The shaggy-faced rust bucket couldn't help him when he needed really it. Scud would have taken Hoodie without him moving a muscle to help. Sam had no aggressive drive that he had seen. Unless they were out to capture cold cuts, Sam would be of no use.

He turned to open the door and ordered his nursemaid into the backseat.

Sam paused to look at Alpha. He was angry with her. She could not understand why. Her tail drooped and her ears went back. Unhappy Alpha. Unhappy pack.

The loud *mee*-now of protest from the backseat didn't deter Sam. She jumped in and plopped down, taking up all the seat not occupied by the cat cage. This time the protest and sharp claws didn't move her. Instead Sam began thumping the cat carrier with heavy rhythmic swipes of her enormous tail.

Law slid in behind the wheel, suppressing a moan as his stump protested its recent treatment. No time to do anything about it now.

Jori smiled at him as she slid into the passenger seat. The sudden unexpected brilliance of it felt like a light had turned on inside him. She'd never smiled at him like that before.

"You're a hero. Everybody says so. The other police are talking about how amazing it is you could outrun that creep." Her eyes were shining as she looked at him. "I was so scared. But you weren't. Not at all. I watched through the window."

Law scowled, not sure how to take the praise. "You should have kept your head down. You didn't know if shots would be fired."

"I guess you're right. I wasn't thinking of that. I brought you into that. If I'd only been paying attention before I walked in."

"Or stayed in the car and let me get the damn coffee."

"You'd have surprised the thief and could have been shot."

Law shook his head. "I would have looked first. That's my job."

She smiled again. Was she flirting? "You were wonderful."

His knee twinged as he reached for the brace. "I wasn't that great."

"You looked pretty great from where I was standing."

He shrugged, not wanting her gratitude. "I'd have done what I did for complete strangers. That's the job."

"Okay." He watched her think through that. "All the same, it was me and I'm grateful."

"Were you scared?"

"Terrified."

He'd felt it, too, terror for her, standing in the line of fire of a meth head. "By the way, he didn't have a gun. Only a knife." And knives killed, too.

"Did you know he didn't have a gun when you chased him?"

"I didn't. But there wasn't much of a bulge in that pocket when he came out of the store. And he ran. I didn't shoot him, because the parking lot was full of bystanders. If I'd fired someone else might have caught a bullet."

"So you ran him down. That takes a lot of quick thinking and calculation."

"Like I told you, it's the job. If I'd had a real dog with me, I'd have set him on the suspect and saved myself the aggravation." His expression must have revealed his feelings as he glanced back at Sam, because Jori's smile was on the fritz again.

Jori reached up to pet Sam, who'd thrust her head forward to once again check out her Alpha. "Sam has other virtues." Her gaze was reproachful. "You haven't given her a chance."

Damn. He'd done it. Put out the light he'd never thought he'd see in Jori's face. He felt suddenly cold and alone, and very sad. He wanted that warming grateful gaze back.

He reached across the console and his computer and

touched her cheek. It was too pale and chilled. "I'm sorry about . . . everything. My fault, not yours."

She smiled. "Thanks for the apology."

"I didn't—" Too late. He had. He grinned and pinched her cheek lightly. "How about breakfast now? I could use some decent coffee and some eggs."

"Are you okay?" She touched his mouth and blood came away on her hand.

He grabbed her hand and wiped the blood on his uniform shirt. It was just an excuse to touch her. "I'll clean up in the restroom. Okay?"

She nodded. "Whatever you want."

This time he grinned. "Don't offer me open-ended invitations. I'm still the same bastard you thought I was an hour ago."

"Yes and no." She met his gaze with a steady look. "You're that, but more. We need to talk."

He nodded. "Yeah, we do." And she might be revising her opinion of him again after she heard what he wanted to talk about.

# CHAPTER FIFTEEN

"What do you mean, Sam's a thief?"

Jori's voice wafted up the staircase to the loft bedroom where Law had retreated to examine his stump. He had felt it swelling inside his prosthesis during the day. The torque and strain of the tumble he had taken had damaged the socket, making a good fit impossible. But he had been determined to finish his shift. Even if his limp was so pronounced by the end of the day, his colleagues were commenting. Now he was paying the price. The prosthesis hurt like a sumbitch.

But he'd made a collar this morning. First in more than four years. He still had what it took. That was worth the pain.

His cell phone chimed. He glanced at the number. Another news channel. He punched END and put it back in his pocket. Local radio and TV outlets had been calling all day, wanting to interview him. One of the customers in the parking lot had taken a phone video of his takedown and sent it in to the media. It was playing on all the local channels. A fellow officer said it had gone viral on YouTube.

He didn't want anything to do with that. No publicity for doing his job. Certainly not just because he was missing a leg.

"Battise?"

He looked up and smiled. He'd offered to buy dinner, but Jori was downstairs, promising to cook for him if she could find anything in his kitchen. Good luck with that. Best answer her before she came looking for him.

"I taught Sam to bring me a beer while I'm working." He released his prosthesis and pulled it off. "A few days after she mastered the trick I noticed some franks were missing from the fridge. A few days later some sliced turkey had disappeared. Since she'd been with me all day, I figure she raids my refrigerator in the middle of the night." He gingerly peeled off his liner. "Your dog's a Snack Hound."

"You mean *your* dog." She sounded closer. She must have come to the bottom of the stairs to hear him better. "WWP didn't teach her to help herself. You did."

Law hissed in a breath as the stump sock came off. "All the same. If she keeps doing midnight raids, I won't be able to afford to keep her in the style to which she's becoming accustomed."

"Okay. I'll see what I can do about that."

He could hear her climbing the stairs as she talked. Not good. "Can you give me a minute? I'm busy here."

"I'm just bringing that beer you asked for. Sam's good but she can't climb a spiral staircase."

"Jori, you don't need to—" Stripped to his skivvies, Law looked around for something to cover himself but he was in a chair, far from bedding or closet. His hand would have to do.

Her head appeared first. She was still talking. "I didn't expect you to be so modest. It's not as if I haven't already seen—*oh!* You're hurt."

He expected her to stop or at least turn away but she was still coming up, eyes fastened on his injury. "Oh, Law. Are you in a lot of pain?"

"No." He shrugged, spreading his fingers to shield his crotch. All she had to do was walk into a room and his dick went hard enough to pump iron.

She bit her lip as she came closer still. He knew how his stump must look to her, bruised and swollen as if it had been beaten with a stick.

Her gaze met his, her eyes framed by a frown. "It looks really bad. You need a doctor?"

"No." He let out a breath, trying not to groan.

She reached out and touched his bare shoulder, her hand smooth and cool on his skin as she examined him. "You've a nasty scrape on your hip and smaller ones on your torso."

"This is nothing. You should have seen me after Scud and I took down a soldier who'd deserted and was hiding . . ." He stopped and swallowed. Why was he talking to her about Scud?

He looked away and picked up his prosthesis. "This is the problem." He pointed to the crack. "I need it in good working order to pass my physical in two weeks. I can switch back to an older leg until it's repaired."

"Oh, Law."

He watched her with a smile. "That's the third time you've used my first name today."

"Don't let it go to your head." She looked back at him, something new in her gaze he couldn't pinpoint but he sure did like. "Now how can I help? Ice or heat?"

"I'll take care of it later. I've got some paperwork to do back at the office after I drop you back at the motel."

She pressed a second hand to his bare shoulder as if she could stop him from rising. "You're not going anywhere on that leg tonight. You can deal with paperwork tomorrow."

Her hands felt good against his skin. He wished she'd slide them lower.

"Can't I do something to help?"

He ground his teeth. One day ago, he knew he would have answered with a crude suggestion. But he couldn't do that, not when she was looking at him with more admiration and empathy than any other human had in a long *long* time. Something just under his heart drew tight with a pain tougher to deal with than his stump. He knew he would never again hurt or disrespect her. On his life. That realization made him very nervous.

He looked away. "It's no big deal. Just clomping around on a given day, pounding the stump, can make it swell or shrink. See this beauty right here?" He pointed to a bright-red bruised area. "I call them stump hickeys."

"Because the fit wasn't good." She nodded. "An air pocket suctioned the skin into a classic bruise. I read about that. Do you have a lotion or salve for this?"

"Yeah." He pointed to a tube of ointment on the dresser. *She read about it?* She was reading up on the care of amputated limbs? That knot under his heart tightened.

She picked up the tube and came back. "I can put it on for you but you should wash and dry the area first. Let me get something to do that."

She headed for the bathroom before he could move an inch. When she turned her back, he stood up and hopped quickly over to the bed and sat, so that he could toss one end of the comforter over his good leg and hide his hard-on.

She came back with a soapy cloth and a towel. "You clean up while I find some bandages to cover your scrapes."

"Don't have any bandages."

She stopped short. "What about the K-9 first-aid kit we gave you?"

He grinned. "Fast thinking. Under the sink, downstairs."

Jori came back with her booty of gauze, sterile bandages,

hydrogen peroxide, an anti-bacterial ointment, and medical adhesive tape. By then he'd been able to clean his stump.

She examined it and then noticed his complete disregard for the rest. There were a few scrapes he probably couldn't easily reach. "Let me help with the other wounds."

"I can do it."

"Sure you can, but you'll like it better if I do it."

She met his hot heavy gaze, but he didn't say a word. He simply rolled onto his side on the bed.

"*Ow. Ow.* Ouch!"

"What a baby." Jori leaned in close to the abrasion on his hip as she gently applied a fresh pad with hydrogen peroxide. "You're like raw meat here."

"*Uh-huh.* But if you don't stop handling my butt like that you're going to have to deal with the consequences."

Jori laughed. "You're in no shape to make good on those threats just now."

Law chuckled. She had no idea. The shape he was in, covered discreetly by a towel, could have her walking funny for a week.

But he didn't want her to stop touching him. Her fingers were soothing and cool and efficient as she cleaned and bandaged him. She wasn't feeling what he was feeling. But he could so easily change that. A quick flip of his hips and her fingers would slide off his hip and into his groin where she might caress every throbbing inch of him.

Sweat broke out on his forehead. He needed to think about something, anything else. "Tell me about the night Brody Rogers died."

Jori stilled. Her gaze shifted from her work to meet his. Her guard was up. "Why?"

"I read your trial records." Law shifted back so that he could sit up. Talking to her with his bare ass in her face didn't seem right. "It was a lot harder to gain access to the grand jury records. I've learned what I can. But I want to hear your side."

"Why?"

She straightened away from him, arms folding defensively across her chest. "Last time we talked you said you didn't care what I'd done or why. What's changed?"

He pushed a hand through his hair, searching for simple honesty in his reply. "I don't know, Jori. Maybe nothing. Maybe everything."

She gave him a look. He tried to look as innocent as a man with ulterior intentions could. It must have been pretty damn convincing since she finally shrugged. "Finish what you need to do. We'll talk over dinner."

"This is good." Law scooped up another forkful. "What do you call it, friggin' what?"

"Frittata." Jori sat at the table beside him, cradling a cup of coffee like it was the only warmth in the whole world. "I didn't have much to work with, some eggs, milk, a hunk of cheddar, and an onion."

"And peas." He stared at the green spheres dotting the puffy omelet. "I hate peas." But he shoved the forkful in his mouth and sighed in satisfaction.

"You had four bags of peas in the freezer."

"I use them as ice packs."

"Oh." Jori almost smiled. But she couldn't forget the conversation they needed to have.

Argyle had made herself at home in Jori's lap, but kept creeping up to peer over the rim of the table at Jori's regrettably unserved plate.

Jori couldn't even think about swallowing food. Not when she knew Law was waiting for her to tell him her story. If he had done research on her, he must know everything. Why did she need to say it out loud? What did he need to hear?

She watched him eat. He was dressed again in a waffle-weave Henley and sweat shorts with one empty leg. He looked good, as if the pain and bruising hidden beneath his clothing didn't exist.

She'd been startled to see him on crutches but she didn't say anything. What he had done today he had done for strangers, for law and order. It had cost him. But he seemed at peace with that. She was impressed, and wary. She couldn't afford to care so much about him, or his good opinion. Not when she was becoming emotionally involved. He'd warned her away from that. He was law enforcement tough, unsentimental, and probably jaded from years of perp lies. She couldn't expect him to believe a thing she said. Talking about Brody should put up walls for both of them.

She took a gulp of her coffee. "What do you want to know about Brody?"

"I need to know the facts, as you remember them." Law put down his fork, though he looked at the remaining frittata with longing. "Humor me. What happened the night Brody died? Had you seen him earlier?"

"Yes. He came by the apartment but said he was going to a frat party up on Beaver Lake. One of his alumni chapter members has a weekend place up there."

"You get a name?" She shook her head but leaned back, braced for trouble.

Law was choosing his way carefully, in full interrogation mode, planning when to reveal what he'd learned independently as he went along. He was leading her somewhere but he needed to know some things first. So he needed to mix it up, put her at ease. "How did you two meet?"

She didn't say anything for several seconds. "We met at a frat party on campus. Brody was an alum of the fraternity but he said he liked the vibe of campus frat life so he went back to the campus house as often as he could. He'd worked for Tice Industries so he was a bit older. Handsome, funny, definitely more sophisticated than the average frat boy."

"So you fell for him." Law tried to keep his tone light. He'd known and both envied and disapproved of the type while he worked his way through college.

"I did, for a while." She shook her head. "He had dreams, and even bigger ambition. But no patience. He was always looking for shortcuts. He knew how to bend rules and make people like it. Everything with Brody was a calculation. In the end, I realized that I was one of his shortcuts. It changed things."

"In what way?"

She got up, set Argyle on the floor, and began to move around, as if the action helped her think. "We got engaged on Valentine's Day and I moved into his Fayetteville apartment. Brody worked in Fort Smith but kept a place near campus because he was there every weekend to party. He said I should live with him so we could make the most of whatever time we had together. It was my final semester of school. I was starting to cram for my finals and interviewing for grad schools, too. I thought being alone, out of the sorority house, would help. But Brody wasn't very understanding about the fact that I wasn't interested in partying from Friday night until early Sunday morning."

A smile lifted one corner of Law's mouth. "So, you were once one of those wild sorority girls I used to stop for driving drunk? They'd sometimes flash their tits at me in the hope of getting away without a ticket."

"Did it work?"

"Never. But I always enjoyed the view."

Jori rolled her eyes. "That was never me. I was the responsible sorority sister who made certain everyone else got home safe. It was one of the things Brody said he liked about me. He said the fact that I was good at managing chaos meant I'd make a good corporate wife."

Law watched her closely, wondering if she knew she winced when she'd described herself as a *corporate wife*. Maybe that's what she meant by being part of Rogers's calculation. "You did drink?"

"Sure."

"Do a little weed?"

"Once. Didn't like it."

"Brody give it to you?"

"No. It was at a rush, freshman year. Why? You think I'm lying about not knowing he was a drug dealer?"

"I think you were either lying to yourself or ignoring signs you didn't want to think about."

His blunt honesty took Jori's breath away. But what else could she expect? That's what everyone thought. Even her family wondered. And what could it possibly matter now? But she'd had four years to wonder just who Brody's clients were.

"I caught him once with a stack of cash." She made a large C-bracket between fingers and thumb. "He said he was acting as the bank for his fraternity's fantasy football league. He said it was nothing to worry about—an in-house transaction among brothers. Nothing bad could happen. I told him I didn't like it. Gambling was illegal on campus."

"That kind of gambling's pretty much illegal all over." Law reached for the last of the frittata, giving her a second to breathe. "Did you ever see him high?"

"Drunk. Of course."

"Pills or coke?"

"No."

He looked up to catch her expression. "Would you know?"

To his surprise, she thought about it. "I knew casually a few students on campus who did drugs. Mostly to get their party on. But Brody was never spaced out. Sometimes he was wired. All talk and continuous action. He said it was because he'd had a really crazy week at work and needed to work the energy off."

"Then he probably preferred uppers. Businessmen often do."

Law reached for his laptop, shoved his flash drive in, and brought up a page. "The autopsy report says Brody was high on coke when he died."

Jori didn't answer. She'd learned that fact at the same time the public did. Along with the news that he'd been carrying drugs and several thousand in cash. "So I was guilty by association."

"Yes." He didn't sugarcoat it. She'd already suffered the legal consequences. "The law allows persons to be prosecuted simply if they benefited from drug money. Brody made money selling drugs. It's impossible to say which part of that money paid for things like your apartment, your engagement ring, or anything else he gave you. The law takes the broad view and can confiscate it all." He waited a beat before going on. She'd heard it before. Still, he felt like a bully reminding her of it all.

When she didn't respond he looked up. The sight of her kicked him in the gut. She was standing very still, the only movement the fingers of her right hand shifting the loose end of her braid. But her soft mouth was pinched by sadness, the same sadness that slouched through her body and made her seem smaller and more vulnerable. It was as if she'd just heard the guilty verdict delivered all over again.

He wanted to go to her, to touch her, but he didn't dare. He was being a cop now. A professional would just move on. He could only move forward.

"Tell me about your relationship with Erin Foster."

She looked startled to hear the name. But she didn't

question why he was asking about the woman. "We belonged to the same sorority. But she was three years ahead of me. Graduated after my freshman year. She was in law school with my brother. So I saw her only from time to time on campus and at college functions."

"Friendly?"

Something flashed across her face. "We weren't friends. She and Brody were together until just before we met."

"Is that significant?"

"Only that Erin never let me forget it. Whenever we happened to run into each other she made a point to ask about Brody and then imply that she had recently seen him. As if she thought I'd be jealous."

"Were you?"

She just stared at him. Clearly the answer was no. He was pretty sure after what he'd learned that she was wrong about Rogers. It irked him that she still believed the douchebag. "For the record, I think you were used. A man who hides his stash in his girlfriend's place is looking for a scapegoat. Pimps and dealers do it all the time. Rogers had a plan if he was caught. You were his patsy."

He tried to ignore the sick look that washed through her expression. Jesus. He thought what he said would help break the spell of Rogers. But the echo of his words in his ears sounded coldhearted.

Even as he was freaking at the possibility of making her cry, though, the detective part of him noticed that she didn't look so hurt. She did look angry. He watched that emotion smooth the pinched look from her face until her eyes were bright with it.

"I know I was stupid. I was a sorority girl with bleached-blond hair and all the right clothes dating a member of the Tice family. I was self-involved and while not totally an all-about-me girl, I knew that marrying Brody would make me a fixture in society. It was only when I accepted his ring that I discovered I didn't want it, any of it." She looked straight at Law. "I wasn't going to marry him."

Law knew she was talking to herself as much as him. He kept eating, just to have something to do that kept him from staring as he listened to her answers. To his surprise, Argyle appeared on his lap and tried to make herself at home. But she kept sliding off his stump. Law grabbed her and tucked her in his right arm. "Tell me more about the night he died."

She made a turn around the room. "It was late April. I'd been trying to get up the courage to give back the ring almost since the day I accepted it." She glanced down at her left hand, as if expecting to see the engagement ring she'd once worn. "I was glad he wasn't staying regularly at the apartment. He'd begun making excuses about not showing up for the weekend, or until Saturday night. Then leaving first thing Sunday morning. I didn't even ask why. I wanted out." She glanced at Law again. "I didn't love him. Not really."

Law broke off a bit of frittata and fed it to Argyle. "Then why did you go down without a fight?"

"What are you talking about? We had a big wicked fight that night. I threw the ring at him and told him to pack and get out."

This was news. It wasn't in the court record. "What did he do?"

"He said a few ugly things and left."

"What did he take with him?" Argyle purred and rubbed herself against Law's Henley.

Jori frowned. "Nothing." Her voice trailed off in thought. "He did go into the bedroom. I thought he was going to pack so I didn't follow him. But when he came back he had nothing except the leather backpack with his laptop that he carried everywhere."

"How long was he in the bedroom?" Argyle pawed lightly at the hand Law ate with.

She frowned. "I don't remember. I just wanted him to leave."

Law waited a beat. "When did you learn about the accident?"

She flinched. "When the police came to my door at five a.m. with a warrant to search the apartment. I don't even think I heard anything they said after they told me Brody had died when his car went off the highway and crashed." All the blood had drained from her lips.

Ridiculously jealous that a man who'd been dead more than four years could make her so sad, Law pushed on quickly. "Why didn't your attorney use the breakup as motive for you being framed by Rogers?"

"He said what happened between me and Brody wasn't relevant. That I had been found, independently, in possession of illegal substances and that I was being tried for drug possession."

"But they wouldn't have searched your apartment if Rogers hadn't been found in possession first. Your defense attorney wasn't worth spit because he didn't argue cause."

She rounded on him, her face flushed. "My parents hired the best lawyer they could find. They tried everything. It didn't work." She was back on the brink of emotions Law was pretty certain he couldn't handle. So he pushed on, again.

"Did you tell your counsel that Brody was cheating on you?"

Jori waved a hand. "Brody wasn't cheating."

Law licked a greasy finger clean then touched his keyboard until he found what he wanted. "According to the statement of a woman named Erin Foster, Brody Rogers had been with her on the night he died." He watched Jori's expression closely. "Did you know about that?"

Jori frowned. "Where did you get that information?"

"It was in the affidavits presented to the grand jury looking into Rogers's death. In her interview, Foster says Rogers came to tell her that he'd broken off his engagement to you, that he said he'd been having second thoughts for a while."

She was blinking hard. "That's so like Brody!" She paused and jerked her head as if tossing off some burden.

Law was losing patience. "And your counsel never thought it might be a good idea to follow up and see exactly what they were doing together?" He saw her face. "I don't mean screwing each other, Jori. Rogers was high the night he died. Think about it. Some people drink their troubles away. Addicts get high together. Didn't you ever wonder who Rogers's customers were?"

Jori nodded slowly. "I used to lie awake in my cell and think about that."

"My guess is he was the friendly campus drug dealer. The popular frat boy, a known quantity welcome at all parties. He was safe, exclusive." Law fed another bit to Argyle without even thinking about what he was doing. "No clandestine buys on corners in not-so-nice neighborhoods. It must have played well with everyone involved."

Jori's jaw began to work. "Every friend I had deserted me. In the beginning I thought it was because they were shocked and didn't want to be associated with someone who'd been accused of dealing drugs."

"Or maybe they just didn't want their own secrets outed."

She looked at him for confirmation. "They thought I was guilty because *they* were?"

"That's a fair guess. They must have expected you to start naming names to cut a deal with the D.A. and save yourself."

"But I couldn't."

He gave it to her raw. "They didn't know that, did they? Not until you went to prison, anyway," he added under his breath.

She had sharp ears. "You mean they knew I was innocent only because I was found guilty?"

Law couldn't answer that. But it made sense. He did have another theory.

"Don't you think it's odd that no one else was arrested behind the revelation of Brody as a drug dealer? Not one client was discovered? Why didn't your defense attorney at least go after Erin? She could have been drug-tested."

Jori opened her mouth to reply then snapped it shut. For five long seconds she stared at him with a hard expression. He held her gaze with dogged determination. He owed her that.

"Why are you telling me all this now? And what's in it for you?"

Law had to smile. She had finally caught up with him. Smart. He liked that. Liked her. A lot. He owed her his trust, even if it blew up in his face.

"I think there's a connection between Brody, your case, and Tice Industries. Tice and I go way back to my early years as a state trooper. We've suspected them for over a decade of transporting drugs. Twice while I was on patrol we caught a trucker for Tice with contraband. Both times, the trucker was an independent. Tice attorneys successfully claimed the company couldn't be held responsible for what a contract worker did in his spare time. The truckers went to prison and kept their mouths shut. That kind of loyalty requires incentive of both the financial and the physical kind."

"You mean they were paid to go to prison?"

"And/or threatened. That's speculation. That's all the state police ever had."

"What has any of that to do with me?"

"I was hoping you could tell me. Rogers was a Tice relation. And he worked for the family business. If they're running drugs, he'd have had an inside track."

"That can't be true. Maybe Brody was dirty, but Luke Tice always was such a straight arrow his frat brothers called him Mr. Clean."

"The guy now running for the state senate?" When Argyle made a move to hop up on the table and help herself, Law pushed her back into his embrace with a hand.

"Yes. I never knew Luke well. He and Brody were six years older. And they'd had a falling-out by the time we met. Brody said Luke was jealous that he was working with Luke's dad at the company headquarters while Luke spent his time in the D.A.'s office at much lower pay. But Luke will inherit the major portion of the company, so that never made sense to me."

"So Rogers lied to you."

"He didn't lie . . . Right. He lied to me a lot, in a lot of different ways."

"Don't beat yourself up about that. Sociopaths like Rogers are masters at not being caught. You never know you're being lied to because you're never not being lied to."

That statement brought her up short. She turned a gaze on him reflecting her own suddenly darker thoughts. "What about you? You just said that you're after Tice Industries for drug dealing. Is that why I'm here? You hoped I'd be able to name names and give you the inside scoop on how they deal drugs?" Her outrage grew as she said the words aloud. "Oh my God! I'm such an idiot!"

Law stood up, Argyle dumped onto the floor. "Jori, it's not like that."

Trembling, she backed away from him. "I need some air." She turned abruptly away, grabbed her North Face vest off a chair, and headed out his front door.

# *CHAPTER SIXTEEN*

The chill blast of air surprised her. The weather was turning quickly, as it often did in December in the Ozarks. The evening sky was clear but there was a ridge on the northern horizon that spoke of a Blue Norther headed their way. But Jori didn't pause to go back for hat and gloves. She tucked her hands under her arms to protect them, bent her head to protect her eyes, and hurried down the gravel pathway that led back toward the main road hidden by the trees.

Her boots made so much noise on the gravel that she didn't realize she had been followed until a hand snagged her elbow from behind.

She swung around to meet Law staring down at her, his Henley and sweat shorts the only protection against the wind. He didn't say anything, just stood, big and solid and powerful even on crutches, waiting for her to offer some explanation.

Suddenly she was angry, angrier than she had allowed herself to be at any point in four years because it didn't matter. Nothing worse could happen.

She tried to jerk her arm free of his grasp and stepped away from him, putting up a hand to stop him from advancing again. "I kept thinking that if I just held on, held it in, things would get better. Or at least not get worse. I was innocent. I didn't know anything. But that didn't stop anything. My whole life went to hell and I couldn't do anything to stop it. Nothing!"

Law felt her pain like a jab. He knew about how quickly things could go sideways. One second perfectly fine. The next, jagged bits of one's life were flying away, having burst into a million tiny obscenely painful pieces that would never, ever fit back together properly. The difference was he'd known the risks, and accepted them as part of a job he wanted to do. She had never seen disaster coming.

He didn't know what else to do so he held on to her arm. When she tried to pull away again he applied only as much pressure as was necessary to hold her in place.

She looked down at his grip that completely wrapped around her upper arm, and then her cinnamon-brown eyes met his in blazing anger. "Let me go."

"I believe you, Jori. I. Believe. You. Are. Innocent." He said the words separately, hoping they would sink in and take hold in her thoughts.

She held his stare a moment longer. "I was okay when people dropped me as a friend. I'd done something stupid. So maybe I deserved what happened to me. But not my family." The wind was whipping her voice away but she didn't seem to care. "Many of my parents' so-called friends disappeared, too. They found themselves abandoned at so many social functions they simply stopped going. My dad is a director of academic affairs at UAMS so it didn't really make a difference in his professional life, but my mother's clothing boutique suffered. People came to spy on the mother of the felon, but they didn't leave their money. She nearly closed her doors that first year after I went inside. I brought that shame on them. And they did nothing to deserve it."

"Jori." She backed up a step as he took one toward her. "It's over." He took another step. This time she didn't retreat. "You're safe. It's over."

"Don't think I'm feeling sorry for myself. I'm just so damn angry!" She gasped in a breath of icy air as she stared up at him. "I don't know what to do with all the anger."

"Get even." He said it calmly as he reached out and caught a strand of her hair flailing in the wind. He brought it back to tuck behind her ear but it wouldn't stay. Poor ear. It was red with wind and cold. He covered it with his big palm, fingers diving into the hair behind to cradle her head. He didn't know about a woman's pain. Or the death of a lover's dream. But he did know about evening the score. That had been his job all his life, protecting the innocent and getting justice for victims. He was a great avenger.

She still stared at him, but something was kindling behind her eyes. Hope.

"How?"

"We can begin by finding out what really happened the night Rogers died."

"Can you do that?"

"I can." The only way he knew how to seal that promise didn't have words to go with it. He brought her in so that he could cradle her head against his chest. "I'd really like a chance to ask Erin Foster a few questions."

She didn't fight him as he held her close. She was shivering in his arms so he tightened his hold, wanting to give her as much of his body's surface heat as possible. If it was too much, she didn't protest.

"What kind of questions?"

"Erin's affidavit says that Rogers left you and went to

see her. You thought she was a little too flirtatious for an ex. Maybe that's what they both wanted you to think. That she was jealous. You said she was always hanging around, trying to get his attention, drag him away on some pretext. Maybe he was her dealer. Or perhaps they were dealing together."

"I never thought." Jori lifted her head and looked at him. "But Erin's married to Luke Tice now."

"Mr. Clean. I wonder. It certainly ties things up in a neat bow."

He watched the scenario play out behind her bright gaze until the pieces began to lock together in a new design. "You want to meet Erin? I know how to make that happen."

"I thought you weren't in touch with your former friends."

"I'm not. But I have an invitation to the biggest social event in northwest Arkansas this weekend. It's happening Saturday in Eureka Springs."

"What's that?"

"My brother's wedding. I told my parents not to expect me." Her expression sobered. "I didn't want to spoil it with my presence." She told him briefly about the call from Erin a week earlier. "But now I see why my presence might make certain people uncomfortable for a very different reason. I'd be a reminder of all the lies they told."

Law was moving ahead with different calculations. He knew that if they were about to tangle with the Tices, there would be consequences. "Are you sure about this? You've moved on in your life. Nothing they did or are doing can hurt you anymore."

Jori nodded, letting the heat and strength of him shear into and through her fears, making her feel stronger than she had in a long time. She knew not to rely on this feeling between them to last. The one that said they had crossed some barrier between a one-night stand and friends. They had a mutual interest. When that was gone, he might be, too. But for now, when she needed him the most, Law was here smiling down at her. And it was like standing in a spotlight. "Let's do this."

Law saw again the glimmer of admiration and awe that had been on Jori's face after he chased down Hoodie this morning. It felt so good his chest expanded in determination. He wanted to be every single thing he saw reflected in her gaze. He wanted to be that guy. He wanted to be her hero.

Law kissed her with a fierce determination to stamp out, for the moment, every other thought in her head but him. He was pretty sure he was succeeding when he felt her sigh into his mouth and then her tongue slide forward to tangle with his. He could feel hands creeping up under his shirt onto his back, exposing his lower spine to the chill of the wind. Everywhere else in his body the heavy thick tide of desire was rolling through, pumping him up in every vital spot.

When they finally paused to breathe he asked, "What was your college major?"

"Criminal justice." She slid a hand down into the back of his pants and gripped a naked butt cheek. "I wanted to be an attorney. Do something for the greater good."

He hissed in a breath as she slid that hand forward. "And now?"

She smiled against his warm mouth. "I just want to be bad."

He could definitely help with that.

For the first time in what felt like forever, he had hope, and that scared the hell out of him. But he was going to make it right for her. Because he could.

He kissed the tip of her nose. "I'll stand here with you

all night if that's what you need, Jori. But my balls are turning blue. Can we take this indoors?"

"Just so you know. There've been no other women. Since you."

Jori frowned at him. They were back in the cabin, in that moment between decision and deed. "You don't need to say things. Just don't lie to me."

"I'm not lying." The look on her face made him blush. "I tried. Okay? I picked up a woman but—it didn't feel right."

Jori just folded her arms and waited.

Law shook his head. 'Try to tell the truth." He should have kept his big mouth shut.

He went toward the fireplace. He'd meant to light it when they came in but his stump was hurting something fierce. He'd had to take the prosthesis off. Now he wanted to set the mood.

The wood was all laid out. He often preferred a real fire to the more efficient central heating. All he had to do was reach down and get the electronic starter. He shifted both crutches into one hand and balanced on one leg as he bent down.

Sam came running. She saw what he was reaching for and swooped in and scooped it up and turned to him, tail-wagging proud.

Law felt his face go red a second time as he snatched the starter. "I can light my own damn fire without help!"

"Sam! Come here, girl." Jori clapped her hands. Sam's tail drooped as she turned toward the female.

Jori bent down and gave the dog some long heavy strokes that began at her head and reached all the way to her tail. It was a comfort rub, much as Sam and her littler mates would have gotten from their mother's tongue. "Good girl, Sam. You're such a good doggy. Yes you are." Over the top of Sam's body she aimed an arched gaze at

Law. "A fire is a nice idea. But won't we be spending the evening under the covers?"

Law had been leaning against the mantel, willing the kindling to catch fire. He looked up and caught her gaze. It was he who combusted. Grinning, he reached down and grabbed the pail of sand he kept for emergencies. In about ten seconds, the kindling was out.

When he looked up, Jori was gone. But there was a vest lying on the floor that led to the bedroom on the main floor. He grinned. Thank goodness he wasn't going to have to haul himself up the spiral staircase again.

She was already under the covers when he got there. He could see the straps of her bra. Her boots and jeans were on the floor. Shirt? He didn't give a flying flip where it was. It was off her.

He shucked his Henley and reached for his waistband.

"Wait." He looked up.

She was watching him very intently. "You still go commando?"

He froze. What was the right answer? Hell, he couldn't change it now. "Yeah."

A very naughty smile spread very slowly across her mouth. "Then I want to do that."

He grinned like a man who'd hit the jackpot. "Oh, hell yeah."

He dropped the crutches and dived for the bed.

Jori came up on her knees to meet him in the middle.

He didn't kiss like other men. There was no smooth seduction. No playful interest. No hint of weighing this kiss against the memory of many others. There was something fierce and hungry in Law's kisses. It was like having the front seat on the Batman roller coaster. The overpowering sensation was that of being swept up by a primal force and taken for a ride.

That didn't mean he didn't care about arousing her. He

did that, with every urgent stroke of his tongue. In the way he fit and refit their mouths together as if they were a puzzle he was trying to work out.

He drew in a breath, sucking in her lower lip as his tongue swept into the canyon behind the fullness. She, in turn, bit his upper lip, tiny little nibbles that sent shivers through the powerful heavy body under her hands. They weren't movie lovers, trying for the right angle, the perfect cinematic kiss. They were raw and hurried, a little uncoordinated. They were bumping noses and swirling tongues as they each vied to get enough of the other.

Finally, both breathless, they pulled back for a second of air. Jori opened her eyes first. His were still closed. He kissed with his eyes closed! That moment of knowledge broke her heart. He looked beautiful. Gorgeously male. His mouth glistening with the succulent loving of her own. And she knew, with certainty, that he could break her heart if she weren't very careful, and very smart.

Her stunned realization lasted only a fraction of a second. Then his burning gold-black eyes blazed blowtorch-hot on her face.

Afraid to think about her feelings, she kissed him hard and reached for his waistband.

She heard him groan in relief as his erection was freed. She looked down between them. She'd seen him before. But this time was different. She could barely breathe. He was so hard. Gorgeous, proud, and all hers.

"Condom. Left pocket." Law wasn't a talker. He just went with the basics. He pulled her in, palmed her butt to haul her closer, and returned to kissing her like his life depended on it.

His hands were at her back, releasing her bra, and then he was dragging it off the ends of her fingers. He stared at her so long she began to shiver. Then he looked up at her and the things most men say were all in his eyes. She didn't need the sound. And then he was on her, pushing her back onto the bedding, pushing his knee between hers as he balanced himself over her on his hands.

He paused. "I'm going to need a little help here."

"With what?"

"Your panties."

Jori looked down her body and then up into his face just inches from hers. "Use your teeth."

She didn't think his gaze could get any hotter or his breath harsher. But every muscle in his body flexed as he hovered above her and then he was back crawling on hands and knee down the bed, using his tongue to leave a long wet trail down the middle of her body.

He took her waistband in his teeth and pulled. It was the sexiest sight she'd ever seen. But his actions didn't get the job done. He released the waist and looked down. "Spread your legs. Wider. A little more."

He dipped his head and grabbed the seat of her panties in his teeth. He jerked it to one side and then again. The third time she heard something rip. And then she forgot about the panties. His tongue, hot and wet, was sliding up into her folds. Her eyes fell shut then opened again as she gasped out his name.

After that she pretty much forgot to do anything but breathe. He was in charge. Without laying a finger on her he pushed and pulled, teased and nibbled, surged and retreated until she was dancing, hips off the bed, on the tip of his tongue. She came so hard it almost hurt. She was gasping and crying, sipping hiccupy breaths of air as she rode his mouth through the climax.

As soon as Law felt the last hard ripple flow over his tongue, he surged back up the bed, gliding every hard inch of his torso over her body. The room was chilly but her skin was hot. Almost as hot was he was. He reached for a condom and held it up. "My turn."

He didn't ask for her help. He slipped into it faster than she could have managed and then he scooped her up and flipped them both over. He set her upright, astride his lap and then let go.

For a moment Jori felt self-conscious. She had been on top before but the lights were out. Not now. She could see every gorgeously muscled inch of him. His mouth glistened with her essence. His belly rose and fell like a bellows. The dark smoke of hair that arrowed from his groin out over the sculpted mesas of his chest glistened, too, where he'd rubbed himself over her on his path up her body.

He stacked one hand and then the other behind his head. He looked perfectly at ease. Except for the hard demanding pressure surging between her thighs. And the hot look in his dark eyes. He was exerting all his will, waiting on her decision of how to proceed.

She wanted this as much as he did. She needed to own that for both their sakes.

She leaned forward, one hand pressed to his chest, and lifted her hips up a few inches. She watched his eyes widen and then stretch more as she reached back between her spread thighs and gripped him. He was full and hard, a pulsing, alive thing in her fist. Smiling into his eyes, she rolled her hips, just grazing his tip. She watched him draw a quick breath between parted lips and smiled. Oh yes, two could play this game.

She rolled her hips in the opposite direction, sinking down a little this time so that he moved into her entrance. His eyes were black, the pupils obliterating all the gold. With each roll she sank down, inch by inch, seating him a little deeper before rising again.

An arm slipped from behind his head and he flung it across his eyes as a sound of torment groaned out of him. She repeated her actions more slowly, drawing out the plunge and the rise. This was a test of wills she wanted very badly to win.

"Jori." Her name was nothing but a gust of need. And then he moved so quickly she didn't have time to react. His arms came forward and gripped her waist as he levered his hips off the bed, forcing her down on his full length. He slid in, deep and hard, all the way until she was filled to the limit.

Jori sucked in air, trying to catch a breath and control the moment. But his hips pumped deeper and rougher and quicker than her thrusts had been. He was in charge and determined not to let her find another moment of command of herself. All she could do was bend forward, brace a hand on each of his wide shoulders, and ride him for all she was worth. When she shattered again, the million little pieces of bliss rippled out from their joining, over every inch of her and out through her fingertips and toes. It was a full-body release.

Law made love like he did everything else, full-out and with everything in him. When he came it was with a pounding fury just short of pain. And the sound that came from him was part ferocity, part desperation, and a whole lot of ecstasy.

And that, a faint thought warned him, could be trouble. Because now all that hope and fear and longing were bound up in the woman gone liquid in his arms.

"Do you really think it's possible to learn the truth?"

Law blinked, rising up out of a dark quiet peace he'd never known before. How long it lasted he didn't know. But it felt precious and he didn't want to lose it, or the woman who'd given it to him. He lifted her up and draped her across his naked body.

She put out a hand to stop him. "Wait. Your poor bruised body."

"Can take a lot more than what you can dish out." He settled her tighter against him, locking his heel behind her knee to hold her in place. He smoothed a hand repeatedly down her back, as if she were the only blanket he'd ever need.

Her body on his body—it felt so good.

She lay her cheek on his chest, her unbound hair sliding over his torso. She was the best thing he'd ever held in his arms. How was he ever going to walk away? But she'd asked him a serious question.

"I can't promise I will answer every question. But my gut tells me there's a lot to learn."

She raised her head and placed a hand on either side of his face. "I trust you."

*Don't.* He wanted to warn her but the word wouldn't get past his teeth this time.

For the first time in his life, he wanted the truth about himself—that he was insensitive, untrustworthy, possessed of a quick temper, and selfish—to be a lie. Thirty-one years was a lot of life to live down. Maybe he couldn't do it.

He hadn't told her everything. He didn't tell her that he knew who had searched his cabin. Sam's reaction hadn't meant anything to him at the time. But after a while, he realized the dog had been taught to search for intruders. No intruder. No reaction. Instead, she'd alerted. That must mean she recognized that someone besides him and Jori had been there. Even though the intruder was gone, his scent remained.

It was enough to send him back through the records until he discovered something that he hadn't checked on the first time because it seemed unimportant: the name of the state trooper who had come upon Brody's wreck. Trooper Ronald Becker.

It was The Pecker who had come to his cabin looking for something. And Sam knew it. Law smiled to himself.

A guilty conscience was a terrible foe. He would never have made the connection between Rogers's death and Becker if Becker hadn't sought him out first. By coming into the Springdale office, Becker had not only put Law on alert, he'd given Sam a chance to learn his scent.

But what was Becker after? And what was his connection to Tice Industries?

Jori sighed in her sleep and hung a hand over his shoulder as she snuggled closer.

Law sighed as well, thinking he'd better let her get her rest. Besides, he wasn't done thinking.

He was going to have to be very careful as they went forward. If Becker was on the Tice payroll—even off the books—there would be clues. And rumors of someone in law enforcement on the take. Those rumors were always spoken as hints with no attribution. The Thin Blue Line of law enforcement conduct held true, but it was also permeable. It allowed the truth through even as it shielded it.

Law smiled in the dark, the scent of the hunt strong in his nostrils. He was a detective, a hunter of bad men. Becker's actions confirmed that he was up to something. He didn't yet know what. In a case like this, it was best to seed the ground with innuendo and wait to see who reacted. Jori's brother's wedding would be the place where he started.

After a minute Jori's hand crept between their bellies. "Just for the record. I never got involved in lady love. I'm too partial to this." The way she handled his package, all possessive and greedy, left no doubt.

Much later Sam, who had been discreetly absent during their lovemaking, made her way into the bedroom and up to the head of the bed on Law's side. She stared at him, nose pushed forward. He was sleeping. After a few seconds, satisfied that whatever odors she'd absorbed—Alpha smelling of the woman and her of him—were good ones, she padded down the foot of the bed and climbed up on the mattress. She made two turns and then slid into a prone position.

Half awake, Law reached down and brought the quilt up across all three of them. Sam didn't mind.

When all was quiet again, Argyle appeared. She didn't make a sound. Her weight made no impression when she jumped up on the bed. Her paws left shallow impressions on the quilt as she picked her way carefully among the lumps, human and canine. She was looking for a spot. That perfect spot of heat and comfort that only felines require.

She found it on Law's pillow.

She kneaded the softness a few times, and then rubbed her forehead against his hair to mark her spot. Leaning up and over, she sniffed his breath to see what she'd missed, if anything. Man didn't smell of food. Too bad. Everything else about him was irrelevant. Except his warmth. She still didn't like him but he was warmer than her own female.

She curled softly around his head, bracing her sheathed paws against his crown in case he decided to move, and closed her eyes. Maybe the male had a usefulness after all.

# *CHAPTER SEVENTEEN*

Law didn't know where to look first. Formal occasion, she'd told him. Tuxedo a must. He figured he'd look like a gorilla in a penguin suit. But he wasn't prepared for what formal looked like on her.

The sleek braid Jori most often wore had been swept up into a high shiny ponytail that cascaded down her back in a sexy mane of loose curls on her shoulders. The tiny chandeliers hanging from her ears were catching brilliant bits of light and casting rainbows on the wall. Her dress, a stretchy lace thing the color of pearls, clung to her curves. Bands of fabric hugged the corners of her shoulders, anchoring the plunge of her neckline. Modest yet sexy as hell. That dress made him itch to snag a finger in the crisscross lacing cinching her waist, drag down her zipper, and peel her out of it. But mostly he was fascinated by her legs, looking a mile long in gold sandals with ankle straps and fuck-me heels. Her face was shadowed and mascaraed and lipsticked just enough. He'd known she was a pretty woman. He hadn't realized she was a gorgeous one.

Just as quickly, he realized he would have competition for her attention this evening, and probably every day after.

"Do I look okay?" She did a little turn for him, a hopeful smile on her red mouth.

"Yeah." He looked away, feeling the rare sensation of intimidation. Hell. He'd already made love to her and knew she liked it. Why was he feeling out of his league when he looked at her now?

*This is the real me.* He'd said those words to her about his state police uniform. Was this the real Jordan Garrison, the former sorority college girl at home in expensive clothes, polished makeup, and mile-high stilettos?

"You don't like it." She sounded surprised, and just a little bit hurt.

"No." He looked back at her, unable to keep his hunger from showing. "I like it. A lot!"

"Oh." She said the word softly, as if it hadn't occurred to her before that she might have taken his breath away. She had no idea the power she possessed. He knew he'd get on all fours—threes—and crawl to her if she asked. Which she never would. She wouldn't see her influence over him as power to be used to gain the upper hand. Lucky him. Even so, he rented a damn tux!

He looked to lighten the moment. "Your shoes match."

Jori looked down and cocked her foot to show off a heel. "I thought, for the occasion, I'd try to be normal."

She looked up at him, a little secret smile on her face. "Actually, I've made a vow to myself to never wear completely matching clothing."

"I noticed. Want to tell me why?"

A tiny frown deepened between her eyebrows. "Last time you said it didn't matter."

"It didn't. Then."

Jori took a careful breath. She shouldn't read too much into that statement. Yet she felt it, too. Things had changed between them. "Since prison, I can't stand the idea that someone else decides what I wear and can't wear. That was the toughest part inside. Having no control. Once out, I felt the need to do things daily to remind myself that I was back in control."

Law got that. A little bit of rebellion every day to remind herself that she had her freedom back. "I used to count my fingers and toes after every surgery. Just to be certain nothing else had been taken from me while I was unconscious. Those remaining five ugly toes were sometimes the best sight I'd see all day."

Jori let herself absorb that confidence without comment. No one needed to tell her Law didn't give away pieces of himself, even the tiny ones, easily or often.

"So, what doesn't match today?"

Jori offered him a flirtatious smile instead of an answer. "You're not dressed."

He looked down at himself. He wore a stiffly starched shirt hung open over his impressive bare chest, and the pants to his rented tuxedo. Filling one leg was his second-best prosthesis. His bionic wonder was on its way to the manufacturer for repairs. This one didn't fit as well as it should because of the residual swelling. But he wasn't going to meet a Tice on crutches.

"There aren't enough buttons on this shirt. And I don't know what I'm supposed to do with these." He opened his fist and held out a palm full of studs and cuff links.

Jori smiled. "Want some help?"

He gave her a short upward motion with his head.

His lids fell half shut as she approached him and took a piece of metal from his hand. "These are called studs. They take the place of buttons."

As she worked the first stud into the hole in his shirt, the knuckles of her hand skimmed the trace of dark hair on Law's chest. He sucked in a shallow breath, not wanting her to know how much her nearness affected him. She smelled of jasmine and vanilla. Jesus. She was killing him.

To keep herself from turning her hand around and skimming the broad shadowy contours half hidden by his shirt, Jori made herself talk. "You really never wore a tux before?"

"Never."

She slanted a questioning look up at him. "What about prom?"

"What about it?"

"You didn't go?"

"No."

Jori thought about that answer as she worked the second stud through the shirt fabric. She and her girlfriends had planned for her prom for three solid months. The guy who took her wasn't nearly as interesting to her as getting the right dress and heels. They had pored over the wholesale catalogs in her mother's dress boutique, making sure they each picked out the absolutely most sick dress of all. "Where did you grow up?"

He looked down at her, his lids nearly closed. "The Alabama-Coushatta Reservation in east Texas near Livingston."

"Reservation?"

"Shocked?"

"No." Jori studied his face. It gave away no clues. "I know about Native American reservations. I just never met anyone who grew up on one."

"In your world, I'm not surprised."

She ignored the jibe. "Didn't your father make a big deal out of his Cajun background?"

Law nodded. "Yeah. He liked to do that. Called himself the original coonass." Some emotion crossed his face but disappeared too quickly for Jori to read it. "I wasn't reared to share his heritage." At her raised eyebrows he added, "My mother was a temporary sidetrack for him. One of many."

"You share his name."

"Yeah. She got him long enough to make it legal. Most women didn't."

"So your mother is Alabama-Coushatta?"

"Was. She's dead."

"I'm sorry."

"Why? You didn't know her."

"But I know you."

Law grunted and looked away. That empathetic impulse of hers had a way of catching him off guard. Her fallback position was open. His was clamshell-shut.

Jori took the last stud from his hand and began working at his chin. His skin was warmer here, and she couldn't help but notice the steady pulse beating in the hollow of his throat. She longed to stroke the pulse point with her finger. But she knew that would prove disastrous to their evening plans.

She moved her gaze a few inches upward. He had shaved very carefully. His jawline was satin-smooth. She lifted a finger to touch the shiny flat scar curving down from the left side of his chin onto his neck.

"Stop." She met his gaze inches from her own and got a jolt. He looked annoyed, but she knew now that it was an indication of how very much he kept himself under control.

She tucked her lips together as she finished buttoning the stud. He wouldn't like it if she found humor in his predicament.

There would be time after. And after, she was going to do a lot of things to him she could not let herself think about at this moment.

"Now the cuff links."

He held out his arms. His wrists were thick. The cuffs barely met around them.

When she finished the second cuff, he leaned forward quickly and sniffed her hair. "You smell nice."

She glanced up, straight into those dark-golden eyes shadowed by a thicket of black lashes. "Thank you."

"Where's the cummerbund?"

"Not wearing a sash." His expression was priceless.

"Fine. But everyone else will be wearing one."

"Two words. Black belt."

Jori grinned and then helped him slip on his jacket. For a rented garment it looked ridiculously good on him. She smoothed his lapels with her hands. "Very nice."

"What about this thingy?" He held up the bow tie by its cord.

"Not an option for the wedding." She took it from him and began to attach it around his neck. "You can ditch it at the reception."

"Promise?"

"I'll remove it personally."

He reached up and closed his hands over her waist. "Want to practice removing things now? You still haven't told me what articles of clothing don't match."

It was a hot lick of a moment. The air sizzled and snapped. He didn't look at ease in the tux. He looked like a heat-seeking missile dressed up as James Bond. All bad-ass attitude and yet coolly watchful. His golden-black gaze was leaving heat streaks on her skin.

"We can't . . . not now."

He smiled. It was something she was beginning to think of as a reward because he did it so rarely and felt so good. "Later."

Jori nodded, not daring for both their sakes, and the wedding, to say another word.

Law watched her gather up her purse and a wrap that

looked like a sweater with long tails she wrapped around her waist and tied. She didn't look dressed warmly enough for the weather. He should insist she put her coat over what she had on. Maybe he should get the blanket off the bed.

When he suggested the latter idea, she laughed and ran her hand down his jacket front. "You'll find ways to keep me warm. I'm counting on it."

Law grunted and swung his hand out for her to go ahead out the door. He'd find ways all right. Spend the entire trip thinking about them. He was already hot enough to burn down the cabin around them.

Once they were both in his truck, she turned to him, her eyes a little bright. "Thank you. I wouldn't have the nerve to do this alone." She leaned over and kissed his cheek near the corner of his mouth.

Again, he only allowed himself a nod. Anything else would be a disaster. He didn't know how to cherish. But he did know how to protect. If anybody said or did anything today to dim the light in her eyes or stiffen the soft beauty of her smile, he would pound them into the ground.

Law turned on the ignition, threw his beat-up truck into gear, and stomped on the pedal, sending gravel flying.

Sam looked up from the backseat, curious about the cause of the excitement. All she noticed was two Alphas on high alert. But not the scared or angry kind. That other kind she hadn't quite figured out. But it made the air between them fragrant with happy.

At least Cat wasn't with them. The last glimpse she'd had of the feline was as she was being shut into the downstairs bathroom with a tray of something even Sam wouldn't eat.

Samantha lay her head on her paws and sighed. Alpha happy. Pack happy.

# *CHAPTER EIGHTEEN*

"Looks like Santa farted Christmas all over town."

Jori laughed. "That's a terrible way to put it."

Law wagged his head in disbelief as he inched his truck along Spring Street. The narrow winding lane through downtown Eureka Springs was clogged with shoppers and holiday guests drawn by the town's monthlong celebration, and the chance to purchase one-of-a-kind artwork, jewelry, and crafts.

"Just look at that." He pointed to a storefront window where a young man sat wearing a Santa's elf costume. Holding a huge peppermint lollipop, he waved at passersby. "That's just freaky."

"They call them living windows, Law."

Law grunted. "I'd say a man dressed up like that lacks a certain amount of self-respect."

Jori landed a playful swat on his arm. "Some people have a better-developed sense of play. I bet you'd make a wonderful elf."

He scowled at her, but it was halfhearted.

"Now, that's more like it." He pointed to a young woman standing on the curb at the Basin Street Park, right in the middle of town. She wore bright-red Heidi braids and a Santa's helper costume that consisted of a lace-up bustier, a very short skirt with ruffled panties, and thigh-high white stockings with Christmas bows as garters. The sign beside her said she was handing out fudge samples from Two Dumb Dames Fudge Factory.

He turned his sludge-gold gaze on her. "Would you wear that for me?"

Jori laughed. "No way. You're hell on lingerie."

"Damn straight."

Jori turned away from his wolfish grin, a little stunned that the man she'd once thought had no sense of humor was teasing her. Better to concentrate on the scenery.

Law was right. Eureka Springs's Old World spa village facade of original nineteenth-century Victorian houses and storefronts did look like a Santa's Christmas Village come to life. Every store window and restaurant and bar entrance that wasn't swagged and wreathed was strangled with tinsel and ornaments and lights. But the town lost its starchy appearance after dark, becoming the most open-minded in the state.

She had often walked the meandering slope of Spring Street on a weekend getaway from the University of Arkansas with friends. There were bars for every taste. Her favorite had been the Rowdy Beaver Tavern, which offered karaoke as well as live bands. Other bars catered to bikers. Some welcomed doctors, lawyers, and business-people styling the "Born to Be Wild" swagger of their lost youth. Others, like the Cathouse Lounge, served the hard-core one-percenters. Both groups shared a love of the challenge and the thrill of riding the steep twisty roads leading into town. For the moment, the celebration of

Christmas had brought everyone into cheerful coexistence.

Jori glanced at Law, who was intently watching holiday shoppers cross the street without even acknowledging traffic. This would be her first Christmas in five years to celebrate as she wished. So what did she wish for? She mustn't wish for him. If history was any judge, she didn't make good decisions where the men in her life were concerned. The jump from outlaw businessman to wild-man lawman sounded a lot like rebound.

Lost in thought, she didn't realize they had climbed past town and up through the residential area until they came out of the final steep, twisty turn of the street at the entrance to the Crescent Hotel. Here the crowd swelled again as people milled around the Christmas Tree Forest of lighted and decorated trees on the east lawn. The hotel built on the mountaintop rose out of the woodland darkness as majestic as any Old World castle.

But it was the laughter that caught Jori's attention as they pulled into the curved drive before the multistoried hotel. Carefree and joyful laughter.

Jori pushed back against the seat. There were people dressed for a party thronging the entrance. Many of them had to be wedding guests. Her mom had said small wedding. Her eyes did a jittery dance over them, seeking yet fearing recognition.

The spinning sensation was back. The quivery feeling that her compass was shot and that, if she moved, she would simply dance off the edge of the mountain.

That's when Law's headlights caught a woman.

Jori couldn't catch her breath. No, she'd stopped breathing. Memories quaked through her. They would know. They would all remember when her life had become a one-minute news spot on the local channels for weeks.

*Bail denied. Flight risk.*

*A risk to whom?*

*Shame, thick and corrosive, coursed through her. She was going to be sick! No, that might be seen as an admission of guilt.*

*She'd not even been allowed to attend Brody's funeral. What must his family think of her? Not her fault, his, that she was stuck in a jail cell.*

*Guilt—oh God! She'd been found guilty. Guilty, of what?*

"Jori."

Jori realized Law was saying her name. Had said it three times. She turned to him. In the gloom of the truck cab, it took her a moment to see the hard stare he bent on her.

"Have you changed your mind?" His tone was low and neutral. "We can go get a beer instead."

A way out. He was offering it. But she wasn't as much of a coward as that. "No. I've come here for answers. Let's get them."

He watched her for several long seconds, as if guessing her thoughts. "They can't hurt you unless you let them." He reached over and unhooked her seat belt and then grabbed her chin and planted a swift hard kiss on her mouth. "Let's go get these bastards."

Jori smiled. "You always talk as if you're going to war."

Law shook his head. "I've been to war. This is the opposite. We're investigating a crime. Cool heads required."

"You're never cool."

"Around you." His face sobered with emotions at odds with his gentle tone. "You haven't seen me doing my job. The Hoodie robber doesn't count, either. Most of my job requires this face."

Jori watched as every emotion but sharp watchfulness

drained from his expression. Hard eyes, harder mouth. She shivered. He was right. She'd never seen that face. Someone was about to be in a world of trouble. She was glad it wasn't her.

"Jori! You're here." Despite the crush of people in the columned lobby, cordoned off in the middle for a huge decorated tree, Heather Garrison spied her daughter the second she entered the hotel lobby.

Her mother threw her arms around Jori's neck. "It must have been the traffic. I told everyone you'd come. I told them!"

Her mother's voice squeezed Jori's heart. It had not occurred to her that her mother would make believe that she was coming up until she could no longer hold on to that lie. For the first time it occurred to her that maybe not showing up would have been worse than being here. And that she had been unkind and thoughtless to think otherwise.

Heather released her daughter, her blue eyes swimming in unshed tears. "Let me see you. Yes. You chose the absolute best dress. It suits you perfectly." Her mother rotated her fingers to make Jori twirl around. "Have you been to the gym? Your figure looks better than ever."

Jori blushed as her mother's joyous tone drew glances her way. "Work keeps me active. And look at you. You look like you could be the bride, Mom."

It was true. Taller and slimmer in physique than Jori, her mother looked wonderful in her formfitting, blush-colored sequin mesh gown.

"Sorry we're late."

"We?" Heather Garrison's gaze widened as she looked fully at the man who stood a little behind her daughter with his back angled to the wall. Her gaze stayed wide as it shifted to the shaggy dog the color of barbecue sauce wearing a service dog vest who sat beside him.

Jori reached back and snagged Law's arm to pull him closer. "Mom, this is Lauray Battise." She left out his title. Considering recent circumstances, mentioning that he was an officer of the law might not be considered a good thing. Sam pushed her head under Jori's hand, reminding her. "Oh, and this is Sam, his service dog. I hope it's okay that she's with us."

"It's fine." Her mother's voice sounded pleased and girlish. Law was having that effect on the other women in the hallway, too. "Welcome. Mr. Baptist, is it?"

"Battise. Just call me Lauray." Law held out his hand but Jori knew her mother wasn't about to miss an opportunity to hug a good-looking man.

Sure enough she scooted under his arm to hug him, saying, "Oh, we aren't a formal family, Lauray. I'm Heather, Jori's mom."

She gave him a quick squeeze and then backed up before her friendliness could be misinterpreted. "We're happy to have any friend of Jori's with us on this special day."

"Thank you, ma'am."

She gave Law's arm a pat, her eyes widening perceptively at the hard muscle underneath his tux coat. She turned to Jori and gave her a raised-eyebrow smile. "We have so much to catch up on later, don't we?"

Jori smiled back. "Yes we do, Mom." How could she have ever thought otherwise? "Where's Dad?"

"Keeping Kieran company until it's showtime. Which is in . . ." She twisted the diamond watch on her wrist around to see the dial. "Oh my. Ten minutes! There's still so much to do. Kaitlyn wanted a small ceremony but Kieran wanted a party. So they compromised. The wedding is in the Conservatory. Only immediate families. The reception will be in the Crystal Ballroom with all three hundred guests. Go through there," she pointed down a hallway to the right. "I left space on the second-row groom's side for you. Just in case."

"I like your mom."

"Everyone does. Dad likes to say that God sprinkled a little bit more positive dust on Mom than he did the rest of us. She never sees a negative."

Law grunted noncommittally. "I see where you get your legs from." He pushed open the doors to the Conservatory.

The first things Jori saw past three short rows of chairs were her brother and her dad. They were standing next to the priest under an arbor of white poinsettias.

Kieran saw her first and came charging up the shallow aisle. "Pima!" He swept her off her feet and swung her around, knocking over a white folding chair in the process. Neither cared.

"Put me down, Kieran. You're ruining my dress." But Jori had wrapped her arms around her big brother's neck and held on.

He deposited her on the floor but then threw a possessive arm around Jori's shoulders as if he wasn't ready to let go. For a second they just stood staring at each other with stupid grins on their faces.

"Pima?" Law's voice broke the spell.

"Stands for pain in my ass," Kieran answered easily, giving the stranger a quick up and down. "She wasn't an easy child. I'm Kieran, the big brother." He stuck out his hand.

Law took it. "Lauray Battise."

Their grins were friendly but Jori saw the momentary struggle as those hands locked in contest. They were nearly the same height but Kieran was built leaner. Kieran shared Jori's open face and easy smile yet his gaze was nearly an even match with Law's in steely determination.

"Army?"

"Ranger." Kieran jutted out his jaw. "Two tours."

Law nodded. "Afghanistan. Three tours. I lost the last time."

Kieran's gaze dropped to the dog Law petted with his left hand, noted the canine's vest, and moved on to Jori, who was blushing. "Not where it counts."

"Jori?"

She turned toward that bewildered voice. "Daddy!"

"Hi, Kitten." He pulled her close to him, mercilessly crushing his boutonniere. "Finally listened to your mother, huh?"

"Mostly." She stared at her father, a slightly shorter, grayer version of her brother. "You look good, Dad."

"You look better." He palmed her head and kissed the crown of her hair and then held out a hand to Law. "Time for introductions later. Right now everybody grab a seat so we can get this party started."

The ceremony was short and sweet. Kieran and Kaitlyn looked like everyone's idea of the topper on a wedding cake. His grin revealed a man so proud and happy, he was about to bust his studs. And she, all blushing teary bride in a simple elegant gown, had eyes only for her new husband.

Jori kept her eyes on them, ignoring the shocked, round-eyed glances of the maid of honor. There'd be time to deal with Erin Tice later.

# CHAPTER NINETEEN

Law stood back from the other guests at the reception, observing. No one seemed to mind that, an hour after the nuptials, they were still waiting for the arrival of the bride and groom.

Samantha sat beside him, nudging her head under his hand from time to time as they waited for Jori. Law petted her, the rhythmic action soothing the tension of exposure. Jori had said she wanted to speak privately with her parents, but Law suspected she just needed to catch her breath. He couldn't blame her.

Crowds made him edgy. The large Crystal Ballroom had too many exits and windows. The music was too loud. The laughter was too high-pitched. And the food. The mountains of what was probably delicious, expensively arranged gourmet fare—still untouched—reminded him of a Kandahar province food bazaar. The aromas made him slightly nauseated. He was way out of his comfort zone. If not for Jori, he would be long gone.

Finally, he saw her. She paused in the doorway, her eyes roaming the group, searching. God, he hoped it was for him. And then he remembered. She had yet to face all these people who, for him, were like so many bleating sheep. No way would he let her run the gauntlet of curious stares alone.

He moved quickly and quietly along the perimeter of the room, his discomfort at being bumped and jostled by other bodies forgotten. He wasn't sentimental. He'd never understood other guys in his unit getting all moony-eyed over face time with their girls or wives. But the sight of Jori standing proud but uncertain got to him. This wasn't about him. This was about keeping her strong, and watching her back.

Jori felt all eyes on her as she stepped into the Crystal Ballroom. Even looking directly ahead, she could see some of the guests elbow others to draw their attention her way.

"This sucks."

Jori glanced sideways at Law, who had stepped up behind her. He placed a hand on the small of her back and urged her forward. "Let's get this over with."

She knew he didn't like being on display, either. "I'm sorry."

"You should be." He slanted a glance down at her as they moved into the throng of guests and toward the champagne fountain. "I know I look good in this tux but I didn't think I'd cause a scene."

Jori choked on her laughter and misstepped. But Law was there, a strong arm around her waist. "How about some champagne?"

Jori nodded. She could use a little liquid courage at the moment.

Erin must have been waiting for her. As soon as she and Law had snagged glasses of champagne, Erin floated up to them in a bridesmaid dress a little shorter and a little better-fitted than any of the other attendants'. Her hair was cut in long layers in shades of blond from champagne to butter, gold, and honey. A marathoner, she was toned, lithe, and tan.

In purely female fashion, Erin gave Jori a down–up glance, assessing her critically. "Wow, Jori. That is you. You're the last person I expected to see today. How are you?"

"Peachy, Erin. And you know what they say about bad pennies."

Erin frowned, as if not familiar with the cliché. "I almost didn't recognize you." She touched one of Jori's curls. "You were blond last time I saw you."

"But you're still the same." Jori let her puzzle on that for a second. She might have known, Erin's attention didn't stay on her. She was now looking up at Law with a flirtatious smile.

"I'm Erin Tice, Luke Tice's wife." She held out a slender hand that barely seemed capable of managing the chunk of diamond that was her engagement ring.

"Lauray Battise." Law engulfed her hand in his much larger one. She practically purred.

"And what do you do, Lauray Battise?"

"State trooper, ma'am."

Jori saw Erin wince at his use of *ma'am* but she recovered quickly. She turned to Jori. "I didn't know you still required an official escort to functions these days."

"She doesn't." Law waited until Erin glanced back at him. "I'm screwing her three ways from Sunday. And, yes, she's that good in bed. So I'd do just about anything for more. Including coming here."

Erin's mouth fell open. So did Jori's.

"Well, hello." Luke Tice had appeared out of the crowd and put an arm around the waist of his wife. With his commonplace handsomeness and a politician's assuredness that he would be a welcome addition, he offered Law a big grin. "Hey there."

Erin, who had been staring at Law like he was a cross

between Chris Hemsworth and Darth Vader, cleared her throat as she glanced her husband's way. "Luke, I'd like you to meet—"

"No introductions necessary, Erin." Luke grinned like a big kid. "I know who this is. Trooper Battise, right? Saw your picture in the *Democrat-Gazette* the other day." He offered his hand. "You have my heartfelt gratitude for your service and sacrifice to our country."

A floating photographer began taking pictures as the two men shook hands. It was the cue for Luke to continue. "This man's a bona fide hero, Erin, a decorated veteran. Lost a leg in Afghanistan. But that hasn't stopped him, no sir. This past Thursday, Erin, he stopped a robbery in progress in Springdale and then outran the fleeing robber. On one good leg. The video of it is amazing." Luke reached up to pat Law's shoulder. "This is a real American hero." He spoke loud enough that all nearby could hear. "What brings you to Eureka Springs, Trooper Battise? In need of a little R and R?"

"I'm here with Jori Garrison."

Law reached out to snag Jori by the waist, just as Luke had done his wife. "She's asked me to look into the events surrounding her incarceration." He felt Jori stiffen beside him but ignored it. "I might have a few questions for you at some later date, Mr. Tice. We are, after all, celebrating tonight."

Luke's eyes narrowed on Jori for a microsecond before slipping back into political mode. "Right." His gaze shifted to Jori and away then back, as if he couldn't decide if by looking too long he might imply something unwholesome. "Glad to see you looking so well, Erin." He held out his hand.

Erin forced herself to smile but she wasn't about to shake hands in a staged photo op with the man who'd helped put her in prison. "Hello, Luke."

Luke glanced at the photographer and smiled. "I understand. I'm probably not your favorite person. But in all fairness, I was junior counsel and only doing my job. You've paid your dues and I'm hearing great things about how you've turned your life around. See, I do keep up. I always thought you were a decent person who took a momentary wrong turn. You're now working as a trainer for Warriors Wolf Pack. Am I right?"

"Yes." Jori let the word hang as Law's hand moved from her waist up to her shoulder. The implication: *Take it easy.* But she was out of the cage of wanting to simply be left alone. Now she wanted, no, needed answers. And she wasn't going to play nice to get them. But Luke was still talking.

"So then you'll be happy to hear that I've been talking to my dad about Tice Industries making a sizable contribution to so worthy a cause. Training dogs to look after our wounded vets. Can't think of a more noble aspiration. Glad to know you're part of it. We here in northwest Arkansas take care of our own."

Jori felt as if she were going to choke. He was using her to make political points with the reporter who had joined the photographer.

"I'd like to talk with you, Luke." Law moved one aggressive inch toward the politician. "I can call you Luke?"

"Absolutely. Call my office and we'll get you set up. Always a pleasure to talk with a veteran."

"Privately would suit me better. You, too, probably."

Luke stared for a second then glanced around, seeking an out. "Ah, that'll be my aide looking for me. You'll have to excuse me. Jori, Trooper Battise, a pleasure." Not waiting to see what Erin might do, Luke pulled her along with him.

The minute they were abandoned by the photographer and reporter, who trailed after the candidate, Jori turned on Law. Her voice was low but full of heat. "Oh my God.

I can't believe you said that about me to Erin. My reputation is ruined."

He glanced down at her, his cop face in place. But there was a glint of gold in that implacable stare. "What reputation?"

As always, his raw brand of honesty carried a punch. This time it punched a breath of laughter out of her. He was right. At this point, what else did she have to lose? As long as her parents never heard about his remark. "What happened to cool and professional?"

"Shock and awe." Law steered her toward a more private corner of the room. "It's a cop tactic, too. I wanted to rattle her. I also made her jealous as hell."

Jori crossed her arms to keep him from taking her hand. "What makes you think that?"

Law's mouth stretched just short of the smile as he reached out to entangle his fingers in the lacing at her waist. "I might not know much about social graces. But I know when a woman's coming on to me."

Jori's eyes widened. But then, how could she be surprised? Erin always wanted to be the center of all men's attention. It seemed as if marriage hadn't changed that.

Law lightly pinched her elbow and nodded in another direction. "Friend of yours?"

Jori turned to the group of people her age casting glances in their direction. One of them, a redhead, waved. Jori looked away. Her nerve had completely deserted her. She just hoped Law wouldn't notice how rattled she was.

"Chelsea Bennett. We were once friends."

"Then let's go over there and let her be your friend now. You need one."

He had noticed.

Half an hour later, as the guests drank and waited for the bride and groom to appear at their reception, Jori had had enough. Even though her friends were being nice, the strain of them not asking where she'd been or what she'd been doing made everyone's smile brittle and the conversation as stilted as if English were not the first language for any of them.

Law was just plain furious. He wanted to wad the group into a ball and drop-kick them into Beaver Lake. He couldn't for the life of him understand why Jori had cared so much what any of them thought about her. None of them had half her character or courage. But then, he supposed, it must be about her parents. She cared for their sake. So he'd remain on his best behavior as long as Erin Tice stayed away from him.

Finally the bride and groom appeared.

Jori and Law took seats at her parents' table to eat and listen to speeches, some heartfelt, others hopelessly inept, and then watched the cutting of the cake. Jori was pleased to hear her father's calm voice chatting with Law from time to time. She didn't know what her father said but Law seemed to relax and respond with more than his famous one-word answers. Maybe he was enjoying himself. Or maybe he was just doing it for her. Either way, she was grateful.

Her mother, on the other hand, seemed to be trying to cram six months' worth of gossip and family news into their first chat. Jori couldn't help being a little overwhelmed by the sheer energy of her mother's enthusiasm. But it also felt better to be face-to-face with her than avoiding her. She'd been wrong to do that. Even if, she realized, she was going to have to limit her exposure to all that joy. A lunch here, a dinner there, sprinkled out over weeks. Little measurable dips into the family pool until she was comfortable with full immersion.

She loved her parents dearly. But they were seeing her as the daughter she had been four years ago, just finishing college, not yet on her own. She could hear it in the way they talked to her. For them she was still a woman-child who wasn't quite ready to launch. But she wasn't that person anymore. She was different. Not bad different, just different enough that their experiences of the world no longer matched. She was going to have to give them time and exposure to learn the new her. And accept it.

A couple of times she caught her brother's eye from where he sat with his bride at their private table. Each time he winked then rolled his eyes. He understood.

Law had waited for his moment to talk with Erin Tice. It came at the end of the evening. Jori had wandered away to find the ladies' room. So he was, for the moment, on his own. His stump throbbed. He'd been standing too long on a prosthesis that didn't fit as well as it once had. When he moved, his limp was more pronounced. He was going to ache all night. Or not. Maybe he'd bury all his troubles in the sweet warmth of Jori and his pain would no longer rule his dreams. Something to look forward to. That was a novelty, and a welcome one.

The bride and groom had departed and the lights in the ballroom had been turned down and tables pushed back in order for the younger guests to finish getting their dance party on. Things were about to get drunker and looser, and certainly more interesting.

But he couldn't very well just approach Luke Tice's wife, even if they had been introduced. He'd have to bring her to him. He knew just how to do that.

As she danced with a stranger, he gave her a hot hard glance, eyes stopping at her breasts and then hip level before sliding away. She bristled, but she glanced back after a few steps. Law looked away, no trace of his real thoughts on his face. Enough eye contact, and she'd find a way to wander over to him. Eventually.

Eventually lasted only five minutes.

Erin came dancing up to him at the end of a song, a bottle of champagne in hand and eyes wide with me-likey avarice. "You've been watching me, Mr. Battise."

Law met her flirtatious smile with a bland expression. "Have I?"

Her smile turned up at the corners. "I might be married but I'm still a woman. I notice these things."

"If you say so."

"Dance with me." She grabbed his wrist and pulled. He didn't move. Not even an inch. "Oh, come on. Don't be shy."

"I don't dance." Law patted his left leg. Sam sat up.

"Oh, right." When Erin looked up from his leg, he noticed her pupils were unusually wide even for the lighting, engulfing the blue of her eyes. "How about we find a quiet place to chat?"

"Can't do that."

She frowned. "Does Jori keep you on a tight leash?"

He smiled just a bit. "No one will ever do that."

Erin's smile returned. "So you were just throwing her off the scent before?"

"How's that?"

"By saying she's the best lay you ever had." She turned her head to cast a glance around the room before looking back at him and sliding a hand up his arm. "I think you were really issuing me a challenge."

"Honey, if that's your idea of flirtation, you need to meet a better class of men." He casually brushed her hand from his arm.

She smiled slowly, her gaze drifting below his waist as she replaced her hand on his arm and squeezed. "I do like a challenge."

Law looked down at her hand where a four-carat diamond sparkled and then back at her. Her lipstick was smeared and her mascara had gone cakey from the heat of dancing. She was not yet thirty but there was a hard edge already to the curve of her smile. Something was riding her, but it wasn't going to be him.

"Is this the game you played with Brody Rogers? Or were you more than fuck buddies?" He leaned in so that he couldn't be overheard. "Rogers was high the night he died, Mrs. Tice. He'd just come from your place. Did you two do a few rails to celebrate his broken engagement?"

She snatched her hand back. "Who are you?"

"Just an officer of the law. If you'll excuse me."

Law walked away before she could rally. He held himself militarily erect, trying to suppress his limp as he crossed the ballroom. His leg was hurting like a sumbitch. So were his hip and half a dozen other bruised places. He began swearing under his breath, viciously and methodically, as he left the room.

He needed fresh air. Quiet. A place away from people until his temper cooled. Then he'd find Jori and they'd get the hell outta Dodge.

He'd lobbed a few live grenades tonight. He would just have to wait, and be ready, for what sprang up in retaliation.

He had reached the first of the wide front steps outside the hotel when he heard the sirens. Before he could steel himself, the yelps of the approaching ambulance quickly gained intensity as strobe lights appeared out of the night, eclipsing even the Christmas decorations in their blood-red flashes.

The siren's wail merged into screams of incoming rocket fire. The chill of the December night ruptured. The scene exploded into the blinding brilliance of a desert sun.

*His body jerked as the echo of a ghostly rifle shot crackled around him.*

*He pedaled back until his back touched cold*

*stone, halting his retreat. One hand scrambled desperately for the M4 carbine that was always strapped across his torso when on duty.*

*The sickening punch of an explosion rocked him back on his heels. His heart began to race. The explosions of firepower erupting around him had one purpose. To kill.*

*He willed his knees not to buckle as he fought for control of the pain and panic engulfing him. Scud was nearby, barking excitedly, frantic for his leadership. He tried to call him back. He mustn't fail Scud. Not this time.*

*Something exploded in his chest. It was his heart. He could feel the blood spewing out through his chest wall as the searing heat of a mortar ripped into his gut.*

*He smelled death.*

# *CHAPTER TWENTY*

Erin turned her back for her husband to unzip her. "I think that trooper named Battise should be fired. He insulted me."

"Can you wait until I've won the election before you start handing me your personal vendetta list?"

She danced away from him when he'd dragged the zipper open. She'd had enough champagne and pills to feel bold. "Would it matter if I said he stuck his hand down the front of my dress?"

"Did he?"

"Maybe."

Luke snorted. "You're an incorrigible flirt, Erin. Unless you've got two witnesses who'll swear to what you just told me, no. I can't afford to alienate a decorated veteran who's just been all over the news as the new local hero."

Erin shimmied out of her dress and kicked it out of the way. Bending over required too much effort. "He wasn't very nice to you, either."

Ignoring the jibe, Luke turned to look out of the windows of the governor's suite at the Crescent Hotel. It was a spectacular view. Below lay the glittering Christmas lights of the town. Being a Tice, he didn't need to deal with many of the mundane concerns of life. For instance, the need for the ambulance arriving in the parking lot below. If ill or injured, Tice Industries would send a helicopter to zip him over to a Fayetteville hospital. But how wrong people were to think he didn't have problems. He had masters he served, just like everyone else.

He turned back from the strobe lights pulsating through the darkness and smiled at his wife's beauty. For her, anything.

"I smile every day at people I despise because they are useful to me. At the same time I avoid former associates because I'm advised it would send a wrong message to be seen with them. The best way to stop trouble is to avoid it. Dad was right about this Garrison wedding. I should've listened."

She shrugged and subsided into a chair, feeling the buzzkill of reality setting in. The highs weren't lasting as long as they had even a few weeks ago. "I hate your campaign."

"You think I get any joy out of it? I'm busting a gut trying to build something here. Do some good. Make some changes. But first I gotta pay my dues. And that can be tricky. That's why I'm always telling you to stay out of the public eye when you're not prepared. When you do show up, smile and look pretty. And when anyone brings up a political matter, you refer them to me."

Erin adjusted her demi-cup bra and succeeded in capturing her husband's eye. "You mean keep my mouth shut."

He smiled and came toward her. "Pretty much. You're gorgeous. The love of my life. I'd do most anything for you."

"You would, wouldn't you?" She gave him her best smile, thinking she'd chosen the right cousin after all. "So, about Battise?"

He shook his finger at her. "I can't slay that particular dragon, sweetheart. Sorry."

She looked away. "He mentioned Brody."

"What?" Her husband's tone made her look up. "Why would he have any reason to mention my cousin?"

His eyes scared her, making her back off. "Oh, you know. I guess Jori's been spinning lies about us."

"Why would she discuss Brody to Battise?"

Even through the haze of booze and pills, Erin realized she couldn't very well tell her husband what Battise had implied. That she had been Brody's customer. It might remind him of other promises she'd made and broken since. "I have no idea. Swapping love stories with a new boyfriend? Who knows what goes through a convict's mind."

"Battise did say he wants to meet with me."

"Don't do it, Luke. If he's following up on something Jori said, it can only mean he'd like to make trouble for you. Maybe *she* wants to make trouble. Now that she's out of jail, maybe she wants revenge. And she's screwing a cop to get him to help her."

Luke frowned. "I wonder. You ever think about Brody?"

"Of course not." Her high, veering sharply toward itchy-twitchy, made her voice sharp. "Why would I?"

"What if Brody hadn't died?" He was watching her now, still a little jealous after four years whenever his cousin's name came up. "He sure had the charm."

She ran her nails up the nape of her neck, trying to distract herself. "He was engaged to Jori."

"He said he'd broken it off with Jori that last night."

"I was there, if you recall."

Luke's expression turned grim. "I recall a lot of things."

Erin popped up from her seat. "Oops. Almost forgot my meds. Pour me another glass of champagne while I get them. I ordered room service to bring more up."

Luke followed her. "You shouldn't mix alcohol with your medication. You know you're vulnerable."

"I know. And I don't, usually." She avoided his gaze. "It's just that my knee hurts like hell. My orthopedist says I tore something in that last race and may need surgery. Still, I had to look beautiful for you tonight, didn't I?"

She kicked up a leg sporting a five-inch heel held in place by a tiny rhinestone strap. "I do this for you, sugar."

Luke grabbed her foot and kissed it just above the strap. "Did I ever tell you you're the most beautiful woman I ever saw?"

"Every day, baby. That's why I married you. Now let me take the edge off and show you just how much I appreciate you."

"That's right, Dad. A state trooper named Battise wants a private meeting with me. He was here with Jori Garrison. How the hell should I know? They just showed up at the wedding together."

Luke moved his cell phone from one hand to the other as he pushed open the door. "Nobody ever heard of him until he made the papers this week as a one-legged hero. Now everyone's talking about him. What I want to know is who the hell this Battise guy really is."

Luke moved out onto the balcony just outside his suite, not wanting Erin, who appeared to be asleep, to overhear his conversation. The air was frigid, smelling of snow, but he couldn't wait until morning to get a few answers from his father. He didn't rattle easily. But the mention of Brody had unnerved Erin. Now he was worried, too.

So far, however, his father sounded like an adult dealing with an overwrought child.

"So, you do know him? How? No, I'm not overreacting." He hated that soothing let-me-take-care-of-this tone. "Oh, really? Then did you know he's asking questions about Brody?"

Luke smiled as he held the phone away from his ear. That had gotten a rise out of his old man. Brody continued to be a sore spot for his father.

When the expletives on the other end of the phone subsided, Luke was more calm. "Like I said, Jori must be thinking of protesting her verdict. That's the only thing that makes sense. If that's it, maybe I should talk directly with her. No, I know I can't appear to be backing down on a verdict that's part of my tough stand on crime."

Luke began to regret making the call.

"You say that, Dad, but you don't mind me owing favors across half the state for other considerations. How is this different?"

More political advice he didn't have time for.

"No. Of course, there's nothing more for the state police to learn about Brody's death. Why would I try to hide anything from you after all this time?"

For the first time his father paused to think. Good. He'd called him for some of his bedrock cut-your-losses advice. What he'd gotten so far was nothing close to that.

"No. I don't want you anywhere near this, you hear me, Dad? Handle it wrong and it could blow up in my face."

Luke ducked back into the main room of the suite, his ears, nose, and fingers tingling from the cold. "I was hoping you could fill in a few blanks for me. But since you can't, I'll take care of this. I have resources, too. I am your son. Right. Right. I just thought you should know. Yes, I'll keep you informed. Good night."

Luke punched END and tossed his phone on the sofa. He might just have made a mistake.

"Goddammit all to hell!"

Harold Tice tossed the Waterford crystal sniffer of Tennessee whiskey at his fireplace, where it shattered into a hundred tiny prisms. Luckily, his wife was away visiting her sister in Bentonville and wouldn't be home until morning. By then the maid would have cleaned up. Meanwhile, he was going to have to do some cleaning up of his own. For Luke's sake.

He should have followed his instinct when he'd first learned that Battise was looking into his military records. He'd had all the pieces. Wounded jobless veteran. Angry and antisocial. Suffering PTSD. Easy enough to stage something. People would have done no more than wag their heads and say *What a waste*. But now Battise had gone and made himself a front-page news hero right in Tice Industries' backyard.

Worse still, he'd joined up with Jori Garrison.

"What the hell is going on?" Harold looked about to reassure himself that he was, really, alone. The maid might have heard that crash and come running. No one.

He subsided into his favorite wingback chair, but there was no peace of mind to be had tonight from staring at the mounted twelve-point buck he'd killed at age sixteen.

Becker's phone call a few days earlier had caused him to look into what Jori Garrison was up to. What he'd learned had soothed his concerns. She was now a service dog trainer at Warriors Wolf Pack. That's where Battise had gone to get a service dog to help him deal with his PTSD. Pure coincidence the two should meet. But nothing to worry about, until now.

Harold looked around for the whiskey he'd poured.

Right. Smashed. He sighed, too preoccupied to pour another.

Maybe Jori had convinced Battise to look into her case. But that had nothing to do with Brody's death. Or had he missed something?

Harold thought about Becker. Becker hadn't been on his private payroll for four years out of charity. The dickwad had extorted enough money from him. It was time he earned his keep.

A man couldn't control every eventuality. But he could prepare to avoid disaster.

# *CHAPTER TWENTY-ONE*

Sam didn't pay any attention to the sights and sounds until she heard Alpha moan. She turned to him. He was suddenly awash in hormones. His heart rate was accelerating. His breath coming in short staccato rhythm. His fear flowed into her, stunning her with its intensity. This was bad.

She realigned her big body in front of Alpha's, whimpering and shaking as she balanced her paws against his hips and butted his chest with her big head, trying to draw his attention. This was her job, what she was trained for. Pull her Alpha out of his nightmare. Make the fear and anxiety stop.

> On autopilot, Law reached out to stroke his dog as he had every other dog in his life who had done a good job. "Gute Hund. So ist Brav, Scud. Gute Hund. We're going to make it this time."

Getting no response, Sam jumped up with paws against Alpha's chest, making soft nasal sounds as she pushed her muzzle forward, her nose taking in short quick sniffs of his scent. He didn't smell right. There were odors of fear and the rank sweat of a body pushed to its limits. She could smell in his sweat traces of blood from his scrapes, a hint of pus, and the white blood cells making scabs to heal over the raw places. Even the bruises inside the metal and plastic leg he wore had a ripe flavor. He was sick, very sick.

Her Alpha's body jerked. More sweat poured from him, vinegary with a cocktail of full panic.

She pushed in closer, leaning her warmth against him, and nuzzled his neck. She'd been taught to be pushy, force her body and presence on her Alpha until he focused on her. It wasn't working this time.

Sam pressed on, licking his face in long hard strokes that insisted he give her even more of his attention. Happy Alpha. Happy pack. Alpha needed to be okay. She would make Alpha okay. Then she would be okay.

*Law stroked his canine partner, the automatic physical motion somehow soothing as he struggled with the vivid sights and sounds and smells overlaying his reality.*

*After a few seconds, the attack ceased. There were voices now, shouts and cries. And pain. Always pain.*

*It didn't matter.*

*Law wrapped his arms around his K-9 and breathed deep. Scud was alive! Everything was going to be all right.*

The room came into focus. Not any room Law had seen before. It was dark but for a fire blazing from the hearth in front of him. Someone was sitting beside him. Talking. A woman's voice. Talking about . . . blueberry muffins. How to make them.

"Two cups of all-purpose flour. I never sift. Aunt Suze says you should but I don't . . ."

He blinked against the dimness, as if there were a shade over his eyes. A living room appeared with a two-story bank of windows open to the night. He could just make out the pale planks of a deck beyond. He sat on a small sofa that he shared with—he turned his head toward the voice—Jori.

She smiled tentatively. "Are you back with me?"

"What happened?" His throat felt as dry as if he'd been licking asphalt.

"Nothing. Much." Jori glanced at the front door as she heard footsteps crunch past the cottage. "You, ah, had an episode. Water?"

She offered him a cold bottle of water, which he gulped in big slugs that splashed around his mouth and onto his shirtfront.

Jori was ready, mopping up the water with a napkin and then adjusting the blanket she must have thrown around his shoulders sometime earlier.

"How did you find me?"

"I was looking for you. One of the bellboys told me he'd seen a man with a service dog out on the front veranda. I couldn't find you at first. There was a lot of confusion out on the drive. One of the hotel guests, not a wedding guest thank goodness, had a medical emergency. The EMTs had been called. Finally I saw Samantha. She was jumping on you and barking. As I got close I could see something was wrong. You had that thousand-yard stare I've heard about."

Law absorbed this information without responding.

"I didn't know what else to do so I brought you here."

Law's gaze did a jerky hyperalert perimeter check. "Where is here?"

"It's one of the private cottages on the grounds of the hotel. Mom and Dad rented it for the newlyweds but they had other secret plans. Mom gave me the key so we'd have a place to stay for the night."

"She saw me like that?"

"No, Law. I got the key at the reception. No one saw you. I doubt anyone would have noticed anything wrong but me."

Law looked away. He could just imagine everyone staring as she'd led the zombie away from the front of the hotel. At least he hadn't passed out.

Cold shame washed through him. He was soaked in his own sweat. He smelled of Scud—no.

He looked down. Sam lay by his side opposite Jori, her big warm body pressed along his flank. She was sprawled as if half asleep. But even in the gloom he could see her big soft eyes gleaming as she watched him.

Not Scud. Sa—Samantha. His heart constricted. Fuck! He'd really gone in deep this time.

He tried to swallow but his throat was still as dry as the desert he'd just left behind.

"This one's not cold." Jori held out a second plastic water bottle.

He took it and drained the contents in one long series of gulps. "Why did you stay?"

"I thought you might want company." She didn't touch him but he could feel the penetrating force of her gaze through the darkness.

"I don't ever want company when this happens."

She nodded and moved to get up.

He grabbed her arm. He didn't ask her to stay, couldn't, but after a second of tension against his hold, she relaxed back onto the sofa.

They sat in silence for several minutes before he took a deep breath. Images still slid in and out from the edges of his vision, but reality held. "Did I ask you about baking products?"

She frowned then smiled. "Oh. You mean the muffin recipe I was reciting." He sensed embarrassment in her voice and in her shrug that rubbed her slender shoulder against his arm. "I didn't know what else to do. I thought the sound of a voice going on about something ordinary would help ground you."

"I don't need help. I can handle it."

"Okay." She sounded matter-of-fact, as if they were talking about a sneezing fit instead of a full-blown flash-back that even now kept his heart beating too quickly.

"Still, you've got to admit that fresh blueberry muffins is a pretty good lure away from the blue devils. That's what my grandmother calls sadness."

He scrubbed both hands down his face and noticed they shook. "You think I'm sad?"

"Not exactly." He felt her sigh, the little up–down move-ment of her arm along his. She felt warm. Or maybe it was just that he was freezing.

"I don't know much about PTSD. Can't imagine what you've been through. But I know about wanting to be somewhere else, anywhere else, and knowing you can't get there."

She took a longer shuddery breath this time. "The first weeks I was in prison, I'd forget to breathe sometimes. I passed out once. And I was always holding my breath. I was afraid that when I closed my eyes at night the walls would fold in and swallow me. The counselor said I needed to find a safe place to go to in my head when that hap-pened. A happy place. It took a few tries but I found that when the walls closed in I could go into my head to my grandmother's recipe box. Blueberry muffins is the recipe I remembered best. By the time I'd mentally collected all the ingredients, stirred them up, and they were done bak-ing, I'd moved away from the worst moments."

Law thought about that. He'd had so many worst days

he could mentally bake a bakery shop full of muffins each day probably for the rest of his life.

"Who's Scud?"

He jerked. "What?"

"You were talking about Scud. Was he your last military K-9?"

"Yes." Law gritted out the word.

"He died protecting you?"

"I don't—won't talk about that."

"Okay." But she didn't move away, only rested her head on his shoulder.

After more long moments of silence where there was only her warmth to hold him there, he began talking.

He told her everything he remembered about that day. How bright the sun had been. But not too hot. Afghan winters could be as cold and bright as those in Colorado. But everything remained brown. He told her about the run that morning, how clean and fresh and powerful he'd felt. Those things were as lucid and bright in his mind as if they were today's memory. But he was there with her. He could feel her fingers wrap halfway on his biceps when he began to tremble.

He stuttered now. The story coming in more fragments. Bits and pieces blown fresh of the mooring of sequence.

"Scud died protecting me from my own unit." Law sucked in a breath, pushing against the pain that threatened him. "I should have protected him better."

"I'm so sorry, Law."

Jori reached up to touch his face but he jerked away from her. He could feel it coming. Needed to get away from her, away from the shame of what was exploding inside him.

He tried to stand. But his legs didn't work. His body wasn't under his command. He began to shake with the effort to override whatever had him rooted to the spot.

In panic he felt the eruption within and he couldn't stop it. Anger, fear, grief, and agony were all elements of the wall he'd built to hold it all in. But comfort, as alien to him as love, did him in.

Jori put her hand on his shoulder and leaned her head against his.

His eyes filled. "Fuck."

He held himself rigid, refusing to accept what was happening, a fist pressed to his belly to hold it in. But it came anyway, pain that made a lie of all his years of carefully constructed isolation. A moan escaped him as it gave way like a physical tearing inside. Then the place where he didn't need anything or anyone burst open like a dynamited dam.

Tears spilled over the seam of his closed lids.

He felt Jori's arms go around him, trying to cradle his larger frame to hers. He could so easily have broken her embrace and escaped. But he didn't even try. At least she didn't promise that it was okay. And that everything would soon be fine again. He knew better.

Sam came forward, shaking and whining, ears flat in confusion of the moment. Both members of her pack were hurting. She licked at Jori's face, slick with salty wetness, then lay her head behind Alpha's head in the cradle of his neck and waited for the emotional hurricane to die down.

# CHAPTER TWENTY-TWO

"This isn't going to work." It was just after dawn and Law was slamming into his clothes, at least the tux pants and shoes. Samantha watched from a prone position a few feet away. Her body was taut and ready for action.

"What are you talking about?"

"I lost it. Showed weakness."

"A few tears?" Jori sat up in bed, covers pulled close to protect her nakedness from the cold. "That didn't bother me. I'm a woman. We deal in tears."

He shot her a hostile glance from beautiful bruised eyes. "I don't."

"Yeah, well, get over it. You needed to let the grief out. It will be better now. You'll see."

She saw on his face that she'd said the wrong thing. Offering platitudes to a man who knew better.

He hunched back toward the corner of the room, his chin tucked. He looked exhausted, as if he hadn't slept in a week. His mouth was pinched and his eyes hooded. All that was lacking was raised fists to make him look like a cage fighter at the end of his options. Nothing to do but slug it out. She had no doubt he thought he was fighting for his life.

"I'm too messed up to be with you. To be with anybody." He seemed to wrestle every word out of himself. "I was flashing back half the night. What happened took more than my leg. I'm fucked up."

"Okay." Jori took a deep breath. Maybe she didn't know enough to know if it would get better. He'd probably had counseling that revealed things she might never know. They had been through a lot in just a few days of knowing each other. But there was another side to Law. A side she didn't know at all. She'd seen signs of it twice last night. And both of them worried her.

They had sex in the middle of the night. Long after they'd climbed into bed, too exhausted to even talk anymore. The wind had come up, slamming into the house with a force that was a perfect reflection of the conflict raging inside the cottage as two bodies locked in physical embrace struggled for emotional survival.

It was not fun or amorous but a carnal grappling of dark emotions and hard-edged regrets working themselves out in a quick rough coupling that left Jori sore and unsatisfied.

Afterward, she wanted to curl into a ball at the far edge of the mattress, as far away from him as she could, to try to figure out what had just happened.

But its aftermath dropped Law into an exhausted sleep so quickly and so deep that she couldn't move him an inch off her. He had clamped his body down over hers, as if shielding her from an exploding world. And he never let her go, all night long.

He might not have offered her tenderness but he knew how to protect, even in his sleep.

Now, watching him put on one shoe, swearing under his

breath from the pain his ill-fitting prosthesis caused, Jori couldn't order her feelings, or her hopes.

She had known from the beginning that *easy* wasn't part of his vocabulary. Law was a complicated angry man no longer certain of his place in the world. That lone-wolf image was a good one. But she had thought she could make things better for him.

Last night had shown her, for better and for worse, that being with Lauray Battise was not, maybe never, going to be easy. Maybe not even possible.

"Had enough?"

He stopped and watched her. She just stared right back. There was so much she wanted to say.

*I can't begin to understand what losing a leg and Scud cost you. But I'm proud as hell of you for clawing your way back. Making your body work again. Enduring everything. I want to weep for you but I won't. Because you don't need that. But don't think you're the only one who's screwed up and confused. You came into my private space and shattered my peace. I know I said I could handle it. You, here and gone. I'm not sure anymore that I can handle it. Or you. Or even want to. No. I want to. I'm not at all certain I should try.*

She didn't say any of that.

She came up on her knees on the bed. "Listening to people talk last night about financial investments and charity balls and tailgate parties. Who's on the fast track and who's peaking too soon. Half the time I didn't know what they were talking about. I'm no longer of their world. I don't belong anywhere, either."

He shook his head like a bull annoyed by a biting fly. "You have a way back. You have your family. I saw you with them. I saw how they look at you. They love you. They'll do anything to help you."

*As I would you.*

But she couldn't say that, either. Much too exposure for her. She wasn't sure what love was. But this—whatever it was—felt like something precious, something to hold on to.

Law wouldn't hear it if she said that last night hadn't made him appear lesser in in her eyes. It had made her feel that, at the very least, he trusted her.

She didn't have to hear him say he didn't trust easily. She'd heard it in his explanation of the events in Afghanistan that led to his wounding. His anger at his unit. At what he perceived as a military cover-up after the fact. Even in his grudging respect for his sister and what she'd done for him that was tinged with a resentfulness she didn't understand. Who didn't want help?

She wasn't going to walk away. She just needed to come at him in a way he would understand. And that would give them a chance to move past last night.

She knew this much was true. He was about honor, and duty. And persistence.

She slid off the bed, leaving the protection of the covers behind as she walked naked across the floor and reached for her undies.

When she had that much armor on, she turned to him. "You promised you'd help me clear my name. I want you to keep that promise."

He stared at her, the pain in his expression so raw it made her stomach clench. He watched her for what seemed like forever, his breath coming and going harshly through his teeth.

Finally, he straightened up from the chair on which he sat. "I can't be what you want, Jori. You're starting to dream. I can see it in your beautiful face. I won't do that to you."

"Is this about your dad?" Somewhere in the jumble of

misery that poured out of him during the night he'd even told her about his father's philosophy about women.

Law shook his head. "This is about how I don't know how to be with you. With anyone. I'm messed up."

"Is that what he told you? Then fuck him." She saw his eyes buck wide. "Yes, I said it. Screw your dad for trying to keep you from needing love. That's cruel. Everybody needs somebody."

He looked at her. The hunger for her was so plain on his face, it made her ache unbearably.

She came to stand before him. "You're not like him, Lauray. You're your own man." She reached out and touched his face very gently. "And I like that man."

He gripped her about the waist hard. No lover's touch. He clutched her like a man going under for the final time. "You need to stop being nice to me."

"Why?"

"Because I'm going to start wanting to believe you. And I can't risk that. I'm not ready."

The moment was almost too much. Watching the torment in the eyes of this supremely self-sufficient man made her feel as if the world were about to spin off its axis. But she stood her emotional ground, because she knew he needed her courage more than she needed her fears.

His wanting to believe her was a good thing. Maybe enough to start him on the road back to life. But she needed to put a little distance between them for her courage to survive.

She slipped out of his grasp. "Excuse me."

Jori hurried into the bathroom to wash her face and hide the tears she didn't want him to know about. As she scooped handfuls of water over her flush face, she raced around in her head, trying to think of a change of subject, a safe topic.

"Can we get breakfast before we head back to Springdale?"

"Sure."

Law came to the bathroom door and held out her dress, his expression remote as he focused for the first time on her lacy nothings. Her bra was black and her cheeky panties blush. For a second his eyes darkened and she knew he was remembering her promise to show him her mismatched items of the day. The heat in his gaze nearly caught the fragile strips of lace on fire.

She turned and faced him, waiting for his decision. But after a moment the fire died in his liquid black-gold gaze and he turned, moving quickly away. "McDonald's. Drive-through."

An hour later Law pulled up his truck beside Jori's SUV at her motel. He didn't take his hands off the wheel, or even glance at her.

Too proud to beg him to speak, Jori reached for the door handle.

"Jori." He waited until she looked back. "You know the expression, *kicked a hornet's nest*? I shoved my foot pretty far up Tice's ass at the wedding. So from now on, I work alone. If I get something, I'll be in touch. If not, this is good-bye."

Jori swallowed words of affection and hope. He was gripping the steering wheel so hard she expected it to crack any second under the pressure. He might be sitting next to her, but his expression was as cold and distant as the moon. He'd been through a lot the night before. He needed time. "Oh. What about Argyle?"

"Fuck." He blinked. "Swing by and pick her up on your way home. I'll make sure I'm out of the way. Drive safe."

And just like that, Jori knew it was over.

# CHAPTER TWENTY-THREE

Law felt like a string of live wires stripped of their protective coating. It had been a week. Nothing. No phone calls. No response to his attempts to set up a meeting with Luke Tice. He doubted Tice's campaign office was so dysfunctional that Tice didn't get messages. That meant he was being ignored.

He cut a wedge of his egg-white omelet and put it on a paper napkin before setting it on the floor in front of Sam. She sniffed it and looked up at him, ears spreading.

"Yeah. I know. Tomatoes, mushrooms, and onions. No cheese. No meat. But I've got a physical to pass in a few days. I need to eat healthy."

Sam sighed so deeply her cheeks fluttered. Law had begun to recognize that as her whatever-you-say-boss-but-I-don't-have-to-like-it response to things she disapproved of. That didn't keep her from swallowing the wedge of omelet whole.

Law gulped the last of his coffee and reached for the check. It was his first day off in five, but he couldn't just sit in his cabin all day. Not when too many things in it reminded him of Jori. The upstairs bedroom reminded him of how tenderly and efficiently she'd taken care of his abrasions. The downstairs bedroom was worse. They'd made love in that bed. He'd settled for sleeping on the sofa. He'd slept in much worse places.

He'd looked at her number on his cell a dozen times a day. But he knew he shouldn't do that to her. He wasn't a fool. When a woman looked at a man as she had that last morning, he knew what she was feeling. What was new was that he felt an answering hum in his own chest. But he'd screwed it up.

Shamed himself.

Cried.

She might try to forget. But he wouldn't. He'd broken down in front of her.

He shuddered in remembrance of his weakness. Even he knew a woman wanted a man she could rely on to be strong when all else failed. How her eyes had shone in admiration after he'd taken down that robbery suspect. He'd been Superman and Captain America in her eyes. For a moment.

The goddamn PTSD! If he wasn't one fucked-up bastard before Afghanistan, he'd shown himself to be one now. In front of the only person he had ever wanted to be a better man for.

"Tears. Jesus."

Law wiped his mouth to erase the spasm of self-disgust twisting his features. Sad fuck. He had to deal with himself. But he wasn't going to inflict himself on anyone else.

He'd gone to the gym to do some cross-training, doing as many reps as he could until his muscles trembled so badly he could hardly walk. It felt good to be that tired. He'd do it again tonight. Then lighter tomorrow and feather back on weights over the next few days to give his body a chance to heal and build muscle. His physical was in three days. The Arkansas State Police physical required successive completion of five tasks in order: standing vertical jump of a minimum of thirteen inches, twenty-four sit-ups within a minute, seventeen push-ups within a minute, a three-hundred-meter run within seventy-eight point nine seconds. And finally a mile-and-a-half run within eighteen minutes and thirty-seven seconds. Compared with his military training, it was a cakewalk. But that was before he was minus a significant muscle in one leg to propel him along.

The jump and the mile-and-a-half run were going to be the difference between making it and failing.

Law rose casually, shifting his weight onto his good leg. His fancy prosthesis was due back today. He had called three times to make certain it would be delivered.

He reached for Sam's leash and out of habit—and training—did a sweep of the local coffee shop customers. He had taken the table at the back, near the restrooms, facing the door. He'd noticed everyone who entered while he ate. Nothing out of the ordinary.

Even so, as he approached the cash register to pay, his gaze shifted back to the lunch counter where a man in a suit sat drinking coffee. The guy made eye contact and nodded.

Law went through a split second of scenarios that allowed him to keep control of the situation that might or might not unfold. BE PREPARED was tattooed on his DNA.

The man was a stranger but his gaze had been too direct for casual. Something about those faded blue eyes said he wasn't a businessman. The suit screamed *on the job.* Investigator? Had someone turned him in to IA for his illegal online searches?

He paid, left a tip, and with Sam turned for the exit.

He walked down the block to a hardware store and entered. He made a line for the back of the store, putting some barriers between himself and whoever came through the door next. Ten minutes later, with a bag containing, nails, brads, and a roll of screening to repair a porch door, he stepped out into the December cool air. His hot breath made a cloud before his face. Before it cleared he'd made the man in the suit leaning on the passenger-side door of his truck.

"So it's like that." Law glanced down at Sam. "You keep watch on his flank. I'll do the talking."

Almost immediately Law glanced away from the animal. He must be losing it, talking to a curly-top mutt who couldn't chew her way through anything more dangerous than a cardboard box. As proof, he'd started his morning by picking up wadded-up dog-spit-covered pieces of a shoe box.

"Can we talk?" The man with the faded blue eyes held up a badge as Law neared.

Law halted, legs braced apart, his gaze searching for backup. "Am I under arrest?"

The man watched him steadily but didn't look particularly hostile. "Conversation, Mr. Battise. My vehicle or yours?"

Law reached past him and stuck his key in the passenger-side door.

"Task force?"

"The Central Arkansas Drug Task Force." Faded blue eyes had introduced himself as Detective Wentworth. "We're conducting an investigation in which your name has come up."

"I doubt that." Law stretched out his legs behind the wheel, ignoring the twinge in his stump. "I'm a state trooper stuck behind a desk. The only drugs I deal with are those given to me by my doctor for this." Law thumped his prosthesis.

Wentworth nodded. "Heard about that. Honor to know you."

"Right."

Wentworth sobered. "You've been doing some unauthorized investigation of Tice Industries."

"Who says?" Law didn't as much as blink but his guard was up again, and not just because he'd spied Wentworth's partner loitering in the middle of the block. It was twenty-five degrees outside. No one chose the out-of-doors to check his cell phone for messages. Two detectives gave better odds to this conversation being legit. But then all dirty cops were on the job. Was Becker part of this task force, too? Tice's man inside? He needed to watch his step. He'd give nothing away until he got more intel.

"Are you accusing me of anything, Detective? Or are you just fondling my balls?"

"I've been asked to order you to back off."

"On whose authority?"

"What do you know about Trooper Ron Becker?"

"Not much. I know I don't like him."

"He sure is interested in you."

"Uh-huh."

"Did you know he broke into your home ten days ago?"

"Yeah. My dog told me."

The agent eyed Sam, who was sprawled between them, with skepticism. "What kind of dog is that?"

"Cheez Doodle. Why are you really talking to me?"

"CADTF has been working a wide-scope investigation that includes northwest AR and parts of three other states for more than two years. We're about to move. But we have to know our quarry hasn't been tipped off."

"You think I'm involved." Law didn't make it a question.

"No, sir. If I thought that, you'd be talking to me after I read you your rights."

Law held that clear-water gaze. "So why are you talking to me?"

"You have a pretty high government clearance. CID gets respect with us. So I'm doing you the courtesy of asking you to back off."

"What does that look like?"

"Don't call or try in any fashion to get in touch with Luke Tice, any member of his campaign, or family. And keep off the state and federal criminal online databases."

Law's interest pricked up. "What do I get in return?"

"The privilege of knowing that once again you've served your country in the capacity of law enforcement."

"I do that every day."

Wentworth stared at Law so long he felt the urge to scratch. Finally, he shrugged. "What do you want?"

"You ever come across the name of Jordan Garrison in your investigation?"

Wentworth subjected him to a second, longer stare. "She's an ex-con."

"She's a classic case of the letter of the law being carried out in an unjust way."

Wentworth's mouth turned down. "I see."

"No. You don't. But that's not important here." Law knew instantly that Wentworth knew Jori was—had been involved with Law. For the first time he was glad he'd broken it off with her. He'd expected trouble. But federal trouble was the last thing she needed to become involved with. He was saving her that much.

Law shifted his shoulders, feeling that live-wire edginess that had been with him for a week throw off a few bright sparks. "What's important is that if you come across any information that would appear to have to any bearing on the reopening of her case, I would like to have it."

Wentworth shook his head. "I can't promise anything. This is an ongoing investigation that may take months or longer to process."

"In other words, I scratch your back and you say thank you and walk away."

The man grunted. "Sounds about right."

"Are you after Tice Industries?"

"You know I can't reveal details of an ongoing investigation."

"Yeah, yeah. So then I'll just pretend I'm talking to myself and you can nod if you feel moved to. Is the investigation bigger than a bread box?"

Wentworth shrugged. Law smiled.

"I'm guessing a case that's taken years to put together involves suppliers as well as dealers, and probably the dirtbags on the job who run interference for these good citizens."

This time Wentworth just stared.

"That would include Trooper Becker in law enforcement corruption. Very bad news."

Not even a flicker of an eyelid.

"Our friends at Tice are on the transport and supply side. Get them to talk and a large-scale drug trafficking ring gets mapped, top-to-bottom."

Wentworth rubbed his eyes. "That's a nice story, Mr. Battise. You should write a book."

He reached for the door handle and then turned back. "Saw that video footage of you running down a perp." He cracked a smile, and it brought life to his pallid complexion. "That's the best takedown I've heard about all year. Proud to know you."

He was all the way out of Law's truck before he said. "You might want to keep an eye on the news over the next few days."

Law watched Wentworth wander across the street and slide into a car so nondescript it stood out like a sore thumb.

He shook his head as he ruffled Sam's fur. "We played nice. Now we have to sit it out and wait to see what happens. Waiting. The thing I hate most in all the world."

Sam licked his chin.

"Yeah, I know. You hate egg-white veggie omelets. I guess we can't have everything the way we want it."

# *CHAPTER TWENTY-FOUR*

Jori looked up from reading her notes at a table in the main room of Warriors Wolf Pack. A woman in jeans, a man's oversized pink golf shirt, and black puffer coat came in leading a dog. She recognized her as Sarah, the wife of Mike Williams, a veteran of the Gulf War, the first war in Iraq in the early '90s. Mike's service dog was named Yuki, a shepadoodle who had been placed with them before she came to work here.

The Williamses had become a bit of a legend at WWP. They'd requested three individual home visits since the placement six months earlier. And had been back here once, since Jori joined the staff, for extra training. Kelli had taken them on as her personal crusade.

But to judge by Sarah's mouth, crimped into a tight line, and the determination in her sneakered stride with Yuki in tow, there was new trouble in the wind.

"Good morning." The volunteer of the day at the reception desk greeted the woman with a smile.

The woman didn't smile back. "I want to speak to the person in charge." Her Arkansas hill country drawl emphasized the weight of her life. "Somebody needs to take this here dog off my hands."

Jori stood up and came forward, hand extended. "Good morning, Mrs. Williams. How may I help you?"

Sarah looked her up and down, wariness in her washed-out blue gaze. "You're one of the trainers, right? I need a higher-up."

"I'm sorry, but Kelli's out seeing about another dog right now. I'm sure she'll be glad to talk with you when she returns. We expect her back in about twenty minutes. Would you like a bottle of water? Or maybe coffee. It's awfully cold today."

Sarah shook her head, mouth working impatiently. "I just came to deliver your dog back to you. We can't use him no more."

"Is that so?" Jori looked down at Yuki. "May I pet him?"

The Sarah looked startled. "I guess so. He's your dog."

*And that's the problem*, Jori thought as she knelt down. Sarah hadn't bonded with Yuki. Kelli had just done a workshop for trainers about the wives and mothers of veterans, longtime caregivers like Sarah who had trouble adjusting to the help that a service dog could provide.

As she rubbed Yuki's head with both hands, she sought a casual tone. "How's Mr. Williams?"

"Mike's fine." She glanced back at the door. "He don't want to come in. And I can't stay. So if you'll just . . ." She extended Yuki's leash to Jori.

Jori stood up, pretending not to understand the gesture. "Why don't you and Yuki come with me?" She turned and began walking away, gambling that Mrs. Williams wouldn't just abandon the dog in the middle of the room.

Once inside the privacy of Kelli's office, Jori waved her hand toward one of the chairs. "Have a seat and tell me what's wrong."

"Like I told you, I can't stay. Mike's in the truck." Sarah sat down, pushing her fingers through short silver hair that Jori was almost sure was self-cut.

"Yuki's a nice dog, and all. Quiet, easygoing. And he don't shed, just like you said. Only he's interfering with my schedule. I can't have that."

"Of course not. What's Yuki doing?"

Sarah's combative expression eased a bit at the sound of Jori's sympathetic tone. "He's got it in his doggy head that he can tell Mike when his medicine's due. I came in the other day from shopping to find Mike had already took his meds half an hour early. He said Yuki had brought the medicine organizer and put it in his lap so he thought it must be time."

Jori nodded, giving herself a moment to think about how to phrase her reply. Yuki was one of those dogs who was a self-starter, able to learn routines to the point where it seemed he could even tell time. Some saw that as a blessing. But other caregivers saw the service dog as being in competition for the attention and affection of the client.

"You know, there's another way to think about that. Yuki was taking care of Mike. What if you'd been delayed in traffic?"

Sarah shook her head and frowned. "I learned a long time ago to shop at odd hours, after eight p.m. or before six in the morning. I got to know there's no traffic so I can get back in a hurry." The tension in her voice said more than her words.

"You worry that Mike might not be able to get or do something he needs to while you're out."

She jerked her head once in agreement.

"So, in a way, isn't it nice that Yuki has paid enough attention to realize then Mr. Williams needs his medication?"

"The dog was half an hour too early!" To Jori's surprise

Sarah blinked back big crystal-bright tears. "Not that anyone cares, besides me. Mike thinks that damn dog hung the moon. Won't even allow me to help him in and out of the shower no more. Tells me to leave him alone. He and Yuki can manage. After all I done all these years." She bit her lip and dug in her pocket for a tissue.

Jori offered one from the box at her elbow and waited for the woman to calm a bit.

"Sorry about that." Sarah offered Jori a small smile and, without seeming to realize it, reached down and began stroking Yuki, who had stood up to lean against her leg. "It's just a bit much what with a dog to look after on top of Mike."

Jori almost jumped in, but Sarah looked like she had more to say so Jori sat on her impulse.

The older woman looked at the floor. "It's not been easy since Mike come home from the Gulf War. Never been able to hold down a job for long, on account of mobility issues. So, I worked and looked after him and the kids." She looked up suddenly. "But I never minded that. The kids are grown up now and need their lives to be their own. Me and Mike have a routine."

Jori nodded.

"Then along comes this dog." She gave Yuki a sorrowful glance. "Yuki takes away from me the fun part of being with Mike. She makes him laugh."

She glanced at Jori, eyes red with the strain of holding back tears. "It sounds stupid. But it's like Mike's suddenly got someone else on the side. Don't that sound crazy?"

"No." Kelli had said it wasn't unusual for family members, especially wives, to resent the intrusion of a service dog into their lives. It was especially true for those who had done the caregiving for so long that to think of relinquishing any part of it seemed like failing or cheating.

Sarah sniffed a couple of times then gave herself a little shake. "I can't have that dog in my house. Not when Mike lavishes more affection on him than he does on me in a given day. Mike's even talking about them going fishing in the spring. For years I couldn't hardly get him outta the house for nothing. Even church. But give him a dog and he's thinks he's Huckleberry Finn!"

So the problem wasn't Yuki's failure to bond with Mike, but his success.

Jori watched the fissures form in the woman's mask of resentment. Behind it lay years of worry and weariness, and neglect.

Her instinct was to reach out and hug her. But she suspected proud and stubborn Sarah Williams wouldn't welcome sympathy. Still, she took the chance and reached her arms toward the woman.

Sarah surged into them, hugging her tightly as she broke into tight little sobs.

Without letting go, Jori stretched out her leg and pushed the door shut.

They held on to each other for a little time until Sarah let go first.

When she had mopped up her face, Sarah stared off into space for a moment. "I told myself I wasn't going to make a scene. Now I've gone and made a first-class fool of myself. Jealous of a dog." She glanced at Jori. "You must think I'm Looney Tunes."

Jori smiled. "I think you're strong and hardworking. I think you love Mike. And I know you're exhausted. You need some time for yourself."

"When am I supposed to do that?" The defiant Sarah was back in charge. "Where's the hour in a week for me to do anything more than I'm doing?"

Jori glanced down at Yuki. There were a dozen practical suggestions she could make, but she doubted that the exhausted and combative woman in front of her would hear them.

"I've got an idea." Jori stuffed two more tissues in the woman's hands. "I'll be right back."

Jori opened the office door and glanced around, hoping one of the men who worked or volunteered at WWP would be around. Maxine, who'd just come in from the back, intercepted her. "You got your hands full there."

"Yes. I need you to do something for me. Find Jake. Tell him there's a man in a truck parked outside. And could he take him somewhere, buy him a meal? Talk to him? Do whatever men do. I need at least two hours."

"Okay. But what are planning to do about Mrs. Williams?"

Jori smiled. "Do you know a beautician who could work a client in ASAP?"

An hour later, Sarah Williams was laughing and gossiping with the other clients in the Cut, Curl or Dye Boutique as if it were a weekly experience. She didn't seem at all fazed by the fact it was a black salon.

"I just love all the pretty things in here. I haven't been inside a woman's salon in ten years."

Leila, the salon owner and Maxine's cousin, met Jori's gaze in the mirror. "Then shame on you, Ms. Williams. You been going to a barber, haven't you?"

Sarah nodded. "I take Mike. After the children grew up I just naturally found myself sitting in a chair beside him. Besides, a woman's salon is expensive and I don't have time to fool with hair."

"You gave up too much. When I finish this cut I'm going to show you how a handful of mousse, the right lipstick, and some mascara makes you good to go."

"No makeup. No time for it."

"Uh-huh." Leila just kept snipping, shaping Sarah's mannish mullet into a softer feminine style.

Five minutes later Sarah was blinking at herself in the mirror. "Is that me?"

"It's you. Only better." Leila held up three items. "For dress you use the same rosy lipstick for your mouth and cheeks. Dab it on the apples just like I showed you. For every day you use clear gloss to keep your lips soft and dab a little on your lids to give you a bit of shine. Apply mascara. Thirty seconds and you're good to go. It takes longer than that to pee. Now give me your cell phone so I can take a few photos for you to show one of those grocery store haircut places what the cut is supposed to look like."

"It's a miracle." Sarah kept staring at herself in Jori's passenger-side mirror on the drive back to WWP.

"You know," Jori began conversationally. "There's another way to think about Yuki. He's not just there for Mike. He's there for your peace of mind, too. You've got backup. Let Mike fuss with her, brush her, feed her, play with her. That gives you time to do other things while Yuki keeps tabs."

Sarah shrugged. "You really think it's safe to trust a dog with all that?"

"I could put you in touch with a couple of our other veterans' wives. They would be able tell you more than I can."

Sarah touched the hair feathered out across her cheek. "I wouldn't know what to do with spare time."

"Time you found out, maybe?" Jori chuckled. "But don't get too relaxed. We can't teach our dogs to cook a pot roast or tell a joke. And they'll never replace a good woman."

As they rounded a corner, Sarah turned to gaze wistfully at the box store they were passing. "Seems a shame not have a new outfit to go with this haircut."

Forty-five minutes later they entered the WWP building. Kelli, Jake, and Mike were drinking coffee and chatting.

"Well now, don't you look pretty." Mike came to his feet on his braces and crutches, a big grin on his face for his wife. "Sarah, you look like a bride."

"You're overdoing it, Mike." Sarah took a friendly swat at her husband's arm. Her smile was as wide as sunshine.

Kelli winked at Jori. "Why don't you both come into my office for a moment?"

Within ten minutes, the Williamses were on their way home, Yuki happily stashed in the backseat of their truck.

Kelli came up to Jori. "Thank you."

"My pleasure. I just took a chance. And I know what you're thinking. A little makeup and a decent haircut won't make her life any easier."

Kelli grinned. "Then you for sure can't read my mind. I was thinking you pulled off a miracle. You've got a knack for dealing with people. Sometimes that's harder than working with the dogs. Good job."

Jori basked in the glow of Kelli's praise all the way home.

It wasn't until she was alone that she allowed herself to even think of how lucky the Williamses were to have each other. Even with the burden of his disabilities.

Ten days and not a single message or phone call from Battise.

He'd warned her. But then he'd called and asked for her to come to Springdale.

She'd seen the real Battise. The lawman who set his own welfare aside to serve and protect others. And the troubled man who wanted desperately to hide his weaknesses. Seeing all that had made her want so much to be with this flesh-and-blood imperfect man. The trouble was, he didn't want to acknowledge that man.

Too bad. She was very much afraid she had fallen for

him. Even with the dents and rust and mileage, he was more of a man than any other she'd ever known. So it might be hard, maybe close to impossible to be with him. But she was going to make him let her try.

"It beats the hell out of being alone."

She was going to give him time, until Christmas Day. By then she might just dress up like that Dutch-girl elf he'd so admired in Eureka Springs, and show up on his doorstep. What would be the worst that could happen?

She knew him well enough to know he wouldn't turn her away if she started undressing. After that, well, one step at a time.

Argyle jumped up in her lap, purring and pawing, looking for the perfect spot.

# CHAPTER TWENTY-FIVE

Law was humming along to Johnny Cash's version of "I Won't Back Down" on the radio as he turned off High Sky Inn Road onto the paved strip of road that led to his cabin. It was raining and the forecast promised sleet then snow as the day wore on. Right now there was little to see beyond fine mist blowing in the beams of his headlights. Though the sky had shifted from navy blue to sullen gray, the hollows in the winding road were still pitch black. He'd worked a night shift at his desk. But he didn't mind. Two things had him smiling.

One, he'd be taking his physical the following morning. After he passed it, he'd be fully reinstated and ready for active duty.

Two, the morning's headline news story was fresh in his mind.

NORTHWEST ARKANSAS DRUG SWEEP ARRESTS DOZENS.

Even as he started to go over in his thoughts the details of the earlier newscast, the radio station news came on.

"The Central Arkansas Drug Task Force, assisted by other local, state, and federal agencies carrying warrants, arrested sixty-seven people in the early hours of this morning. Warrants were issued as part of a sweeping federal investigation into corruption and drug trafficking. Several additional people were arrested in Missouri and Oklahoma. The Arkansas arrests include four law enforcement officers who are accused of accepting bribes to watch over drug shipments crossing state lines. Further arrests are expected. The major surprise of the drug bust is Harold Tice, majority shareholder and CEO of Tice Industries. Mr. Tice, sequestered in his home, is expected to turn himself in at the courthouse later today. Three other men and a woman are still at large as of this newscast. Their names will be released at a task force news conference scheduled for eight a.m."

Law turned off the radio. So Faded Blue Eyes was telling him the truth. Too bad he couldn't have been in on that.

He glanced over at Samantha, dozing peacefully on the seat. Since the major meltdown in Eureka Springs, he'd been feeling stronger. The daytime flashbacks were all but gone. Even the night terrors had lessened in frequency and intensity. He supposed he had Sam's diligence to let him know that was true. That didn't mean the worse attacks were gone forever. No one could promise that. Still, he couldn't very well go back on patrol with a doodle as backup. He had a decision to make.

He'd given it some thought. He didn't want another K-9 assignment. Something had changed with the loss of Scud. He couldn't put his finger on it. He'd thought it was anger and grief and guilt making him reject the thought. It was those things. They didn't, however, entirely explain the reason he didn't want to have another K-9 partner. Something inside him just felt . . . different.

Images of Jori kept him company when he did feel— what did she call it? The blue devils. A sissy name for what he dealt with but, strangely enough, the name helped.

Several counselors he'd dealt with in the early days had suggested he visualize pleasant memories to counteract flashbacks. They'd never worked for him. Perhaps because he had so few. Until lately.

Imagining himself lying next to Jori, naked and sated from making love, gave him peace of mind, and a hard-on. Oh well, nothing was perfect.

He glanced at his cell as it vibrated. Jori. This would be her fifth call of the morning, after a week of asked-for silence. She probably wanted to talk about the news, and ask him about Tice.

He didn't have anything for her yet. Until he did, he wasn't going to risk talking with her. It would be their final conversation. He wasn't ready for that. Wasn't at all ready to let go of the best thing that had ever happened to him.

Still, he knew how to sacrifice for the greater good. That good, being her. He'd be a burden. She deserved better. He wanted her to have the best. That wasn't him.

He grunted. Guess he'd learned not to be so selfish, after all.

Except he wasn't ready for that final conversation.

He turned off the blacktop onto the gravel drive leading up to his cabin. The sight of a strange truck in his yard didn't alarm him. He'd been avoiding reporters for two weeks. He'd just have thought the news of Tice's imminent arrest would have outstripped a two-week-old story about a one-legged police officer.

His headlights gave him the first clue.

Missouri license plates. Not a reporter.

Law rolled to a stop fifty feet short. All his senses on alert. He lived in the woods for privacy. But that same privacy had liabilities. Whoever drove that truck would have heard him coming long before he saw that he had company. That didn't mean he didn't have a few advantages.

The obvious advertisement painted on the side of his vehicle: STATE TROOPER. Being the law had its uses. Even with perps.

His headlights on bright to illuminate the area ahead, he waited a few seconds to see if anyone would exit the truck, or his front door. When that didn't happen, he reached back to release the safety on his holster then eased out of his cruiser, leaving the door open as a shield.

His guest might be some innocent civilian. Whoever it was, he was about to scare the bejabbers out of his uninvited guest.

"State police. Show yourself." At that moment he heard Sam's low growl and swung around. But it was too late.

"Stop right there, Battise. Don't make me shoot you."

He couldn't see the face of the man who'd been lying in wait for him. The guy had used the bright shaft of a high-beam flashlight to momentarily blind him. But he did recognize the voice.

"Pecker."

"Turn around real slow. You know the drill."

Law didn't move, hand still on his holstered weapon, though he could not make out the barrel of Becker's drawn weapon in the light. "You're one of the fugitives, are you?"

"You don't want to test me, Battise. I'm cold and getting wetter by the second. I want to talk to you. That's all I came for. Talk. Now turn around. Hands on the back of your neck."

Law turned around slowly. He'd have another opportunity.

"Kick your door shut. I don't want to have to shoot your mutt."

"No. She'll freeze out here."

"What the fuck am I supposed to do about that?"

"Let me call her. I'll put the leash on her. You've seen her. She's harmless. Sam! Heel, girl."

Even as the words left his lips Law hated saying them. Every K-9 he'd ever partnered with would have had Becker already on the ground and subdued without his command. It was an innate instinct in most dogs, even pets, to defend the pack. Sam was growling. But she lacked the bite drive of a German shepherd or Malinois. He wouldn't risk her going for Becker and getting shot.

Sam leaped out of the car, head low. "Sam, heel." Her gaze still on Becker, she moved to Law and bounced up on his chest to check him out.

Law looked down. "Good girl. Down. Heel. Now I'm going to attach her leash, Becker. Don't get squirrelly on me while I reach in my pocket."

"Use one hand. And move slowly so I can see everything." Becker watched Law attach Sam's leash. "Now move away the hell from the cruiser. Three easy side steps. That's right. Take off your rig. Use only your left hand. No, fuck. You're left-handed, aren't you? Right hand. That's right. Now extend the belt out the full length of your arm. Drop it and take three steps forward. Two more. Nice and easy."

Becker moved in behind Law, careful to maintain his distance. "Now head for the house. I'm only going to warn you once. Make a move of any kind and I'll shoot you and your dog."

The rain was already changing to ice. Law could feel it freezing on his face and on the ground. It caused his prosthetic foot to slide ever so slightly on the gravel as he resumed the walk toward his cabin. He had to concentrate not to slip. Becker wouldn't get far if this kept up. Winter in the Ozarks could be as dangerous and sudden as anywhere in the Lower Forty-Eight. Mountain roads and ice did not mix well. Add in the winds that whipped through the narrow hollows at fifty-plus miles an hour and the roads became deadly.

They reached the porch, Law six feet ahead. He thought

about pushing through the door and taking his chances that he'd make it to the hearth and the loaded pistol he kept in the stack of firewood before Becker got to him. Lousy odds.

Once inside, Becker lowered his gun. But he didn't holster it. "Now, this is better. Been freezing my nuts off waiting for you."

Law turned around slowly. "What's this about?"

"I need to get out of Arkansas."

"I can't help you."

"Oh, I think you can. And you will want to when you hear what I've got to say. Now get down on your knees."

"I can't do that. Prosthesis."

"I saw that video of you chasing the robber. You two were rolling around on the ground like a couple of puppies. You'll find a way." He raised his weapon. "Now. If you touch the knife strapped to your leg I will shoot you."

"In the back? That's a damn cowardly thing to do."

"I'll shoot your dog."

Law stiffened. Not Sam's fault she didn't have a killer instinct. "Let me sit in a chair."

"Okay. But slow. I swear, one move and I'll plug that curly bag of bones and tag you, too."

Law made his way to the kitchen table, hands still behind his head. He could judge by Becker's footsteps that he was staying far enough away to have a clear shot if he moved to attack. But Becker sounded exhausted. He'd probably spent hours in the cold and dark. That would make him distractible, but also unpredictable. He wasn't about to underestimate a longtime trooper like Becker.

When Law had seated himself, Becker moved in behind him and placed the barrel of his gun against the nape of his neck. "I'm just going to cuff you so we can talk without a problem. I'm trying to do the right thing here." He cuffed Law, hands behind his back, with flex cuffs.

When he was done, he moved back in front of Law and said, "I've had nothing to do with the drug trade. I'm a cop. Traffickers are the scum of the earth. Those other officers they arrested this morning have no honor."

"It's me you're talking to, Becker. I know you're on the take with Tice. I know someone sent you to the Springdale office to spy on me. And I know you broke in here looking for something. Was it evidence I was collecting on Tice? You were helping him cover up drug dealings."

"No. It wasn't like that. I had information the Tices were willing to pay me to keep quiet about. Nothing to do with drugs but good enough to ruin a political career." Becker grinned, looking a little more relaxed. "That's what I want to talk to you about. It'll cost you your truck, some cash, and a twenty-four-hour head start to get my information. Then I'll give you enough to ruin Tice."

"No."

Becker smirked. "You think you're too good to do a deal?"

"What deal? I let you get away and you promise to phone me from Brazil and tell me about the Tices? A six-year-old could see the problem with that bargain."

Becker nodded. "What if I could guarantee that Luke Tice will end up in jail?"

"The feds are taking care of that as we speak."

Becker shook his head. "That'll never stick on Luke. His dad, maybe. But he can buy enough lawyers to keep this mess tied up in court for the next ten years. Luke is slick as shit. He'll rally sympathy. Might even win the election because his poor daddy's been indicted. You've seen stranger things happen."

Law didn't argue. "Why do you care?"

"I hate to see a bad man get away."

"Since he's no longer paying you."

Becker's face went crimson. "I was holding them to

account." He thumbed his nose. "You know, it was so simple. I didn't have anything but a hunch. But I worked it out in such a way that I could benefit on both sides, father and son."

"That must have been some hunch." Law was watching Becker's every action, calculating the odds of which chance to take when. He needed to keep him talking while he did that.

"I need money and your vehicle."

"I'm broke. My truck is yours. Keys in my rig outside."

Becker swore under his breath. "I'll give you this much, Battise. The father was paying to keep the son out of the news. The son was paying to keep the father from knowing the truth."

"I'm impressed you could play the pair off each other like that."

Becker nodded. "What I got could get your girlfriend what she wants."

"What do you think that is?"

"Revenge. Papa Tice says your piece of ass wants revenge for her time behind bars."

"Unlike you, she really wasn't guilty."

Becker's face swelled again with anger. "I don't have time for this. You interested in a deal or not?"

"Not."

"A regular Boy Scout." Becker glanced around the room as his thumb played with the safety.

"If you've got information, take it to the feds, Becker. Cut a deal. Lighten your sentence."

"No deal will keep me out of prison. I can't go to prison. I'm a cop. You know what'll happen."

"The feds could send you out of state. Give you a new identity in prison. If you know enough you can make that deal."

"No." He slid the back of his hand over his mouth. "I'm

not going behind bars like the scum I put away. Douche-bags getting to see me locked up? I can't do that. If you won't deal, then I need a hostage."

He raised the barrel and thumbed the safety, then palmed one into the chamber. He aimed his weapon at Law's good leg. "Don't make me regret what I'll have to do next if you don't cooperate. I'm going to need your leg."

"Fuck you."

Becker chuckled and moved in behind him.

"Sorry about this, Battise. I kinda always respected you. Guess I still do, you son of a bitch."

Becker's left arm encircled Law's neck. Law braced his feet against the floor and kicked hard. Overturning the chair and himself, and causing Becker to fall. But the bastard had him. Becker had placed the palm of the hand against Law's shoulder. As he applied pressure on both sides of his neck. Law felt the white-hot shock of rage before he passed out.


Jori was surprised to see Law's truck pulling out on the highway just as she approached. She honked, trying to get his attention, but the truck turned off in the opposite direction.

She'd tried calling him half a dozen times on the drive but he wouldn't pick up. She doubted he'd even listened to her messages. Stubborn man!

The news of Tice's arrest had stunned her. She had a dozen questions and she was certain Law had information the public wouldn't get. So here she was, two hours later, arriving just as he was leaving. The ice had begun to build up on the trees, rain freezing on contact. Another hour and she wouldn't have attempted the trip.

She blew her horn a second time as she passed the turn-off, following the truck instead.

To her surprise, the truck speeded up.

"Dammit, Law. Stubborn male."

He didn't want to see her. Well, tough. She'd driven all the way up here to—A cursory glance in her rearview made her foot reach for the brakes.

Sam was galloping down the road behind her. Why would Law leave Sam behind?

Jori pulled over and opened the passenger-side door.

Sam bolted into the front seat, shaking rain and sleet from her coat. And then she barked.

Jori looked up. Law's truck had disappeared around a bend.

Jori shut the door and put her foot on the gas. The SUV tires spun before getting traction.

"Dammit. It's icing up." Jori looked at Sam. "Sorry, it's going to be rough."

She put her foot more carefully on the gas, increasing slowly only as she felt the SUV roll forward. It was well past daybreak but it seemed like dusk with the deep shadows of the mountainside surrounding her. She could hear the sleet pinging softly on the windshield as she edged her way along in second gear.

The road took a sharp turn, the grade climbing upward toward a sharp drop-off. She had passed an earlier highway commission warning sign about the steep grade coming up, telling truckers to shift to lower gears. She was already in second on the climb up.

She held her breath as she edged her car forward. She didn't like ice. Drove on it only when absolutely necessary. Seeing Law seemed absolutely necessary until this moment.

She made it to the top of the grade by sheer will at a crawl of less than four miles an hour. But her stomach dropped to her feet as she crested the top and stared out across the edge of the curved road, about to head steeply downward.

There were skid marks on the road and a gap in the railing on the outside. Bare broken branches still swayed, flinging icicles onto the road. Out and beyond the break and drop-off was a pair of high beams arching through the darkness below.

"Oh my God. Law!"

# *CHAPTER TWENTY-SIX*

Jori's hands shook as she fumbled to plug her cell phone into its charger and punched 911 for the third time. Maybe more juice would help the call get through.

*Don't think about what just happened. Don't think about it. Don't think.*

There was a single ring this time. Even before she could react in joy, the line went dead.

"Oh, come on!" She glanced at the bars, swinging her phone around on her extended arm inside the SUV, seeking a stronger signal. One bar, then the NO SERVICE message came on. Hills made a joke of wireless coverage claims.

Jori closed her eyes then opened them immediately. Mistake.

*Don't think about what just happened. Don't think about it. Don't think.*

She couldn't call for help. She needed to go for help.

Jori stepped on the gas. The SUV jerked forward.

"Crap!" Too much, too fast. The road was slick from rain, and getting slicker from the fact that the water was turning to ice on contact with all surfaces.

Yet even as she applied the brakes softly, the SUV continued to roll because she was now over the crest of the rise. The grade was steep. Too steep for her to attempt. She applied a tiny bit more pressure and felt the back end began to fishtail.

*Take your foot off the accelerator.* She could practically hear her father's voice in her ear as he taught her to drive. *Don't apply the brakes until tires regain traction.*

In the time it took to think those two thoughts, the SUV found traction and slowed as the rear tires grabbed asphalt. But now her vehicle was smack in the middle of the road and turned almost sideways, pointed toward the outside edge.

"Oh God! Oh God! Oh God!" Heart thundering in her chest, she glanced over the hood and down over the edge for the first time since she'd seen the accident. Her heart nearly stopped.

Fifty yards away and maybe two dozen feet down, blazing headlights illuminated a swath of evergreen trees, the only indication in the gloom that there was a vehicle down below. Law was down there. He needed help but she couldn't get it.

Sam whimpered, scratching at the passenger-side door as if she sensed something had happened and what needed to be done.

"I know. I know. It's going to be okay." Jori gave her slow hard strokes from neck to tail. A frantic dog wasn't going to help. "I'll think of something."

Sam was shaking, a combination of her own exertions, her wet fur, and the anxiousness pouring from Jori.

Even as she tried her phone for the fourth time, texting a message in the hope it might get through when a phone signal would not, she noticed that her windshield wipers were no longer able to scrape away all the ice from the glass. She looked at the thermometer. Thirty-one degrees, the magic number for disaster. The severe weather was arriving earlier than forecast. She had to get Law help.

She knew he must be hurt. Equally, she refused to even acknowledge the possibility of anything worse.

She needed a plan. She needed to get to him. To tend to his injuries. Keep him warm until help came. Three things.

"I can do this." She said the words aloud to help make herself believe them.

Except help. What would bring help if her cell phone wouldn't work down at the crash site?

Inventory.

She needed to think about what she could carry with her to accomplish her goals before she stepped out into the sharp cold slowly encasing her world in ice. Once she was out, every second counted. The freezing rain was forecast to change into snow, eventually. Snow would be easier to deal with.

"Please, let it snow." The thought came and went. She had to deal with what was, not wishes.

"Inventory, Jori. Think."

But nothing came to mind. Her heart was in that wrecked truck below. Her brain was stalled. Nothing else came to mind. She was wasting precious seconds.

She thumped the horn, making long hard blasts. "Dammit, think!"

Whining in distress, Sam leaned in and licked her face. "Stop. I don't have time for a dog—" A lightbulb went on. She grabbed Sam and hugged her neck. "Thank you!"

Working with dogs for a living made her more prepared for emergencies than most pet owners. Training included first aid for dogs. Like Law, she carried a full canine first-aid kit and two blankets. There was also the roadside emergency kit her father had sent her when she bought this SUV. At the time she'd wondered when she'd ever need it, other than maybe the booster cables. But canned compressed air, bungee cords, and flares? Flares! Flares were good. They could be used to mark the way.

But first she needed to find Law.

She leaned across Sam and opened her glove compartment. A big heavy flashlight rolled out into her hand.

As she stuffed the flashlight into a pocket of her micropuff jacket, she gazed at the goldendoodle with misgivings. Service dogs were taught to find things when given a direct order. Sam would certainly help her find her way to Law. But the weather would be hard on her. Sam didn't have protective clothing.

Jori pulled up the hood of her jacket and tied it tightly around her face then leaned her head against Sam's. "You have to stay here. I'll crack a window but leave the engine running for you for heat."

Why was she talking to a dog? Because she badly needed to bounce her thoughts off someone. And Sam was watching her with the intensity she displayed when learning a new game. Her ears were up, eyebrows twitching, her body ready to react as her gaze shifted intently with Jori's every move. As if she might be asked to repeat them. Sam was more than a warm body. Sam knew things.

Jori pushed open her door. As she did so, she heard sounds of an engine close by. Her heart stumbled and she scrambled out onto the road. Another car. Someone to help her.

She moved to the front of her truck so she could be seen, head swiveling left and right to catch sight of approaching headlights. But nothing moved in either direction through the dreary blue-gray morning misted by sleet. The only light, other than her own vehicle, came from a house across the valley. That faint light might as well have been from a star. Too far away to help her.

After a few miserable seconds more, Jori realized the engine sounds she heard were coming from the wreckage.

That sent a shudder through her . Movie and video images of exploding autos papered her thoughts. Fuel leaks igniting. Greasy engine parts catching fire.

"No. Focus, dammit." The shouted words brought her back to reality. An empty freezing stretch of roadway. Sheet bouncing in micro beads off her face. No other human sound in the world. Only the musical tinkle in the overhead branches of freezing rain turning into ice crystals.

A shudder of cowardice quaked through her. She was already cold, scared, and clumsy. She wasn't very brave, and she certainly wasn't a trail climber or outdoorsperson. She might only end up another casualty. But she was all the help Law was going to get. For now.

Until she got to Law. Law would know what to do. But she had to get to him first.

Holding that thought in her mind, Jori made her way to the back of her SUV. She had on boots, but they weren't especially helpful with traction on the slick road.

She shoved her cell phone into her pocket and discovered long-forgotten gloves. Happily she tugged them on.

Sam barked as she opened the hatch, and jumped with paws over the backseat.

"No. Sam. Stay."

She began sorting through things. Yes, the first-aid kit was there. And the bulkier auto emergency kit. And two blankets. She set the first two items on the ground and tucked the two blankets under an arm.

As she reached up to close the hatch Sam launched herself across the backseat and out the rear of the SUV.

"No, Sam." Jori turned to go after her and nearly lost her footing.

Sam stood watching her for a second then barked and headed off down the road, nose to the roadway.

Jori shook her head. She didn't have time to chase Sam. With luck the dog would follow her.

She picked up her kits and moved to the edge of the
road. The first few feet of the drop-off were steep, as if a
giant shovel had gouged a piece out of the hillside.

Sam barked. She was twenty feet away, back toward the
curving crest where the truck had left the highway. She
barked again, several excited barks, and began pacing back
and forth in a lazy eight, spinning once, then retracing
herself and shaping a zigzag pattern of sniffs as she walked
toward the rim.

Jori knew what Sam was looking for. The same thing
she was. She could only guess that perhaps Sam, familiar
with Law's truck, had found the smell of Law's tires on
the roadway, recognized them, and knew the trail went
downhill. The dog might not know there was a wreck
ahead. But she scented something that had her dancing as
her barks became more strident and urgent.

Jori half walked, half slid her way up to where Sam
stood on the roadway, trying to find a way to step down into
the valley.

"Okay. Okay." She was yelling because she had moved
out of the sheltering mountain's curvature. The wind
whipped up from the valley, hitting her full in the face.
Perhaps Sam had caught the scent of Law and/or his truck
in the wind. Sam's scent base would include things like
Law's truck in which she regularly rode.

Jori turned her back and moved to the edge, off the roadway. There was a narrow strip of black-tarred gravel, not
even enough to call a shoulder, and then nothing. She put
down her things and reached for the flashlight. The beam
showed her a sheer drop of about six feet, the same as
before. She couldn't handle that.

She began walking the rim, pointing the flashlight over
the edge. Sam danced along beside her, barking occasionally, as if to hurry her along. Finally, about ten yards farther, she found a slope of earth. Not more than two feet

wide. It angled downward like a ramp dug into the hillside.

Sam at her heels, Jori hurried back to pick up her things, swearing when she nearly fell again. The road's smooth surface was quickly becoming a skating rink. Surely once she was off the road into the dirt and trees, the ground would be drier, not yet frozen and thus easier to navigate. She thought for two seconds about putting Sam on a leash. But if she fell or Sam did, and they got tangled up in the underbrush, the leash could break Sam's neck or strangle her. No, the dog was better left off leash.

Sam watched her, head down and still, as Jori touched first one boot and then the other over the edge. Her arms were full. She held her flashlight in the same hand as the auto kit. No way to catch herself if she went down. But she needed the supplies.

Her right foot slipped a little in wet mud but her left foot found solid footing in rougher rutted ground strewn with gravel, sticks, and leaves. Slowly, one foot at a time, she moved down the makeshift ramp until she was only head and shoulders above ground.

This seemed to be Sam's signal that it was time for action.

Sam moved in behind her, snuffling as she went.

"No, Sam. Stop." Sam was prodding her, nose at the middle of Jori's back.

"Okay, good girl. Go slow, Sam." Jori spoke automatically. Her concentration was on the ground in front of her. Or rather below her. The ramp didn't extend very far. About four feet ahead, it sluiced back into the hillside.

"Crap." Jori froze. What was she going to do now?

Impatient with the delay, Sam barked and pushed past her.

*"Aaah!"*

Dumped off the trail by the dog, Jori fell several feet

and began sliding on a combination of rain, mud, and soaked leaves. First on one knee and then on her butt, she pinwheeled down a steep slope interspersed with tree trunks, leafless limbs, and vines that looped through the undergrowth like trip wires. A tree limb struck her right wrist, forcing her fingers to open and release one of the kits.

"Crap!" Angry tears filled her eyes.

With her free hand she grabbed a vine and jerked herself to a stop. It happened so fast she couldn't process it all. She felt nothing for a second but relief that she wasn't dead.

Then pain flared to life. Her wrist. Her shoulder. Her knees.

"Dammit, Sam!"

She sat up and looked around. She could still see the rim of the road backlit by the gray sky maybe twenty-five feet above her. She hadn't fallen that far. But she'd lost the auto emergency kit. No flares. No blankets. She didn't want to waste time looking for them.

Her flashlight lay farther down the slope, its light half buried in a tangle of dry brush. She climbed to her feet, ignoring the pain in her ankle, and flexed her hand around the first-aid kit. She had that much.

The silence was suddenly split with a dog's excited barks, from below her.

"Sam! Law?" Sam had found Law. She was sure of it.

Jori scrambled to stay on her feet as she began moving through the treacherous but less steep woodlands. The sounds of Sam's barks were her beacon. Sam had found Law. Law would know what to do. All she had to do was get to him.

She paused when she finally saw the truck. It had landed on or rolled onto its roof. The front end was crumpled and the tires were all shredded. But the cab remained intact. Everything was still. No Sam. No barking. No sounds but the moaning of the wind high overhead and the growing silvery jingle of icicles.

Why wasn't Sam still barking?

Jori moved forward slowly. She just knew it was going to end well. That Law was hurt maybe. But surely, he would be okay. She forced her feet forward. Her heart thumping so hard her body shook with each beat. The wind shoved her along, almost against her will. Whatever was here, whatever she found, she'd have to deal with it.

"Oh, Law."

Jori approached the passenger side, set her teeth over her bottom lip, and ducked her head to aim her flashlight into the truck cab. All the windows were broken out, making access easy.

Law lay on his back on the roof at an awkward angle. Another man's body hung, nightmare-like, from the front seat on the driver's side. But her only focus was Law.

His face was wet with blood. Sam had wedged herself in and around him for protection. But it was the look in his eyes when he recognized her that stunned her.

"Jori? What the hell are you doing here?"

# CHAPTER TWENTY-SEVEN

"Nice to see you, too."

Jori's reply was pure reflex. Nothing close to the got-my-act-together quip it seemed to be. Her voice was hoarse from the cold. She was soaked and shaking. Her thighs trembled from exertion. Her shoulder and left hand ached from the fall she'd taken. She hadn't any expectations beyond hoping to find Law alive.

Was he even glad to see her?

Law blinked, as if he didn't trust what he was looking at. Then his expression turned grim. "As long as you're here you can be useful. First, move this doodle off me." His voice was curt but calm.

Still reeling from his lack of welcome, she crawled in far enough to reach out and grab the edge of Sam's service vest. She tugged. "Come on, Sam."

Sam wiggled back, ready to stand her ground. She could probably smell Law's injuries and wanted to protect him.

"It's okay. You're a good girl. Yes, you found him." Jori's hand went to her pocket where she kept treats. It was an automatic move made dozens of times in a day, yet she was surprised to find a few nuggets. She held out one. "Good Sam. Get your treat."

Sam nosed the nugget in Jori's palm but then looked back at Law.

Law spoke up. "Yes. Good Sam. You get a treat."

For the first time since she'd known him, he'd used the high-energy excited voice of a K-9 trainer to motivate Sam. It worked.

Sam crawled forward and took the treat. As she reached for several more, Jori noticed that Law wasn't looking at her. In fact, he seemed oddly still. He didn't try to shove Sam or even pet her. His body was at an awkward angle, his hands out of sight. Just how injured was he?

Frowning, Jori tugged on Sam's vest harder. "Come on, girl. Move over here."

This time Sam did move. Six inches. Then she looked back over her shoulder with twitching nose and ears on full alert.

Jori looked at Law. "How badly hurt are you?"

Instead of answering, he half rolled onto his stomach so that Jori could see his hands were bound by flex cuffs. "Find something to cut these with. I need to get to Becker before he bleeds out."

For the first time since crawling into the cab, Jori let her gaze move from Law's face. The first thing she saw was that she was kneeling not in just rainwater but in mud mixed with blood. Something awful had happened. Law was cuffed. A prisoner.

A strong reaction spasmed her stomach. For one wild second she thought she might be ill.

"Jori. Jori, look at me. It's not my blood."

She opened her eyes to focus again on Law. Rolled back onto his bound hands, he stared at her with a steady penetrating gaze.

"Go to the truck bed. Open my toolbox. Find pliers, wire cutters. Something with a sharp edge."

Jori crawled backward, sparing only a quick glance at the man strung upside down in his shoulder harness and seat belt. There was blood dripping from his shoulder but it came from higher up. His eyes were open but he didn't seem to know she was there. A dozen questions about why he had done this to Law flashed through her mind, but it wasn't time to get answers to any of them.

One more quick glance at Law's grim face and she was backing out into the cold.

The rain had shifted over to sleet. BB-sized bits of ice on the push of the wind whipped and stung her face. The ground around her was growing white. As she moved toward the bed of the overturned truck, steadying herself on the damaged metal side, she realized her right hand was bare. She hadn't noticed when or how she'd lost her glove. It didn't matter. Nothing else mattered. Not even Law's less-than-happy-to-see-you greeting mattered at the moment. She had a job to do. Find a tool that could free him.

She had to drop to her knees to get in under the bed to locate the toolbox. The lid was bent, and when she pulled on the latch nothing happened. She tugged twice more, her cold fingers beginning to cramp.

"Crap." She shimmied back on her knees and looked around for something she could use as a lever to pry it open. A few feet away she saw what looked like a jack handle. She stood up and took a few hurried steps. And fell.

"Shit!"

"Jori?" She heard worry in Law's tone but she didn't have time to reassure him.

She came to her feet, trying to dig her heels into the freezing ground with each step. *Get the jack handle.* It became her entire focus. Five steps and she had it.

She made it back without falling again, and ducked under the side of the truck bed. She jammed one end of the tool into the latch of the toolbox and jerked. Nothing. She jerked several more times. It wouldn't give.

"Screw this. Open up!" This time she half stood and as she jerked she added the full weight of her body to the jack handle.

The truck rocked back and forth, making sickening sounds as metal ground against metal—and then the truck began to slide.

Frightened, Jori fell back, bumping her head on the lip of the truck bed as she scrambled crab-like for safety. She heard Sam bark and a man cry out in pain. Almost as quickly as it began, the trunk shimmied to a stop barely a yard away. It was enough to reveal the ground scattered with the contents of the toolbox.

"Yes." Jori pumped her fist in the air and then grabbed up an assortment of wrenches, wire cutters, pliers, anything that looked like it might cut something. With an armful of items, she scrambled back to the passenger side and knelt down.

"Having fun?" Law's voice sounded strangled.

"Fuckin' dandy." She couldn't see him well. The flashlight she'd left in the cab had rolled into the front section during the slide.

She dropped her tools, moved to the front, and reached a hand under the headrest to retrieve it. As she did so the man in the front suddenly reached up and grabbed her by her hoodie.

"Who are you?"

Startled, Jori blindly grasped the first thing to come under her searching hand and swung hard. Her assailant cried out and released his hold. She snatched up the flashlight and shone it in his eyes. "I'm the idiot trying to save your life, asshole!"

She scuttled on her knees to the back section again and shone the light on Law.

This time there was a look of doubt on his face. "Jori. You seem a little overexcited."

"You think?" Her breath was coming quickly, taking in the cold that made her chest ache.

"Ease back, just a tad, before you wear yourself out."

"Turn over. Now."

The light caught a flash in his eye, something she didn't have time to process before he began squirming to turn onto his stomach. The entire time, Sam lay beside him, whining softly as if cooing to a child.

Jori pointed the light on her collection to choose a tool. But the light bounced around. She grabbed the flashlight in both hands to steady it. Of course, she was bordering on hysteria. She could feel it creeping in. But she pushed it back down into whatever hole in her psyche it had slunk out of. Time to fly apart later.

She chose the oversized wire cutters and, going flat on her belly, slid in beside Law. That's when she realized his prosthesis was missing. No time to wonder. She felt with her hands for a spot to cut and then slid the blades in under his right wrist.

The cuffs came off with ease. Two quick snips.

The first thing Law did was lever up, grab her by the shoulders. Hard.

Furious with him, she tried to push him away. He held her tight. His eyes were bright but his face was pale.

"You're no illusion." For the first time he looked close to happy to see her. But Jori was too cold, achy, tired, scared, and worried to accept his version of an apology.

"Lucky for you. Now let go of me. I've got to go find help."

"The hell you are." She tried to move away but he continued to hold her in place with what seemed like very little effort on his part. "You aren't dressed for a long hike. You don't know the terrain. You could get lost."

"Or fall and break a leg, and freeze to death. I know that." Her voice sounded so reasonable. As if she were saying second place wasn't so bad. She didn't know why.

"Look at me, Jori. You're not going. And I don't have a goddamn leg to stand on—literally. So we're both going to stay right here until the storm blows through. At least we've got some shelter."

Jori's gaze went to the man watching them both with hot feverish eyes of pain. He was breathing in short rapid gusts.

"You've got to help me get him down and find where he's bleeding. We can ride this out together."

Jori held his gaze. She suspected Law could very well take care of his former kidnapper, or whatever he was, alone. But she wasn't perfectly sure she could find help.

"Maybe I'm not equipped to go for help. But I know who is."

She looked at Sam, who came instantly alert as if she'd called her name. "Sam's been taught to go for help when her owner is in trouble. We can send her for help."

Law shook his head. "I know search-and-rescue dogs. Sam's not the type."

"Yes, she is. She will find another human to help. That's what she's been trained to do. Even if her owner can't send her for help, she knows to go and seek it."

Jori scrambled back on her knees, making space. "Lie down, Law. And close your eyes."

He watched her for two seconds then went prone.

Jori turned to Sam. "Look, Sam. Law is hurt. We need help." She nudged Law. "Now your turn."

Law opened his eyes and looked at Sam and said in a sharp voice. "Sam. Find help!" He gave the hand signal for *help* Jori had taught Sam.

Sam jumped to her feet, turned and sniffed Law's prone body, stopping at his hip, his left shoulder, and sniffing both wrists. Whatever she read coming off him was enough to convince her to act. She licked his face twice then turned and jumped past Jori to get out.

Jori crawled out of the tiny cramped cabin after Sam into a swirl of ice and tiny flakes.

She stood up and watched Sam orient herself.

The dog stood for a moment, nose up, ears lifted. Jori wasn't at all certain of what Sam was listening for and sniffing out. But she trusted that training and instinct were working together.

Sam barked a couple of times and started off in the direction they had come. But then something—a sound perhaps?—made her stop. She lifted her nose again, ears pricked forward, and turned slowly in a circle until again something caused her to pause. After alerting with rising tail, she ran off in the opposite direction, down the slope.

Jori watched the rusty-red dog, a bright moving blot against the creep of white over the gray landscape until she disappeared below the slope.

"It's a hell of a day to send her out into." Jori had shimmied back through the cab's window.

"We didn't have a choice." Law's tone was grim.

Jori nodded and bit her lip, wondering if she had just sent a wonderful dog on a suicide mission. The weather was brutal. The ice would damage her paws. If she didn't find someone quickly she might not have the stamina to lead them back when she did find help.

"Now you will help me." Becker was pointing his hand with a gun in it at Jori.

# *CHAPTER TWENTY-EIGHT*

*Find Help.*

Sam knew those were very important words. It was a game she had played most of the two and a half years of her life with her trainers. *Find Help* was the toughest game. It meant Alpha was down. Alpha was sick. Alpha was in trouble.

It meant locate and bring back a human, sometimes a stranger, to where Alpha was.

"Find help. Sam."

Sam looked back. The trainer woman was watching her. She would give good treats for the completion of her job.

But treats weren't the only motive in Sam's eagerness. There was a stronger force pushing her. The innate instinct to defend the pack.

Alpha was down.

She could smell anger and fear on Alpha even before she'd found him in the truck. Only it wasn't just from him. A flurry of odors created by injuries blanketed the truck as she'd neared it. Some were from the man with Alpha who had tried to take Alpha away.

Alpha did not like the man. Sam did not like the man.

Sam lowered her head, approaching the driver's side of the truck. She ignored the woman's calls and stuck her head in through the broken window to sniff the man.

Yes, bad man.

He had attacked Alpha.

An attack on Alpha was an attack on the pack.

Alpha down.

Sam would act to defend the pack.

*Find Help.*

Sam circled the truck several times and then ran back the way she had come. But the odors died that way.

She paused and pushed her nose into the cold air. Surprise. The cold wet wind was now spitting ice.

She did not know what it was. But it worried her. Like a horsefly that once stung her nose and eyes and ears.

She stopped to snap at the white stings before she again put her nose into that cold wind.

She turned back from the woods. There were so many new smells on that stinging airstream. Cows and goats and chickens were known. A feral cat family burrowed in an outcropping of rock nearby. Rabbits, beavers, raccoons, squirrels, and deer. All known. But there were spoor of things she'd never even seen.

The cold seem to be crystallizing them before her. She licked at the air. The cold stings landed on her tongue. She tasted plowed fields and wheat chaff and a scrap of corn husk. Things not known.

This new frigid wind bathed her nose in the giant perfume bottle of the earth.

She danced in a circle, breathing in delight. But she soon pulled out of the overwhelming need to catalog every new and old scent.

*Find Help.* That meant human scents.

Humans had odors different from cows and chickens. So many chicken scents in the wind today.

Sam paused and sneezed twice to clear her scent palate. Then she licked her nose and pricked her ears. Humans made sounds, too. It took several seconds to catch the sound's orientation. Yes. There it was. That faint wail of a police siren, followed by several short whoops. It sounded like Alpha's cruiser. He'd turned it on only once. But it was enough.

Sam wheeled and headed out in the opposite direction from the one she and the woman trainer had come.

Find Help was this way.

The white air pelted her, becoming more and more annoying. That and the ground. It was cold, getting harder to sink her claws in for traction. She could not run long.

The white air stung her insides, too. Made white stuff come out of her mouth.

Sam crossed a field and then a ravine, stopping only for the scent of human and the sound of the Alpha cruiser. The ravine was not wet. It was smooth like glass and crusty in places. In one place it gave way, plunging her up to her underbody in a current of liquid chill.

Sam scrambled out and made it to the other side. There she paused and shook herself, trying to make the cold leave her. She licked at her paws, trying to dry them and make the sting of cold go away. But they didn't feel right. And her tongue dragged across hard pads.

*Find Help.*

She shook herself again and lifted her nose. This time human scent. But not in the same direction as the siren. Siren was closer. Human unknown.

Sam did not make a decision so much as follow the instinct bred in her dozens of generations ago.

*Find Help. Help is what you identify with.*

Alpha was siren.

Go to siren.

Sam took off toward a line of telephone poles. The decision made in a fraction of a moment.

A minute later she found a road. Veering left toward the direction where she'd last heard a siren, she picked up speed.


"You sure they'll try to get away in this storm?"

The detective nodded at the trooper as they stood at the roadblock intersecting two rural roads. "They'll definitely try it. Less traffic on the roadways. Easier to slip through. Our tip said they'll use the state roads in this weather."

"Yeah. Remind me how good a capture is going to look on my record, Detective."

"Makes it worth the blue balls, Trooper."

"I'm already afraid to sit down." Another of the task force operatives cradled his weapon to his chest. "My ass is frozen solid. Might crack right off if I apply pressure."

The detective shared the laugh, though he envied the SWAT team member his tactical high-visibility parka. As a detective, he wore his own clothing , but he'd been caught flat-footed by the sudden winter storm and had to borrow a goose-down vest and knit cap. The suit sleeves weren't holding up their end against the sleet.

"No one's been through here in the past twenty minutes. I think I'll duck into my car to check in with the other details to see if they've made a capture."

The state law enforcement officers nodded but exchanged glances that said they knew the fed needed a moment out of the cold. They were made of hardier stuff, drinking scalding coffee from thermoses held in waterproof gloves.

No one noticed the dark red speck coming up the road until they heard a bark.

"Damn. Is that a dog?"

All members of the roadblock turned to look. One trooper pulled high-resolution binoculars from his pocket. "It surely is. And booking it toward us."

"Probably hoping for a cozy lap to curl up in."

"Or a piece of your sandwich."

"I don't think so." The trooper adjusted his binoculars. "She's wearing a service dog vest."

At about fifteen yards out, the dog suddenly stopped and began barking like crazy.

"Something's got her riled."

"Who's in charge of something like this?"

The SWAT guy kicked his head toward the detective's auto.

A trooper knocked on the glass and explained the situation.

The fed stepped out of his car. He stared for a second at the rusty-red dog in a service vest. Fine icicles hung from the fur around her eyes, ears, mouth and beard, and the curly fur on her legs. She was still barking but now running a few feet away and then looking back over her shoulder, as if to signal the need to follow.

"I know that dog." One of the troopers who'd been checking in joined the group. "She belongs to Trooper Lauray Battise."

"That's right." The detective nodded. "I've seen her with him, too. Sam, right?"

The younger trooper started jogged toward her, calling, "Here, Sam. Here, girl."

Sam began barking frantically, backing away as she did so. She stopped and executed a couple of bouncy turns, her barking thinning out from the cold. Then, when the trooper got close, she turned and shot away back down the road she'd come up.

The other men turned to the detective for advice.

He nodded. "One of you better follow her in a car. Service dogs are trained to get help when there's trouble."

"Jori, back out."

Becker held the gun closer to his chest to steady it. "If she moves I'll shoot her."

"If you shoot her, Pecker, I won't just kill you. I'll let you bleed out. Slow." Nothing in Law's expression said he could be moved from this position. "This is between you and me. Jori just made it possible for me to save your life." He tapped the K-9 first-aid kit. "You're bleeding pretty good. There's a tourniquet in here. She goes free. Then we deal."

Becker was sweating even though his every breath was frigid. Finally his gaze shifted to Jori. "Get out."

"But—"

"Jori. Get out. Now. Take cover and wait until I call you. Now." He didn't raise his voice. He didn't have to.

Jori sent one wild pleading look Becker's way and began sliding backward out of the truck's cabin.

Law reached for the tool kit.

Becker jerked away. "What the hell do you think you're doing?"

"About to cut you down, you bastard. Unless you'd just rather die."

"Why would you help me?"

"Because so far, you're just an extortionist asshole. Do you intend to up the ante? If not, put the goddamn gun down."

The two men eyed each other for a long moment.

Becker swallowed. "I've got grandkids."

"Sounds like you're not ready to die."

Law held out his hand.

"It's my leg. I think it's crushed."

"Not a problem. I'm an expert at being a gimp. Teach you all the ropes."

Becker let go of the gun.

# CHAPTER TWENTY-NINE

"*Ahhh. Ahhh.* It hurts like a—"

"No sympathy here, Becker. You threatened to shoot me." Law had loosened the tourniquet a bit to make certain blood was still flowing.

Satisfied, he retightened the strips of cloth. "I don't think Jori is feeling very friendly toward you, either."

Law winked at Jori, who was huddled with them under the truck bed while he worked on Becker.

She didn't smile but he couldn't blame her. It was snowing now, soft flakes that turned the world into a winter wonderland. Gorgeous, but dangerously cold for three people who were not prepared for the exposure.

With Jori's assistance, he'd cut Becker loose. Not having his prosthesis meant he'd had to ask her to help him shift a few things around when he would have preferred she stay dry and huddled out of the wind. But once he'd gotten Becker on the ground, he'd dragged himself and the trooper under the shelter of the truck bed where he could work on him. Jori assisted him with the things he needed from the first-aid kit. But he'd rather she'd taken shelter in the cab. There wasn't enough room for all three of them in there but she refused to leave him.

The tourniquet was tight enough to stop most of the bleeding. To do more without knowing the extent of the injury might cost The Pecker his leg.

Once he'd gotten the man's bleeding under control, he'd butt-scooted back over to the cab and torn out the seats. With Jori's assistance he erected a wall around them. The fortress didn't stop all the wind, but every little bit helped.

Help, Law thought grimly. They needed help to come. Soon. For Jori.

"How far do you think Sam had to go for help?" Jori was looking at him, her lips pale as she huddled in the blanket he'd found behind one of the seats when he tore it out.

"Not far."

"Maybe she gave up and took shelter."

Her voice wobbled. It twisted his gut. But he couldn't let himself dwell on any of the things he'd been thinking about for a long time, until they got out of this mess. He hardened his heart.

"I can't believe I said to send her out in this storm." Jori was genuinely worried.

"Not your choice. Hers. Either way, she'll be fine." His voice was steeled with certainty, but he didn't glance at her again.

For a police officer, lying to get the needed response to keep a gnarly situation under control was practically mandatory. But he wasn't certain he could keep the truth out of his eyes. They were in a significant amount of trouble. And Sam, bless her, wasn't likely to be their salvation.

"You're right. Sam's smart. She will be fine."

Poor Sam. Law felt a beat of guilt about the way he'd treated that curly-haired rust bucket today. She was a faithful dog. A good companion. A help when he didn't know he needed her. But she was a lover, not a fighter. He hoped she was holed up somewhere warm. Unlike Jori, he wasn't at all confident of that, either.

Law adjusted the tourniquet he'd applied to Becker's leg again. The accident had gouged a hole in his right calf and probably nicked an artery. The ground behind them had grown slick with blood before he'd been able to get the tourniquet from the K-9 first-aid kit in place.

Law glanced up from the wound he was watching to his own empty pant leg. The bastard had choked him out and taken his leg before he could regain consciousness.

But he was an officer of the law. Had taken a vow to protect and defend. That meant saving a life. Becker was a shithead but he was a human, and he didn't want that life on his conscience.

"Do you hear a siren?" Jori was suddenly alert.

Law listened. "Yes." But that didn't necessarily mean anything. As a trooper he knew law enforcement was out in full force, prepared to take care of many accidents and other problems associated with the winter storm.

But the siren was coming their way.

"Stay put."

Law scooted to the edge of the overturned truck, grabbed the edge, and pulled himself to his foot with a biceps flex.

"I'm coming, too."

He made eye contact with Jori, worried about the smile blooming on her face as she scrambled toward him. "No. This may be nothing. Either way, I want you safe. Don't move until someone comes to you. Got it?"

She looked at him then slowly nodded.

Law hopped away from the truck toward the sound. The siren was echoing around the valley but the Doppler effect told him it was coming toward him. About two hundred yards out, a state trooper cruiser appeared on a rise in an unseen road. If he'd had his prosthesis he would have made a run for it, hoping the sight of a man in motion would catch the trooper's attention.

Instead, Law looked around for something to flag them down with, in case they sped by without noticing the wreckage. But then something caught his eye.

A rusty-red speck was bounding across the open ground ahead and at an angle to the cruiser.

Law smiled. The doodle had done it!

He saw the cruiser slow to a stop and a trooper popped out, megaphone in hand. "Trooper Battise?"

Law waved both arms back and forth over his head, balancing on one leg.

"Sit tight. I've got backup coming."

Law nodded but he really wasn't listening. He was watching Sam, now about fifty yards out, slow down, wobble around in the snow, and then collapse.

"I'm not getting a pulse." Jori looked at Law, who was kneeling in the snow holding Sam in his arms.

He didn't look up. "Get a thermal blanket from the trooper. Get it here fast."

He saw her wheel away from him. She'd helped him get to Sam, acting as his crutch, but this was his dog, his responsibility. It tore him up that he had to ask for help when he should be the one helping others.

Jori was headed for the cruiser while the trooper was calling for an ambulance after checking out Becker's condition. Everyone was doing their share.

He glanced down at Sam. She was lying lifeless in his arms. Ice crusted her muzzle and face. He ran a hand gently over her head to dislodge icicles. She was suffering from hypothermia. He needed to get her warm.

Unable to carry her, he sat in snow and tucked as much

of her body inside his jacket as he could manage. He knew about K-9 care. As Jori and the trooper came running back, he went over the treatment in his head to keep from going crazy with worry.

He had time. Minutes. Even if she wasn't breathing.

*Wrap the dog in a blanket. Find a warm place.*

He began to rub her body vigorously with his hands, trying to get the blood flowing. She'd run a long way. He was careful not to touch her ears, nose, ears, or feet. If she had frostbite, this would only make things worse.

Sam shuddered in his embrace, her body fighting for its life. He could hear her gasping.

"It's okay, Sam. I got you." Law hugged her tighter, letting her chill wet fur soak his shirt. At least she was getting some heat from his body.

"We've got a thermal blanket. And some instant heat packs." The trooper began tearing open the blanket packet while Jori squeezed the packs to activate them.

When the trooper had spread the thin Mylar blanket on the ground, Law lay Sam on it. She was still now, no breath sounds coming.

*Still time.*

Law grabbed Jori's wrist and shook his head as she would have placed a warming pack next to Sam. "Wrap the packs in something. If they get too hot next to her skin we'll have other problems."

"Right." Jori tore off her only glove, stuffed the hand warmer into it, and handed it to him.

"I'll find something else." She turned away and headed for the truck.

Law wrapped Sam up and leaned over her.

"How you doing, Sam?" He rubbed her roughly through the blanket. No response. He felt for her pulse but couldn't locate it.

He checked her pupils. They were dilating. Sam was unconscious, going into a coma.

"She's dead." Jori had fallen onto her knees beside him.

"No. Not yet." Law heard his own voice as if from a distance. "I'm going to use CPR." He'd done this before, when his K-9 had jumped a fence in Kandahar and landed on a live electrical wire. The shock had stopped his heart. Hypothermia was a bit trickier. Sam had exhausted herself.

The blast of a siren close by made the little party jump. Another state police auto and an ambulance were arriving.

"Here comes the cavalry." The trooper sounded relieved.

Law didn't respond.

He stretched Sam out carefully, tucking a second hand warmer Jori gave him under her shoulder. He noted in passing that the cover looked an awful lot like a bra but made no comment. He was running the scenario in his head. It had been nearly four years since he'd practiced this technique.

He gently tried to open her lower jaw but met resistance. She was stiffening up. He needed to move more quickly. He didn't smell vomit and hoped her passageway was clear. He aligned Sam's head with her back and tilted it a little more to open up her airway.

His hand was large enough that when he placed it under her jaw, he could use his thumb as a clamp over the top of her nose so that no air could escape through her mouth.

Moving quickly but methodically, he bent and placed his mouth over Sam's nostrils and blew into her five quick breaths.

"Her chest moved." Jori was crouched down beside him, watching.

Law placed his free hand lightly on her chest, waited three seconds, and repeated the five quick breaths.

He needed to get her to a vet. But that wouldn't help if she wasn't breathing. And she was so cold. He'd read that resuscitation of a hypothermic dog could take up to an hour. They needed to move while he gave her CPR.

Five quick breaths. Her chest moved with his hot breath.

"I can't find a pulse." Jori sounded scared.

Law looked up. "Go to the ambulance. Get me a dextrose drip." He didn't wait for her to respond. His three seconds were up. He blew another short blast of breaths into Sam's nose.

All around him he felt and heard people, and then more people. At some point an EMT bent down next to him. "What do you need?"

"A ride to the vet. Or an emergency room."

"I know just the vet." The EMT slapped him on the back. "Let's get you into a squad car."

"I can't stop."

The EMT nodded. "Bring a stretcher over here."

Law stopped listening. He was minimally aware of being lifted, along with extra hands to hold Sam, while he continued mouth-to-mouth. Once started, he couldn't stop until they got to the vet.

He and Sam were hand-delivered into the back of a cruiser. He was only dimly aware that Jori had scooted in beside him, holding Sam in her lap.

The sound of the siren surprised him but he was grateful.

"Damn ice." The trooper driving threaded her cruiser around several other vehicles. "You both buckled up? Then hold on, we're going to get your dog help as fast as humanly possible."

Law didn't say a word. But in his head were all the words he couldn't say aloud as he continued CPR.

*Come on, Samantha. Don't go all squirrelly on me now.*

*You're a brave girl. Strong and courageous. As much a self-starter as they come.*

*I'm sorry I doubted you. I'm sorry for every slight. Every single thing I ever did wrong by you. I'm sorry.*

*I couldn't have gotten a better dog. I see that now. You're the best damn Cheez Doodle dog ever born.*

*Today you put your life out there for me. As much as any K-9 I've ever owned. And you did it without your Alpha with you for backup.*

*You've got a strong heart. You make it keep beating.*

*Don't you die on me before I can thank you. Don't you die.*

They were near Springdale, the streets abandoned to accumulating snow, when Jori spoke for the first time on the drive. "Law, I think I feel a pulse."

Her voice was only a whisper as she massaged Sam under the blanket. "No. Maybe."

Law shut out her voice. It took concentration to keep up the rhythm.

As he came to the end of the three-second rest, Sam's body jerked. Then again. She opened her eyes, stared at Law, and then moved a paw to place it against his heart.

"I've got a pulse!" Jori's voice was as excited as any kid on Christmas.

Law nodded. "I know."

# CHAPTER THIRTY

"I'd like to thank you, Detective, for going out of your way for my dog." Law sat in a chair in the waiting room at the vet's.

The detective smiled. "You can thank your dog. She found us. We were about three miles away. We'd received a tip about two of the suspects we missed during our night raid and set up roadblocks, hoping to catch them. You even did part of our job for us."

"Glad to help."

The detective nodded. "When you're feeling up to it, I'd like to talk with you. I won't say you're wasted where you are. But you've got the kind of skills we could use. Two captures in less than two weeks? It's getting so the rest of law enforcement in northwest Arkansas feels redundant."

"Just doing my job."

"I can up your pay grade. For now, I need to go to the hospital. I plan to interview Mr. Becker as soon as he's out of surgery. Ma'am." He smiled at Jori, who occupied the chair next to Law, before walking away.

Law watched the detective through eyes of exhaustion. Sam was going to be fine. The vet doctor said she was making a remarkable recovery. They were still warming her up and giving her IV fluids and nutrition to replace what she'd lost on her trek for help.

Yes, there were some signs of frostbite, but they'd keep her until they had assessed that, which would be a few days. Even so, she'd be fine.

Maybe. But Law wasn't going anywhere until he saw his K-9 again.

Law drew in a breath, his shoulders arching, as the sound of voices rose at one end of the hall.

It wasn't unusual to see a hospital corridor full of uniforms when one of their own had been wounded. But the veterinary hospital had never seen anything like this. State and local law enforcement had turned out to stand vigil for the dog who had saved three people, including one of their own, from what the news was calling the Blizzard of the Century. So far. When they got details of a hostage situation . . . Law sighed. He hated being in the media.

Yet suddenly Sam was a celebrity, and very much a member of the Troop L Springdale office.

"*Oooh-whee.* I never saw anything like it. That dog has heart. She gave it everything she had." The trooper who had followed Sam in his cruiser was gracing the vet staff with his version of events.

Another trooper chimed in. "Don't leave her owner out of it. Mouth-to-mouth resuscitation. On a dog!"

A third added, "Trooper Battise is one of us, all right. Captures a fugitive. Rescues the girl. And saves his dog's life. All with his leg missing."

Law scowled. "That's not exactly how it happened."

"Be quiet, Law." Jori snagged his arm. "They're building your legend. And just think of all the bragging rights this is going to earn you!"

Law ducked his head, but a smile tugged at his mouth. "I don't like things getting built up all out of proportion."

Jori gaped at him. "To what?"

"You found us. Sam went for help. I was tied up." Law shook his head.

"You came through when it counted. Ask Becker. And Sam. You're amazing."

"I don't see it like that." Law reached up to brush a thumb down the side of her face. They'd been given fresh clothes by the troopers who'd come to the vet's office to check on them. They'd washed up as best they could in the restroom. But Jori's face was still pinched with cold, and her eyes were dull and her mouth drawn with fatigue. He was going to get her to an emergency room to be checked out as soon as he saw Sam. Turned out, he was feeling pretty territorial, too. "I'm nobody's hero."

"Sorry. No. Get used to the role." Jori drew up her feet and snuggled down closer to him. "You saved Becker. After you talked him out of killing us. Sam went on your command to get help. When she couldn't go anymore, you saved her. You're awesome."

"It's not that simple, Jori. Never simple with me."

He rubbed his thumb alone her jawline, his sludge-gold gaze following its path. "I thought I was a goner when Becker skidded off that rise. We bounced around so much we should have been on the obit page tomorrow. Guess I've got a few lives left, after all."

"Don't say that." She touched a finger to his lips for a second. "I don't like to think of how much you risk on the job every day. And I know, before you say it, that it's not my business."

"I wasn't going to say that." He didn't smile at her, not quite yet ready to tell her everything he thought.

"It seemed like a miracle when Sam showed up. But I could deal with that." He paused again, his face going serious. "However, I thought I heard the underbrush crackling under footsteps a few minutes later. I almost shouted to alert that someone that we were alive. But then I noticed Sam wasn't responding to those sounds." His voice dipped. "So I chalked it up to . . ."

*Flashback. Hallucination.* They both knew that's what he meant.

"Sam and I were together. She knew it was me." But Jori didn't want this bright moment in a tough day to turn dark. Not after all they'd been through.

She put a hand on his chest and began smoothing it across the one ab. "In other words, you would have been dreaming it was me, if I hadn't actually showed up?"

Law looked into her eyes with a heated intensity that was impossible to misunderstand, but said nothing.

So she plunged on. "Sorry, you don't get rid of me that easily."

"Mr. Battise?"

Law looked up, relieved to see the veterinarian coming toward him. "You can see Sam now. She's feeling pretty frisky, considering what's she's been through."

That drew a shout of joy and relief from the throng of his fellow officers. "Way to go, Doc!"

The veterinarian nodded in acknowledgment. "Don't be alarmed that we have her restrained. Don't want her to damage her paws before we're sure about the possibility of frostbite issues. If you'd like to follow me."

Law looked down at his missing leg. He had come in on the backs of two colleagues. Getting to Sam was getting to be a burden for others.

"Got your back, Battise." One the troopers appeared with a pair of crutches. "One of the vet's assistants broke her ankle at Thanksgiving. She says you can borrow these until you leave."

Law stood up on one leg as easily as most people do on

two to accept the crutches. He tried them out. But they were so short he had to hunch over.

The trooper laughed. "Did I say she's five foot two? Improvise, Trooper. Improvise."

Law looked back at Jori. "Coming?"

She shook her head. "You first. She's your dog."

He nodded and moved to follow the doctor.

Jori sighed and watched Law navigate the crutches. He should have been a foolish sight. But she'd learned the first time she'd met him that Law didn't have a disability. All that tough male grace was an innate part of him that went deeper than two legs. Lauray Battise was a force unto himself.

Her heart shuddered.

*Oh no.* She'd skipped over all the steps between attracted—things such as "like," "fond of," "comfortable with," "connected to," "starting to see a future"—and love.

She swallowed and pulled her legs up in her chair then wrapped her arms around them and rested her chin on her knees.

It was a stupid thing to do. He'd warned her. She'd seen him in action. When things got tough, he pulled so far inside himself that up until a few hours ago, he had probably been determined never to see her again.

That thought gave her palpitations.

Regardless of all that had happened he had yet to ask why she was here.

And until this moment, she hadn't been sure, either.

Whatever was going on inside her had nothing to do with his feelings, or even his approval. It went deeper than that.

This feeling was wild, tough, unreasonable. The kind of love where you know that, whatever happens, it will remain.

Even if he didn't.

It felt scary but good, certain and real. It was an out-flow of emotions from her heart toward the heart of this hard-to-love man. It was unconnected to the hope that he might, should, must return it. No, this kind of loving was a gift.

*Hold what you love in your open palm. If it remains, it's yours.*

She'd heard that somewhere, or words to that effect.

Law's head might not ever get to *love* with her. But it was enough for now that she was there. *Now* was all any-one every really had.

And it felt so damn great.

She was grateful for the now of loving Lauray Battise.

Jori looked up. Where had everyone gone? The hallway was empty. Except for Law, standing at the counter.

Her heart flipped over at the sight of him. Lust stirred much lower. But in her gut, fear flickered. She didn't have a prayer.

"You are an idiot, Jori Garrison," she whispered to her-self. She wanted him, all of him, and for him to want her back.

The phone in her pocket chimed. She looked at the number. It wasn't one she knew.

"Hi. You must be Wonder Woman."

"Uh, I'm Jori Garrison. And you are?"

"Jori. He never told me your name. I'm Yardley, Law's sister."

Jori's eyes got big as Battise came toward her. She put a hand up to block her voice and whispered, "Law told you about me?"

"Let's just say that I heard what he wasn't saying. Heard about your adventure today. You and I have lots to talk about. Privately."

"Okay. Then I'll have to call you back." The legendary Yardley Summers had called her!

Law thumped his way over to her chair. "Sam looks good."

"I can tell. You're perfumed with her tongue."

He smiled a little through his weariness. "Want a kiss, babe?"

Jori held up her hand. "Later. You're a few Tic Tacs short of yummy."

"Let's go."

"Where are we going?"

"I've called in a favor with a fellow trooper. You're going to the emergency room."

Jori stood up. "Think again."

Law stared at her. "I don't have a vehicle. You don't have a vehicle. It's still snowing. What do you suggest?"

"I need a bath and dinner."

He studied her for a long moment, noting her color, her breathing rate, and the pulse beating in the hollow of her throat before nodding. "Got it."

# CHAPTER THIRTY-ONE

"This isn't exactly what I had in mind."

Jori looked around the neat but too-frilly-for-her-taste bedroom of the B&B. It was the place Troop L used when an officer who lived in the county needed to stay close to the office overnight. It had been years, but Mrs. Watson remembered Law and readily agreed to give Jori a room.

Law stood just inside the door, looking about as comfortable as a six-year-old in a crystal shop. "The owner says she's got a can of soup she can heat up for you. I've arranged to have your car towed here as soon as the roads are passable." Something struck him. "You didn't leave Argyle in your SUV?"

"No. I didn't think I'd be staying overnight. I left her at WWP." She hadn't thought through a lot of things. For instance, how Law would react to her presence. She'd used her need to know about the Tices as an excuse to see him. Now it seemed like the ridiculous errand it was.

She started to sit on the bed but then thought better of it. She dropped into a small wicker chair next to a matching wicker table. "Make yourself at home."

He let out a long breath. "I'm not staying."

Jori popped up. "You're not thinking of going back out in that storm?"

He came close and pushed her back into her seat with a palm to her shoulder. Efficient but not very lover-like. "*Shh.* You're exhausted. I don't want to argue. I'm not staying with you."

She gave him a doubtful stare from her seated position. He had developed a black eye, and the vet had glued the cut over his eye shut. Even so, he looked dangerous, and sexy. She immediately regretted that selfish thought. He held his left shoulder hitched a fraction higher than the other when he used the crutches. How badly did it hurt him? He looked ready to drop.

"Where are you going to sleep?"

"At my desk, eventually." He shrugged only his right shoulder. "I've a mountain of paperwork to fill out about what happened today. The feds have questions for me. My captain has his own set. My truck's been totaled so I have to see about that, insurance, towing. And then I'll need to withdraw from the state police physical tomorrow." He looked down at himself. "It's not going to happen. My prosthesis may not fit for a few days."

Jori's gaze dropped to the pinned-up leg of the sweatpants he wore. He must be in a lot of pain, but he wouldn't admit it. "It doesn't seem fair. You worked so hard."

He shrugged. "I've waited this long."

She reached out as if to touch him but stopped short at his backward step. She wondered what constellation of bruises lay underneath the Trooper L sweatshirt he wore. He'd been tossed like a salad in that tumbling truck. He probably needed first aid more than she did. But she saw it in his gaze. She didn't have permission to invade his space just now.

Law was grateful for every inch between her hand and his body. If she had touched him . . .

He looked back at the window where winter was doing its best Disneyland version of *Frozen.* "It's still snowing."

"I noticed." She rubbed her brow. "You should at least get a shower."

He stared at her until her head came up and a little smile appeared on her face.

"I promise I won't attack you. I'm too exhausted."

He didn't smile. "I can't make the same promise."

That brought color to her cheeks and reminded Law that even battered and bruised, he still had the capability to rise to the occasion of Jori. "I'll take my chances."

He shook his head. "No. You called me five times this morning. Yeah. I got the messages before my run-in with Becker."

He pushed back against the hurt that suddenly shadowed her gaze because he hadn't returned any of them. He needed to be very clear. He was an officer of the law at the moment with business to finish. "Why were you coming to see me this morning?"

He saw her reach back through the long hours of this day. It was only one thirty in the afternoon. "When I woke up I saw the news about Harold Tice being arrested as a suspect in a drug trafficking ring. I called because I thought you'd know more."

"So did Becker." Law let out a long sigh, the only indication that he was so tired he was practically asleep standing up on insufficient crutches and one very sore good leg.

"When you didn't answer I couldn't wait. I needed to know what you knew. That's why I drove over. To talk."

He knew she added those last two words as a defense, because the flush creeping up her neck was working on him, too. For that reason, he owed her a glimpse of what was on his mind. Now that they were safe. He was running an operation in his head one step after another.

"Becker was rattled when he came to see me today. He got the drop on me as I was coming off night duty. But it had nothing to do with the task force roundup. He claims that was a mistake. He isn't part of a trafficking ring."

Her expression perked up. "Then why was he running?"

"For reasons that I'm still piecing together." Those reasons might turn out to be important to her. Maybe not. No way to know until he talked with Luke Tice.

"You know something." She was reading him. He must be more tired than he realized. He ached everywhere.

"I need to go."

She stood up, this time folding a hand over his wrist where he held the crutch. Her hand was cold but her touch lit him up. He could see worry, strain, and exhaustion in every line of her face and posture. "You promise you'll let me know if you find out anything important? To me."

"I promise." Not going to touch her. Absolutely not happening. He really couldn't understand why his arm wasn't listening to his head. His left hand moved so quickly that he couldn't prevent it from cupping the back of her neck to pull her close to his chest. "I thought I might die today. For the first time in a very long time, I cared about not doing that. Don't read too much into this, Jori. I'm feeling my way here."

He couldn't believe how grateful he was that she didn't say anything. Didn't even embrace him. Just let him hold her. Maybe she understood him better than he did himself. That wouldn't be difficult. Coming in out of the cold, his self-inflicted need for solitude, was going to be every bit as hard as anything he'd ever done. And it scared him shitless.

He kissed the top of her head, released her, and headed for the door, all in one long motion.

When he was gone, Jori stood at the window and watched him maneuver his way on crutches through the snow back to the waiting trooper's cruiser. The image of the weary warrior had never been more clear in every line of his body. Yet even in that weariness he reflected the primal masculine instinct of a survivor.

Jori turned from the window as the cruiser pulled away. She was living with her palm open. She hoped she hadn't just watched love fly away.

Law rechecked all his facts on the screen at his Springdale desk. He'd been through every piece of intel until what had been staring him in the face finally began to make sense.

"Got the bastard."

He ejected his thumb drive and reached automatically under his desk to tuck it into Sam's vest. But Sam wasn't there. The absence caused a pang just behind his rib cage. Damn. If he hadn't gone and fallen for that shaggy Cheez Doodle after all.

He reached for his phone and dialed. The veterinarian's office assured him, again, that Samantha was doing well. She'd drunk water by herself.

Law smiled. He'd have to get her a purple heart, no, a purple paw to sew on her vest to show she'd been wounded in the line of duty.

His smile dimmed as his thoughts turned to Jori. He'd have to do better than that for her. She had brought Sam along. She, too, was responsible for saving his and Becker's lives.

His phone rang before he could reset it. "Battise."

When he hung up he was smiling. The Pecker had come through. Spilled his guts to the task force detective in the hope of getting protective custody.

Law drummed his fingers on his desk. Change of plans.

He didn't have much time before matters were taken out of his hands. He'd played poker in the barracks to pass the time in Afghanistan. Not so much for the money, but to keep his wits sharp. He'd need to pull to an inside straight on this play, one of the toughest gambles. But he had nothing to lose. And he wanted very much to win something for Jori.

He picked up the phone and dialed Luke Tice's home phone number. It was listed in the police reports. After what had happened in the wee hours of the morning, Tice wouldn't dare ignore a call from state police headquarters.

"I'd like to speak with Luke Tice. Tell him Trooper Battise has a message for him from a mutual law enforcement officer friend. He's probably seen the news reports. No, I'll wait."

He'd just about finished his cup of coffee when someone picked up. Waiting was the second thing law enforcement officers learned to do well. It gave your opponent a false sense of power.

"Yes?" Tice sounded tense.

"You want to talk to me. Today." He gave an address and time and hung up. No way was he going to allow Luke Tice to get the upper hand again.

"Let's keep this short and to the point." Luke sat behind a desk at his empty campaign headquarters. Not even the media had sought him out in this weather. He was dressed in a heavy sweater and ski parka. "What did Becker tell you?"

"Not as much as I've discovered on my own this afternoon." Law remained standing, having traded his girl-sized crutches for man-sized ones. And borrowed sweats for the uniform he kept at work for emergencies. "Trooper Becker seemed to think I'd pay for what he had on you."

Luke smirked. "Which is nothing."

Law smiled. An innocent man might have wanted to know what Becker could have said. Tice seemed to think he knew, and whatever Becker had couldn't touch him.

"It took me a while to put it together. Brody Rogers didn't have an accident."

He paused to allow Tice to say something. But the politician seemed comfortable with silence. "It was the tire marks. No one thought anything of them at the time. Becker made certain of that."

It was a micro expression of fear that Law would have missed had he not been watching for it. The hook was set. Now he was going to play Tice until the man wore himself out from avoiding the truth.

Law leaned an elbow on top of a tall file cabinet. "It was easy to understand why law enforcement ruled it an accidental death."

"You mean because Brody was high on coke." He made a dismissive gesture. "He was an idiot. I'm amazed he hadn't killed himself before."

"Yes, Mr. Tice. The fact that the first officer on the scene found evidence of illegal drugs gave that possibility the appearance of truth. Don't know how much you know about law enforcement procedures. But the way in which the first responding officer handles a crime scene can direct how things go in the overall investigation."

"You're saying Becker mishandled the *accident* scene?" Luke looked smug. He had balls, Law gave him that.

"How long was it before Becker got in touch, Mr. Tice? The next day? Two or three days later, once he knew the department was going to write up the death as an accident?"

"I don't know what you're talking about. I never met with Becker in the days following Brody's death. It was a tragedy. The family was in mourning."

"It's been four years but phone records can be pulled, Mr. Tice."

For the first time, Luke Tice blinked. "I don't recall meeting Becker. He might have called for information about Brody. I am family."

"And that's the thing that makes this so bad. You ran your cousin off the road. I don't know why. Neither does Becker. But I bet I will find out. Given time."

Tice stood up. "You're wasting my time and yours. Do your worst. I've got bigger problems than you right now."

Law nodded. "Your father's arrest. That should put a crimp in all this." Law looked about the campaign office.

"Not at all. People will rally. Someone's always after you when you live at my level, Trooper Battise. It will come to nothing."

"Don't bet on it. Becker's been talking. To the task force people."

"Are you threatening me? You're going to spread lies about me, too? Becker can't hurt me. He's been arrested for drug trafficking. He's a dirty cop. The public will say he's doing this to make himself look better. And you."

He came slowly around his desk, a man who'd faced down the worst. "You may be a war hero but I've been doing some checking up on you, too, Trooper Battise. You have been diagnosed with mental instability. PTSD. You see and hear things, isn't that right? Your emotional state is unreliable."

Law smiled back. "That's why you should listen to me. I'm not reliable. I don't care if no one else believes me at the moment. I don't care if they don't believe Becker. Because he has planted the seed. And I'm going to be its Farmer Brown. I will nurture it until I've grown a case that can't be ignored."

"You're an officer of the law. You can't begin a vendetta against a citizen. That's illegal."

Law ignored him. "I will make it my life's work to dig up every bit of evidence that went unfound because Becker helped you escape. There are other people who were out that night. People you don't know about who may have seen things they were never asked to report. Where were you that night? We know Brody went to see the woman who is now your wife. Were you there, too?"

Law straightened away from the cabinet, wishing like hell he wasn't encumbered by crutches. "What happened to the car you were driving during that time? Did it have repairs done on the front fenders right after Brody conveniently went off the cliff? I'm sending pictures of the tire tracks I found in the original investigation file to the FBI for better forensics analysis. Will they discover they belong to two different vehicles? I'm going to crawl over every piece of evidence until I've built a case for the fact that you killed your cousin. And when I'm done, you'll wish you'd made another choice today."

"Why are you doing this? I never did anything to you."

"No. But you killed a man. And in doing so you cost a young woman the first years of her adulthood, which were spent behind bars for a crime in which she had no part."

"Wait just a minute. Is this about Jori? Drugs were found in her apartment."

"Drugs you knew Brody was dealing and never told anyone about. Why was that? Who were you protecting?" Law saw Luke's gaze flick to the picture on his desk. And then he knew.

"Your future wife. It's on record that Brody went to see Erin the night he died. Did they do drugs together that night? Is that why you went after him? Did you walk in and find them high and maybe a little too friendly?" He saw the color rise in Luke's face. He had the bastard.

"You were seeing her by then. And Brody was supposed to be getting married. Did you have a fight? Maybe when he left and you went after him. Caught up with him on an empty lane and saw your moment."

Tice's jaw had hardened, his eyes like pale granite. "What does any of this get you? You have to want something."

"Justice. For Jori Garrison."

"I didn't kill him. Brody lost control and ran off the road."

"Because you were chasing him. There are two sets of skid marks in those pictures. I'd bet my left leg on it, if I hadn't already lost it. So I'll go with my hunch. My hunch says you drove him off the road."

Luke began chewing his lip. "I might have been behind Brody. He'd been to see Erin and upset her. I wanted to catch him to tell him to leave her out of whatever he was doing." He glanced up at Law and then away. "I might have seen what happened. There was nothing I could do. He died instantly."

"How do you know that?"

"The coroner said no one could have survived a drop like that."

Law smiled. "Becker and I just did. This morning. Haven't you been watching the news? Your luck's run out. You just admitted you left the scene of an accident without even bothering to call for help."

Tice looked away. "A smart man would bet on a winner. He would want to see me succeed. It's the only way to help Jori. Once in the legislature, I might be able to influence a way for Jori to receive a pardon." He looked up, a glimmer of hope flaring to life. "You need me."

"I'll settle for a few years of your life. I'm coming after you with everything I've got. And don't let an empty pant leg fool you. I will stomp you flat."

"What is this about? A piece of ass named Jori Garrison?"

"It's about justice. First, for your scumbag cousin. If convicted you'll probably get a deal similar to the one Jori got, an opportunity after a few years behind bars for parole so you can start over from way behind. Maybe you'll crawl past your mistakes. Maybe you won't. At least Jori can look the world in the eye because she was innocent."

Luke licked his lips. "We can make a deal. Twice what I gave Becker?"

Battise slowly drew in a lungful of air and turned toward the door. He might never be able to successfully back up every aspect of his bluff. But at least he had finessed the truth. Luke Tice had run his cousin Brody Rogers off the road out of jealousy.

How did a man live with guilt like that?

He didn't have to wonder if Erin Tice would be able to. Whatever people believed or didn't believe, he doubted she'd stay with a man who had killed his rival.

But then, he didn't understand women well. There was one waiting for him now, though she hadn't said so.

Law shook his head. He'd done nothing to deserve a woman as good as Jori Garrison. In fact, he had disappointed her more than pleased her. And yet she had come here, in an ice storm, to find him.

Fuck it. It was the way she looked at him, those big eyes that held a wonder and womanly affection he'd never before seen aimed at him. She thought he was a hero.

Maybe it was time he tried acting like the man she thought he could be.

# CHAPTER THIRTY-TWO

"We're getting lots of inquiries about our service dogs. And many new donations. Samantha's heroism has raised Warriors Wolf Pack's profile. So we need to discuss how to behave with the media." Kelli looked up from her notes and smiled as Jori entered the staff meeting. "And here she is, our heroine of the hour."

Jori blushed as she slipped into the room. "Sorry I'm late. I had to drive in from Little Rock this morning." As soon as the snow had stopped the day before, her father had driven to Springdale and brought her back to her parents' home in the capital city. She'd lost the rest of the day by sleeping it away. "What have I missed?"

"Only your face on every media outlet." Maxine grinned. "The phone has been blowing up with questions about you, and what we do here. You're a media darling."

Jori noticed the other staff members were looking at her with a combination of awe and envy. It didn't make her feel good. It made her feel different, not one of them any longer. Her parents' faces had worn that same expression, mingled with worry.

"But we know the truth. Mostly, she takes up space," offered Jeff, the only male staffer there. The jibe struck the right tone to bring the group back to earth with laughter.

"Which brings me back to what I want to stress this morning." Kelli crossed her arms on the boardroom table and leaned forward. "We have several members of the press coming in to do interviews with us over the next few days. I'm concerned about how they're already portraying Samantha in the news. What she did was extraordinary. Feel free to show off what our service dogs are trained to do. It's quite impressive. But we don't want to oversell their capabilities. It wouldn't be fair to our veterans and their dogs. Is everyone in agreement?"

Everyone nodded. Maxine raised her hand. "So, like, are we to dress up a bit, for the interviews?"

"I'm wearing my best pair of jeans and a 'cute top.'" Jeff raised his voice to falsetto on the last two words. A man who worked with women, he'd become a quick study in their vocabulary.

After going over the more mundane but vital weekly operational issues, the meeting broke up.

"Jori, do you have a moment?" Kelli pointed to her office. Once there she took up her preferred position on the edge of the desk. All three lights on her phone were blinking. With a sigh she moved to her doorway. "Maxine, hold all my calls for ten minutes."

She returned with a frown for Jori. "How are you feeling? Any injuries?"

"Only a couple of bruises. I'm fine to work. I want to work."

"Good." Kelli resumed her perch. "Because I've got a proposition for you. As you know, service dog training programs nationwide can't keep up with the needs of our veterans. I'd like to raise our graduation number from thirty-five dogs a year to fifty-five. To do that I've had to think about the financial resources that requires. Because of recent events, we're being approached with funding proposals from foundations both private and public. There are two proposals that will take me to D.C. next week. Even the governor's wife called to inquire how she might get involved. Frankly, all this has my head spinning. I can't run this place and do all the socializing required to keep money flowing in." She paused. "You're a good trainer, Jori. Sarah Williams called this morning to thank you because she'd seen your picture in the news."

"My picture's in the news?" A cold feeling slid down her back. "What pictures?"

"Some taken at the rescue site of you and Sam and Trooper Becker. I suppose you were busy with other things to notice. And, yes, there are photos of you taken from our website."

"You mean pictures of me in prison garb." She hadn't even glanced at TV or the Internet yet.

Kelli nodded. "You're a media sensation. They grabbed what they could find."

Jori subsided into a chair. "My poor parents."

"No." Kelli shook her head. "I'll bet that's not what they'll say if you ask them. I'm proud of you. I'm doubly proud of our program at the women's prison. Those women need to see rewards from hard work and determination. I'm so certain of your abilities that I'm trying to work up to asking you to become the spokesperson for WWP."

"Me?" Jori laughed.

"After all you've done to bring our attention to the public. You're a good trainer, but you're equally good with people. I saw you work with Mr. Battise, a hard case if there ever was one. And the other day you were great with Sarah and Mike Williams. I need someone who's articulate and can think on her feet to go out and talk to church groups, garden clubs, Rotary, Kiwanis, heck, anyone who wants to know more about what we do here. We need to be on everyone's charity list. I'm already stretched to my limit."

"I'd have to think about it."

"You do that. Now, being a spokesperson won't substitute for being a trainer. It'll be in addition to. I'll try to scrape together a little additional money for you. But you won't be out of pocket for speaking and traveling."

Kelli stood, an indication that she was done.

As Jori came out of the office Maxine and the other trainers were staring at the flat-screen TV in the main room.

Reluctantly, Jori moved toward them. "What's up?"

"Luke Tice has withdrawn from his senate race, citing family issues."

"I guess he does have issues. His father's been portrayed as part of a drug trafficking ring." Jeff shook his head. "Some people never have enough."

Jori turned away. She almost felt sorry for Erin.

He was waiting for her by her SUV at the end of the day. The weather had tempered a bit in the wake of the storm. The sun had shone all day, enough radiant heat at thirty-eight degrees to make life normal again. But the heat she was feeling had nothing to do with the day or the sun. Its source was the man she was walking toward.

He looked better than he should have after all he'd been through. Had it only been two days ago? And not a word. She hadn't expected anything else. Even so. Damn.

Jori took her time walking up to him, looking her fill. He was off duty in jeans, a dark cord shirt, and a well-worn puffer vest that looked like he'd owned it next-to-forever. Tall and broadly muscled and on two feet again, even if one was state-of-the-art tech. The absence of a beard still surprised her. But she liked his bare face just fine. In fact, she liked several things about him bare. Maybe not the thought to be having while he was staring back at her. Better to think of something else. Like, if not for the black eye, a stranger would never guess he'd recently been in a near-fatal accident.

Her heart lurched in her chest, knocking aside lust. It would be a long time before she could think about that day without her breath catching. Probably never.

She stopped a few feet away. Time for honesty. "I didn't know if you'd turn up."

Law noticed she said *if*, not *when*. Did she really think he could keep away from her after all they'd been through? "How are you?"

He reached out and snagged her chin, turning her face one way and then the other. "No bruises on the face. What about your wrist?"

"All better." She held up her arm as proof. "Where's Sam?"

"Still at the vet's. She's his star patient so he's taking extra-special care of her."

Her chest squeezed tight. "Is it the frostbite? How bad is it?"

"The doc assures me it's minimal. Her paws, mostly. But it can take up to five days to be certain of the extent, so she stays so he can treat her for a full recovery."

She swallowed. "Maybe we shouldn't have sent her out."

"No." His voice was strangely gentle. And the hand at her chin had become a caress. This was not the Battise she knew. "Don't second-guess yourself. We could have been stuck out in the cold overnight. Becker wouldn't have made it. It was the right thing to do. And Sam was the right dog to send for help."

Jori glanced at him skeptically. "Am I hearing praise for the Cheez Doodle from you?"

He ducked his head, but his expression was warm. "I guess you are. She's got miles of heart, that dog. Nobody could have asked more of a canine."

"Then you're going to keep her?"

This time his expression wasn't mild at all. He lifted his head so she got the full effect. It singed her ears. "I'm thinking about keeping everything I picked up at Warriors Wolf Pack. If that's okay with you."

It didn't take more than a single heartbeat for her to give up being cool and lift her arms about his neck and kiss him. She meant it to be a flirtation. But the moment she touched the hard reality of him, she remembered she was dealing with Battise, a law unto himself.

He swept her up in an embrace that lifted her off her feet and engulfed her mouth with his in a kiss that was hungry and demanding and completely sexual.

When she lifted her head, his eyes were molten and her feet still hung off the ground. "I owe you something."

She tightened her arms around his neck, wondering if the staff of WWP was looking at them through the windows. "What would that be?"

He glanced at the windows, too. "I could show you here but it might get us arrested."

He saw her smile fade, and his heart sank. "You should know, Lauray Battise, that what you think you owe me and what you want from me aren't the same thing."

He set her very carefully back on her feet but couldn't quite let go. His hands gripped her waist. "How's that?"

"You said you'd let me know if you found out anything important. You didn't call about Luke Tice giving up his candidacy."

He nodded. "I was going to do that, in a little while."

"What about Erin Tice admitting that she's going into rehab because of her addiction to painkillers?"

"Where'd you hear about that?"

"The sorority grapevine. You remember Chelsea Bennett from the wedding? She called with the news. She said everyone knew Erin had a problem since college but she'd cleaned up her act to marry Luke. She claims a sports injury is to blame this time for her addiction. Chelsea thinks she's just using it as an excuse to hide out while Luke deals with all the fallout that's coming their way."

"She has no idea. Unless Luke told her what I did."

Jori looked up at him. "What did you do?"

"Told him I was going to nail his sorry ass to the wall for running his cousin off the road."

"You threatened him? No. Wait." Jori gave her head a little shake. "You think Luke drove Brody off the road?"

Law nodded slowly. "He did it, Jori. I got it out of him. And I think I can prove it."

"Wow." Jori thought she probably shouldn't feel anything like happy, considering the revelation that Brody had been murdered. But there was a relief in knowing what happened. There had been so many unknowns in her life during that time. "I've always wondered what would have happened if Brody hadn't missed that curve. Now I'll never know."

A spasm of pain crossed Law's features at her wistful tone. "If Brody hadn't died that night, he would still have been out of your life. You'd already given him back his ring. You would have moved out. You would never have been searched and arrested, and all the rest." He leaned down to rest his forehead against hers. "It was just pure bad luck, Jori. It should never have happened to you. But at least now, we know the truth. I promised you that."

She leaned back so that she could see his face. "You did all that for me? A man who never gets involved."

He lifted his head, his heart in his eyes. "I'd do just about anything to make you smile."

Jori smiled. "You only have to show up, Law."

# CHAPTER THIRTY-THREE

"Twenty-two. Twenty-three." Law was panting. Counting had never been such hard work, or so much fun.

"Twenty- four, -five, -six." He flexed his hips in quick succession, burying himself deep inside Jori each time.

Jori's little cries of pleasure were his reward. She was stretched out beneath him, her thighs locked around his waist. He held her hands, fingers intertwined flat against the bedding on either side of her head. He was completely in charge of her pleasure. And he had every intention of delivering each and every one of the one hundred strokes he'd promised her.

He took a deep breath, withdrawing his penis until her wet flesh held just the thick tip in its embrace.

Jori looked up at him. He was sweating; every taut line of his face and bunched muscle of his arms and shoulders glistened with his exertions. And she'd never been happier to see anyone struggle so hard.

One hundred strokes.

That's what he'd promised as compensation for the night in Eureka Springs when they'd come together as much out of desperation as desire and he'd taken what he needed and left her marooned. She didn't agree with his interpretation of that night. But only a fool would argue with a man as eager and well equipped to pay as he was.

"Twenty-eight."

"Twenty-seven." She grinned up at him. "Circling doesn't count."

He laughed, a husky deep sound that came from somewhere just north of his navel. "Twenty-eight, now. And twenty-nine. And now thirty."

Jori gasped as he plunged in so deep, her body fluttered and gripped him. Then she dug her heels into the mattress and lifted up off the bed, following his withdrawal.

"Damn, Jori. You're pushing me." The admission seemed wrung out of him.

"You didn't say I couldn't play, too."

Law flung his head back and flexed into her again, wondering how anything that ached so bad could feel so good. He felt like he was going to explode. Not just the very lucky inches of him buried in her wet heat but his entire body would participate in a climax that was seventy strokes away. If . . .

"You need to talk to me. Now."

His grumpy demand, so at odds with the liquid ripple of his back, butt, and thigh muscles, made her smile. "What do you want me to say?"

"Anything. Please. Distract me." The last came through gritted teeth as he made his way stroke by delicious stroke through the thirties.

"Tell me about your tattoo." The first time she asked, he'd ignored her question.

He took a deep breath and opened his eyes. "It's called the Twin Water-Fowls. It's the symbol of the Alabama-Coushatta Tribes."

His rhythm slowed, adjusted for thought. "It represents

the gift of free will from the Great Creator. We believe each individual makes his own choice between 'good' and 'evil.' Forty-three. Forty-four . . ."

"So they are like yin and yang?"

"More than that." He paused and gave her a sly glance. "Want to ride awhile?"

"And do your work for you?" She smiled and shook her head.

"There's a chair over there." He turned his head to the wooden straight-back chair that served as her vanity stool and dressing chair. "Forty-eight, forty-nine. Fifty!"

"Oh!" Her fingers clenched over his. He'd found it, the rhythm that was going to take her over the edge. Fifty-two, -three, -four, -five. Fifty-five was a winner.

When she came back to the present Law's forehead lay buried in the hollow between her shoulder and neck, and he was whispering, "Sixty-two, sixty-three, God, Jori. You feel so good. I'm sorry, I can't—"

She blew out her breath, rubbed her cheek in his hair. "You were telling me about, oh, good and evil. Is that all?"

"No." He paused, threw back his head as he arched into her, and sucked in a long deep breath. "The Twin Water-Fowls represent the positive and negative elements of polarities: day and night, sky and earth, life and death, man and woman, alpha and omega, the beginning and the end."

"Circle of Life." Seventy-seven. Long slow seventy-eight and seventy-nine.

"That's—oh yes, like that." She rolled her head back and forth, wanting so much to dig her nails into his ass and ride him home. But they were almost there. "That's pretty profound for a lone wolf."

He looked down at her, lifted himself as much as possible without losing their vital connection, and took in her nakedness just for the pleasure of it. "Is that how you think of me? Lone wolf?"

"It's how you think of yourself." Jori paused to take in the pleasure of his deep slide back into her body. She'd lost count. The tension was rising again, the sweet twisting need that bound two bodies in mutual hunger. But he was moaning. Keep talking.

She opened her eyes and forced herself to focus on his left biceps while the deep slow grind of his body on hers could so easily have stroked her blind. "It's so intricately patterned. There's got to be more."

"Eighty-five. Eighty-six. Okay. Remember, you asked. See the four diamond-shaped symbols in the mouths of the birds? They represent the four elements: air." Stroke. "Earth." Stroke. "Water." Hip rotation and deep plunge. "Fire. Things that make life possible." He was grunting now between words.

Jori relaxed, listening to his voice coming from deep within. Her body had begun to flow with his, an adjustment to the rhythm of his voice.

"The four points represent all important things symbolized by four. Four directions." Hip thrust. "Four seasons." Oh, so good. "The four phases of man."

She closed her eyes. So close. So very close. "What about the feathers?"

"The seven feathers and black points represent the seven sacred fires and the seven ceremonial pipes."

"Keep going." Oh God, yes. Her bones were melting. Seven more should get her there.

"Ninety-one."

Law smiled. He was going to make it. "Seven times seven is forty-nine, the age at which a man or woman is recognized as having survived all tests and difficulties of life and proven through deed, reaching the peak of his or her spiritual power."

"The peak. Yes, please. Let's do the peak. Now!"

The slow glide of his body in and out of hers altered.

The slow grind became a series of deep hard quick thrusts that forced grunts of need from Law and cries of need from Jori.

She came first, the release this time like an assault of sheer pleasure. Hard, bursting ripples that seemed too much.

Law rode her through her climax, taking her long past pleasure to a new intensity that set off a second orgasm before the first had left her.

She cried out, "Enough. Oh please, Law."

Smiling, he buried himself deep, pumping hard and fast until there was nothing left but the hunger denied and inflamed by one hundred strokes.

In the silence that followed, their slick bodies glued together chest and belly, his soft penis still stirring inside her, Jori heard his voice as deep and soft as the night.

"One hundred and nineteen."

"For a man who walks alone, that's a lot of community commitment you've inked permanently into your body." Jori watched Law towel off from the safety of her bed. They'd showered together, satisfied to do no more than fool around under the water, kissing and touching like necking teens.

"I never said I didn't feel things deeply." He flexed his arm and looked at his tattoo.

"Maybe so deeply you must protect yourself?"

He didn't answer.

Then he dropped his towel and came toward her, the intent in his eyes reflected in his amazingly resilient body. Well, one particular part.

When he had climbed in beside her, he flipped over on his back and tucked an arm behind his head. Maybe a man who'd accomplished 119 strokes needed a bit of rest.

"Can I scare you a little bit more?" She rolled over onto

her belly and half on top of him and propped her arms on his chest.

"I like you, Lauray Battise. A lot. I know. You did everything your father told you to do to get rid of me. I'm sorry. It's not working."

He watched her, his eyes darkening with that golden glint of fire in their dark depths. "Why not?"

"I told you before. I don't like being told what I can and can't do."

"It wasn't a challenge, Jori. It was a warning." His voice was no more than a deep breath of air.

"That you're unlovable?" She lunged forward and kissed his jaw. "They lied. Everyone who ever said that lied. Look in my eyes and tell me you still believe them."

He did look, looking so far and deep into her open gaze that he began to see something he did not know he wanted until now, a future.

"What if I screw it up for us?"

"You can't screw it up. If it's what you want." Her turn to whisper. "You get to decide."

He felt her warm breath stir his chest hair, the fragrance that was Jori already familiar to him. He'd never been this close to another person before. Not in this way. He stopped breathing. "I do want it, Jori."

"Good." She slid back down to snuggle against his warmth.

There was a long silence before he said, "So how will this work?"

"Don't worry, I'm not going to go all nesting pigeon on you. Your cabin is safe. I have a job nearly two hours away. Your solitude is safe, except maybe on the weekends."

"You may have a job. What if I don't? I didn't get to pass the trooper physical." A beat. "I'm not even sure I want to be a trooper any longer."

"No biggie. Mr. Task Force guy practically offered you a job at the veterinarian hospital. You can still be in law enforcement if you want."

"Maybe I don't want that anymore."

Jori stilled. "If this is about what I said a few days ago about not liking the idea of you risking your life I—well, honestly? I meant it. But that's not my decision. It's what you do. It's who you are. I'll figure out how to live with it."

He turned and came up on his elbow. "I have problems, Jori. It's why we met. I'll be a burden."

"Says the cop whose girlfriend's an ex-con."

He laughed then, like a man who needed that cleansing relief in his life a lot more often. "So, it's going to be that way? I'm unemployed and you're a felon, and life will be just one happy dance."

"No." She rose up on her knees, bending over him and putting a hand on either side of his face. "It's going to be hard. But we will find moments. And those moments of happiness will grow and expand until we can hold the dark places at bay most of the time. I want to try that with you. If you want it, too."

"Dance with you?" His eyes turned soft into liquid gold currents where the dark shadows shimmered. "Anytime. Anyplace. Anywhere."

She kissed him and it was warm and soft and so very nice. The hum of passion never left him but this time it was muted, a part but not all of his need for her.

Much later, when her phone rang, Jori was reluctant to answer but when she saw who it was, she had to. Yardley Summers. They had talked twice in the past two days. She supposed she should have told Law. But both brother and sister were hard to slow down, impossible to stop once they were on a mission.

"Hi. Yes, Yardley, he's here." Jori rolled over and handed Law her phone.

He frowned and didn't take it. "My sister? Why is she calling you?"

"You'd better let her tell you herself."

# CHAPTER THIRTY-FOUR

Jori sighed in gratitude when the Albuquerque VA Medical Center came into view through the cab window. Albuquerque was clear and as cold as ice the week before Christmas. If not for the cold, it was easy to imagine it was summer. She doubted the season changed the brown desert landscape very much.

She glanced at Law, who sat next to her with his legs spread and his arms relaxed, but the pose didn't fool her. The lines around his mouth were deeper than usual. His gaze unfocused. Only the presence of Sam, who had recovered surprisingly quickly, seemed to hold him in place. He rhythmically petted her while she leaned fully against his good leg. Everyone at the airport had smiled at the rusty-red floppy-eared dog wearing a service vest with a purple paw, and camo-print protective booties.

Jori looked away. She hoped she and Yardley were doing the right thing.

When the car pulled up to a parking lot near the main building, Jori sat forward, looking for the woman Law had earlier described as tall and striking, with

deep-mahogany-red hair. The moment she spotted Yardley standing on the shallow steps of the main building,
Jori knew she could have picked her out in a crowd of
hundreds. She had an Elle Macpherson curviness about
her. And hair like a horse's mane. Jori was glad she was
Law's sister.

When they had exited, Jori went ahead while Law paid
the driver.

Jori held out her hand to the beautiful woman who
shared Law's sludge-gold eyes and direct gaze. "Hi, I'm
Jori."

Yardley looked at her and then embraced her. "You're
a miracle worker. I could never have gotten him to do this."

"I just hope we did the right thing."

Both women turned to watch Law approach. He and
Sam were truly an inseparable pair these days. They had
arranged for Law to spend three days here to take part in
the Native American healing ceremonies at the VA center, where PTSD issues were treated with a holistic approach and ancient Native American ceremonies.

Yardley embraced her brother, whispering in his ear, "I
like her. She can handle you."

Law smiled. "You have no idea."

Then his gaze shifted to the two men who stood a little
to one side. The taller of the two, a man with a deeply lined
tanned face, long gray ponytail, and plaid shirt, came forward. Silver glinted on his wrists and his bolo. He smiled
and nodded politely at the women but he reserved his attention for Law.

"Welcome, warrior Battise. I am John Ayze, one of the
traditional practitioners. You understand what we do here
today?"

Law nodded. "I know the sweat lodge ceremony."

"Yes. But this is a special ceremony for Native American war veterans. Before a soldier goes to war, you are

given the ceremony of training and armor and comrades so that you can protect yourself in battle. But when you return, there is no ceremony to remove these things, and all the spirits you have collected at war. Many suffer because of this rift between war and peace. It goes by many names. Here we remove that armor in ceremonies meant to honor your service and allow you to return to us in peace."

The man touched Law's arm. "You were wounded. Western medicine has healed what is possible to physically heal. Here we deal with spiritual matters. We begin with a sweat lodge ceremony. Afterward we will conduct the first 'enemy way' ceremony. It is the traditional ceremony for countering the harmful effects of the spirits you collected in battle. In three days we will have completed the ritual. You may come back as often as you need to until body, mind, and spirit are one in peace. Are you ready?"

Law took a breath and nodded.

They followed John Ayze to a spot near the parking lot that had been walled off. As they stepped through the gate, Law stopped short. There were other men present, some clearly Native Americans. Some not.

Law didn't recognize the others at first, dressed as civilians. It wasn't until one of them raised a hand in greeting that Law knew who they were. Four men from his old squad stood waiting with hands folded before them at military rest.

He stopped short, his gaze going hard, his stance rigid.

Jori moved in and squeezed Law's hand. "They wanted to be part of this. To share the healing. They have a story to tell you, Law. We thought you should hear it."

He looked at her, his mouth hard. "Whose idea was it that they come?"

Jori held that daunting gaze. "Mine. Don't be angry at Yardley. When we planned this, with the healing ceremony, I asked her to contact them, too. You told me you thought they were responsible for Scud's death. Let them tell you their side."

His body stayed still, rigid, but his eyes were alive as he continued to look at her. "You thought of this?"

"I want to help make it better. After Yardley told me about the healing ceremony, I knew it would help to have other men you know to share it with. I hope it's okay."

He turned to stare again at the men who waited for him to approach then slowly nodded. "You will be here when it's over?"

"I'll be here as long as you want me to be."

A faraway smile curved his mouth. "Thank you."

He squeezed her hand so hard she would have protested at any other time. But the emotion coursing through him was more important.

Law looked down at Sam and nodded. "*Hier*, Sam. We've got some healing to do."

Jori watched them head toward the sweat lodge but she would not stay to watch. This was not for her. This was for Law.


"You're not keeping up." Yardley pushed another tequila shot under Jori's nose.

Jori stared at the row of four shot glasses on the table before her. "How many am I behind?"

"Two."

"Didn't we order food?"

Yardley laughed. "Yes. Meanwhile, don't embarrass me. Drink up."

"Right." Jori reached for another shot of clear liquid. She wasn't much of a drinker. Two shots and her eyes were doing independent rotation. That old saying, *One tequila, two tequila, three tequila, Floor*, now made a lot of sense.

They were seated in a private corner of a dimly lit bar in Albuquerque that Jori would never have had the courage to enter on her own. Yardley's declaration that she knew the owner/bartender wasn't as reassuring as it might have been. She was waiting for Law to return from his first day of healing.

She hoped they'd done the right thing. Yardley was positive Jori had. But then she learned in a very short time that Yardley was a force of nature much like her brother. She seemed never uncertain about anything she said or did.

Jori glanced at her drinking partner, who had consumed all four shots. She didn't appear the least bit affected. Dressed in slim jeans and a tailored white shirt with turquoise snaps and cuff links, she was a Ralph Lauren dream come true. The silver earrings dancing against her dark-red hair made Jori green with envy. The woman was gorgeous without trying. And every man here was aware of that fact.

Only Jori was close enough to notice the strain around Yardley's eyes. Something was definitely worrying her. Was it Law? Or something else? Jori decided it was not her place to ask.

The sound of male laughter across the room shifted Jori's sideways as she fingered her still-full glass.

Across the room a group of men wearing turquoise bracelets or bolo ties, sporting long luxurious hair that flowed over the shoulders of their plaid shirts, were playing pool. Sort of. Mostly, they were using pool as an excuse to keep an eye on the two women who were very close to being "drunk available." At least their frequent glances told Jori they were hoping that was so.

Jori smiled to herself. Wasn't going to happen.

She glanced again at Yardley, who was fishing in her pocket for her beeping phone. "Yes?" Jori watched Yardley's face go slack as whoever was on the other end began to talk. Then her dark eyes flared. "That's not possible!" The panic in Yardley's voice was like a punch in the chest.

Jori reached out to touch Yardley's arm. "What's wrong? Is it Law?"

But Yardley was already sliding out of the booth. "No. Not Law. I need to take this." She turned and hurried toward the restroom.

Jori swallowed her unease. What on earth could alarm a woman like Yardley? Maybe she would tell her when she came back.

She pushed the third undrunk shot back beside the fourth. No more until food came.

She felt more than saw Law enter the bar. It was the way the men at the pool table suddenly shifted their focus from her to the door, alerting her to their interest in the new arrival.

He was alone, except for Sam. Her heart sank. She had hoped he'd be with his squad, a sign they had settled things.

He looked around, giving a chin-up greeting to the bartender. And then he looked straight at her.

Jori lifted her hand in greeting, unable to guess by his expression what he was thinking and feeling. It was his professional face. But Sam looked at ease. A good sign.

His slow deliberate movements betrayed a trace of weariness. Yet it was the stride of a man on a mission as he came toward her.

He slid into the booth beside her, not quite touching her but close enough to leave no doubt for anyone who cared to notice that they were together. He didn't look at her at first, just stared at the men, who suddenly found their game of pool much more interesting than anything going on in her booth.

After a moment, he reached under the table and grabbed her knee and squeezed. Hard.

She stared at his profile. It was that of a man hard, determined, whole. Her heart flipped over. Oh God. She had fallen so hard in love with him.

When he finally spoke his voice was low, steady, deep. "Scud wasn't an easy K-9. Most military handlers refused to work with him. But we were a good team. He was wounded, too, in the blast that took my leg. He went berserk when he realized I was down. Wouldn't allow my own squad to touch me. Bit two of the guys. I saw the marks. I was bleeding out. They had no choice."

He turned to her, a smile at last edging into his expression. "Thanks to you, I now know the truth. And I can live with that."

Jori held the weight of his gaze as long as she could, choked by happiness and the realization that he really was grateful. Yet she knew not to make too much of it in public or she'd embarrass him.

Instead, she pushed a shot of tequila in front on him then picked up her own and held it up. "To Scud."

A look intimate enough to set the liquor on fire entered his gold-black gaze. He picked up the shot glass and touched it to hers. "To Scud."

# EPILOGUE

Sam awakened in the night. The cabin was quiet and dark, except for the tree glowing in the corner near the fireplace.

She pulled herself to her feet and stepped out of her new bed, a fluffy round thing Alpha had given her when she came home. It was better than the floor on chilly nights. But not as good as the foot of Alpha's bed. Still, there were different rules when Jori came to visit. At least she had not brought Cat.

Sam stretched her back, paws pushed forward while her rump and long tail thrust toward the ceiling. She still wore protective booties. Law said she was "Good Sam" because she did not chew them. It was not a difficult command to master. They did not taste good, and they did keep her paws warm.

She looked toward the refrigerator, as usual, and then toward the tree. The lights on it were still bright.

A few days before she and Alpha had gone into the woods nearby. He had hacked at it with a long sharp object until it fell over. Then he had dragged it back to the house, set it in a pan of water, and wrapped lights that twinkled all around it. He seemed very proud. Sam did not know why.

Earlier today, it had been surrounded by boxes of bright colors with shiny strings. Jori and Alpha had played with them until the strings came loose and the boxes broke. Then they took what was inside and played with that.

Sam did not understand why until they offered her a bright paper with strings. She tore at the paper as they had done. And out popped a ball with a bell. That was a good thing. It made a good treat.

*Treat.*

Maybe there were more treats. She'd checked regularly throughout the day. It paid to be sure.

She padded over and sniffed the tree. It smelled of pine resin, old bird droppings, the accumulated debris that had once been a nest, the shells of several cicadas, a few tiny insects burrowed in for the winter, and a faint whiff of bear urine that was more than a year old. All things Sam had smelled on an outside tree before.

The pair of cat eyes staring back at her from the interior was a new addition. She woofed her opinion of Argyle's commandeering of the center of the tree. Better there, however, than in Alpha's bed.

There were also shiny globes and hooks of sugary candy in the tree, hung too high for her to reach.

Alpha said No.

Sam huffed and turned toward the refrigerator. Since her return from the vet she did not have to hunt for midnight snacks anymore. There was always some tidbit of meat left unwrapped on the lowest shelf for her.

She pulled open the door and slid her nose inside. *Treats!*

Her mouth began to water. There were several small chunks of ham from dinner and two slices of turkey that Jori had brought with her the night before.

Jori made Alpha happy. Sam liked Jori.

Finally, when the treats were gobbled up, Sam closed the door and slowly made her way into the bedroom.

There were no noises now but those of sleeping people in the room, the signal that she could enter.

She went to the head of the bed on Alpha's side. He smelled calm, without pain, and of Jori. Satisfied, she moved to the foot of the bed and climbed up, one leg at a time so as not to disturb the sleepers.

She found a shallow place between the humans, inviting from their warmth, and lay down.

She huffed a great sigh. Her new bed was nice. This quilt was nicer. It smelled of Alpha, and Jori, and Sam.

Alpha Happy. Sam Happy. Pack Happy.